355: THE WOMEN OF WASHINGTON'S SPY RING

KIT SERGEANT

THOMPSON BELLE PRESS

CONTENTS

ALSO BY KIT SERGEANT

Historical Fiction: The Women Spies Series

355: The Women of Washington's Spy Ring

Underground: Traitors and Spies in the Civil War

L'Agent Double: Spies and Martyrs in the Great War

The Women Spies in WWII Series

The Spark of Resistance

The Flames of Resistance

The Embers of Resistance

The WWII Women Spies Series

Marie-Madeleine

Virginia Hall (Coming soon!)

Be sure to join my mailing list at www.kitsergeant.com to be the first to know when my newest Women Spies book is available!

***

Contemporary Women's Fiction:

Thrown for a Curve

What It Is

This book is dedicated to all of the women who lived during the Revolutionary War and whose talents and sacrifices are known or unknown, but especially to the real-life women upon whom these characters are based.

GLOSSARY OF TERMS

Claret: a type of red wine

Dragoon: a member of the British cavalry

Fichu: a small triangular shawl that women wore around their shoulders

Hessians: German mercenaries who served with the British Army

Laudanum: a form of opium used for medicinal purposes, especially pain relief

Lobsterback: derogatory term for a British soldier; similar to Redcoat

Loyalist: an American colonist who remained loyal to the British Crown; aka "Tory"

Madeira: a type of dry wine

Men-of-war: British naval ships

Mob cap: a type of head covering with a ruffled brim worn in the 18th century

Oberstleutnant: a commissioned officer in the German Army

Queen's Rangers: Loyalist military unit fighting for the side of the British

Rebel: a term for Colonists who rejected British rule; aka "Whigs" and "Patriots"

Stomacher: a panel that fits in the bodice of 18th century dresses

Tory: an American colonist who remained loyal to the British Crown; another name for Loyalist

Waistcoat: a men's vest worn under a coat for formal attire

Whig: a term for Colonists who rejected British rule; opposite of "Tory" and "Loyalist"

"I intend to visit 727 before long and think by the assistance of a 355 of my acquaintance, shall be able to outwit them all."

— -ABRAHAM WOODHULL, AKA SAMUEL
CULPER, SR.

PROLOGUE

JUNE 1930

*M*orton Pennypacker's hands shook as he opened the package and retrieved the envelope sitting on top. Decades of research might be vindicated by the contents of the letter inside. Or those decades might have been all for naught, resulting in yet another dead end.

The letter, written by one of the world's preeminent hand-writing experts, was predictably neat, the writer careful not to give away any trace of emotion in the curves of his lines. As Penny-packer scanned it, a hint of a smile appeared on his wrinkled face. Phrases such as "the same weight and style of paper," and "the same flourishes on the cursive d's," jumped out at him before he read the words, "These are definitely written by the same man."

Pennypacker carefully set the letter on his desk and picked up his red pencil with one hand as he flipped to a dog-eared page in his ledger with the other. In the blank space beside the words *Samuel Culper Junior,* he wrote the name *Robert Townsend.* He sat back in his

1

chair, allowing himself a long-awaited moment of triumph before retrieving the other items from the box.

For years Pennypacker had been collecting information on the members of the Culper Spy Ring, General Washington's main source of intelligence on British troop numbers and movements during the Revolutionary War. He told others that his interest was mainly academic, but he had to admit to himself that he was out to beat the rest of the amateur enthusiasts in naming every Culper constituent. Some of the ring's members had been much more forthcoming after the war: Benjamin Tallmadge had written about his leading role in his memoirs, and Caleb Brewster, purveyor of the secret intelligence, bragged about his adventures to anyone who would listen. It was not until Pennypacker was able to get his hands on a trunk from a widowed relative of Townsend that he was vindicated in his long-held suspicion as to the identity of the elusive Culper Junior. The trunk proved to be the mother lode: it contained ledgers, drawings, and old documents that had once belonged to the Townsend family.

Pennypacker gingerly examined the century and a half old cipher he had sent off to be compared with Townsend's account book. The printed numbers and the names they stood for were as familiar to him as Culper Junior/Townsend's cursive loops. Although the Culpers also used code names and, occasionally, invisible ink, they would substitute numbers for common words, names, or places in case their missives were ever intercepted. Each member —as well as General Washington himself—had a copy of the cipher written in Tallmadge's handwriting, but at some point Townsend had made his own copy. The number 721 coded for John Bolton (Benjamin Tallmadge) while 726 was for James Rivington, the Tory printer and business acquaintance of Townsend. Samuel Culper Senior, the founder of the ring, was referred to as 722 but was known in life as Abraham Woodhull.

With the revelation that Townsend was Culper Junior, there was only one ring member whose identity remained a mystery. Pennypacker picked up the copy of a letter Woodhull had written to General Washington in August 1779 and read it aloud, enjoying the way the words echoed off the walls of his office. "I intend to visit 727 before long and think by the assistance of a 355 of my acquaintance, shall be able to outwit them all."

727 was code for New York City. Woodhull was from Setauket, but he had often traveled to Manhattan under the guise that he was garnering supplies for his farm, picking up intelligence and passing it on to Tallmadge by way of Brewster and his whaleboat.

Pennypacker exchanged Woodhull's letter for the Culper cipher, and, for perhaps the hundredth time, ran his fingers down the sheet until he reached 355 and the word adjacent: *lady*. Who was this lady of Woodhull's acquaintance that he was so confident could outwit his enemies? The reticent and paranoid Woodhull did not have many contacts outside of the ring, and Pennypacker concluded that it was more than likely she had been recruited and cultivated by one of the other members.

Now that he had confirmed Robert Townsend's participation, perhaps he could coax 355's identity into light. Maybe Townsend had even made the copy of the cipher for 355 in order to decode his messages. Based on his research thus far, Pennypacker had narrowed the enigmatic 355 to three possible women—Margaret Moncrieffe, Elizabeth Burgin, and Sally Townsend—but from there, he'd reached another impasse. With a sigh, Pennypacker turned back to Townsend's trunk and the documents it contained.

CHAPTER 1

MEG

*M*eg stared at the bayonet blade, now only inches from her breast, and felt beads of sweat form under her bonnet. She met the eyes of the bayonet wielder, the shorter of the two men—one could hardly call them "gentlemen," though they were wearing the red regimentals of the King's army—before taking a step backward. She forced her voice to take on a demanding tone. "Sir?"

The short man narrowed his eyes. "Stealing apples, eh?"

Meg hid the hand holding the offending fruit behind her voluminous skirts. "I was going to give them to my horse."

"Those apples belong to the British army." The short man stepped forward, narrowing the gap Meg tried to put between them.

"Sir, my father serves the King as well. Captain Moncrieffe." She glanced across the channel to Staten Island. Her father was on that island now, too far away and too occupied with fighting the Patriots to come to her rescue.

"Haven't heard of him." The short man straightened his arm, aligning the bayonet with Meg's eyes.

Her heartbeat, already at a canter, quickened even more. The other soldier stepped closer to peer into her face. He flicked his hand out, forcing her bonnet back before he pushed his partner's musket away. "Leave her alone. Can't you see she's a child?"

Her hand tightened on the apple as she refrained from stating her customary reply: that she was no longer a child.

The bayonet wielder seemed inclined to agree with her. "She's old enough to provide me some relief."

Panic rose again in her chest. She had heard of women being raped during this infernal war, but usually by the rebel army, not her own countrymen. Thankfully the other man replied, "Save yourself for the whores in New York. If her father is indeed a captain and gets word that one of his own spilled his seed in his daughter, you'd hang from that same apple tree."

Meg took the deepest breath her stomacher would allow as the men left the orchard. Mrs. De Hart was right: this was no place for a woman, especially not one without a chaperone. She went into the house to fetch a sheet of paper and quill.

No man in the world had more of an attachment to King George than her father, but that created a difficult living situation for her in the midst of the revolution. Since Meg had returned from Europe, it seemed she found herself thrust upon Whig host after Whig host, all extolling the evilness of His Royal Highness.

She'd been with the Bankers in Elizabethtown and accompanied them when they departed for the countryside after the British Navy arrived in the Lower Bay. But Meg had soon grown tired of hearing Mrs. Banker's list of complaints against the Crown and the army that served it, including Meg's father himself. She'd fled the company of the Bankers while they were at church and rode out to the De Hart's farm on the coast. The De Harts, like the Bankers, were patriot sympathizers, or Whigs, while Meg and her father were opposed to independence and known as Loyalists or Tories. Nonetheless, the De Harts had been friends with her late stepmother.

Mrs. De Hart was reluctant to take her in at first, stating that, since her husband had been called away to help draft the state constitution and her youngest son had joined the Continental army, she could offer Meg little protection. Mrs. De Hart eventually relented, herself frightened by the presence of the warships stationed across the bay, and the two of them had fallen into a peaceful routine, at least until the scene earlier that morning.

Meg composed a hasty message to her father, imploring him to find a safer place for her to reside, preferably with a family affiliated with their own cause.

A few days later, Mrs. De Hart and Meg were sewing in the living room when they heard a horse approaching. They exchanged looks of alarm as someone's fist rapped on the front door.

Mrs. De Hart rose to open the door. "Yes?"

"I'm looking for a Miss Moncrieffe," a gruff voice stated.

"For what purpose?"

"I am Major Aaron Burr, aide-de-camp for General Putnam. He has sent for Miss Moncrieffe on orders of Captain Moncrieffe."

"Father got my letter!" Meg exclaimed as she walked to the door.

Major Burr looked to be around 20 years old. His facial features were even and lean but for his cheeks, which still held a boyish roundness to them. He wore the navy blue uniform of the Patriots, his dark hair tucked under a tri-corner hat. His eyes, black as pitch, fixed on her as he bowed. "Miss Moncrieffe?"

She curtsied toward him in the manner she'd been taught at her Dublin boarding school and offered her hand. "Indeed." His skin was softer than his appearance, bronzed by many months spent outdoors, would have avowed.

His hand freed of Meg's, Major Burr put both arms behind his back and drew his legs together. "I am to convey you to General Putnam's residence on Manhattan Island."

"Manhattan!" Mrs. De Hart repeated. "With all of the British warships in the harbor?"

7

"I will make sure Miss Moncrieffe is safe at all times," Major Burr replied.

Putnam was a rebel, but at least she would be under the protection of a general, Meg surmised. Her relief at being sent for was being quickly eclipsed by exhilaration at the possibility of riding alone with the handsome Major Burr. "Is it far to the city?"

"About ten miles. We must leave soon, my orders are to have you at the Putnam residence tonight."

Mrs. De Hart beckoned him inside. "Let's get you some food and drink while Meg packs her things."

"I shan't be long," Meg promised as she hurried to the guest room. She had not brought much to the De Hart's as she had not had much time to pack when they originally fled Elizabethtown. Most of her fine gowns were still at the Bankers' house. Meg threw the only riding dress currently in her possession on the bed. It hadn't been cleaned since she had last worn it and dust still covered the burnt orange fabric. She shook it out and sneezed. Despite its state of unwash, the close-fitting dress would both make riding easier and show off her womanly curves. She added an ostrich feather onto the matching bonnet and tucked her blond hair underneath it.

When Meg returned to the kitchen, she noticed Major Burr had removed both his sword and hat. He had fine hair, she noticed. Dark and thick, it curled underneath the blue ribbon that held it back in a queue. "Ready, Miss Moncrieffe?"

"Please, Major Burr, call me Meg." The white edge of his forehead, previously hidden under his hat, spoke even more of long days in the sun.

His smile lit up his face, including those dark eyes. "If you would call me Aaron."

"Aaron it is." Meg turned her shoulders as she moved past him, offering him a glance at her décolletage. When she turned to get his reaction, she noticed the smile had left his face.

"How old are you?" he asked.

"Why, Aaron, I am a woman of seventeen."

"Not much of a woman," he grunted, rising from the table.

"How old are *you*?"

"Just shy of 20." He gave her a meaningful look before putting his hat on and tucking his sword back under his belt.

"That is not so much older than me."

"Older in years, and in experience." He picked up her valise from the doorstep and walked out the back door.

"Have you seen many battles?" Meg fell into step with him as they headed to the stables.

"I was with Benedict Arnold in Quebec."

"I see." She assumed he knew where her loyalties lay, her father being a British captain and all.

"Do you have a horse of your own?" Aaron asked.

"Yes. Father brought him over from England."

"Is he as majestic as his master?"

"Of course." She turned toward Aaron and batted her eyelashes. "And yours?"

"My horse was dispatched to me by General Washington himself."

"Oh!" she exclaimed. "You are an important man."

They reached the stables. Normally Salem wouldn't let anyone else handle him, but Aaron gave off a calming air that seemed to charm her horse. He expertly saddled Salem and then led him to the side of the house where a brown steed was tied to the fencepost. Aaron handed Meg Salem's lead as he mounted his own horse.

Mrs. De Hart came to give her a hug and Meg thanked her profusely for her kindness in taking her in. The elder lady waved from the front porch as they departed. Despite their differing viewpoints on the outcome of the war, Meg hoped that she would remain unharmed and that Mr. De Hart would soon return from Trenton.

"I actually came from Washington's staff," Aaron said casually after a few minutes of silence.

"You were under the direction of the leader of the Continental army?" Despite herself, Meg was impressed.

"Indeed. But I resigned and began working for General Putnam a few weeks ago."

"You didn't like working for your Commander-in-Chief?"

Aaron shrugged. "Our Commander-in-Chief has little military training. He fought in the Indian wars, but has yet to win a great battle. And he's a slave owner."

"I suppose you have extensive military expertise."

He shot her a sly smile. "I did go to Princeton." His gaze traveled from her boots up to the fichu that barely covered the bodice of her dress. "I suppose you are one of those English-educated girls, er, women."

"I went to boarding school in Ireland," she told him proudly. "And I was raised by General Gage until I was three."

Aaron leaned over to spit onto the ground.

"One of my stepmothers was the sister of William Livingston, the governor of New Jersey, the other stepmother was the sister of John Jay," Meg continued.

"All Whigs. Why did your father marry so many women whose families spoke out against the Crown?"

It was her turn to shrug.

"And yet your father espouses a futile cause in the King's name," he continued.

"The King is the anointed ruler."

"He is not my anointed ruler."

"Clearly not."

Aaron rounded his steed as they approached the checkpoint into the city. One of the men in charge stuck his fingers into his mouth and gave a loud whistle. Other men in blue uniforms quickly mounted their horses and fell into line behind them. "A cavalry charge?" Meg asked Aaron with a slight hint of mock to her tone.

"An escort," he replied. This time Meg was the first to break eye contact as she felt her face heat up under Aaron's searching gaze.

Another rider came beside Salem and Meg. "That is a fine horse you have, miss."

"Thank you." She glanced over at him. His face bore smallpox scars, but it was still well-shaped. The epaulets on his shoulders revealed that he was an officer. He nodded back at her staring. "Captain Webb at your service, miss."

"Watch it, Webb." Aaron called from the other side of Meg. "She's only seventeen."

She squeezed her legs, causing Salem's pace to quicken, and glanced back at the rebel soldiers. Aaron held a tight smile, but Captain Webb made no secret of the fact his eyes were fixed on her backside.

The City of New York at present had changed much from her youth. Meg was fourteen when she had returned from overseas. At that time, Father had been married to Catherine Livingston, daughter of the Whig judge. Meg hated her—she wore a permanent frown and, worse yet, was staunchly in favor of breaking from the King. Luckily Meg spent most of her time under the care of a governess, but she cannot say she was sorry when Catherine died a year after her arrival, leaving part of her immense family fortune with Meg's father.

Back then Meg had been shocked at how many slaves wandered the broad streets, performing various tasks for their masters and dampening a vision that had otherwise been unmarred by the handsome residents and grand brick houses. New York had been bustling with trade and shipbuilding.

Now the harbor was occupied with warships instead of whaling vessels. The wide expanse of Broadway, still bordered by mansions interspersed among the oak and hickory trees, seemed deserted.

Aaron halted his horse at the corner of Reade Street in front of Number One Broadway, a grand two-story brick house with carved Palladian windows.

"We've arrived." Aaron dismounted, handing the reins to Captain Webb as he came to stand by Salem. He pulled off his riding gloves and offered Meg his hand. She took it, trying to not reveal the swelling of emotion the simple contact had stirred in her. Despite her supposed youth, Meg was well acquainted with male attention and welcomed it for the most part, the British brutes in the garden notwithstanding. But Major Burr, with his distinguished record and handsome countenance, was at a level she was unaccustomed to. *Not to mention he fought for the other side.*

Aaron, for his part, also seemed to be affected. His already weathered face grew even darker as he put his arm around Meg's waist and helped her down.

They were greeted at the door by Mrs. Putnam, who exclaimed that they had arrived just in time for the evening meal. She had a wide, honest face and stocky figure. She introduced Meg to her daughters, Belle and Molly, both who appeared to be in their early 20s. They paused in their fussing over Meg as a large, rotund man with long gray hair entered the room. His face was as well-worn as the battle maps that hung from the walls. His uniform was ill-fitting, the buttons that attempted to hold their own over his protruding belly on their last threads. Like his wife, there was a kindly air about him.

"General Putnam." Meg approached him and reached for his hand, which he promptly grasped. "Thank you for your hospitality."

"Nonsense," he said, his voice lisping slightly over the s's. "I have nothing but the utmost respect for your father. We fought on the same side during the French and Indian War. He is only my enemy on the battlefield. Privately, he can always command my services. And that of my family," he said, dropping her hand as his wife stepped forward.

"Come, Miss Moncrieffe, let's get you settled in your room before supper," Mrs. Putnam said.

"Please call me Meg."

"And I'm Dolly, not Mrs. Putnam." She gestured toward her husband. "You can call him Old Put. Everyone else does."

Old Put placed an arm around his handsome aide-de-camp's shoulders. "Fancy a drink after your journey, old boy?"

"Yes sir," Aaron replied, his gaze following Meg as Dolly led her up the stairs.

CHAPTER 2

ELIZABETH

JUNE 1776

"*T*he commander of the British army, General Howe, has left Virginia," Elizabeth's husband Jonathan told her as they sat down to dine.

Elizabeth motioned for their maid, Abigail, to serve her more stew. "What does that mean?"

Jonathan sighed and rubbed the graying whiskers on his chin before he answered. "It means if he has any thought to him, he has his spyglass set on Manhattan."

"Why is that?"

He waved toward the window that looked onto the East River. "The ports. The fact that New York is in the middle of the country. If he closes down the harbor, the Continent will suffer greatly."

"Thus the reason for the Yankees' arrival." Since the spring, the city had been filled with soldiers in a rainbow of neutral colors: brown, light gray, buff, and even green. "Food's been hard enough to lay hold of without these New Englanders coming for it." Elizabeth took another swallow of stew. She hadn't had much of an appetite at this time during her other pregnancies, but for some reason she was perpetually hungry with this one.

"Hush, woman. Them New Englanders are the only chance we've got in this Loyalist city. New York City didn't come to the aid of Boston, yet here Boston comes to aid us. Makes a man think real hard about where his priorities lie."

"Jonathan," Elizabeth's spoon clattered in the silver bowl. "You can't possibly mean— "

"That's right." He plunked his wineglass down resolutely. "I'm thinking about joining the army."

Fear began to rise in her chest as she contemplated the next few months without Jonathan. She was nearly seven months pregnant. And then there were the other children to think of: Jonathan James, who was almost six, and Catherine, now four.

Elizabeth turned her back to her husband while she fed the remaining scraps of bread to her hound dog and thought of a suitable reply. Her brother James had been killed last year during the Siege of Boston. Jonathan was an intensely religious man, and if Elizabeth brought up James's death as an argument, Jonathan would simply tell her that if he were to die in battle, it would be due to God's will. She swallowed back her next rebuttal—that Jonathan was too old. He was nearing fifty, which was how she convinced him not to join the Continental army when the first shots had been fired at Lexington and Concord over a year ago.

She decided to reason with him, a policy that she learned, after eight years of marriage, worked the most often. "Who will take care of the shop?"

"You must." He gestured toward Abigail. "Abby will help with the children, right?"

As Abigail nodded, Elizabeth couldn't stop her mouth from dropping open. Jonathan was of the mindset that women were not to be involved in financial affairs. It did not seem prudent for Elizabeth to remind him of the fact she had no idea of how the shop was run. "And you?"

"If I die, I will have died for a great cause rather than as a coward in my bed."

She wanted to say, "A coward that still could have provided for his family," but she realized the futility of it. It had not been a marriage of love—Elizabeth's father had arranged for his daughter to wed the wealthy merchant, Jonathan Burgin, on his deathbed. He wanted to assure that someone would look out for his oldest daughter—a girl of only just sixteen—after he had passed. But, despite her initial reluctance to marry him, admiration had grown out of trust and reliance.

She wondered how she would survive without Jonathan. Ever since the war began, Jonathan had complained of a lack of customers at his store and that money grew tighter. She felt a swell of indignation: she had already lost her only brother due to this conflict and now she was being asked to sacrifice her husband as well?

Elizabeth marveled at the changes that overcame her native city as more Yankee troops arrived from Boston. Because the family quarters were located on the second floor above the Queen Street shop, they had a good view of the city below from both the east and west. The harbor, which had been practically deserted in the spring with the arrival of General Lee from England, now teemed with American soldiers. It seemed a company was always conducting drills outside their building, their fifes and drums audible long into the night.

After the British settled on nearby Staten Island, Jonathan had officially enlisted under General Woodhull and was ordered by the Committee of Safety to help garrison the East River beach. Jonathan would often come home exhausted and sunburned. Gone was his previous reticence to talk politics with his wife. He filled her in on what was happening outside, including a supposed plot by the Loyalists to kidnap General Washington, which resulted in the hanging of a man in the gallows near Bowery Lane. Every day after that he had stories of Tory turncoats being tarred and feathered or dragged through the city while straddling a fence rail.

Confined to her apartments and the store below it, Elizabeth could still feel the tensions rise in the streets of New York City. She was not opposed to war. She had read snippets of Jonathan's copy of *Common Sense*, and agreed with most of what Thomas Paine had written, specifically that England, so far removed, had no right to govern America. But with the conflict building right outside her window, Elizabeth began to question whether it was worth her and her family's lives.

The military occupation, thankfully, brought business to the shop. Jonathan owned a dry goods store that sold such necessities as stationery, tobacco, and tea (the local herbal kind as Jonathan had refused to sell Bohea after the Boston Tea Party), along with a few other various items such as walking sticks, ribbon, and scraps of cloth. The first morning Elizabeth opened the shop, she was relieved to see Jonathan's longtime friend Hercules Mulligan enter, ducking underneath the doorframe as he did so.

"Hello, Elizabeth," he said warmly, taking both of her hands in his. Hercules's palms, like the rest of his body, were massive. In addition to his height, he had a girth that could have been imposing; his manner, however, had always been most affable to Elizabeth. "How long until the baby comes?"

"About two months," she said, retreating back behind the counter. With her previous pregnancies, Elizabeth went into a self-imposed confinement at this stage, but the necessity of making money meant appearing in public with her swollen belly.

"I have to pick up some things." The stocky Irish immigrant would have made a hardy soldier, but instead he owned the finest clothier shop in Manhattan. "Do you have any sugar?"

She glanced down at the ledger in front of her. "Sugar?"

Hercules set a few items down on the counter. "If you do, it would be in the back room."

She nodded and ducked underneath the curtain that led to the stockroom. There she was confronted with an endless sea of objects wrapped in brown packaging. The bell on the front door of the shop rang as she fumbled with a packet similar in size and shape to what she imagined a bag of sugar would be.

"Never mind, Elizabeth," Hercules called out.

As she reappeared in the front of the store, she noticed Hercules eyeing the new customer with disdain. The unfamiliar man wore a powdered wig and a well-cut suit. He had a long, crooked nose and shrewd blue eyes. "I'm looking for ink."

"To print more of your treasonous lies, Rivington?" Hercules asked, a growl in his voice.

"Actually," the man called Rivington turned to his accuser, "it's for personal correspondence." He faced Elizabeth. "I would like to purchase some ink."

She looked helplessly at Hercules. He inclined his head toward a shelf on her left side. She grabbed a pair of inkwells and placed them on the counter.

"Three," Rivington stated.

She retrieved another before opening the ledger to a fresh page.

"I'm on credit here," Rivington said.

"I hardly believe Jonathan would let you purchase on credit." Hercules walked to stand at Rivington's side. "Not with your Loyalist tendencies well-known."

"They are so well-known because I have a readership that numbers in the thousands, which leads me to conclude that there are plenty of people still loyal to the King in this town, despite what you may see outside." Rivington lifted his chin as a regiment of soldiers in green coats marched past the door. "Credit, then?" he asked Elizabeth.

She nodded her acquiescence, mainly because she had no idea what to charge him. "For now. I will speak with my husband later about settling your debts." She was aware that Rivington ran the *Royal Gazette*, the city's most popular Tory rag. Once she'd seen one lying in the street, a headline about Washington's supposed illegitimate children marching across its front page.

Elizabeth noted, *Rivington, 3 inkwells*, in the ledger as the printer left the shop.

"How are your wife and daughters?" she asked Hercules when she'd finished writing.

"Safe, thank you. They have gone to live with my mother in New Jersey."

She took stock of the goods he had helped himself to as he continued, "You ought to think of leaving the city, too. It's getting very dangerous for women and children."

Elizabeth closed the ledger. "I must look after the shop. If we leave, chances are it will be looted and everything we have will be lost."

Hercules grabbed his purchases. "Challenging times we live in nowadays."

"Indeed," she agreed as he walked out, the bell ringing behind him.

July 9th was yet another sweltering day in summer full of hot days. Elizabeth threw open the second-floor window, but no breeze rustled the trees. The west windows of the apartment showed ominous storm clouds approaching.

Jonathan appeared from the bedroom clad in his blue uniform. Since housing for the troops was scarce, his superior had allowed him to remain living in his own home, but every morning he rose to continue building the fortifications on Broad Street. Tonight he had been called to the Commons for the reading of a declaration from Congress.

Despite his age, Jonathan had taken on the manner of a giddy schoolboy. He twirled Johnny around the room, shouting, "Free men, my boy, we're free men!" Johnny joined in his father's giggling.

A blessed wind finally stirred the room, but with it came a clap of thunder. "Must you go out in this weather?" Elizabeth asked.

"I've been ordered by General Washington himself." Jonathan set Johnny on the couch and picked up his hat. He gave her a quick peck on the cheek. "I'll probably be home quite late." A bolt of lightning flashed as he left the apartment.

. . .

The storm finished as evening fell. The sudden silence previously occupied by thunder was soon permeated with shouting and drumming that continued all night. True to his word, Jonathan stumbled into the apartment, still slightly drunk, near dawn. He filled Elizabeth in on the words of what was being called The Declaration of Independence, an assertion that the American colonies were free from British rule.

"When the whole of the army in New York cheered, we were louder than the storm overhead." After it was read, Jonathan told her how he'd followed a group of men, led by Hercules Mulligan, down Broadway to the statue of King George that stood in a nearby park.

"I know it," Elizabeth stated. "The one near all the mansions."

"Aye," Jonathan agreed. "We then knocked down the statue and drew arms upon it, cutting off the metal head. It was almost as if we had pulled the King himself from his pedestal."

"An act of treason," she murmured.

"It's not treason in America," Jonathan corrected her. "The metal will be melted down into bullets for our army. A fitting end, I should think." He grabbed his wife's hands in his. "Just imagine, Elizabeth, the glory that shall be our new nation once this war is over and we are forever freed from England's grasp."

Elizabeth nodded wearily before getting up to return to her bed.

CHAPTER 3

SALLY

JULY 1776

"*R*obert!" Sarah Townsend exclaimed on catching sight of her youngest son striding up the path.

His father, Samuel Townsend, clasped Robert on the shoulder as he ascended the steps. Robert's clothes, tattered in spots and clearly in need of a wash, were in stark contrast to Papa's smart wardrobe, complete with his ever-present gold-tipped cane. Papa's blue eyes held an uncustomary look of worry as he asked Robert, "What has become of Staten Island?"

Robert shook his head. "Howe's now got Hessians fighting for their cause. The Island is lost, the Bay nothing but a sea of British naval brigades. Manhattan Island is still ours, but likely not for long."

Papa's frown deepened as Robert peered at his mother and middle sister, Sally. Sally was aware that most other Quakers would have shooed the women away, claiming that this was "men's business," but Robert believed that war affected all of his family. Papa claimed to be one of the few townspeople in Oyster Bay who hadn't

21

taken a side, but Sally knew others whispered of Samuel Townsend's rebel leanings.

"The Loyalists are informing on their Whig cousins." Robert leaned back on the portico column and folded his long arms. "Men and their families are fleeing Long Island in droves, leaving behind their houses and farms."

"Worldly goods," Papa said. "Still, our Friends might do with a word of warning."

Robert straightened. "Your cousin, George?"

Papa nodded. "Especially after that stunt he pulled in the spring."

Sally glanced back and forth between her father and brother, trying to follow. She knew that Oyster Bay's Committee of Safety, of which their relative George Townsend was a member, had arrested several of their neighbors a fortnight ago and accused them of being loyal to the King, and therefore anti-American.

Feeling suddenly smaller than her eighteen years, Sally slipped her hand into her father's. "Papa, are you in any danger?" Everyone in town knew of Papa's arrest during the French and Indian War years earlier when he had protested against the way the prisoners of war were treated. For his crimes, Papa was jailed for a few days and forced to pay a hefty fine.

He squeezed her hand before letting go to ruffle her copper curls. "Of course not, little Sally." He turned back to Robert. "Probably John Kirk as well."

As if to match the solemn mood that had descended upon them, the sky opened and a torrential rain began to fall. The four of them huddled closer underneath the portico that offered little protection as the rain blew sideways. Mother and Sally ran inside, leaving Papa and Robert to endure the soaking downpour.

Like many of their Oyster Bay neighbors, the Townsends owned slaves, but they were usually kept for outdoor work, such as caring for the livestock and helping with the harvest. The regular household duties fell to Mother and the Townsend girls, although Sally would much rather have been outside with the horses and chickens.

The night Robert returned, Audrey, the eldest Townsend sister, and Phoebe, the youngest, helped their mother prepare dinner while Sally set the table with earthenware plates. There was a time when the Townsend meals had been clamorous and full of entertainment —three of Sally's brothers, with the exclusion of the reticent Robert, were boisterous and quick-witted, and spent their mealtimes exchanging jokes and laughing loudly. Visitors, either out-of-town patrons from Papa's store or friends and family, often joined them as well.

But now, with the war dividing the neighborhood into Tories and Whigs, guests were a rarity. The oldest Townsend son, Solomon, was currently away at sea and Samuel Junior, Sally's second oldest brother, had passed away a few years ago. There was plenty of room around the pinewood table in the kitchen, where Papa nowadays preferred his family to dine. The crackling of the fire didn't much compensate for the solitude of these new family dinners.

Whenever any of Sally's brothers were present, the dinner conversation characteristically turned to war. Tonight was no different. William, older than Robert by three years, asked his father what he thought of Congress's Declaration of Independence.

Papa chewed and then swallowed before replying. "I think this has turned what some thought was a rebel skirmish into a real war for the new America, where one side struggles for the right to be free and the other for the right to oppress."

Robert nodded. "I fully agree. And with that, I am ready to take up arms for our new country."

"No, Robert." Papa reached for his son's hand. "You cannot. You know as well as I do of the strict pacifism we adhere to as Quakers."

Robert pulled his hand back. "But Papa, as Paine wrote, we must follow our own Inner Light."

Sally glanced at William, whose face looked blank. Papa had given both William and Robert a copy of *Common Sense*, the pamphlet advocating independence written by fellow Quaker Thomas Paine. Sally had been curious as to what part had gotten the residents in Oyster Bay so divided. She had snuck into William's room one night and grabbed it, intending on returning it as soon as he noticed it was missing. It had been several months and she had read the now dog-eared copy front to back at least six times. Each time she read it, she became more in favor of America eschewing the monarchy and becoming its own republic. Sally knew—and William clearly didn't—that Robert was referring to the part where Paine urged his readers to follow their own conscience.

Papa took a sip of ale and then set down his mug. "I can get you a position in the Queen's County militia that does not require you to fight."

Throughout the meal, Phoebe and Audrey had been quietly focused on the food in front of them. Sally guessed that her sisters were too preoccupied with the thought of their childhood friends marching off to war to worry much about Thomas Paine. But their mother's head, like Sally's, had been volleying between the men as they spoke.

"Samuel," Mother put her spoon down and wiped her mouth. "I'm not sure I want Robert involved in the war at all."

"But Mother," Sally replied, "Robert has to do something. I would too, if I could."

"What would you do?" William guffawed. "Ride off into the night like Paul Revere? Take up arms against the Redcoats?"

Sally flipped her hair and glared at her brother. "Just because I'm a female, it doesn't mean I can't serve my country."

"Actually," William said, picking up a forkful of food, "that's exactly what it means."

Samuel Townsend had been elected to the fourth Provincial Congress and was summoned to White Plains, New York in mid-July. A few days into his journey, Papa, sensing the frustration from his middle daughter on not being able to contribute much to the rebel effort besides sewing uniforms, sent word for Sally to come to White Plains to hear the reading of the Declaration of Independence. Robert volunteered to be her chaperone.

Sally had always sensed that she was Papa's favorite daughter. The Townsends believed an education was necessary for all of their children, and, consequently, the three girls had attended school and learned to read and write. Sally was particularly good at math, and Papa often asked her to assist with his ledgers if she was not preoccupied with climbing trees or catching frogs with her brothers.

Audrey, however, was more adept at womanly duties such as sewing and baking. She planned on marrying James Farley, a captain who sailed with their brother Solomon, as soon as she turned twenty-one and Sally had no doubt she would excel at her household obligations as a matron. Phoebe was only sixteen months younger than Sally but she took after Audrey and was already a much better cook and spinner than her middle sister.

Sally was thrilled at Papa's invitation and had her portmanteau packed days before she and Robert left. Although they would only be spending one night away, she stuffed her bag with combs, petti-coats, and jewelry. Sally normally could not be bothered to worry about such accoutrements, but this was a very special occasion: the Provincial Congress was tasked with adopting the Declaration of Independence for the state of New York. Only days ago, General Washington had read it aloud in Manhattan, and she was eager to hear for herself what Thomas Jefferson had written.

She chose to wear her best day dress, a hand-me-down from Audrey. Ever since the boycott of British goods, Sally had refused to buy new clothes and settled for either homespun, or—more likely since her sewing skills were somewhat lacking—castoffs from her older sister.

The Dosoris ferry took them across Long Island Sound, which Robert told her his friend Caleb Brewster called the Devil's Belt. After they disembarked on the mainland, the final leg was to be accomplished on horseback. Confident in his sister's ability to prop-erly ride a horse, especially since he himself had taught her, Robert rented Sally her own bay instead of having her ride with him on a pillion.

They finally dismounted at the farmhouse of her uncle, James

25

Townsend, in mid-evening. Exhausted from the long trip, Sally fell asleep right away.

A crowd had already established itself in front of the White Plains Courthouse when Robert and Sally arrived the next morning. A fife and drum corp played "Yankee Doodle," while a boy waved the flag of the local minute men to the beat. Unlike the divided neighbors of her hometown, the hordes of people gathered around her all seemed to be Whigs and buzzed with support to sever ties with the King.

Suddenly the courthouse doors opened and the delegates emerged. Everyone around them gaped at the men blinking in the sudden sunlight. Even the band members stopped to stare, holding drumsticks paused in mid-air and fifes to frozen mouths.

After a moment, the rumble of the crowd quickly filled the silence that ensued when the music ceased. Robert, standing behind his sister, whispered some of the delegates' names in her ear. "That's John Jay and Lewis Morris."

Sally stamped her foot and glared at her brother. "I know."

Robert, too caught up in the excitement, ignored her. "Look, there's General Woodhull—the elected president of the Congress. And there's Papa." The drummer resumed his beat and Sally's heart thumped in time with it. A man dressed in a dark blue coat and tan breeches climbed to the top of the steps of the courthouse.

"That's John Thomas," Robert murmured before the entire congregation hushed.

Mr. Thomas's voice rang clear and loud against the still summer air. "When in the course of human events…"

Sally hung on every word of the document, trying to process what it all meant. Her chest swelled with outrage as Mr. Thomas read a list of complaints against George III. When he spoke about the inalienable rights of "life, liberty, and the pursuit of happiness" that Parliament and the King had previously deprived the colonists from seeking, some of the crowd members shouted their agreement. Mr. Thomas concluded the reading by proclaiming that the

Convention had unanimously resolved to ratify the Declaration of Independence. At this, the throng of people broke into two factions: those who cheered enthusiastic "huzzahs!" on their way to the pub to continue the celebration and those so overcome with emotion they were sobbing openly outside the courthouse.

Sally was among the latter; as she wiped her eyes, she noticed her normally stoic older brother doing the same thing. He too, had been moved to tears by the powerful words that finally set them free from the King's tyranny.

CHAPTER 4

ELIZABETH

JULY 1776

*O*n the evening of July 12, Elizabeth was at supper with Abigail and the children when Johnny spotted a fleet of ships passing by.

"Look, Mama!" The excited little boy got up to point out at the harbor. "Are they American ships?"

"I don't think so," Elizabeth replied, knowing there was no American navy to speak of.

"Are they British, then?" Catherine, astute for a four-year-old, and even more for a girl, asked.

In lieu of replying, Elizabeth scooped more soup into both of their bowls. "Eat up, now."

A loud booming noise shook the panes of the window. "They are firing at us!" Johnny shouted.

Elizabeth felt the now familiar terror rising as she lifted her heavy belly out of the chair and went to the window. Below them, neighbors were fleeing from their houses. As if pulled by the shrieking below, Abby and the children joined her at the window. Catherine pushed in front of Elizabeth and she put her arms upon her daughter's tiny shoulders.

In a matter of minutes, the crowds below were packing up wagons with household goods and heading toward King's Bridge, the only land bridge leading to the mainland. Troops moving in the opposite direction rushed into the throng of people. The soldiers, finally arriving at their destination on the shore, seemed dumbfounded. A few of them peeled their guns off their shoulders and fired at the ships, to no avail.

Another boom caused Elizabeth to abandon the window and take the children to the interior of the house.

"Missus, we need to go now!" Abigail shouted.

"How?" Elizabeth frantically gestured to her belly. She knew it was probably wisest to leave the city, but at the same time, she didn't know how two women would manage to convey Catherine and Johnny to safety, especially given her condition.

"Maybe the Fraunces can help? Or the Underhills?"

Elizabeth nodded toward the kitchen window. "They are probably fleeing the city with the rest of them." She met the eyes of her maid square on.

Abby's normally stoic brow was furrowed with worry as she hugged Johnny to her. "Missus, the baby. Your midwife?"

Elizabeth shook her head. "Gone too, I'm sure. But I've still got time to figure that part out."

Abigail took a deep breath. "I can do it. I helped Madame Nance a few times when she delivered babies in the log huts behind the Commons."

Catherine flew into Elizabeth's arms as another cannon sounded, this one even closer than the ones before it. Again, the two women met each other's eyes over the heads of the little ones in their arms. Abby had grown up in the unpaved back streets of the Holy Ground, the slums near Trinity Church, the daughter of a prostitute who had wished for a better life for her progeny. Elizabeth's friend Mary Underhill had once cared for Abigail's mother and suggested to Elizabeth and Jonathan that they hire her daughter. Thus, Abigail had come to serve their family at the age of thirteen. Even when times were tough, like the past couple of months, Jonathan made sure he could at least provide Abby with food and a roof over her head, less she suffer the fate of her mother and countless scores of other destitute women in the city.

CHAPTER 5

MEG

JULY 1776

*I*n the same fashion that her husband commanded the troops, Mrs. Putnam ordered her female servants and daughters to spin fiber to make shirt cloth for the infantry.

"Do you not spin, Meg?" Belle asked one morning in the parlor-turned-sewing room.

"No, I've never learned." Meg couldn't ignore the look Belle gave her sister.

"Such as happens when one loses a mother at an early age," Molly whispered back, loud enough for Meg to hear.

"I was taught to embroider, however," Meg told them. "And I can sew buttons." She wasn't exactly eager to repair uniforms for the enemy, but desired to make herself useful to the general, or at least his family, for hosting her.

The living room was comfortable, warmed as much by Mrs. Putnam's genial personality as it was by the warm summer air. The pleasant smell of the servants cooking dinner wafted in.

When they returned to their tasks after a satisfying lunch, sans the general and Major Burr, Meg didn't feel the need to put on her usual airs. She filled Molly and Belle in on some of the pranks she had pulled on the head mistress in Dublin, such as the time Meg put ink in her powder so that her hair turned the color of pitch for weeks.

"What did you learn there if not how to spin?" Molly asked.

"Needlework," Meg said, holding up the frame on which she was embroidering a handkerchief for Old Put. "My headmistress was French. She thought that English gals were boring, and was determined to teach us how to make good conversation, so we were exposed to some reading and poetry. Mostly though, we learned traits that would make us a good wife: dancing and singing."

"How does singing make you a good wife?" Belle asked.

"Apparently French gentlemen like to be sung to sleep after dinner," Meg replied.

"Do you suppose Major Burr likes to be sung to?" Belle inquired. Molly seemed to find that extraordinarily funny.

Upon hearing his name, Meg could feel her face grow hot under her mob cap. "Ouch!" she shouted, looking down at the dot of blood that now graced her finger.

Molly giggled again. "Try to keep your mind on the task at hand, Meg. That way you won't prick your finger while thinking of a handsome soldier."

Thankful for the distraction, however painful, Meg rose from the chair. "I'll just go upstairs and fetch a washcloth." She hastened from the room and climbed up the grand staircase. While she was looking for a clean rag, she noticed a door off the hallway. She headed to it, bloody finger forgotten, finding that it was unlocked. It led outside to the gallery on the flat roof of the house. She fiddled with the knob on the door, and once she was sure it wouldn't lock behind her, ventured outside.

With no trees to provide shade from the mid-afternoon sun, it was quite warm. She walked to the balustrade that bordered the edge of the rooftop, kicking something in the process. Awkwardly she bent down, casting her hands underneath her skirts to find the object, which turned out to be a small spyglass. She lifted it to her eye and peered across Manhattan. The Gothic Trinity Church, on the corner of Broadway and Wall Street, dominated the skyline with its steeple, the highest on the island. At Bowling Green, she could see the empty space where a statue of King George had once stood. The statue had been abased by ruffians upon the announcement of the Declaration of Independence just a week before. On the other side of the Mall, near Broad Street, she could see soldiers in green jackets cutting down the beautiful trees that shaded the avenue. Across the way, other men were busy digging trenches next to the cobblestone street.

She moved the spyglass to the wide beach that led to the East River. Beyond that she could see the British men-of-war, the *Asia* and the *Phoenix,* docked at the harbor. She wondered if her father was among the men on either one of those ships.

A voice from behind Meg knocked her out of her revelry. "They say an invasion is imminent."

She took a step back from the edge of the roof, wishing her wide skirt would have allowed her to sit. Her knees had weakened, either from the heat of the day or from the fact the voice belonged to Major Burr.

"So that is the cause for all the ruckus." Meg gestured toward his fellow countrymen below in the act of destroying the charming avenues of his adopted neighborhood. "Will they evacuate the city, then?" She felt sad that she'd finally found a decent home—even if it was occupied by the enemy—only to be forced to leave it again.

Aaron shrugged, taking the spyglass from her to train it on the British ships. "Your father and his friends have their guns pointed at us again."

"If the rebels would halt their crazy dreams of independence, maybe they would point them elsewhere."

"Not a chance." Aaron tossed the spyglass a couple of feet away. He glanced at her. "What are you doing up here, anyway?"

"I could ask you the same question."

"I'm stationed at the old Webb mansion." He leaned over the balustrade to point at a narrow bridge that connected the Putnam house to its equally stately next-door neighbor. "The Kennedys—

35

the ones who owned this house before Putnam confiscated it—and the Webbs used to host opulent balls, and wanted an easy way to get to and fro."

"That doesn't necessarily answer my question."

"I saw you up here, and didn't think it was a ladylike thing to do, spying on warships."

"I wasn't spying. I was trying to escape the sewing circle downstairs."

Aaron let out a laugh before catching himself. He straightened his facial features as he looked at Meg, his eyes scanning her face. "You know General Washington is coming for dinner tonight?"

"I didn't."

"Well, he is, along with some colonels and other higher-ups. I'd curb your Tory talk if I were you."

"I don't talk like a Tory."

He started toward the entrance to the roof. "You do, but I suppose one can't be blamed if they are the daughter of a traitor."

Meg turned in his direction. "My father is loyal to his King. It is your Commander-in-Chief that is a traitor."

He opened the door. "Even if you think that, I wouldn't mention it to the Commander-in-Chief himself."

"We'll see about that," she told him as she stalked past him.

"Indeed we will." Meg couldn't be sure, but she detected from the sound of his voice that his grin had returned.

George Washington was as tall as the rumors had said he was. He wore no wig, choosing to powder his graying brown hair and style it with curls above each ear. His uniform was the same dark blue as Major Burr's, but with gold epaulets at the shoulders. His long face held no hint of a smile. It was well-known that he spoke rarely so Meg was shocked when, as the meal began, General Washington asked her why she didn't drink her wine.

The truth was that the toast had been to Congress, and Meg didn't feel the need to drink to the health of the redundant governing body. Aaron's earlier warning froze her reply in her throat and she cast her eyes around the table helplessly. Everyone seated gazed back at Meg, waiting for her response. She picked up her glass and took a cautious sip. "To Parliament and Admiral Howe," she said quietly.

There was an audible gasp from the direction of Lady Washington, a stocky, regal woman in a simple dress and cap. Meg looked over at Aaron, who stared back at her with his black eyes narrowed, his chiseled jaw set.

Old Put, seated beside General Washington, let out a hearty guffaw, the kind that came straight from the gut. "Forgive the child, she does not mean to offend." He patted the general on his shoulder. "Anything from the mouth of such a young innocent should be an amusement, not an insult."

General Washington set down his wine glass and turned his steely blue eyes to Meg. "Miss Moncrieffe, I will overlook your... indiscretion, provided the next time you are at Admiral Howe's table, you drink to my health."

The rest of their company let out uneasy giggles.

Despite her heated face, the general's words produced hope that Meg would soon be reunited with her father. "Sir," she said, interrupting the cautious conversation around her. General Washington once again glanced in her direction. "I will do anything you ask provided you permit me to see my father again."

He exchanged a look with Old Put, who furrowed his brow. "I will do what I can," the general consented, picking up his fork. "But as of right now he's on the other side of the water from us."

"Have you ever been to an American ball?" Molly asked Meg the next day.

Meg set down her embroidery frame. "No. I suppose the brink of war is not exactly the time to have balls."

"It is not, but there is one anyway next Friday night."

"I wouldn't exactly call it a ball, more like a social gathering," Belle added. "And the price of the ticket goes toward raising money for the troops."

"You have to come, Meg," Molly insisted. "I'm sure Father will pay for us all to go."

Mrs. Putnam didn't pause in her spinning, but Meg noticed her eyebrows raise slightly.

She swallowed the lump of nerves that had appeared in her throat. "Do you suppose that the local officers will be there as well?"

"If you mean a certain Major Burr, I believe so," Belle replied.

While the city readied itself for the suspected arrival of Admiral Howe and his troops, the Putnam sisters and Meg occupied themselves by preparing for the ball. It was to be held at Fraunces Tavern, on the corner of Queen and Dock streets.

Most of the merchants in that area had vacated the city, including, unfortunately for Meg, those that ran the best dress shops. The next few days were blissfully free of spinning as the Putnam girls and their maids set about turning last season's dresses into a more current style.

Belle lent Meg a dress of rose silk. Meg tried to hide her dismay: the color was pretty, but the dress had the wide skirt of two years ago instead of the form-fitting gown with a higher waistline she had come to prefer.

Belle pulled up the mountain of fabric in the back. "Don't worry, Meg, you can alter the farthingale into a bustle."

Meg sat on her bed. "I can't alter anything." She had never wanted for many material things in her short years. Her father, far away though he was, always provided her with whatever toiletry and clothing materials she might have needed. But she was forced to leave all her beautiful dresses when she evacuated and the blockade meant that new and alluring things were not easy to come by.

Belle sat beside her. "Molly and I can help, as can my maid, Eunice. And wait until you see how good Eunice is with hair. We'll literally be the 'belles' of the ball."

Meg looked at her gratefully. Her mother had died in a drowning accident when she was two and her father had sent her brother and her away to school shortly after that. He had remarried twice, but both of her stepmothers had also died. Most of her life she had been passed from one caretaker to another. Belle and Molly were the closest Meg had to any female relatives for a long time. "Thank you," Meg told Belle as she pulled her up from the bed.

The day of the ball was a flurry of activity. At Belle's insistence, the girls indulged in a large breakfast but skipped lunch. They hid away from the heat of the day by taking a nap indoors, cooled by the pleasant breeze that entered through the open windows.

Near evening, Eunice was employed to coax and tease the Putnam sisters' hair high on top of their heads, in the style of the new French queen. Eunice braided Molly's hair with pearls while Belle's coif was adorned with fresh flowers. Meg preferred to keep hers simple, asking Eunice to just use the curling tongs on the wisps of hair that hung down from her unadorned chignon.

The heat had lessened considerably when the Putnams and Meg left One Broadway. Old Put wore his uniform while Mrs. Putnam was in green brocade, of a darker shade than Molly's dress. Belle was a vision in blue.

As the ball was only a few blocks away, they decided to forgo a carriage. Meg peered at the house next door as they set off, wondering if Major Burr was still getting ready. She couldn't discern any activity inside and set her eyes to focus on the sidewalk in front of her.

The tavern was a red-bricked building in the Dutch style with a flat roof and a portico held up by white pillars. The liveried butler greeted the party by offering his arm to Mrs. Putnam as she made her way up the cobblestones, the general on her other side. As they entered the building, he announced, "General Putnam, his wife, his daughters, and..."

"Miss Moncrieffe." Aaron appeared by her side. He wore his blue and buff uniform, but had added lace cuffs underneath his coat and a cravat at his neck.

"Miss Moncrieffe," the servant echoed.

"How do you do this evening?" Aaron turned to look Meg up

39

and down and she thought she saw a look of appreciation appear on his face. She noted that he looked even more handsome and dashing than the first time they met.

She flipped out her fan and held it in front of her mouth. "Fine," she replied from behind it. She glanced around the tavern, taking in the small tables covered in white tablecloths and the well-dressed Americans filling them. Candles blazed from every available space, renewing the July heat that the evening had cooled off. The smell of cooking meat and stale beer filled Meg's nose with every movement of her fan.

"General Putnam, sir, do you have a minute?" Aaron asked, turning to Old Put.

"Oh, Burr," he sighed. "Always working. Yes, I suppose." He put his arm around Aaron as an older man in a powdered wig approached. "Ah, Black Sam," the general extended his hand to the man. "Let us get a libation."

"Why do they call him 'Black Sam?'" Meg asked Belle as the trio walked away. The man named Sam's ruddy color was similar to Major Burr's.

She shrugged. "His real name is Samuel Fraunces. He is the proprietor of this tavern."

Meg folded her fan and turned toward the main reception room, darting her eyes across the patrons. "Look at all the macaronis," she said disdainfully.

"The what?" Belle whispered as Molly walked off to greet a dark-haired girl in a yellow gown.

"The macaronis. You know, like Yankee Doodle?"

Belle shook her head.

Meg stepped closer to her. "Take that man over your left shoulder, no, don't look yet. Look now." Belle cast her eyes to a middle-aged man wearing a miniscule tricorn hat that topped a powdered wig a full foot above his head. He wore striped silk knee breeches below his unbuttoned coat, which had a red carnation tucked in the pocket. "That's a macaroni."

Belle giggled. "I prefer a man in uniform."

Meg unfolded her fan once more and covered her face, trying not to be obvious about her search for Aaron.

She located him at one of the tables in the corner, conferring with Putnam. Two other soldiers had joined them, one of whom she recognized as Captain Webb from her journey a few days ago.

Belle grabbed Meg's arm and pulled her to where her sister was engaged in a whispered conversation with the dark-haired girl. "I see Alexander Hamilton is here tonight," Belle stated, gesturing to her father and the group of young men. She turned to the other girl. "Meg, I'd like to introduce you to Angelica Schuyler, daughter of General Schuyler."

"How do you do?" Meg curtsied prettily.

"Meg is a Loyalist, but we don't mind," Molly added.

"Indeed?" Angelica asked.

"My father is Captain Moncrieffe of the British army."

Angelica nodded before catching sight of someone over her shoulder. "Captain Webb!"

"Ladies." He extended his hand toward Meg. "Would you care to dance, Miss Moncrieffe?"

As he led her to the dance floor, she snuck a glance at Aaron, who was still huddled with Old Put and the other man.

"I trust you are getting along well in New York?" Captain Webb asked as they touched hands and got into the rhythm of the gavotte.

Meg circled around him before their hands met again. "I am. Old Put and the missus have been quite gracious."

"They always are," Webb said as he shifted down the line.

A fop in a bright blue coat met Meg's hand and introduced himself briefly as a Mr. De Lancy before the line moved again.

Half an hour later, Meg was finally able to sit down. It seemed she had met all of New York society's leading men in the short time she'd been at the ball.

Captain Webb appeared with a mug of cider. "Here, you look like you could use this."

"Thanks," Meg told him gratefully. She took a ladylike sip,

though what she really wanted to do was devour the drink, slam the silver cup on the table, and demand more. Aaron was still in the corner, only now he was surrounded by women. He moved slightly to the side of one woman and her towering hairpiece, meeting Meg's eyes before narrowing them at Captain Webb.

She took another drink and then stuck her hand out to the captain so he could help her to her feet. As she was suitably emboldened by her ale, she decided it was time to approach Aaron. "If you will excuse me for one moment," she called over her shoulder.

Upon closer scrutiny, the women surrounding him seemed ages older than herself. "Major Burr, would you accompany me outside?" Meg flicked her fan out. "I could use some air and would like a military escort."

He excused himself from his hangers-on to take her arm and lead her out the back door. His hand rested on her elbow as they walked on the herringbone patterned pathway, but he dropped it when they paused beside a fence surrounding the grassy knoll that sloped toward the East River.

"Captain Webb could have escorted you out here," Aaron said finally.

"I am aware. But I wanted you."

Aaron blew out his breath and rested his hands on the fence. Meg noticed how strong they appeared underneath the frill of his sleeves. "It seemed to me you could have had any available man in that room." He turned to face her. "Or any man in any room. Why don't you find a kingsman to align yourself with?"

Meg reached for his hand. "Why should I when I can have a perfectly good rebel?"

He stepped closer. "Meg, this isn't going to work. You are so young, and I might be called off to war at any moment."

"I'm not so young. Many people my age are already married. And who knows what tomorrow brings? Maybe General Howe will not attack Manhattan and all of those soldiers making preparations can go home."

"Would that make you happy?"

She shifted her hand so that their fingers were entwined. "Being with you would make me happy."

"Would you change your alliance for me? Would you betray your father for my hand?"

"Do I have to?"

He dropped her hand and turned toward the river. "Yes. I'm Putnam's aide-de-camp, and he assures me that a promotion is forthcoming. Being tied to the daughter of a captain on the other side would not do me any favors."

"I would never forsake my father. Or my King." Meg's voice wobbled as her eyes flooded.

Aaron pulled a handkerchief from his sleeve and shook it out. He wiped her eyes tenderly before he said, "And I won't abandon my career."

"So that's it then." Meg moved his hand away from her face, the tears suitably dried.

He tucked the handkerchief into his pocket. "I guess so."

"Can I just ask for one thing? Can I have a kiss from a handsome officer in the garden on a summer's evening?"

Aaron looked around. The doors that led to the tavern stood open, the laughter and gossip of the room floating out toward the few couples strolling along the promenade near the river. He opened a small gate and led her under the shade of an oak tree. Meg leaned up against it as he asked, "Are you sure you want to do this?"

In lieu of a reply, she pulled him toward her. When their lips met, it felt as though her whole life paraded before her in mere seconds: the death of her mother and her father's next wives after her, the lonely times in Dublin, the fearful scene with the soldiers in Elizabethtown. She was tired of being abandoned, tired of being alone. She may have been a child by some people's standards, but the want coursing through her veins was a woman's need. She wanted to be with Major Burr more than she had ever wanted anything. But was she willing to give up her King and family in order to do so?

43

CHAPTER 6

MEG

*T*he morning after the ball, Meg arose late. She hadn't gotten much sleep: when she lay on her back in her bed, it brought to mind Aaron's soft lips when he kissed her last night. Turning onto her side only served to remind her of the chasm between them. Her last thought before she finally fell asleep was that the chasm could miraculously disappear once this silly war ended.

After breakfast, she was commanded into yet another seemingly endless sewing session. In mid-afternoon, Eunice entered the room to announce a visitor for Miss Moncrieffe.

"Who is it?" Meg was thankful at any rate for the interruption.

Eunice frowned. "A Redcoat captain."

Belle put down the wool she was carding. "A Redcoat? Here?"

Meg rushed to the door. She was pleased to see her old acquaintance, Thomas Walcott, standing in the front hallway.

"Thomas!" she cried, extending her hand. Thomas kissed it obligingly and then gazed over her shoulder. Meg followed his eyes to see Aaron, dressed in riding breeches, leaning against the door-frame outside Putnam's office.

"How is your family?" Meg asked, taking a step closer to Thomas.

"My sister and mother are well. Father is with His Majesty's navy. As was I." He took another glance at Aaron, who now had his arms crossed in front of him.

"The navy? Do you have news of my father?" The Walcott's had been family friends in England and Meg had attended boarding school with Sarah, Thomas's younger sister.

Thomas shook his head.

"What brings you to New York?"

"Well," Thomas shoved his hands into his pockets. "Actually, I'm what you might call a prisoner." From the end of the hallway, Aaron coughed. Both Meg and Thomas ignored him as Thomas continued, "I was captured in the Battle of Bunker Hill."

Conscious of Aaron's eyes on them, Meg put her arm on Thomas's sleeve. "Are you well then?"

"They are treating me quite fine. I have been staying at the home of Hercules Mulligan, the tailor. I believe Major Burr is acquainted with him and his old tenant, Alexander Hamilton." Another cough sounded from Aaron's direction as Thomas stated, "Hercules mentioned that your father requested your residence be here with General Putnam."

At this Meg peered back at Aaron, her hand still placed on Thomas's forearm. Aaron pretended to study the wall in front of him.

"I'm afraid I must return to Mr. Mulligan's at this time," Thomas said, returning Meg's arm to her. "They allow me to come and go as I please. Of that I am grateful, but I wouldn't want to stir their suspicion." Thomas paused as Aaron cleared his throat loudly. "Mayhap I can call on you tomorrow, Meg? We can catch up with old news."

"Of course, Thomas." She turned so that Aaron could see her profile before giving Thomas her sweetest smile. "I'd like that very much."

"Then I shall take my leave of you for today. G'day, Miss Moncrieffe," Thomas said, tipping his hat toward her. "Major Burr." He turned to give Aaron the same gesture, though this time with slightly less enthusiasm.

After he left, Meg put her hands on her hips and glared toward the end of the hallway. "What was that all about, Aaron? Are you coming down with a cold?"

He sauntered forward. "I heard Eunice announce the Redcoat and I wanted to make sure you were not cavorting with the enemy."

"He's no enemy of mine," Meg replied pointedly.

"Yes, I noticed. How do you know him?"

"Not that it's any of your business, but our fathers are old friends."

"I see." Aaron grabbed his knapsack from the hook next to the door. "This conversation has been titillating, but I'm afraid I will have to take my leave of you as well, Miss Moncrieffe."

She pursed her lips before asking, "Are we back to Miss Moncrieffe now?"

Aaron's face seemed to redden slightly and Meg wondered if he was recalling, as she was, their kiss under the stars last night. When he didn't reply, she inquired where he was off to.

"The general has asked me to survey the works around the island."

Meg knew he was referring to the construction of the barricades Old Put had ordered in case there was a British invasion. "I'll come with you," she offered. "The general has given me permission to exercise Salem on occasion in exchange for letting him use him if the need arises. That is," she continued coyly, "after he promised Salem wouldn't be shot down by his enemies."

"Your fellow countrymen," Aaron added. "And it would not be appropriate for you to accompany me."

She tossed her hair back. "Since when have I given heed to what is appropriate?"

At that moment, Old Put exited his office. "Burr, are you still here?"

Meg curtsied as he came toward them. "General Putnam, I'm

47

sorry to say it is me who has detained Aaron in his errand. I noticed that Salem is in dire need of exercise, and I've asked Aaron if I could join him on his ride."

Old Put cocked an eyebrow. "And what did Major Burr say?"

Aaron stood straighter. "I tried to convince her it was a poor idea."

Old Put threw back his head and laughed. "Something tells me there is no convincing this one once she has made up her mind."

"Indeed, sir," Aaron agreed quietly.

Taking the general's comment as permission, Meg ran up the stairs to change into her riding habit.

They rode down Broadway and turned east, crossing New Street. As they approached Smith Street, Meg saw a white figure running toward them, screaming in pain. When they drew closer, Meg could discern that it was a man covered in feathers. The men chasing him were shouting and throwing small pebbles at him. The man tripped over a loose cobblestone and fell, a plume of down scattering in the dust as he hit the ground. Two of his pursuers caught up to him and then bound his arms in rope as the other men looked on.

"What goes?" Aaron asked one of the accomplices as he and Meg halted their horses.

"Another Tory spy, sir," the man replied, doffing his tri-cornered hat.

Meg watched as they led the man away. He was still screaming in agony and she could see that the skin that wasn't strewn with feathers was either blackened with pine tar or blanketed in blisters.

Aaron gave her a worried glance, but once he realized she was more curious than horrified, he motioned for his horse to move onward.

"What was that all about?" Meg inquired.

"Punishment for spying," Aaron replied, his eyes on the path in front of him.

"Spying? How do you know there are spies?"

"We've intercepted a few communications that prove the British have pretty accurate knowledge of the activities of the Continental Army. There are Loyalist spies as well as Patriot. The Sons of Liberty are rooting out what they call the 'Tory Nest' on Manhattan."

"But how do these spies deliver their information?"

Aaron shrugged. "They know someone who knows someone who is able to get the message into the right hands." He turned to look at her. "I can't think of a more repugnant occupation than pretending to be on one side while working for the other, all the while living under the threat of a barrel of hot tar, or, worse yet, the hangman's noose."

As they traveled toward the East River, Meg marveled at the breastworks at the end of Queen Street: large wooden trunks stacked ten feet across, the crevices between each trunk filled in with earth and mud. Aaron pulled his horse to a halt at Whitehall dock. Despite the presence of the British warships in the middle of the river, the wharf was bustling with merchants unloading their trade, the smell of spice and rum filling the air. Aaron focused his eyes on the heavy cannons that faced the river. "Intimidating, isn't it?"

Meg reached over to nuzzle Salem's nose. "I'm not sure it's enough to stop the British navy if they decide to invade."

Aaron sighed as he looked downriver. "Here we go again."

"Aaron." Meg adjusted her seat on the saddle to face him. "What if this war ended as quickly as it had begun? We could marry in peace."

"Quickly in whose favor? Your father's? The King's?"

"In anyone's favor," she replied. "Just so long as we could be together. But, you have to admit, the British have the might: the navy, the cavalry, the money. What do a rag-tag bunch of colonists have against the most powerful empire in the world?"

Aaron glanced over at her, a scowl darkening his handsome face. "I wouldn't be so quick to preclude the result of this war. We might not have the naval strength that the King does, but we have the will and the desire to be free."

"Freedom does not put a penny in your pocket." Meg maneu-vered Salem so that she and Aaron were nearly touching. "Aaron, I could get my father to give you a commission in the British army." She reached out and took his hand. "You could be a colonel instead of a major. And then, when this ridiculous skirmish is over, we could go back to England and raise babies on a fine piece of property."

He yanked his hand back. "Meg, that's treason talk. And besides, I would never give up my taste of freedom, not for land, not for a commission—"

"Not for me," Meg filled in.

He glanced at her before moving his gaze once again to the river. "I don't know what more you need from me. We want two different things."

"But we both want to be with each other."

Aaron clicked his tongue, causing his horse to move forward. "That's not enough."

Meg led Salem into a gallop, her tears blurring the barricades before her. She'd never met more of a stubborn man than Aaron Burr. He was never going to waver from his precious rebellion. *If only there was a way to end this war quickly,* Meg thought as she headed back to One Broadway.

Meg was still thinking the same thoughts that night as she sat down to write a letter to Mrs. DeHart in Elizabethtown. Instead of filling the page with descriptions of last night's ball, she began to sketch the fortifications she had seen earlier. Gun batteries covered the Hudson side of the island and there were more cannons down by the Battery and at Coenties Slip, a block north of Broad Street.

When she was done, she was looking at a map of Manhattan, diagramming most of the defenses she had scouted with Aaron. She crumpled up the paper in her hand, hearing Aaron's voice speak once again of treason. She nearly lit it on fire with the candle beside her before she heard Aaron's other words from earlier: "They give it to someone who knows someone who can get it into the right hands." If the British were somehow informed of the American defenses, maybe they could find a vulnerable place to invade and end this conflict once and for all. Defeated, Aaron would have no choice but to follow her and her father back to England, where the captain would give them some of his extensive land as a wedding present.

"Indeed," she said to herself as she ran her fingers along the paper, smoothing the creases, thinking that she would do anything to be with Aaron. And she knew just the person who could get this report into her father's hands.

Aaron was mercifully absent the next morning when Thomas Walcott came again to call on Meg. It was a warm, sunny day and she invited him for a stroll in the gardens.

After a few minutes of pleasantries, Meg asked Thomas about being a prisoner. "I thought that meant you'd be held in a jail."

"Yes, thankfully not. Because I am of nobility, and not much of a threat, according to the rebels, anyway, they let me walk free. But I'm not allowed to leave the city."

"Are you a threat?" she asked, a note of sincerity underneath her teasing tone.

Thomas glanced quickly at her and then focused back on the path in front of them. "That depends."

"On what such matter?"

He shot her a smile that didn't reach his eyes. "It depends on who is asking."

"Suppose," Meg bent down to sniff a hydrangea bloom. "Suppose I had some information to get to my father." She straightened back up.

"What sort of information?"

"Some might call it 'intelligence.'" She looked Thomas in the eyes as she reached into her bodice and pulled out the folded slip of paper.

Thomas grabbed it from her before peering around the garden. "Miss Moncrieffe, you need to learn a bit more discretion. What if someone saw you hand this to me?"

51

She clasped her hands in front of her. "You could just say it was a love poem."

He colored slightly. "And if I was searched, what would they find?"

She leaned in to whisper, "Information about the rebel's defenses. Can you get it to my father?"

Thomas nodded discreetly. "I know a few Loyalists who are in contact with Governor Tryon. I think I can pass this on. Will there be more of the same sort in the future?"

She stepped back. "Mayhap."

"And how will I get this information?"

"You could call on me again," she replied.

"Don't you think that would arouse suspicion?" He ducked as they passed underneath an arbor. "What would your friend Major Burr say?"

"He might just have to turn the other cheek. This is for his own good, though he doesn't know it yet." She bent down to pluck a rose from the vine trailing up the arbor.

"You do know you are playing a dangerous game."

"Why, Thomas, I am just a lowly woman. They would hang you over me any day. I could just claim I had no idea that information was treason."

He narrowed his eyes. "For a woman, you seem to know an awful lot about treason."

Carefully, so as to avoid any thorns, Meg tucked the rose behind her ear. "I'm not sure what you could possibly be referring to."

Sunday morning, Aaron and Meg accompanied the family to Trinity Church off Broadway. As the Putnam contingent filed into the seats, Meg glanced around the regal edifice to take in the décor. The scattering of light filtering through the gridded windows would have resulted in a dim room had it not been for the massive chandelier hanging from the nave. She mused that there must have been more than a hundred candles in it. The pews were constructed of dark hardwood; a grand organ ornamented with angels and cherubs was placed near the pulpit. A fine bouquet was perched atop the stately altar, the vines trailing across it and downward. More flowers and shrubbery sat on either end of the Lord's Table and the scent of lavender and lilies filled the air.

Meg's assessment of the interior was interrupted when Old Put leaned over his pew to grasp the shoulder of the man in front of him. She caught his profile when he turned to pat Putnam's hand. It was the Commander-in-Chief of the Continental army himself.

After the army's arrival in the city, most of the clergy had removed their Royal coats of arms and ended their tradition of praying for the health of King George at the conclusion of their sermon. Charles Inglis, the rector of Trinity Church, however, had refused to, even under the threat of lynching. Aaron raised his eyebrows at Meg as he sat next to her in the pew. He seemed to be wondering what she was: would Inglis dare to speak of the King with General Washington in attendance?

Tensions rose as the time for the litany grew closer. Meg detected the faint sound of fifes and drums outside. The sounds became increasingly louder until the church doors were thrown open and the band of men entered. She peered behind her. The green uniformed soldiers stood in between the pews, brandishing muskets, their bayonets gleaming in the candlelight. Meg started to rise to get a better view, but Aaron pulled her back down. On the other side of her, Belle murmured, "If he prays for the King, it won't be long until he finds his own eternity box."

Meg reached for Aaron's hand. He squeezed it reassuringly but his eyes were on Reverend Inglis. A few men in front of them stood up and both Meg and Aaron leaned to opposite sides to see what would happen next. She winced upon hearing the reverend's voice —in a booming, clear tone—declare, "Heartily we beseech thee with thy favor to behold our most gracious sovereign lord, King George."

Aaron's grip on Meg's hand tightened as she heard Belle gasp. On the opposite end of the aisle, Putnam rose to bark commands: Molly had fainted. Mrs. Putnam pulled smelling salts out of her bag and shoved them underneath her daughter's nose, all the while her eyes never left the podium. The rest of the congregation was in a similar uproar, but Inglis, unharmed and still at his position at the pulpit, droned on. Meg breathed an inward sigh of relief and couldn't help thinking, *God protect the King and his faithful servants.*

The service continued without further incident, save for the men with pointed bayonets standing in the aisle and the loud whispering from the congregation.

Afterward, Meg lingered behind to make sure that Molly, who had come back around, was able to walk on her own. Aaron and most of the other men had rushed out as soon as Inglis had stepped down. When Meg finally joined them in the sunshine, she found the scene outside to be much calmer than the one during the service. Many of the patrons had headed home already to their Sunday suppers; only a scattering of families remained, lingering to gossip in the church gardens. Meg caught sight of Reverend Inglis being escorted into a carriage by a handful of Whigs. When she finally located Aaron, she found him deep in conversation with Old Put under the shade of a group of locust trees. She was too far away to hear what they were saying but she felt the heat rise to her face nonetheless. Was it her imagination or did both of them keep glancing at her throughout their exchange?

She was about to interrupt their hushed conversation when a loud hammering deterred her. A man dressed in a clergy uniform was standing next to the church doors. After he finished his task, he hurried away, leaving Meg to approach his vacated spot. A large chain was strung through the handle of the door and a proclamation declared that, by order of the vestry, the church had been closed until further notice.

CHAPTER 7

ELIZABETH

AUGUST 1776

he movement of the British men-of-war proved that the Redcoats could strike at any point in the city. Jonathan's commander decided to have his troops sleep out in the open at King's Bridge, in case the enemy resolved to cut Manhattan Island off from the mainland. Throughout August, the British ships kept arriving. The few customers at the shop—the numbers had dwindled yet again with this latest evacuation—filled Elizabeth in with news of the Redcoats' position. Most citizens were convinced that the British would attack the city, but the questions remaining were when and where.

The family dog, Jonathan's since before they were married, stared out the window that overlooked Queen Street, searching for his missing master. Johnny and Catherine frequently joined the hound at his post, their sweet little voices continuously asking of the whereabouts of their father.

As Elizabeth swelled into the final stages of her pregnancy, the summer heat grew even more oppressive. Terse notes from Jonathan stated that he was exhausted from being outdoors all day and night, and felt inferior to the more able-bodied young men in his troop. He wrote in mid-August that dysentery and smallpox were running rampant in the camps. Unsure of where the enemy would attack, Washington had decided to divide his reduced army between the two shores of the East River. Jonathan's was among those troops transferred to guard Long Island.

And still the city waited.

CHAPTER 8

MEG

AUGUST 1776

*L*ike wax from a slow burning candle, worry dripped into Meg's heart. Every day her spyglass revealed more British warships arriving in the already packed harbor.

She was not alone in her gazing—onlookers equipped with their own spyglasses also dotted other housetops at all hours and the wharves were crowded with bystanders. No one—American, British or any other nationality—had ever seen so many ships in one place.

The men refrained from speaking much about the threat of war in the presence of women, but Meg could tell by Aaron and General Putnam's increasingly prolonged meetings that something was happening. Not to mention that General Washington himself was a frequent visitor to One Broadway Street.

She had no way of knowing whether Thomas was able to get the information she gave him to British commanders. He had not come to call after that fateful meeting in the garden.

"Meg?" Old Put poked his head out of his office to find her

creeping near the staircase, trying to avoid the sewing circle in the living room.

"Sir?"

"Can you come in here for a minute?"

"Of course, General." She strode in, skirts swishing. The effect was somewhat wasted since Aaron was not in the room. However, the insides of Putnam's office could not exactly be termed "empty." Heaps of paper covered the mahogany desk as well as the hard-wood floor.

Old Put gestured at the mess. "Since Major Burr is currently occupied, I was hoping you'd be able to help me organize some of this paperwork."

Meg curtsied. "I would be delighted, sir." She glanced at a nearby paper. It was signed by the Commander-in-Chief and her hands itched to see what more information she could glean from her errand.

"But first things first," she told him as she walked toward the window. She pulled back the heavy velvet drapes and secured them with cords.

Both Meg and the general blinked in the sudden light that bathed the dark room and softened the olive walls. The gilt-frames of the portraits—presumably long dead ancestors of Captain Kennedy, the previous occupant—lining one wall now looked grimy. She sneezed at the dust particles dancing in the sunlight while Old Put grabbed a caned wooden chair and set it in front of one of the piles.

"No need for this anymore, then." He extinguished the candle on his desk. "It's all kindling at this point, anyway."

"What is all of this?" Meg asked as she picked up a single sheet off the top of the pile.

"Old orders, commands of troops, requisitions of supplies. Just boring war stuff."

Her heart sank at the word, "old." She peered at the date on the paper in her hand. *April, 1776.* "How would you like me to sort it?"

"Keep any bills or lists of payments for Congress's records.

Everything else can be burned. We must prepare for the off-chance that the British invade New York City."

Meg feigned surprise. "Do you think they are coming?"

Putnam set down his bifocals and rubbed at his eyes. "Those ships in the harbor are probably not just for show. Whether they attack here or Long Island remains to be seen. General Washington must prepare for both possibilities."

She looked up as she heard a door rattle. Aaron, clad in his full blue and buff uniform, entered the room. "Sir, I don't think we need to ponder Howe's course of action anymore."

"Oh?" Old Put dropped the paper in his hand. "What news of Howe?"

Aaron glanced at Meg before replying, "He removed his troops from Staten Island and placed them at Gravesend, on Long Island." He moved forward and handed the general a sealed letter. "Orders from General Washington. General Greene has fallen ill and you are to be in command of the army on Long Island."

Putnam sat back. "I will go willingly, but I do not have much idea of the terrain."

Aaron moved a stack of papers before he unrolled a map on the table in front of Putnam. Meg retreated into a corner, trying to remain as inconspicuous as possible. Both men were too preoccupied to notice her.

Aaron pointed to the map. "The British are entrenched at Flatbush."

"And if we are to keep them there?" Old Put replaced his bifocals to peer at where Aaron was pointing.

"We will need men here, at the Narrows to the right, and here at these passes."

Putnam ran his finger in a semi-circle on the far left-hand side of the map. "What of this one?"

"That's Jamaica Road, sir. It is a narrow road on rough terrain, set by heavy pines on either side."

Old Put shook his head. "We need more men on the easier routes. Spare a few for that road, but put Lord Stirling's men on

Gowanus Road at the Narrows and Sullivan's troops at Flatbush and Bedford Roads."

Aaron nodded and rolled up the map. He started in surprise upon spying Meg in the corner. "Sir?" He turned back to the general.

Old Put had pushed his bifocals to the top of his head and his forefinger now occupied their place at the bridge of his nose. "Hmm?" he replied, obviously lost in thought.

"What of Miss Moncrieffe?"

Old Put sat up in his chair and cast a glance at his charge. "I suppose it is now time to return her to her father."

Her heart leapt at the comment, then immediately fell as she realized the full consequence of his words.

She gazed helplessly at Aaron. His face had hardened. "Indeed, sir." He directed his reply to the general, but his eyes were focused on Meg. "It is much too dangerous for her to linger here. I will make arrangements and then see to making sure Mrs. Putnam and the girls have a place to stay outside of the city."

The general nodded and Aaron left. Meg's eyes remained on the door, hoping he'd come back and declare that, in fact, he was taking her with him.

"I'm sorry, Meg," Old Put stated wearily.

She sunk her weakened body back into a chair. "For what, sir?"

"I know that you love him."

She turned to him, her mouth dropping open in a most unlady-like manner. "General?"

The old man's lips turned upward into a hint of a smile. "You young people think everything is so new, that no one before you has been in the throes of love. I've seen it all, been through it all, watched my men become arsy-varsey with the opposite sex. Even been head over heels myself." He reached out his hand and she came forward to grasp it. "But you are indeed young, Meg, and do not fully realize the consequences of your intended affair."

"But I do sir, and am prepared to follow Aaron wherever he is stationed."

He dropped her hand. "Are you aware that your father and

Aaron fight for different causes? If given the chance, Major Burr would not hesitate to run a sword through your relations in honor of this new nation. And so it would go with your father in regard to his misguided loyalty to the King. I know—I fought by his side during the French and Indian War."

She lowered her gaze. The thought that Aaron and her father might meet in battle had never occurred to her. "Still, I would choose Aaron over my father's allegiances."

"Nonsense," he barked, folding his arms across his broad chest. "I will not allow you to make that decision." His eyes softened. "Hence my sorrow. Major Burr would have been the ideal choice for you in every other respect but for this one unavoidable fact. As a friend of your father's outside of this war, I must order you to return to him and forget about Aaron. I'm sure that once Captain Moncrieffe's attentions are not otherwise distracted, he will find a fine fellow countryman for you to marry."

Meg burst into tears as she rushed out of the room. She ran up the grand staircase and threw herself on the bed to cry for everything that she had lost.

Eunice was ordered to Meg's room to commence packing. Meg stared despondently out the window, willing her love to come rescue her. It was pouring rain and, as she was unable to escape to her rooftop post, she felt even more trapped than she had that afternoon when General Putnam declared his orders to send her back to her father.

After Eunice left, Meg cried herself to an uneasy, restless sleep.

When morning dawned, Meg dressed in a spring green traveling dress tied in the back with a flourish. The slighter skirt would allow her to be more comfortable on the rig that carried her away from her love.

He was standing in the hall when she went downstairs. "Aaron! Have you come to spirit me away?"

He frowned, a muscle twitching in his cheek. "Meg, don't joke."

"I wasn't," she said sadly as she passed by him. She went into the kitchen to say farewell to the family. General Putnam had already left for his post on Long Island and Mrs. Putnam and her daughters were going to stay with friends in Connecticut.

After tearful goodbyes with both Belle and Molly promising to write, Meg once again ventured to the hall. Her bags had been loaded into the carriage waiting outside.

Aaron had not moved from his spot.

"Are you at least going to convey me to my father's ship?" Meg asked.

He nodded. "I've been ordered to join General Putnam, but he gave me leave to see you off. I can only go as far as the docks. Colonel Webb will take you from there. The general also asks that you pass this note to Admiral Howe." Aaron bent down to tuck it into Meg's traveling purse before he hoisted the bag onto his shoulders. He held the door open as Meg left One Broadway for the last time.

The coach began its journey in silence. Meg stared out the window, tears running down her face.

"Meg."

She looked up at Aaron. He looked as sad as she felt as he stated, "I'm sorry."

"Will you come for me after the war?"

He sighed. "I don't know how long that will be. You will probably be married with nine babies by then."

"I will wait for you. All you have to do is ask."

"I cannot ask that of you."

"Will you not wait for me?" She paused as a thought occurred to her. "Let's just tell the coachman to turn back. We can find a clergyman and demand that he marry us straightaway."

He shook his head. "I am a soldier, and ready to die for my cause. But I don't think I can give myself fully if I fear making a widow of you." Every word he spoke emphasized how willing he was to sacrifice himself for his country, at the same time, widening the gap between them and cutting loose the thread that bound their love. "Every time I see your beautiful face, I also see the tyranny of England. I see lordships and titles and privilege. The Continental army does not pay well. If we were to marry, you would be forced to live in poverty and I would have to turn my back on all that I have come to believe in. General Putnam was right: our love can never be."

The carriage came to a halt and Meg rose from her seat. "You might one day know the blessed feeling of independence, Aaron. But I, as a woman, will never be free to make my own decisions."

Colonel Webb helped her out of the carriage and down to the dock while Aaron loaded her bags onto the boat. The wharf was mercifully empty of the onlookers that had graced it for the past few days. Most of the American soldiers had been commanded to Long Island and the rebel sympathizers had evacuated to other parts of the country.

Meg looked at the vast ships that stood at the entrance to the harbor. Her father was aboard one of them, titled the *Eagle*, but she had no idea which one that was.

A seagull landed nearby and pecked at the wood of the wharf before cawing mournfully. In due time her bags were tied onto the skiff. Colonel Webb stepped into the boat as Aaron came to stand beside Meg.

She turned and hugged him hard. The tears were threatening to spill again, but she forced them back. She did not want Aaron to remember her as a sobbing, weak fool. "Take care, Aaron. I fear you will come to harm in the next few days. For your sake, I hope the British leave New York City alone."

"I shall burn the island myself before I let the British take it over." Aaron's voice was muffled.

Meg drew back. "Would you cut the ties that bind you to this city so easily?" she asked, knowing they were not speaking of the city itself.

He nodded and cast his gaze out to the warships bouncing in the gray, rippling water of the Hudson.

Meg reached up to touch his face. "I will love you forever."

He did not reply as he descended into the skiff and held out his arm.

Gently he conveyed her into the boat and led her to a seat, arranging her skirt so it would not get wet. He kissed her cheek before he stepped back onto the dock and nodded at the oarsman.

As the boat pulled away, Aaron stood motionless, as if he were a statue adhered to the dock. The tears could now flow freely. Colonel Webb handed Meg a handkerchief but said nothing.

She watched the figure of Aaron Burr grow smaller and smaller, half hoping he would dive into the water and swim to the boat, declaring that he changed his mind, that he would marry her after all. A tiny smile emerged on her lips. Aaron was too much of a gentleman to put on such a scene. The smile faded as quickly as it had appeared as Meg cursed the fate that brought so fine a man into her life only to let her be torn apart from him.

As though nature had sensed her mood, it began to rain. The waters were rough and Meg's stomach dropped. "Is it much farther?" she asked Colonel Webb. Now that her providence had been determined, she was anxious to see her father again.

Colonel Webb narrowed his gaze and looked off to the distance. "I see a British barge approaching under a flag of truce."

"Are we not to reach the *Eagle*, then?"

"No, miss. My orders were to meet your countrymen. We cannot board a British man-of-war, no matter what the circumstances are."

Meg sighed. As the small skiff pulled up next to the barge, a red coated arm was extended. She grasped it as she stepped across the boats.

"I am Lieutenant Brown," the officer said once Meg was secure aboard. He wore a full uniform, complete with powdered wig. His face was round, his beady eyes eclipsed by the chubby cheeks of a young man. "I've come to convey you to the *Eagle*." He turned toward Colonel Webb. "Sir, I also bring a letter." He bent down to pass it to the colonel.

"This envelope is addressed to George Washington, Esquire," Webb stated.

"Indeed," Brown replied. "Can you present it to Mr. Washington?"

Webb frowned. "I know no one in the army of that address."

Perplexed, Meg stared down at the rebel. His face was tight with anger. "Surely you know it to be the Commander-in-Chief!" she cried.

Webb looked up at her. "You must refer then to *General* Washington."

"This letter is not of a military nature," Brown spat out. "Hence the address."

Webb handed the envelope back to Brown. "I'm sorry, I cannot deliver this letter. As an Englishman, you should know the necessity of proper titles."

Brown tucked it back into his breast pocket. "As an impertinent rebel, you should know the insult you have propagated on your army's behalf."

Colonel Webb sat down in the boat and the oarsman began to row away from the barge. Meg turned away from the railing and, thus, turned her back on America.

Meg was dismayed to find out her father was not aboard the *Eagle*. He had remained on Staten Island to supervise the redoubts.

Admiral Howe had extended an invitation to dine at his table so she put on her finest gown, the same one she wore to the ball only a fortnight ago, and arranged her hair in a similar style.

Twenty or so impeccably dressed guests were seated at the long mahogany table. Most of the men wore British uniforms and were adorned with powdered wigs. Meg was relieved to see that she had been placed next to Major Montresor's wife, whom she had known since she was a little girl.

"Such a beautiful dress, Meg," Mrs. Montresor said, bending

her gray head in closer. "Were you much taxed to be forced to bunk with a rebel leader?"

"No, missus." Meg stabbed at her chicken. "General Putnam and his family were very kind to me."

"Nonsense," a man clad in a brown coat and waistcoat sitting across from her replied. "The rebels have not enough manners to be kind to anyone."

"A toast!" Admiral Howe stood and raised a crystal goblet. "To the King. May the sun forever rise over his vast empire."

"To the King!" his guests cried, lifting their glasses.

"May reason return to these wretched colonies," Howe continued. He turned in Meg's direction. "I welcome Margaret Moncrieffe, returned to us at last from the Americans' grasp. Who do you drink to, m'dear?"

Meg recalled her promise to toast to Washington if she ever found herself in the company of her countrymen. "Cheers to General Putnam, my protector," she declared instead.

The guests paused, their glasses still in the air, unsure of whether to drink to the enemy. "You must not name him here," Mrs. Montresor hissed.

Admiral Howe spoke from the head of the table. "By all means, we may drink to him, if he be the lady's sweetheart."

The guests tittered and lifted their goblets to their lips. Meg's face flushed. Everyone must have been aware of Putnam's advanced age. "Don't mind Admiral Howe," Mrs. Montresor whispered. "We all know that his brother, the head of the army, has his own mistress. And a married one as well!"

The champagne left a bitter taste in Meg's mouth. She was relieved when the men rose from the table. Howe's close confidants adjourned to his parlor to enjoy brandy and cigars while the other, lesser guests, attended to their wives and departed for the shore. As she had the night before, Meg threw herself on this new, finer bed, and cried.

·   ·   ·

The day after Meg arrived on board the *Eagle*, Admiral Howe, via Lieutenant Brown, summoned her to his office. Hastening to get ready, she searched her reticule for a brush to tame her curls. Her fingers bumping the letter Aaron had put there only yesterday. It was addressed to Admiral Howe, she noted before tucking back into her bag.

Lieutenant Brown was waiting outside her cabin and accompanied her to Howe's office. He knocked and then opened the door when the admiral's voice rang out to come in. Brown bowed to Meg but remained at his post in the hall.

The admiral's office was small and dark, the walls papered in navy silk. Bookcases filled with thick books on the art of war adorned the wall, but the room was void of furniture save for a desk, which Admiral Howe sat stooped behind, and a scattering of chairs in front of it.

Meg studied him as she approached the desk. His gray hair needed no powder though a few frizzy pieces had escaped from its ribbon. He wore a black coat trimmed with gold braid. Up close, his face bore the wear of a man near fifty. His brows were thick and heavy but his brown eyes were not unkind.

"I have a message for you from General Putnam," she said, tentatively extending it toward him.

"Oh?" The admiral accepted the envelope. His large hands tore back the seal and he perused the paper inside. Suddenly he roared in deep laughter. He handed it back to Meg. "Go ahead and read it. It concerns you."

It was written in the general's own hand and contained his atrocious spelling.

Ginerole Putnam's complermints to Major Moncrieff. He presents him with a fine darter. If he don't leike her, he must send her back agin. And he will pervade her with a good Twig husband.

Israel Putnam

She sighed as she folded the letter and handed it back to the admiral. *By Twig he must have meant Whig, and by that, he must have been referring to Aaron.* "What news of my father, sir?"

"He is to join the troops at Flatbush."

Meg's heart felt as though it had been pierced by a bayonet. Perhaps the general was right and Aaron and her father would indeed come upon each other, fighting for opposite sides.

The admiral gestured for her to sit at the wooden chair across from his desk before he opened a drawer and took out a folded paper. "Miss Moncrieffe, that correspondence is not the only one I've received from Putnam's household." As he unfolded it, Meg was surprised to see her map of the fortifications in New York City. "I also was privy to this, and I am told that you were the artist."

"Yes, sir." She sat in the chair. It was made of exceptionally hard wood and pressed into her spine.

"This will be of much benefit when the time comes for us to arrive on Manhattan." Her chest grew tighter as she remembered Aaron's promise that he would burn the city he loved so the British could not occupy it. "Do you know of any more information that could help our cause?"

She folded her hands on her lap as she tried to recall those muddled moments in Putnam's office. "Something about roads and passes on Long Island."

"Yes?" the admiral prompted.

"They are sending troops to protect them. Except, there was one they didn't think needed much defense."

The admiral shouted for Lieutenant Brown. When he entered the room, Howe demanded a map of Long Island. Brown fetched it from a corner and then stood over Meg to unroll it onto the desk, setting a silver mug on one side and an inkwell in the opposite corner to hold it taught. She felt a pang of sadness—the scene reminded her of the one in Putnam's office only a few days ago.

"Do you remember the name of it?" Admiral Howe asked.

Meg peered at the map, but couldn't make out anything from it. "It sounded foreign. Jamba. Jericho."

"Jamaica?"

"Yes, I believe that's it."

Brown pointed to a black line that curved around a green area. "This pass is the Jamaica Road."

She closed her eyes, remembering how the general's hand had

been on the left side of the map. She opened her eyes again. "Yes, sir, I believe that's it," she repeated, this time with less hesitation.

"Thank you, Miss Moncrieffe." The admiral sat back in his chair to light a pipe. "Brown, we will prepare to descend through Jamaica Pass. We will do it in the dark of night. The Americans will be taken by surprise."

Meg leaned forward. "Sir, can I get your word?"

Admiral Howe blew out a ring of smoke before nodding.

"There is a man. He fights with Putnam by the name of Aaron Burr. If he is captured, will you spare him his life?"

The admiral nodded again.

"I suppose you want us to have mercy upon Putnam as well," Brown said, his beady eyes appearing even more narrowed as he squinted at her.

"Yes, please." Meg's heart began to hammer as she realized she had just placed both Aaron and Putnam in imminent danger.

"We will do everything we can to honor your request," the admiral said. "When we arrive in New York City, I will release you to the safety of your father." He nodded at Brown, who went to the door and opened it.

"Thank you, sir." She curtsied before exiting the room.

Lieutenant Brown led her back to her cabin. He bowed before saying, "I must take my leave of you, Miss Moncrieffe. I'm afraid we have an army to destroy."

Panic rose once again in Meg's chest. She tugged on the lace sleeve of the lieutenant's uniform. "Aaron Burr. Remember the name."

Brown's face twisted cruelly as he shrugged her off. "No rebel needs to be spared. Especially not one that thinks himself in love with a proper English lady."

69

CHAPTER 9

SALLY

AUGUST 1776

*T*rue to his word, Papa used his political influence to secure Robert a position as commissary with General Woodhull's army. From what Sally understood, that meant Robert supervised the troop's provisions on Long Island. He and Papa left for Queens County in mid-August to protect the cattle. To Sally it seemed such a trifling task, relocating livestock when a British attack seemed imminent, but Robert impressed upon her the importance of protecting their food supplies. He reminded her of the year before when the British had confiscated and then hoarded the cattle of Gardiner's Bay, on the eastern side of Long Island, while the locals starved. *At least it meant that Robert and Papa would not be involved in the fighting,* Sally told herself. *If it came to that.*

Papa returned home a few days later, saying that the mission had been somewhat of a success. Robert was moving eastward with what were left of Woodhull's men, for many of them had deserted. Mother commanded her daughters to pray for their brother's safety.

CHAPTER 10

ELIZABETH

AUGUST 1776

A few hours before dusk on August 21, Elizabeth was startled to see a massive thundercloud form over the North River. As it started to rain, the thunderclaps boomed with seemingly no break in between, and sounded louder than even the British cannon had been outside her window.

The cloud hung overhead for hours, emitting the worst lightning storm Elizabeth had ever seen. The baby inside of her seemed to have the hiccoughs, its rhythmic movements matching the staccato of the lightning. Later Elizabeth would hear of people in the street being struck down by the bolts, which blackened their bodies and melted the coinage in their pockets.

As if pulled by the same magnetism that kept the cloudburst from moving past the city, Elizabeth and Abigail stayed near enough to the window to watch the storm light up the night sky, but far enough away to give some measure of protection. Although she knew Jonathan had installed one of Franklin's lightning rods atop the roof, Elizabeth's heart still pounded every time she saw a bolt streak across the darkened horizon.

When she finally went to bed, Elizabeth had a sleepless night, kept awake by the tossing and turning of her son and daughter on either side and the kicking of the baby in her womb.

The cloud had completely disappeared by the next morning, which dawned clear and bright. But before long, Elizabeth could see a massive cloud of smoke rising across the river.

The British had invaded Long Island.

CHAPTER 11

SALLY

AUGUST 1776

*I*t was a rainy afternoon in August and the Townsend women were in the midst of making strawberry preserves when Robert burst into the kitchen. "Long Island is lost!"

Sarah turned to her son, her hands red with strawberry viscera. "What?" Audrey put a chair directly behind her and her mother sank into it. "Samuel!" she shouted.

Papa, who had been in the parlor going over his books, rushed in. "Robert?" he asked, his face white.

Robert gestured toward another chair. "Sit down, Papa. The news is not good."

Robert relayed the story of the capture of Long Island. "General Woodhull was stationed at Jamaica with less than a hundred men. He had sent most of us on to convey the stock eastward. Somehow the British knew that the Jamaica Pass was left unguarded."

"And then?" Papa asked wearily.

"A British victory," Robert replied in a soft voice. "And a massacre of the American army."

"How goes General Woodhull?" Sally was aware that he knew the general personally, as Woodhull's first cousin, Mary, was married to Robert's friend Amos Underhill.

Robert shook his head. "No one is quite sure of his fate."

"How did you escape?" Sally asked as his mother handed Robert a wet rag to mop his face.

"It wasn't easy," was all he said before he buried his face in the rag.

CHAPTER 12

ELIZABETH

AUGUST 1776

*E*lizabeth waited in vain for news of Jonathan. Gossip at the storefront, as repeated by the middling amount of customers she had that week, was of a near annihilation of the new army of the United States of America, but there were no specifics about how many men were lost, let alone the names of any of them.

Elizabeth had woken up early on the morning of the 30th to prepare breakfast when she caught sight of movement on the streets below. The fog, thick as a blanket when she awoke, had thinned enough for her to make out the parade of soldiers beneath her window. Her hands on the curtain began to tremble as it occurred to her that the British might have invaded Manhattan, but after a moment of worry, she could see that some of the men wore Continental Infantry uniforms.

Contrary to the times that she had watched them march past her apartment in the summer, there were no fifes or drums playing now and these soldiers half-heartedly plodding by were in no discernible formation. She crept into her bedroom to grab a cloak before rushing downstairs to study each man as he passed by her, hoping to spot her husband's form among them. A few met her eyes, and Elizabeth could see shock registered in their sleep-deprived faces. Many of them appeared malnourished, their clothing soaked through by the recent rainstorms.

"Ma'am?" A young man in an officer's uniform paused in front of her.

"Yes?"

He clicked the heels of his boots together and folded his arms behind his back. "Ma'am, General Washington ordered our evacuation from Long Island last night, and my troops have been up since then. Would it be possible for some of my men to catch a smattering of precious sleep in your apartment?"

Elizabeth was taken aback. She fussed with the ribbons of her cloak, closing it tighter around her body, while she thought of a reply. She wanted to say that her husband would think it improper for strange men to be in their house when he was not home. But then again, if Jonathan were somewhere else, she would hope that another woman would be willing to supply him a quiet place for a few hours of rest. "You can have my children's room," she finally replied. Since Jonathan had left, Catherine, Abigail, and Johnny were all sleeping in the master bed anyway. "There are two beds in there. I can get bedding so that some men can sleep on the floor as well."

Relief flooded the young man's tired eyes. "Thank you ma'am. You do a great service to your country."

The men did not stir until midday. Elizabeth had let Abby know of their presence behind the closed bedroom door and instructed her to have supper on hand when they woke.

Elizabeth went down to the store, but, after several hours of not receiving any customers, went back upstairs to find the four men seated at the table, a meager spread of bread, salt meat, and ale before them.

"What news of General Woodhull's men?" Elizabeth asked the table as she refilled their mugs. "My husband was among them."

The men exchanged uneasy glances with each other. One fair-haired young man ventured to say, "General Woodhull's men were on cattle duty."

"Cattle duty?" she replied.

Another young man stood up to offer her his chair. "Yes'm. General Washington wanted to keep the livestock from getting into the Redcoats' hands. So he had the general round them up."

Elizabeth sat down, relieved. She could nearly picture the disdain on her husband's face when he found out that his charge was not to press through the British lines, but to play cowboy to roaming cattle.

The seated men exchanged another tense glance as the blond one continued, "General Woodhull and some of his men spent the night in a tavern to keep out of the rain. They were captured there the next morning."

"Captured?" Elizabeth sat up straight.

"Captured," the blond man repeated. The other men nodded.

"Where is General Woodhull now?"

Another man ventured a guess. "The lobsterbacks have probably taken him prisoner."

Her hand reached out to grip the blond man's arm "My husband is Jonathan Burgin. Do you know his whereabouts?"

He shook his head slowly. "I'm not sure, but I can ask when I return to duty."

"Please do," Elizabeth said, dropping the man's still damp sleeve.

Heretofore, most of New York society would have considered it improper to explain what happened on the battlefield to a woman and her maid, but the war had ended all thoughts of decorum, especially in the minds of these young men. Using halting, defeated language, the men filled Elizabeth and Abigail in on what they called the 'Battle of Long Island.'

The British had waited five days before firing any shots, lulling the

American troops into a false sense of security. The men at Elizabeth's table were from General Sullivan's division. They had been stationed at Flatbush Pass when they were surrounded by British and Hessian soldiers. Their leader had been captured along with Lord Stirling and General Woodhull. The men mentioned that some of their fellow soldiers had been run through with bayonets by Hessians after they'd already surrendered. They'd received word that all of Washington's army was to evacuate Long Island for Manhattan earlier that morning.

"We have lost one island and now we are trapped on another," one of the men stated sourly. "And those Redcoats across the river can strike here at any moment."

"So we are still in danger," Elizabeth said quietly, with an eye on her children playing in the corner of the living room.

"Indeed," another man agreed. "You should leave the city as soon as possible. There's talk of burning it down to the ground so the British can't occupy it."

She exchanged a panicked look with Abigail as the maid cleared the plates. Both had lived in Manhattan all of their lives, albeit growing up under different circumstances. Elizabeth put a hand on her swollen belly. "We know how to survive in times of crisis."

"I certainly hope so," the blond man said. "We hadn't slept for three days before you were so kind as to give us quarter." He wiped his mouth and set down his napkin before nodding at the soldiers still seated. Simultaneously they rose from the table.

Elizabeth also got up to see them out. "Jonathan Burgin," she repeated to the men at the door. "Please find out where he is."

The blond man put on his tricorn hat and said, "I will do my best," before he left with his company.

CHAPTER 13

SALLY

SEPTEMBER 1776

*A*s the British presumably planned their siege of New York City, Papa and the rest of the Provincial Congress were summoned to meet in Fishkill.

The morning before he set off, Papa wore one of his finely cut suits, his gold tipped cane perched next to him as he wiped a spot off the large buckle adorning his shoe. Some of the Friends from church were known to criticize Papa's finery as unbecoming of a Quaker, but he never paid them much mind. He'd even bought Sally an outfit from White Plains. It was in the newest fashion—the yellow skirt gathered just below the bodice, revealing a blue and white striped petticoat underneath. At first Sally had refused the dress, stating she'd rather stick with her homespun and hand-me-downs, but decided to keep it when Audrey and Phoebe each begged to have it instead. The lack of a hoop skirt allowed Sally to join Papa in sitting on the portico as he waited for their servant, Caesar, to bring his mare around. They both looked up as the sound of horses grew closer. A black stallion topped by a British dragoon stopped outside the gate.

Papa held his hand in front of his eyes to keep out the glaring sun as the officer dismounted. Although it was early in the morning, the temperature was already well above what it would have been for a typical September day. As the Redcoat approached, Sally wrinkled her nose in response to the smell of sweat and muck that clung to his uniform. Her eyes were glued to his brass helmet, which was topped with a mane of red horse hair and featured a menacing cross and bones on the front.

"Sam Townsend?" the man demanded loudly. Sally recoiled inwardly at the casual shortening of Papa's Christian name.

"I am that man," Papa replied as he stood.

"You are under arrest."

"On what cause?" Papa asked as Sally gasped.

"Anti-loyalty to the Crown."

"Ah, I see." His voice held no surprise and Sally recalled Robert's words two months ago about villagers reporting their neighbors. Papa gestured toward Caesar, who had dismounted Gem and now stood awkwardly looking on from the side of the house. "Shall I ride my own mare?"

The great man threw his head back in laughter. After he'd regained his composure, he spit on the ground and cursed.

"Go inside now, Sally," Papa said.

But Sally's backside seemed adhered to the porch as her father asked the dragoon if he could have a few minutes to gather some personal items.

"Don't take long," the Redcoat replied before spitting again. "We have many other rebel obstinates like you to arrest today."

Papa took Sally's hand and dragged her inside the house. He headed up the stairs and Sally followed, blinking against the sudden dim light. She paused, dropping Papa's hand as she heard the front door slam shut another time.

From her perch on the stairs, Sally watched that same Redcoat gaze around their living room, a sneer on his face. She angled her head, trying to see what it was about the plain Quaker house that seemed to offend him. He marched over to the fireplace and pulled the small musket that Caesar used to hunt waterfowl off the mantel.

"Sir?" Robert asked as he entered the living room from the kitchen. Mother and Sally's younger sister Phoebe stood just behind him.

"No rebel should own such a weapon." He rammed the stock against the floor again and again as Phoebe screamed. Mother reached around to put her hand over Phoebe's mouth. "Hush now, Daughter."

The gun destroyed, the Redcoat threw it down. Next, he stalked over to the other side of the living room and stood in front of a painting of the oldest Townsend boy, Solomon. Robert joined him, half-blocking the portrait from the Redcoat's angry stare with his body. Robert's lean form and dark mane contrasted with Solomon's fair hair and stocky build. Sally wondered what the real Solomon would do if he were there, deciding that he'd probably do something stupid to get them all killed. On that matter, it was a good thing William, the next brother after Solomon, was absent that morning as well.

For his part, Robert remained outwardly calm. "You would be pleased to be informed that my brother is supporting the British Island on the *Glasgow*," he told the officer softly. "It is not within your power to wreak your vengeance on this painting of a fellow Loyalist."

Despite Robert's reassurances of Solomon's position, the Redcoat seemed inclined to reach for the portrait and treat it as he did the fowling gun. At that moment, Papa came down the stairs. "I am ready," he announced.

"Samuel?" Mother asked, glancing between the officer and Papa.

"Sarah." Papa approached her and Phoebe and embraced them both at once. "I won't be long."

"You won't be long for this world," the Redcoat sneered, advancing toward the door. "A life in prison awaits you. Perhaps your fate includes one of the ships moored in Long Island. But first, to the field headquarters in Jericho."

Not the floating prisons, Sally thought as her legs regained the ability to move. The conditions aboard the decommissioned ships were said to be deplorable. If Papa was to be sent aboard one of them, it was as good as being sentenced to death.

Needing to get away from the Redcoat's damage to their home and the reminder of the power of the Crown, Sally fled outside. As she ducked past the officer, she felt the yellow ribbons on her hat loosen from their bow.

More Redcoat dragoons had arrived, Sally saw as she secured the ribbons under her chin. Neighbors had gathered outside and loitered in scattered groups, sweating from the heat. No one dared to say a word as long as the British cavalry towered over them.

Tories, all of them, Sally determined sourly as she looked upon her neighbors. Old Lady Wooden stood with her arms crossed and seemed pleased by Samuel Townsend's predicament, although her eldest daughter, Mary, looked on sadly as the officer marched Papa out of the house. *If only they'd use some of their Loyalist influence to help Papa.* Her steps grew faster as a radical idea popped into her head. She had to refrain from running to the side of the house where Caesar had taken Gem, lest she call attention to herself.

Their next door neighbor, Thomas Buchanan, was a staunch and outspoken Tory and well respected by the other Loyalists in the area. He was also Papa's best friend. That very morning, Sally's older sister Audrey had accompanied Thomas and his wife, their cousin Almy, to Norwich to go shopping. They hadn't left too long ago, and, since they were in a carriage, they might not have gotten far. Norwich was on the road to Jericho. If Sally could catch up to them, perhaps she could convince Thomas to use his influence to help free her father before they reached the military headquarters.

"Miss, I'm not sure this is a good idea," Caesar said as Sally grabbed the reins of the still saddled Gem from him. "Your father—"

"My father needs me."

"But miss..."

"Shh." Sally touched a finger to her lips and nodded toward the front of the house, where, from the rise in commotion, it sounded as though the Redcoats were preparing to march, with Papa in tow.

Sally led Gem on foot to the edge of the meadow until they were out of sight of any onlookers. She was once again thankful for the lack of a hoop skirt as she mounted the horse. She triple knotted her bonnet before racing Gem the long way around, avoiding the main road for fear of meeting the British troops.

As Sally reached Front Street, she quickened her pace. She finally caught up to Thomas and his band as they were descending the hill on Pine Hollow Road.

"Sally?" Audrey asked incredulously.

"It's Papa!" Sally cried as she pulled Gem to a halt. "They've taken him prisoner."

"Who?" Thomas asked as he exited the carriage.

"The Redcoats. They're taking him to Jericho."

Thomas looked down the road, but Sally gestured behind them. "I got ahead of them. Please, sir, you have to help Papa."

"I will certainly try." He nodded at the coach driver, a Negro slave, who directed the horses to turn around.

Sally rode beside the coach at an agonizingly slow pace. When the cavalry came into sight, their numbers even larger than before, she edged Gem into the woods, the dread of seeing the Redcoat from the house winning over her wanting to catch a glimpse of Papa.

As they came closer, Sally realized that there were more captives sprinkled in with the dragoons, John Kirk and Papa's cousin George among them.

The slave brought the Buchanan coach to a halt as the soldiers encircled them. Sally saw Thomas approach the lead Redcoat. Even before he spat, she recognized him as the man from that morning's nightmare. The Redcoat's harsh voice indicated he was not going to agree with Buchanan's attempts at mediation. When the dragoons again took up their march, Sally dismounted Gem and handed Thomas his reins.

As he took off in the direction of the brigade, Sally joined Almy and Audrey in the coach, the three of them staring after the retreating band of British dragoons and American prisoners in silence. Sally's heart sank as they disappeared beyond another hill.

No one said a word on the way back to Oyster Bay. The tears flowed freely down Sally's face. She had hoped that Thomas would have been able to use his Loyalist influence with the soldiers, to no avail. Now she could only pray there would be a senior officer more willing to negotiate when they reached Jericho.

As soon as Sally arrived home, she saw Robert and William standing on the portico.

"Papa?" William asked, pushing his floppy blond hair back off his forehead.

"Thomas Buchanan is with them now," Sally answered, shaking her skirts out. The pretty yellow gown was now covered with dust and her petticoat clung to her sweaty legs.

"It was a good idea to enlist Thomas Buchanan's help, Sally," Robert said approvingly. He handed her a handkerchief. Although neither brother had commented on her appearance, Sally could well imagine that the tears she'd shed after Thomas's failure at negotiation had left trail marks down her dirty face. "Perhaps Thomas can still convince those lobsterbacks to release Papa after they realize he is no threat to them."

"If they can discern anything through those thick helmets, they will see that Papa is innocent," William added. "I wish I would have been there."

"It's a good thing you weren't," Robert replied. "Your beetle-headedness would have ensured that you'd have ended up a prisoner, too. And the Buchanan ploy would have never worked."

William waved his hand, the lace sleeve billowing in the breeze. "You're right. I guess Sally's plan was the best we could have done." He turned to his sister. "Who would have thought you inherited the Townsend savvy, after all?"

She shrugged off William's attempt at a compliment and went upstairs to join Phoebe and Mother in praying for Papa's release.

· · ·

A few days later Sally's efforts were rewarded when Papa and Thomas Buchanan returned to Oyster Bay. As soon as she spotted Papa walking Gem up the front path, she ran to him. The fine lace of his undershirt was tattered and his clothes were covered with dirt, but he seemed unharmed. After he gave Gem's reins to Caesar, Sally followed him into the house.

Mother and Phoebe were in the living room, attempting to needlepoint. Mother rose and hugged Papa. Phoebe, never one to wait, embraced both of them. After more hugs and greetings, Mother assisted Papa upstairs to nap.

At dinner, Papa explained to William and Robert how Thomas had secured his discharge through a hefty payment, what Papa called a "baron's bribery." He also had to assure the Redcoats that Papa was not of Whig tendencies. Thomas offered yet more money—several thousand pounds in fact—for the release of George and John Kirk, but both men's previous actions toward their Tory enemies spoke more than Thomas's reassurances could.

"Now what, Papa?" Robert asked.

"I must go before the magistrate."

"They will probably have you swear an oath of loyalty to the Crown," William said.

Papa sighed. "Indeed. But it is against all of my beliefs to swear allegiance to an unjust government."

"But Papa, if you do pledge allegiance, does that mean that you will be safe from the charges against you?" Phoebe asked.

Across the table, Robert raised his eyebrows thoughtfully but said nothing.

"Husband, if you comply with what they have asked of you, you could avoid the fate of John Kirk and your cousin George," Mother added.

"I hear they are under the jurisdiction of that bandog, William Cunningham. He'd rather his prisoners rot in hell than feed and clothe them." Robert said, finally ending his silence. "Mayhap we can arrange for you to live with our Connecticut relations."

"No, if I were to flee, they would go after Thomas Buchanan. He would lose the money he put up for my bail. They might implicate him in my escape as well, despite his loyalty to the Crown. Or worse yet, they would come after you boys," he said, casting his eyes to Robert and then William.

Sally sat silently. Of course she wanted a guarantee of safety for her father, but she was not sure if Papa swearing that oath would be worth the sacrifice. The past few years had demonstrated that the British government did not often keep its promises.

Phoebe got up from the table and moved next to her father. "Please, Papa, they are only words. None of our friends will think you a traitor. They know you as an honest man who would do anything to protect his family."

"I will think about it, poppet," Papa said, patting Phoebe's curls.

A few days later, the summons came for Papa to appear before the court. Sally dressed in a red silk sack back gown with a white petticoat. She hoped that her choice of colors would please the British authorities but discreetly tucked a blue handkerchief into her bodice as a subtle act of patriotic defiance.

The magistrate was Judge Whitehead Hicks, a Loyalist, of course. As he began his questioning, Sally's heart sank. Judge Hicks asked Papa about past behaviors that could have been construed as rebellious, including assisting General Woodhull.

Hicks tilted his wigged head in inquiry. "Did you help his troops herd livestock onto Hempstead Plain in August of this year?"

"Yes, sir," Papa replied. "But we did not move more than a couple thousand. Woodhull was cursed with having many of his men desert night after night."

The judge shuffled the papers in front of him. "And your son was commissary to General Woodhull."

Papa gave a brief wave of his hand. From her perch on a wooden chair behind him, Sally could see it shake briefly. "Only for a day. Of course you are aware of the general's fate."

Judge Hicks nodded as Papa continued, "Robert is now living at home, with his family."

The judge pushed the pile of papers to the side and stared intently at Papa . "You are prepared to take the oath of allegiance to his Majesty, the King?"

Sally could feel her brother's form stiffen beside her.

"I am," Papa said loudly.

"I am as well," Robert declared as he stood up.

"Robert," Sally whispered to his back. "Why?"

Robert did not answer. Instead, he strode forward to stand next to his father.

Judge Hicks scrutinized Robert before he finally stated, "Very well, then."

Sally sat back as both her father and brother raised their right hand and repeated the prompts from Judge Hicks. Robert stood erect, but Papa's frame was slouched and his words were lost in the murmurs from the courtroom audience. They were probably wondering, as Sally was, what had possessed her brother to willingly pledge allegiance to a Crown that provided nothing but injustice to its citizens. Sally wondered how her proud papa would bear the shame of standing before Congress now.

In exchange for their vows, Judge Hicks issued both Papa and Robert a certificate as proof of their fidelity to the King.

Later that night, Sally knocked on the door to her brother's room. The door was not shut and it nudged open. Sally caught sight of Robert packing up his things. He looked up as she walked in.

Sally's original intention was to query why he volunteered to take the oath, but she abandoned that line of questioning to ask, "Are you going somewhere?"

"New York City," Robert replied tersely.

"New York City? Now?"

He hefted the bag over his shoulder. "Someone has to provide for this family, and I'm not sure Papa is in the right shape to do it."

She sat down in Robert's wooden chair. "That's why you took the oath—to do business on the island."

Robert patted his pocket. "This certificate will get me past the sentries stationed at Dobbs Ferry."

"For a moment there, I thought you'd switched allegiances."

"I have no allegiance."

"But you worked for General Woodhull. And you gave money to the Sons of Liberty."

Robert looked around the room as if there might be British spies lurking in the corner. "We shouldn't talk so loud about it."

She laughed. "Not even in our own house?"

"No," he said sullenly. "But if you must know, I find it best to remain neutral. That way I can continue doing business with both sides."

"Isn't that a rather cowardly way to look at it?"

Robert approached her. "Not if you want to be able to eat once the British occupy New York. Besides…" he pulled at the skirt of her petticoat, "someone's got to pay for this fine clothing."

"Sell it," she told him blankly, pulling away from him. "I don't care for such things. Papa bought it."

He looked at her earnestly. "And that is why I'm going."

John Kirk and George Townsend were committed to Provost Prison. When Cunningham learned that Kirk had contracted smallpox after a few weeks of ill treatment, he sent the men back to their homes, probably hoping he'd infect the rest of the Oyster Bay Whigs with the dreaded disease. Kirk's wife, happy to have her husband home, nursed him through the illness. Kirk recovered, but his wife and his newborn daughter both died of smallpox a short time later. Their deaths only served to inspire more hatred of the Crown in the townspeople of Oyster Bay, especially in George Townsend, as well as Sally's brother Robert.

CHAPTER 14

ELIZABETH

SEPTEMBER 1776

*I*n early September, Rivington returned to the store. He was dressed similarly to the first time Elizabeth met him, clad in another finely cut suit, this one a sage green.

"Can I help you, Mr. Rivington?" Elizabeth asked. "Do you require more ink?"

Rivington approached the counter and doffed his hat.

She gave him a tight smile as he stood silently, twisting the hat in his hands. "Sir?" she asked encouragingly.

"It pains me to say this, madam, considering your husband's kindness to me in the past. And, also," he gestured to Elizabeth's torso, "in light of your delicate condition."

"Yes?" Her heart was now in her throat.

"I was given a list of American prisoners taken at Long Island to print in my paper."

"Jonathan," she concluded in a whisper. "Where is he?"

Rivington did not reply right away. His hat was now a wrinkled mess. "He is aboard the *Jersey.*"

Elizabeth gave him a helpless look. "Where? New Jersey?"

Rivington flicked his hand toward the East River. "Not New Jersey. The *Jersey.* It's a prison ship. There were not enough places in the city to put all the captives taken in the Battle of Long Island so the British employed decommissioned ships for their confinement." He dug into his pocket to present a piece of paper. "I managed to use my connections to get you a pass." He handed the slip to Elizabeth. "But, Mrs. Burgin, I have to warn you, those prison ships are not pleasant places to be."

She let out a deep breath. "I would think not." She reached out to clasp his hand. "Thank you, Mr. Rivington, for arranging this."

He nodded, pulling his hand back and then taking a step away from the counter. "It was the least I could do. As I said, your husband has always been kind to me."

The next day, Elizabeth set out for the *Jersey*, stationed across the East River in Wallabout Bay. The only other person aboard the small transfer boat, besides the rower, was a tall, handsome man in the blue and buff uniform of the Continental army. He helped Elizabeth onto the skiff before introducing himself as Captain Benjamin Tallmadge.

As they approached the hulking figure of the former battleship, Elizabeth could see that the portholes had been sealed. In their place were small square windows cut into the side of the ship. Iron bars, one vertical and one horizontal, severed the window into four equal parts and prevented any hope of escape. There was no canvas attached to the masts, for the *Jersey* was no longer able to set sail, and served to further illustrate the fact that she was merely a skeleton of a formerly grand man-of-war. The attuned sense of smell that accompanied her pregnancy became a curse as Elizabeth could detect the overpowering effluvia of hundreds of prisoners packed onto the ship. The stench, combined with her nervousness as to her husband's condition, caused her stomach to heave. She clutched the side of the boat and willed herself not to vomit.

The deck was overcrowded with sailors, who went about their

business with barely a sound. Sentries stood by every exit point. The disturbing silence was interrupted only by the waves breaking at the helm of the ship or the officer in charge barking orders.

Captain Tallmadge approached the officer and, in a muffled tone, asked to see his brother, William, before nodding at Elizabeth, who managed to squeak out, "Jonathan Burgin." The officer summoned a nearby soldier and repeated the names before turning to Elizabeth and demanding to see her papers.

The officer glanced through them and then handed them back to her, asking how she was acquainted with Rivington. Captain Tallmadge grimaced at the name as she tentatively replied that he was a customer at her husband's store.

Elizabeth turned as she heard shuffling behind her. She refrained from running to Jonathan as soon as she spotted him. He stepped forward from the edge of the hatchway, blinking at the sudden sunlight, as the guard elbowed him from behind.

She bit back her shock at the change in her husband. A graying, matted beard occupied the lower part of his face; his cheeks and forehead had lost their sunburned ruddiness and now appeared yellow. Every inch of both his tattered uniform and skin was covered in filth. In only a few short weeks, his once stocky figure had become practically emaciated, the manacles at his wrist seeming to be able to slip right off.

Elizabeth heard Captain Tallmadge inquire again about his brother as he pulled the officer aside, affording the couple some privacy.

Jonathan smiled a thin, weak smile that didn't reach his eyes. "Hello, my wife."

"Jonathan." Elizabeth made to hug him, but he ducked, giving the appearance that it greatly pained him. "Lice," he explained.

She settled for grasping his hands in hers. "Are you hurt?"

"Not much." The act of speaking must have also been painful. His lips were dry and cracked, his voice groggy as though he hadn't used his throat in a long time. He attempted another smile as he put a weak hand on Elizabeth's belly.

"Your second son should arrive soon," she told him. "Within a month or so." Of course she did not know the sex of the babe growing inside her, but she knew the thought of it being a son would be a comfort to Jonathan. She began to chat amicably about Catherine and Johnny, trying to ignore her husband's clearly weakened state for both of their sakes. She made no mention of the evacuation of Long Island or the renewed soldiers' presence in New York City. After a few minutes, the officer returned and announced that their time had concluded. The same soldier from before appeared and shoved Jonathan in the direction of the decks below.

Elizabeth wanted to scream at the soldier not to touch Jonathan. She blinked back a tear for her formerly proud, successful husband, now reduced to this miserable hostage. She longed to reach out and grab him—at his attenuated state, she could probably have lifted him, even with her extended stomach—and take him back to Manhattan with her. But she could do none of these things. She watched as her husband went back down the hatchway and felt an overwhelming foreboding that she would never see him again.

They rowed back in silence, both passengers disturbed by what they had seen. As they approached the shore, Elizabeth tentatively asked Tallmadge about his brother. He shook his head as he replied, "Dead."

Elizabeth frowned as he continued, "And I'm not surprised. No one has much chance of survival aboard that floating squalor. They wouldn't let me below, but I could smell enough to picture the putrid conditions they are keeping our soldiers in." He wiped furiously at his eyes before remembering Elizabeth's situation. He pulled out a handkerchief and then reached across the skiff to hand it to her. "I will see what I can do about arranging a prisoner exchange for your husband."

Her attempt at a smile faded as she once again pictured her husband's cracked face and felt that sense of hopelessness as she watched him walk away. "Thank you," she told the captain.

. . .

That night, Elizabeth waited until her maid and children were fast asleep before she crawled out of bed. She lit a candle and went to the window that overlooked the East River. Across the darkened bay, past the myriad of British warships tied at the wharf, she imagined she could see the hulk of the *Jersey*. For the first time since Jonathan had joined the war, Elizabeth found herself breaking down. She tried to keep her sobs quiet, but was unable to stop the flow of tears. Whatever assurance Captain Tallmadge had attempted to provide, given the state of Jonathan's skeletal body and his pallor, Elizabeth knew her husband didn't have much time. Never in her life had she felt as helpless as she did then, practically alone in a deserted city with a baby on the way, her country at war, her husband near death on a torture ship. She felt defeated, much in the way that General Washington must have felt after the Battle of Long Island. Still, Elizabeth thought, the general managed to recognize when it was time to retreat, and rally his troops in order to prepare for yet more battles in this war for independence. Elizabeth wet a linen napkin and patted it under her eyes, trying to keep the swelling down, before extinguishing the candle and withdrawing to her bed.

CHAPTER 15

SALLY

SEPTEMBER 1776

*A*fter the British victory at Long Island, the Whigs, including Samuel Townsend, worried over what would become of their businesses now that their beloved territory was in enemy hands. Stories swept down the island, rumors of Patriots in Setauket, a few miles to the east, having their homes, harvest, and livestock seized by the British.

In late September, Sally answered the door to find a short, broad man dressed in British regimentals.

"Yes?" she asked, trying to keep the fear out of her voice as the uniform brought the nightmare of her father's arrest back to the surface.

"Miss…" he stood up straighter, as if preparing to recite a litany, and then thought better of it. "Are your parents home?"

"No." Sally shifted impatiently. "May I help you?"

The Redcoat's shoulders sank and he seemed to deflate before her eyes. "Miss, my name is Joseph Green. Colonel De Lancey has ordered me to quarter with your fine family this winter. I'm told you have a room available?"

"There is no room," Sally told him resolutely.

From somewhere behind her, a voice piped up, "My brother Robert has only just left for New York City." Phoebe appeared beside Sally. "I suppose you might as well occupy his room."

Sally stood firm at her post at the entryway as the officer transferred his bag from one arm to the other. Phoebe elbowed Sally hard enough that she was forced to step aside. The officer made no move forward as he stated, "New York City. Isn't that quite a dangerous place to be?"

Sally smiled sweetly. "No more so than any other spot on the Continent during this infernal war."

"Indeed." The soldier dropped his bag. "If you don't mind sending your father to speak with me as soon as he arrives, I'll just make myself at home on this stoop." He turned toward the portico steps.

"But Papa is home," Phoebe stated. "I'll get him for you."

Sally shot daggers at her sister's back as Phoebe departed for the interior of their house. *How dare this enemy officer demand to share our home! In Robert's room, no less.* Her eyes threatened to tear over at this newest indignation, but she blinked hard. She would not give this Redcoat the satisfaction of seeing her cry.

Papa gave his second eldest daughter only a brief glance as he passed by, but his meaning was clear: *stay out of this.*

Sally sullenly retreated to the kitchen to help her mother with supper. Presently, she could hear two sets of footsteps in the hallway, and knew that there was no alternative: the Redcoat was going to spend the winter at the Townsends.'

CHAPTER 16

MEG

SEPTEMBER 1776

In mid-September, the British landed at Kip's Bay, an inlet on Manhattan off the East River. The few continentals stationed there fled as cowards instead of fighting and the island was then completely under British rule.

Meg and her father were finally reunited soon after. When she heard the announcement that a few men from his company had arrived on the *Eagle*, she went to ask news of him. Captain Moncrieffe himself was standing on deck and Meg ran into his arms as soon as she spotted him.

"Daughter," he said finally, pulling back to look at her. "I'm glad you are safe."

"Of course, Father. General Putnam and his family were very kind to me."

It had been nearly a year since Meg had last seen her father. He did not look that much different—the face that so many late wives had admired was still handsome, if only a bit more faded. The stern voice, however, had not changed in the least. "Seems like you are not a little girl anymore."

Admiral Howe sauntered over to stand by Captain Moncrieffe. "No, she seems to be quite the woman now. And she's made a few admirers of my men," he continued with a wink at Meg.

She lowered her eyes. "You flatter me, sir."

The admiral put an arm around Captain Moncrieffe. "General Putnam says he could find her a good husband, but I think we would do better to find one of our own."

Captain Moncrieffe shook his head. "She's still too young."

"A bit young in age, perhaps, but not in temperament. Sometimes when she speaks, I think her double her years."

Captain Moncrieffe nodded.

Another man appeared and saluted, his face dark. "Admiral, sir, we are the bearer of distressing news." He gestured toward New York City. "The west side of the island is in flames and the fire is spreading."

The admiral went to the bow of the boat and spit into the water. "Forgive my rudeness, but though they may be British citizens, those rebels are no Englishmen."

Meg placed a gloved hand on the banister and peered at the distant island. She could just barely see a column of smoke rising from the opposite shore. She had heard not a word from Aaron, but knew that, despite his threat, he couldn't have been the one to set fire to his beloved city. She knew, too, that he wouldn't have been among the soldiers who threw down their arms rather than fight at Kip's Bay. It was true that Aaron Burr did not consider himself an English gentleman, but he still had his own sense of worth. She wished she could query the admiral of Aaron's fate, but did not want to face the fatherly inquisition it was sure to incite in Captain Moncrieffe.

CHAPTER 17

ELIZABETH

SEPTEMBER 1776

*T*here were no church bells to warn of the fire. After the British had entered the city, Washington ordered that all bells be taken down and melted for cannon fodder. Elizabeth watched the progression of the fires from her second-floor window. From her vantage point, she could see at least two or three conflagrations, the nearest one off Broadway at the White Hall inn. After the unusually wet August, the September days had been mostly dry. The wells had been wanting of water and the fire spread quickly through the city.

Elizabeth closed her eyes, mentally shutting out the screams and terror of the people running through the streets. If she had time to think of it, she might have been pleased that her beloved New York City, though now even more of a ghost town, was fighting back against the British invasion. But she didn't have time to dwell on anything else: the baby was coming.

Elizabeth steeled her mind away from the thought that the birth of a child often resulted in loss, either of the baby, like her last child who had died shortly after she was born, or of the mother, like Elizabeth's own mother who had died in childbirth. Now was not the time to panic.

"Ooh." she nearly doubled over as another contraction began.

Abigail's eyes widened with fear. "Missus, you've got to get in bed." She cast her eyes toward the window and outside, which, even though it was nine in the evening, was currently filled with more light than at dawn. Abby cursed under her breath as she dragged Elizabeth into the bedroom. She got her mistress settled and then ran for the tureen of water boiling in the fireplace.

The labor pains, as with the fire, continued through the early morning. When she wasn't attending to Elizabeth, Abby paced around the floor in the living room. She instructed Johnny to sit at the table and learn his letters while Catherine played with her dolls. But every time their mother screamed in pain, both children looked at Abby with frightened eyes. Abby knew she needed help, but, from the sound of the chaos below her, it seemed that the few people that lingered in the city after the arrival of the British were finally fleeing as their homes and businesses went up in flames. Abby paused as a thought occurred to her. *Mrs. Underhill!*

Mary Underhill was an old family friend of the Burgin's. She was only a few years older than Elizabeth and they had become fast friends after Elizabeth's marriage to Jonathan. She and her husband Amos ran a boarding house on Queen Street. Abby knew that Mary had two girls in their early teens, so she would be the best person to help with the birth. That was if she hadn't also left the city.

While Elizabeth dozed fitfully, Abby hastened to the Underhill's boarding house. Thankfully the fire hadn't spread to the east side of town, at least not yet. Mary Underhill was seated at one of the tables in the tavern with her husband, Amos, and a few other men.

As Abby rushed toward them, she shouted, "Mrs. Underhill, you must come quickly! Mrs. Burgin is in labor!"

Amos stood, knocking over the wooden chair he had been sitting in. "Is she all right?"

"So far." Abby stooped over, panting from her run. "But Mr. Burgin has been captured and there's no doctor to be found."

Mary grabbed a worn satchel off a nearby hook and went into the kitchen. She emerged a few seconds later, the satchel bulging with cloth. She nodded at Abby and the two women headed back to the apartment above Jonathan Burgin's store, wet handkerchiefs placed over their face so as not to breathe in the smoke that hung in the heavy air.

When they arrived at the apartment, Elizabeth was awake and once again grunting with labor pains. Mary commanded Abby to take the children downstairs to the storefront. She handed Elizabeth a twisted handkerchief and told her to bite down on it when the pain got too much to bear. She wet a washcloth with cool water and patted Elizabeth's sweaty face.

After several more agonizing hours, the baby finally arrived. Mary's expert hands cut the umbilical cord and wrapped him in swaddling before handing him to his exhausted mother. *He possessed a hearty wail*, Elizabeth was pleased to note. He had Jonathan's mouth and eyes and just looking at him triggered both sorrow and happiness in his mother.

"He's beautiful," Mary declared as she came to stand behind mother and baby.

Elizabeth softly rubbed his button nose. "If only Jonathan could see his new son."

"You've still had no word from him?" Mary began gathering up the bloodied linens and cloth.

Elizabeth shook her head wearily as she tried to get the baby to suckle her breast. "Not for a month."

"I know it's not much of a comfort now, but just think—your son will be able to grow up in a free country because of men like his father."

Elizabeth managed a tiny smile as she stroked the head full of dark, wispy hair. "I think I will name him George. George Washington Burgin."

Mary's worn face relaxed into a grin. "I've yet to hear of a finer name." She hoisted a sack of soiled clothing. "If you don't mind,

I'm going to go home to wash up. I'll send Abby back to take the baby."

"Thank you, Mary."

She nodded. "Get some rest. You need to keep up your strength."

CHAPTER 18

MEG

SEPTEMBER 1776

*A*dmiral Howe rewarded Meg's father—and Meg herself, though only the admiral and Lieutenant Brown knew of her assistance regarding the Long Island raid—by giving them a fine brick townhouse on Queen Street. Meg installed herself in the largest of the three bedrooms, complete with a walnut bed frame and pink and white striped chintz curtains. The house had once been occupied by a wealthy rebel merchant who fled the city during the invasion. Like many such properties, the British declared the house to be payment to the King and assumed ownership. It stood near the Hudson in a part of the city that was spared by the fire.

The captain's military duties still required him to be absent quite frequently, so he invited the widow of a British soldier to stay with Meg. Her name was Mercy Litchfield and her house had been destroyed in the fire. Mercy was a true aristocrat: her mother was of Old Dutch stock and her father's Scottish lineage stretched back to ancient times. She lost her husband, John Litchfield, a British captain, in 1775. Mercy was what Belle Putnam would have called a "breath of fresh air." She was devastatingly beautiful, and, despite the dire circumstances of a city under siege, seemed to find humor in everything.

A few days after she arrived, Mercy burst into the townhouse. Her cheeks, flushed from the autumn wind, were a color similar to the damask curtains lining the first-floor parlor Meg was ensconced in.

"Meg!" She fluttered the paper she held in her hand. "We've been invited to General Howe's house!"

Meg hid the embroidery hoop she'd been working on by tucking it under her skirt. "Pardon?" General William Howe was the brother of Admiral Richard—one family member fought the Americans by land, the other by sea.

Mercy sat in the claw-footed wooden chair across from Meg. "A night of musical celebration, hosted by General Howe, is to take place in a fortnight!"

"And what are we celebrating? This incessant war?" Meg longed to retrieve her sewing but she did not want Mercy to know what she had been working on.

"No, silly. We are celebrating the handsome Englishmen that will bring back New York society." Mercy rose elegantly from the chair. "I wonder if Mulligan fled with the rest of them. I wouldn't mind a new frock."

As Mercy flounced upstairs, Meg retrieved the hoop, frowning. She didn't want to celebrate any Englishmen. She pulled at an errant stitch. She had been attempting to sew the initials A.B. onto a handkerchief, on the off chance she'd ever see Aaron again. But the sewing would not have been up to Aaron's fine taste. In a fit, Meg used the tip of her scissors to pull out all of the stitches before crushing the hoop under her satin shoes.

Meg could not have been less enthusiastic about the party. Mercy, in her growing gaiety, did not notice. Normally it would have been unseemly for a widow to be gallivanting around New York, but, with the onset of the war and the fleeing of many of the leading matriarchs, a lot of societal norms had all but disappeared.

The night of the party, Meg and Mercy set out in a splendid coach, which had also been confiscated from a Yankee. When they crossed Broad Street, Meg's eyes did not move from the window. The commercial district, through which she had passed with Aaron less than a month ago, was now a wasteland. Brick chimneys and cellar holes were about all that remained in the smoldering ashes that had once been stately Dutch homes. Tears of relief sprang to her eyes when she saw her beloved Kennedy Mansion, and next to it, Aaron's old residence at Three Broadway, both miraculously spared from the conflagration.

The carriage pulled to a stop in front of One Broadway. "Why have we halted?" Meg asked.

Mercy gave her a quizzical look. "Because we've arrived at General Howe's."

"Howe's residence is the Kennedy mansion?"

Mercy was busy gathering up the skirts of her blue taffeta gown and didn't reply.

Once outside, Meg, dressed in a pale pink sacque dress covered with tiny rosebuds, started. A Union Jack flag, placed in the fore-front of her old safe house, fluttered in the breeze. She felt an unex-pected twinge of sorrow as she gazed upon the flag of her home country. She could only imagine Aaron tearing it down if he saw it in front of his general's former headquarters. The defeat of the American army and their loss of New York suddenly became very real. She hoped that wherever the Putnams—and Aaron—were, they were away from harm.

Accustomed as she was by now to see the tailored red uniforms of the British army, Meg had to blink twice to notice them stuffed into the parlor in which Dolly Putnam had once established her sewing circles. Beautiful women in a rainbow array of chintz, damask, and taffeta sat among the Redcoats.

Meg and Mercy took seats on fine, though unfamiliar, Chippen-dale chairs. Although she could hear the lilting tunes of a harpsi-chord, Meg's view of the room was obscured by the woman in front of her, whose hair rose in a pyramid shape at least two feet off her head and was topped with an ornament that remarkably resembled the *Eagle*.

Mercy caught Meg staring at the unusual coiffure and nudged her with a grin. She put her arm around Meg's shoulders to pull her toward her, giving her a view of the busty woman sidling up to the harpsichord. "That's Elizabeth Loring," Mercy whispered in Meg's ear.

Meg looked at her blankly.

"General Howe's mistress. They say that her husband, Joshua Loring, has been promoted to commissioner of prisoners."

Meg wrinkled her nose. "Seems like an awfully high price to pay for being cuckolded."

Mercy nodded before sitting upright in her seat.

After the rather off-key performance of Mrs. Loring, the parlor was turned over into a dance hall. Besides the Loring/Howe dalliance, gossip that night was of an American man caught spying behind British lines.

"What was his name?" Meg asked a foppish fellow in the red regimentals of an officer.

"Nathan Hale, I believe," the officer returned.

Meg sighed inwardly in relief that it wasn't Aaron. Her relief quickly turned to horror as the man continued, "His body is still hanging outside the Dove Tavern."

Even Mercy seemed shocked and gasped aloud before saying, "Is that not a bit cruel?"

The man shrugged. "It's what happens to spies caught by their enemies."

"Tell me, Major," Mercy said, subtly pulling down on her bodice. "What do you think Howe's plan is now?"

"Besides cuddling up next to Mrs. Loring?" the man asked with a leering grin at Mercy's décolletage.

"Now that they have control of most of New York, do you think the army has plans to invade Philadelphia? Or have they set their sights on New Jersey?"

The man shrugged as he drank Madeira from a cut crystal goblet. "I have heard no plans yet." His mouth turned down. "Why do you ask?"

Mercy gave a dainty roll of her shoulders before placing a hand on Meg's elbow. "If you would pardon us, Major. My throat is much parched." She pulled her companion to the refreshment table in the corner.

"What was that all about?" Meg asked, picking at a display of fruit.

"I have relatives in the Jersey area." Mercy stepped closer to her friend. "Meg, I can't help but notice how many eyes are on you tonight. You could have your pick of any officer in this room."

Meg bit into a grape. It tasted sour and she swallowed it nearly whole, feeling its lump move down her throat. "None of them whet my fancy."

"What about that one?" Mercy used her fan to gesture to a tall, well-shaped man with sand-colored hair. "I hear Major André enjoys his ladies very much."

Though handsome, in Meg's opinion the man called Major André was nowhere near Aaron's caliber. An even lesser-looking gentleman in a double-breasted navy coat who had been conversing with the major caught the women's stare and shoved his way over to them.

"John Coghlan," he stated in a heavy Irish accent, sticking out a pudgy hand. His bald head glistened with sweat and there was a yellow stain on the cream lace of his cravat. His portly stomach seemed to test the strength of the buttons of his vest.

Another macaroni, Meg thought, before she curtsied and then introduced herself.

"Ahh, yes, Captain Moncrieffe's daughter," Mr. Coghlan concluded. "I am acquainted with your father."

"Indeed?" It was Meg's turn to find an excuse to leave the conversation. Unfortunately they were already standing next to the refreshment table. She cast her eyes about the room.

Major André caught her glance and walked over. "Ah, Mr. Coghlan, I see you have wasted no time in finding the loveliest ladies in the room to converse with."

Coghlan frowned as he bowed toward André. "I see you are trying to do the same. I am interested in finding out what other acquaintances Miss Moncrieffe and I have in common."

André bestowed a brilliant grin on Meg and Mercy. *On second thought, maybe he is not so different from Aaron,* Meg thought. "Although I believe it is becoming late. General Howe does not approve of women being out past curfew."

Meg's return smile toward André held a hint of gratitude.

Coghlan's gaze was icy as he must have known that he could not argue with the major. He bowed before saying, "I hope to see you again, Miss Moncrieffe."

As Meg linked her arm through Mercy's, leading her to the door, she whispered, "I hope never."

CHAPTER 19

ELIZABETH

OCTOBER 1776

*D*espite the chaos that had accompanied his birth, George was a surprisingly calm baby. He took to the breast eagerly and expertly. Although he slept in four-hour patches, Elizabeth still felt constantly drained. Abby took Catherine and Johnny out for daily walks and filled her mistress in on what was happening in the city around them.

The fire had exhausted itself, but not before it destroyed nearly every building between Broadway and the Hudson River, save for the Kennedy mansion at One Broadway and a few others. Roughly a quarter of the city had gone down in flames, including Trinity Church.

Elizabeth couldn't muster the strength to go down to open the store, consequently there was no money coming in. Abby usually managed to scrounge up milk from somewhere and Mary Underhill visited daily, often bringing meat and loaves of bread.

One day in early October, Abby startled Elizabeth while George was feeding. "Mrs. Burgin, Mrs. Underhill is here."

"Show her in."

"She's brought Mr. Underhill and another man with her. I told him you were busy, but they insisted on waiting outside until you are ready to receive them."

Elizabeth glanced down. George must have had his fill because he was now sleeping at her breast. She gently broke the contact between the baby's mouth and her nipple. After handing the infant over to Abby, Elizabeth slipped her bodice back around her shoulders and realigned her stomacher, the strings tied loosely now to accompany her wide belly. Mary Underhill was used to seeing Elizabeth half-dressed, but that would be no way to greet a strange man.

She went out to the living room and arranged herself as elegantly as she could before nodding to Abby. "Show them in."

The man who entered with the Underhills was tall and thin, with brown hair tied back in a low ponytail. He had solemn blue eyes above a hawkish nose. His plain dress indicated that he was probably a Quaker. He bowed in Elizabeth's direction before holding up his hand in a clear urge for her not to get up to return the gesture.

Amos Underhill also bowed. "Mrs. Burgin, I would like to introduce you to Robert Townsend." Amos sat down in one of the wooden chairs Abby had arranged in the living room while Mary remained standing by the fireplace.

Elizabeth nodded slowly. She had heard the name many times: the Townsends were Jonathan's biggest competitors. Their import business sold many of the same items, though they operated mostly out of Oyster Bay on Long Island. "What brings you to see me?" She waved her hand toward another chair and Robert sat down.

"I am aware of Mr. Burgin's recent…" Robert paused as if to find the right words. "Capture. I am also aware of your new arrival. I can only assume that things must be challenging for you at this time." His speech was dotted with breaks. It was clear the matters this pensive man came to discuss were difficult for him to voice.

Elizabeth folded her hands over her dress. "Indeed, but I'm not sure what concern it is of yours. Especially given the circumstances betwixt you and my husband."

It was Robert's turn to nod. "I am aware that, in the past, my family's store might have been seen as a rivalry for Mr. Burgin. However, there are affairs that have precluded our business in Oyster Bay. My father was recently arrested, and now we are forced to have the British quarter with us. The army will soon settle for the winter, and I fear that the same might be brought upon your household."

"Soldiers? No one, including General Howe, will be forcing the enemy upon my home."

Mary interceded. "Elizabeth, you haven't been about the city. Everywhere there are doors painted with the black G.R."

"G.R.?" Elizabeth asked.

"For Georgius Rex," Amos spat out. "Indicating that the house has been confiscated by order of his majesty." Amos wiped his gleaming bald head with a handkerchief. For an October day, it was quite warm outside.

Robert steepled his long fingers. "Mr. and Mrs. Underhill mentioned that you are alone here and they worry about you. Some of the abandoned businesses have been looted, and there are riots breaking out constantly. There are stories of British soldiers raping American women."

"The taverns are clogged with enemy soldiers and Loyalists," Mary added. "They are pouring into the city."

Elizabeth went to the window. The streets below were littered with broken glass and trash. "What will become of us?" she asked, more to herself than the room.

"I believe that I can offer a solution."

Elizabeth pivoted her head toward the speaker. "What exactly are you proposing to me, Mr. Townsend?"

"I am suggesting that you might let me run your shop for the winter. With the British occupation, they are in need of worldly goods more than ever. Every day the store remains shut, you are losing money."

Elizabeth glanced at Amos. He and Jonathan had grown up together in Setauket. Amos wouldn't suggest anything to her that

Jonathan wouldn't abide by. "Mr. Underhill, are you in agreement with this?"

Amos nodded. "Mary and I both think it is the best solution. That way you will have protection of a man, and one in good favor with the British."

Elizabeth sat back down. "What have you done to cause such favoritism?"

Robert had the grace to color slightly. "I swore an oath to the King."

Elizabeth's hands tightened into fists. "You are a Tory, and a traitor to your faith." Her uncle had been a Quaker and she knew that the religion specifically forbade taking oaths.

Mary put a restraining hand on her friend's shoulder. "These are trying times, Elizabeth. Many people do things they don't approve of to get by."

Elizabeth took her eyes off Robert to gaze around the room. Many of Jonathan's fine art and trinkets had disappeared—Abigail had to hawk what she could to keep food on the table. Every day she went out into those streets, Elizabeth worried for her. She worried for all of them. Amos was right: Robert's presence in the shop below would offer them some measure of safety, at least until Jonathan returned to take his rightful place. She finally nodded her assent at Robert. "You may manage my store. I expect to get the majority of the profits."

Robert stood to bow again. "Thank you, madam. You will not regret your decision."

Elizabeth also rose. "We all must do what we can to survive mustn't we?"

Robert's blue eyes looked pained as he replaced his cap. "Indeed."

Elizabeth still didn't feel strong enough to venture downstairs, but Abby's daily excursions provided the excuse to spy on Robert.

"He reads a lot, Miss Elizabeth. Whenever the store is empty of customers, he usually has his nose buried in a book."

"And are there customers?"

"Oh, yes, missus. The shelves are stocked again with all kinds of things: tea, perfume, feather pens, even rum."

"Rum?"

Abby nodded, her eyes wide. "Sometimes the Redcoats are queued up outside the door. They love their drink. That's why they are so loud and rowdy in the streets at night."

Hmm, Elizabeth mused, wondering how Robert was able to stock such luxuries. She went to the window. The docks were packed with British warships and she could surmise that the Redcoats were carefully monitoring the harbor. One would think it would be difficult to get items imported from other parts of the world. Either her new business partner had money to bribe British officers, or else he was somehow affiliated with the privateers that roamed the harbors.

Elizabeth thought she'd confirmed her latter suspicion when she finally felt well enough to see the effects of Townsend's tutelage for herself. True to Abby's word, the store was filled with lobsterbacks and commoners alike. Though the shelves were not completely full, a peek inside the storage room proved that it was not because of short supply but more due to people buying items faster than Robert could stock them.

Elizabeth watched from the corner of the counter as Robert served a few customers, the scent of tea and exotic spices filling the room. She held the air that she intended to supervise, hoping that Robert would not guess she was unfamiliar with most of the nuances of being a merchant, especially with the new goods.

"Rob!" a boisterous voice exclaimed.

"Cal!" Robert returned in an equally excited voice. He shook the man's hand before addressing Elizabeth. "Mrs. Burgin, I would like to introduce you to my friend, Caleb Brewster."

She obligingly came forward and curtsied. "Mr. Brewster, how do you do?"

Brewster bowed. He was taller than even Robert and much broader, but he had a disheveled look about him: his unruly brown beard was in need of a serious trimming and his trousers were worn at the knees.

"I knew Caleb before he was a whaler," Robert offered.

"And now, sir, what do you do?" Elizabeth asked. "I imagine whaling expeditions are hard to come by, what with the Redcoat seizure of the harbor."

"Everyone still needs whale oil." Brewster scratched at his beard. "But it's true, madam, that I've parted with my whaling ways. I served the Continentals during the Battle of Long Island."

"And now?" she repeated.

"Now I'm a longshoreman."

Ahh, Elizabeth thought. That's how Robert has access to these items: 'longshoreman' must have been code for privateer, someone who profits from robbing ships of their cargo.

She glanced at Robert. He was noting something in the ledger and didn't look up. The bell rang and all three pairs of eyes watched the newcomer step inside. Now it was Elizabeth's turn to speak a customer's name. "Mr. Rivington!"

Robert's pen paused as he scrutinized the impeccably dressed Rivington striding over.

Brewster's friendly expression became sour. "As in *Rivington's Gazette*? You own that paper?"

Rivington nodded. "I do." He turned to Elizabeth. "Mrs. Burgin, it is a pleasure to see you. Are you feeling well?"

"Well enough, thank you."

"Then, would you mind if I had a word?" He directed Elizabeth to a corner before pulling a folded piece of paper out of his breast pocket. The store had emptied and both Brewster and Robert were watching them, she noted.

The normally composed Rivington seemed nervous. His halting manner panicked Elizabeth as she took the slip from him. "What is it, Mr. Rivington? Is it news of my husband?"

"It is from one of my contacts aboard the *Jersey*."

The store seemed eerily hushed as she scanned the paper. *In response to your inquiries…* she skipped down to the bottom, her heart hammering away in her chest. *Cannot find any trace of a Jonathan Burgin.* Immediately Robert was at Elizabeth's side, grasping her hand to support her weight so she wouldn't sink to the floor. "Is he…?"

Rivington dropped his gaze. "As the letter stated, they cannot find a trace."

"But what does that mean? I saw him with my own eyes on that awful ship."

Brewster shook his head as he went into the stockroom, his baritone voice booming as if he were still in the same room. "If it's the *Jersey* you speak of, he wouldn't have lasted long. He would have died either from the pox or from starvation. They presumably dropped his body overboard once they found out he expired. The same thing happened to my friend Ben's brother." He returned, brandishing a chair which he set in front of Elizabeth. As Robert helped her into it, Brewster continued, "I'm sorry to say, madam, but he's probably shark fodder now."

As Robert elbowed Brewster, Elizabeth buried her face in her hands and wept. Although she didn't fully love Jonathan when he first proposed marriage, she had grown to both respect and admire her husband. Not to mention depend on him. The past few months had been very difficult, and she had to constantly console herself by thinking of how things would right themselves once Jonathan was set free. But now he was gone. He would never meet his new son, never see his children grow up in an independent country, never get the chance to be fully out of England's grasp.

When the tears had finally calmed, Robert handed her a handkerchief. As she wiped her eyes, her sorrow turned to anger. "How dare they?" she demanded. "How do they let such a fine man as Jonathan die and then not even give him a proper Christian burial?"

Rivington picked up the letter and tucked it back under his waistcoat. "I'm afraid that many more men will suffer the same fate."

Robert and Brewster exchanged an uneasy glance. They were probably fearful of Elizabeth losing her composure again. But she was done crying, at least for the time being. Unsure of how she'd found herself in the company of two Tories and a smuggler, she would not give them the satisfaction of seeing her weak. As she rose out of her chair, she informed them, "Not if I have any say of it." With that, the new widow walked out of the store and wearily climbed the steps back to her apartment.

CHAPTER 20

SALLY

*A*s more British troops began moving into town, the Oyster Bay Tories, once too fearful to declare their political sentiments, now pinned red ribbons to their coats and hats in demonstration of their loyalty to the Crown. Thomas Buchanan delivered one such rosette to Papa, who tucked it into a drawer. Major Green, for his part, never mentioned the Townsends' lack of red ribbons.

The same could not be said for the other British authorities who occupied Oyster Bay. One morning, Papa asked Sally to drop off a few items from his store to Daniel Youngs' place on the far side of the Bay. Sally promptly agreed. Even though both Robert and Papa publicly submitted their oath, she couldn't help feeling the Redcoats were watching her father's every move and was eager to keep him out of their sight.

Sally set out on her ride. The fall day was sunny and cool, the yellow and orange leaves falling casually in front of her. She was nearly there when she spotted a British dragoon letting his horse graze in Mr. Titus's field. She rode on without a second glance,

119

but before long, she heard a voice behind her loud enough to resonate over the galloping horses. "You, girl," the officer called out.

Sally slowed Gem but didn't halt.

The soldier pulled up beside her. "I see neither your horse nor you are wearing red in honor of our King."

Sally looked over at the man riding next to her. He was short and squat, his face the same, with heavy cheeks that reminded her of a chipmunk. He returned her gaze, his blue eyes narrowed.

"That's right," she couldn't help telling him. "Gem here happens to have Whiggish leanings and reared when it was suggested he wear Tory red. Besides," Sally patted her horse, "I prefer him as he is."

The dragoon's eyes, for a brief second, seemed to grow even colder as he put spurs to his horse and galloped away. Sally could see that he was also heading in the direction of the Youngs', and her heartbeat sped up, keeping time with Gem's quickened pace. She cursed herself for being so rude, for possibly putting her family in yet more danger.

As she rode up to the property, she saw the dragoon tying his horse to a post.

"Sir." Sally tried her best to sound casual, but the man ignored her.

Just then, Daniel Youngs stalked out of the house and approached Sally. He smiled warmly and held out his arm to help her dismount as the Redcoat looked on. After Sally had gracefully climbed down from Gem, Daniel gave her a hug. As he pulled away from her, Sally figured the dragoon would take the opportunity to tell Daniel about her rudeness, but he stayed silent.

Daniel took the wrapped package from Sally and led her toward the house.

"Daniel?" Sally asked, subtly nodding at the Redcoat, who was examining his horse's shod.

"Ah, yes." Daniel said, his hand placed lightly on Sally's back. "That dragoon is a member of my militia."

"Your militia?"

"Yes. As a Loyalist officer, I have been given command of a unit stationed here at Oyster Bay."

Sally fell silent for the rest of the walk. Susannah had been a childhood friend, and Sally had been fond of Daniel. She supposed he was aware of her family's stance, but that he was choosing not to say anything more, which put only a little salve on her regret that Susannah married such a Tory.

"I hear that you have become hosts to a Loyalist militia unit," Sally stated to Susannah after the Youngs' slave girl had served them tea and pastries. Sally picked up a biscuit, but her stomach was still in knots over the fear that the dragoon outside would speak of her behavior to Daniel, that it would get back to Major Green, or, worse yet, Papa.

Susannah shrugged. "You know how it is." She took a bite of her cookie. "And I hear that your family is hosting Major Green. Tell me, is he good-looking?"

"He is clearly not in want of a good meal."

"Yet I assume he looks handsome in a uniform," Susannah giggled.

Sally wanted to state that it was the wrong uniform, but she bit her comment back along with her biscuit.

An hour later Sally headed back to the Townsend home. Her hackles were raised, expecting to meet yet another soldier on the road who would demand to know why Gem wore no red, but she made it home without incident.

Phoebe met her at the door. "Mother has decided to throw a party!"

"A party?" Sally removed her riding bonnet. "Whatever for?"

"For Major Green, of course."

Sally ran a hand through her dusty copper curls. Major Green's presence was not the nightmare Sally had expected the day she found him on the portico—he had kept mostly to himself and was not altogether unpleasant at mealtimes. He had an unassuming, if aloof demeanor, and allowed the Townsend family to go on with their life as it were. Still, it didn't seem proper to host a party in his honor, given the Townsends' political leanings.

"Papa?" Sally stood at the doorway of the peach-colored dining room that doubled as her father's study, watching him as he leaned over his books. She had to repeat his name again before he finally looked up.

"What is it, Sally?"

She entered the room, shutting the door behind her. She also closed the adjacent door that led into the kitchen and then stood beside his chair. "I was just wondering why we should have a party for Major Green."

Papa set down his quill. "After what happened earlier this fall, I wanted to make sure De Lancey knows that his officer is a welcome guest in our home."

"But if the British——"

Papa placed his hand over hers. "Sally, these are the times we live in. Officers are quartered all over the colonies. It could be worse. Youngs' militiamen are terrorizing the town. I've heard stories…"

"I know." Sally had heard them too—stories of Loyalists plundering their fellow countrymen's farms and homes, and of them kidnapping and raping young women. "I suppose Major Green does offer a bit of protection now that Robert has gone to the city."

"And for that we can be grateful." Papa turned back to his ledger, indicating the conversation was over.

The party took place a few days later. The Youngs were invited, as were Jacob Townsend—Papa's younger brother—and his wife, Mercy, along with a few other Oyster Bay neighbors.

Sally and Phoebe were conversing in the parlor with Major Green, decked out in his uniform, when their cousin Hannah arrived with her sister Almy Buchanan and her husband. Major Green paused what he was saying mid-sentence to peer at Hannah.

"Who is that?"

Phoebe mistook his query. "Thomas Buchanan is a good friend of Papa's. He helped him during Papa's trial."

Major Green did not seem to hear her. He sauntered over to the newly arrived guests and, as custom, politely introduced himself to the married couple before turning to Hannah and bowing. She returned a curtsy, giggling as her cousins watched. Phoebe turned to Sally, eyebrows raised. The three girls, similar in age, had always been close, but Hannah usually garnered the least amount of attention when they were all together. Sally shrugged. She would not have entertained Green's attentions, anyway. From the way Hannah pranced in front of him, Sally figured she'd follow in her sister's footsteps by marrying one whose sentiments went against their newly founded country.

In fact, Major Green, though the celebrated guest of the party, did not leave Hannah's side much of the night until it was time for her to depart.

"Tell me more about Ms. Townsend," Green begged Sally after most of the guests had gone.

"Hannah?" Sally slid a chair back to its customary place in the corner. She briefly considered saying something to avert Green's obvious enchantment with her cousin, but then thought better of it. Hannah was only a year her senior and more than capable of making her own decisions. "Her brother-in-law is a staunch Loyalist."

Green nodded as he moved another chair. His mind seemed preoccupied.

A few days later, the couple announced their engagement. Green was adamant that the wedding take place as soon as possible.

"Why so promptly?" Sally asked him when he entered the kitchen. It was the servants' day off and Sally was tasked with making supper. "Are there plans for winter deployment?" After the words left her mouth, she turned to place a bannock pan onto the hearth, hoping to hide her red face. Her question, though posed out of curiosity, might be taken in offense, as though she were trying to dig up information.

"I know of no such plans," Major Green replied casually. "But, if that were the case, I would like for Hannah to have some prospect of a pension should anything befall me."

Sally turned back toward him and Green nodded at her before swiping a biscuit on his way out of the kitchen.

Her heart was still thumping at the conversation. True, Green had provided no useful information, but what if he had? Sally had resented living in such close quarters with the enemy, but now she began to ponder if somehow she could take advantage of the situation. Perhaps, if prodded in the right way, Green—or any of the other myriad of British officers stationed in Oyster Bay—might divulge secret plans or tactics.

Silly me, Sally thought, wiping her hands on her apron. *What would I do with that information anyway? Whisper it in General Washington's ear?* She pulled the pan out of the fire and set it on the trivet to cool before removing her apron.

CHAPTER 21

ELIZABETH

OCTOBER 1776

*A*s the weather began to cool, life settled into routine for Elizabeth. Although rumors of raping and pillaging spread throughout the city, they were mostly contained to the charred remnants of the west side. The ironically named Holy Ground had been decimated, but in its place sprung Canvas Town, a much more apt epithet. The poor, who had no money to rebuild, spread sails from old boats over the burned-out chimneys and ruins and continued their bawdy revelry. The deluge of Redcoats on the street became a familiar sight to Elizabeth and no longer struck fear in heart.

The loss of Jonathan was not as easy a reconciliation, however. As independent as she had become in his absence, she missed him terribly. As was her custom while he was away at war, every morning she woke up without him, she reminded herself that he'd soon return home. Gradually the realization that he was never coming back would sink in, along with the sorrow. The time between the two thoughts grew closer together as the month went on, but that did not mean the pain lessened.

Mary Underhill stopped by for tea at least once a week. She was well informed of Elizabeth's grievances against Robert Townsend, who had befriended Rivington and started writing Tory trash for his paper. At one such meeting, Mary shrugged off Elizabeth's complaints to ask, "But how goes the store?"

Elizabeth took a sip of tea and carefully set the porcelain cup back on the plate before answering. "Well enough. Mr. Townsend used his contacts at the *Gazette* to secure a contract to supply the British army with stationary."

Mary broke off a piece of scone. "That should bring in a good amount of money."

Elizabeth sighed. "I suppose, but I cannot get the image of General Howe writing orders to condemn a man using ink and paper procured from Jonathan's store." The words, uttered from her own mouth, stung her unexpectedly and her eyes filled with tears.

Mary reached out to pat her friend's hand. "I've said it before, Elizabeth, but we all do what we can."

Mary was a first cousin of Nathaniel Woodhull, the general under whom Jonathan served, and who was tortured in battle, later dying of his wounds. It seemed to Elizabeth that Mary was too quick to forgive traitors. "I just don't understand how Robert Townsend can go about openly associating with Redcoats."

"Elizabeth, things aren't always what they might seem. A lake with calm waters at the surface can run very deep." Mary's voice carried an ominous undercurrent. Elizabeth searched her friend's face to see if her expression might belie her meaning, but the teacup she held to her mouth obscured any telltale sign.

Robert Townsend himself was a contradiction. As much as Elizabeth resented him, he, for his part, made himself useful. It helped that there was a continuous flow of money into Elizabeth's account, which was a double blessing as the price of fuel skyrocketed with the British occupation. The unusually cool October fore-boded an even more frigid winter.

One morning she stopped by the store to check on things while Abby was out on a walk with the children. She flipped uselessly through the ledger while Robert restocked shelves before slamming the book shut with a loud sigh.

Robert turned toward her. "Anything wrong?"

Elizabeth did not want to admit her ignorance, but something seemed off to her. "There are a great many blankets and canned food attributed to a Mr. George Higday, but I don't see any payments, on loan or not."

Robert colored slightly. "No, Mrs. Burgin, that is true. I make the payments from my own account."

"But why?"

Robert walked over and stood on the other side of the counter. "Mr. Higday serves the prison ships."

"The prison ships? How?"

"He arranges a trip out there on a whaleboat at least once a week to offer food and other necessities to the prisoners."

"But why are you aiding him?"

Robert put both hands on the counter. "I consider it my patriotic duty."

"You're no Patriot."

Elizabeth's voice held less animosity than usual, but still Robert visibly recoiled at the harsh words. "I'm a Quaker. I have no side."

"Then you are definitely not a Patriot."

He returned to his former position restocking inkwells. Elizabeth ran a finger across the cracked leather of the account book. As much as she hated his Tory-leanings, she felt badly that she had obviously offended him. "I'd like to meet this George Higday," she said finally.

Robert gave her a long, searching look before he nodded in return.

· · ·

A few days later, Elizabeth was knitting in her apartment when someone knocked at the door. Abigail raised her eyebrows at her mistress, who shrugged. It was not the day of Mrs. Underhill's weekly visit and, besides Robert Townsend, they did not get many visitors.

"Is Mrs. Burgin available?" a rough voice called after Abby had answered the door.

Elizabeth rose. "I am here."

Caleb Brewster, the former whaler and Townsend's probable smuggler, stood in the hallway holding a faded hat in his hands. He bowed. "Mr. Townsend wanted me to inform you that a mutual acquaintance of yours has entered the store."

Elizabeth frowned before remembering her request to meet Higday. "I'll be back shortly," she told Abby. She ran into the bedroom to grab a blanket she had quilted and then followed Brewster as he clomped downstairs.

George Higday was a squat man with a large paunch. His goat's hair wig was too small for his head, revealing his own graying hair underneath it. He stood before the counter as Robert Townsend wrote in the ledger.

"Ahh, Mrs. Burgin, I'm glad you were able to finally make the acquaintance of Mr. Higday," Robert said, nodding at the man.

Higday turned to Elizabeth and bowed. "Mrs. Burgin."

She set the blanket on a shelf behind her before extending her hand. "I hear you do a great service to your country."

Higday glanced at Robert, who returned an almost imperceptible nod. Higday turned back to Elizabeth and gave her a smile that did not reach his eyes. "Oh, I do not do much. I am mostly in charge of the garnering letters from the prisoner's families. Dame Grant and William Scudder are the ones who actually gather the supplies."

Elizabeth could not help noticing that he seemed rather nervous. His glassy-eyed stare bounced from Robert to Brewster and then back to Robert, who had his hand wrapped around his chin while he studied Higday.

"Who is Dame Grant?" Elizabeth inquired.

Again, Higday looked at Robert before replying. "It looks less suspicious if a woman is on board."

Robert coughed and Higday's countenance took on a guilty look, as if he had said something awry.

"Suspicious?" Elizabeth asked.

"He means it makes it look more meaningful," Robert clarified. "The prisoners like to see a cheery female face as it reminds them of their wives and daughters."

Brewster covered up his guffaw by stretching his arms overhead and pretending to yawn.

Elizabeth did not tell them that she was also acquainted with Dame Grant, a corpulent older woman. Although Dame Grant's patriotic blood ran deep, Elizabeth questioned whether her face, with its deep-seated frown lines and heavy jowls, would be considered cheery. There was definitely something the men were not telling her. "And William Scudder?"

"One of my crew," Caleb Brewster drawled.

One of your smugglers, Elizabeth corrected him silently. "And what happens when you arrive at the prison ships? Do you go aboard?"

"No," Higday answered. "It's too dangerous—many of the men have the pox. We anchor next to the accommodation ladder and a guard lowers it for us."

"I am familiar with the dangers of the hulks," Elizabeth said, forcing a vision of an emaciated Jonathan out of her mind. "But how do you know your supplies are actually getting to the prisoners?"

"Well…" Higday gestured toward Robert, who answered, "They have to make sure the guards on duty are His Majesty's soldiers and not American loyalists. Our fellow countrymen are much crueler than their British counterparts. And we have a note from the commissary to prisoners, Lewis Pintard. He is charged with making sure our men receive decent care. As much as can be done in those rotting hulks, anyway."

"The guards will open the letters and read them, but we usually pick up an unsealed reply from the prisoner on the next visit," Higday added.

Elizabeth nodded before remembering the blanket behind her. "Please include this in your next delivery."

"Thank you, Mrs. Burgin." Higday took the proffered blanket and folded it under his arm.

Brewster hefted a box off the counter. "I'll help transport this to your carriage."

"Until next time, then, Mr. Higday," Robert told him.

Elizabeth watched as the two men exited. She was about to demand that Robert explain to her whatever it was Higday was trying to cover up, but the silver bell rang again as a blond man entered the shop.

"Robert!" he exclaimed heartily.

"William?" Robert inquired. "What brings you here?"

The man named William leaned his muscular body over the counter. "Just visiting New York City."

"How did you get past the sentinels near the ferry?"

William grinned. "I have my ways." He turned smoothly to Elizabeth. "And who do we have here?"

"Mrs. Burgin," Robert replied, an emphasis on the *Mrs.* as William extended his hand.

"And you are?" Elizabeth asked.

"William Townsend." He lifted her hand to his lips and kissed it as Elizabeth studied him. He had the same blue eyes as Robert but where Robert's were often guarded, William's were wide and friendly. William was shorter than Robert, but with broader shoulders and a perfectly proportioned face. All told, he reminded Elizabeth of the story of the Greek Adonis that her mother used to read to her.

William turned back to Robert. "Mother and Audrey send their love."

Caleb Brewster reentered the store. "And what about your loveliest sister, Sally?" he asked before embracing William.

William threw his head back and laughed. "Sally's all up in the boughs because of Major Green."

"Major Green?" Brewster asked.

"Of De Lancey's regiment," Robert said tersely. "He's quartering with my family for the winter."

Brewster laughed nearly as loud as William had. "I'll bet Sally is spitting mad."

"Why?" Elizabeth could not help but ask.

Brewster turned to her. "Sally Townsend's as much of a Whig as Washington himself."

"A Whig?" She turned to Robert. "Are the ties that bind you so loose that you and your sister could be on different sides of the war?"

William opened his mouth to say something, but Robert held up his hand. "I told you Mrs. Burgin. I am neutral."

Although she was facing Robert, out of the corner of her eye, Elizabeth could see Brewster and William exchange a quick glance.

Wary of the undercurrents that stirred beneath these obviously veiled conversations, Elizabeth took her leave of the brothers and Brewster. As she ascended the stairs, she couldn't help but hear Mary's warning. Indeed, there was something about Robert Townsend that ran much deeper than what was discernible on the surface.

CHAPTER 22

MEG

NOVEMBER 1776

*T*he cold weather brought a halt to the fighting, and Captain Moncrieffe returned home. Mercy and Meg threw him a small party to welcome him back. Any Loyalist female would have been impressed by the guest list, which included titled lords and heirs to fortunes, not to mention Admiral Howe, his brother the general and, of course, his mistress Mrs. Loring. Standing among the handsome regimentals and gilly macaronis in the Moncrieffe's parlor—and as conspicuous as a babe in the woods—was John Coghlan.

"How did he get invited?" Meg asked Mercy, peering at the corpulent fellow, now clad in a red velvet coat.

Mercy took a bite of cake. "He is of Irish nobility."

"Him?" Meg sneered. "I understand the Irish as I can practically smell the whiskey off him from over here. But nobility?"

Mercy leaned in to whisper, "I hear his father trades African slaves."

Mr. Coghlan spent most of the night trying to engage Meg in conversation, who likewise went out of her way to avoid him.

He followed her into the parlor corner between the refreshments and a potted palm. "So we meet again, Miss Moncrieffe," he stated in an oily voice.

"So we do." Meg's eyes darted around the room, searching for an excuse to take leave of him.

As if he knew of her desire, he took one step closer. "What do you think of our men who now occupy this fine city?"

"Pardon?"

"There are many eligible bachelors in our ranks. I was just curious if you had set your eyes on one. Major André, perhaps."

Meg giggled distractedly as she leaned backward, trying to put as much distance between her and Mr. Coghlan as possible without being obvious. "I'm not quite of marrying age yet."

"And even those who are not so eligible are still an ocean away from their wives and more than willing to spend their wages on a worthy female. If she herself is willing." At this he glanced deliberately at General Howe and Mrs. Loring.

Meg put her hands on her hips. "Why, Mr. Coghlan, are you implying that a maiden would cuckold herself with a man just for money?"

"Not necessarily money. For protection, status, or even just a supply of firewood." Somehow he was able to keep that leering grin as he spoke. "War brings on difficulties only previously imagined."

Meg raised her chin. "I'm perfectly fine under the protection of my father. And I would never marry a man for his money." She thought, as she often did, of Aaron. She would have married him on the spot and lived on a soldier's wages forever, if only he had let her.

"With these trying times, anything could happen," Mr. Coghlan replied cryptically.

Meg bit back another retort as Mercy lived up to her name and appeared by Meg's side. "Meg, there you are. I've been looking for you. I wanted to introduce you to Mr. Mulligan." She turned and curtsied. "Why, Mr. Coghlan, how nice to see you again," she said before pulling on her friend's arm.

"That bracket-face always seems to be cornering me at parties," Meg said as Mercy led her away.

Mercy hooked her arm through Meg's. "You would think you would be used to it, being the most beautiful woman in the room and all. Any of these men would give their eyeteeth to be your husband."

"I don't think I ever want a husband if they are all like Mr. Coghlan," Meg muttered under her breath.

"But you'd be a spinster!" Mercy leaned in conspiringly as she pulled Meg toward a group of men. "Even though I loved my husband dearly, it is not too bad being a widow—you are protected from sullying your reputation by the Mrs. preceding your name." She paused in front of an impeccably dressed, portly gentleman. "Miss Moncrieffe, I'd like you to meet Mr. Hercules Mulligan."

He bowed before taking Meg's hand and kissing it. "Pleased to make your acquaintance, Miss Moncrieffe," he stated with an Irish brogue.

"He is the owner of a tailor shop on Queen's street," Mercy continued.

Mulligan, Mulligan, Meg's mind raced. Where had she heard that name before? "Thomas Walcott!" The words came out before Meg had a chance to think about what she was saying. All three people— Meg herself included—seemed startled by her outburst.

"Why, yes," Mr. Mulligan said hesitantly. "Mr. Walcott was my guest for a few days. How do you know of him?"

Meg thought fast. She couldn't exactly state that she gave Thomas fortification plans to help the British attack the city. Or could she? After all, wasn't this supposed to be a Loyalist affair? "The Walcotts are old friends of the family. I saw Thomas right before the Battle of Long Island. He mentioned that you were acquainted with Alexander Hamilton." Meg hoped that the reference to the known rebel would take the heat off her in case Mulligan knew that Thomas was a spy.

Mr. Mulligan glanced at Mercy. "Captain Hamilton boarded

135

with me while he attended King's College. That is, my wife and I."
He nodded at a thin dark-haired woman across the room. "She is
the daughter of Admiral Sanders of the Royal Navy," he said
pointedly.

Mercy gave a twinkly laugh. "We must judge on people's
declared loyalty, not necessarily on their past actions."

"Or their past acquaintances," Mulligan cut in.

"Right," Mercy said quickly.

Mr. Mulligan held his hands out to Mercy, who grasped them.
"We all know our little Mrs. Litchfield here is one of the biggest
Tories there is, even if her father is a known Son of Liberty and
former member of the New York Congress."

As she regarded Meg, Mercy's smile faded slightly. It then grew
to unnatural proportions as her friend gave her a quizzical look.
Meg barely heard Mr. Mulligan apologize as he took his leave of
them.

"You never told me your father was a rebel," Meg said accusingly as soon as Mr. Mulligan was out of earshot.

Mercy shrugged. "What does it matter?"

"Does he fight for the Patriots?"

Mercy tucked a piece of hair behind her ear. "Yes."

"What battles?"

Mercy's eyes darted around the room before focusing back on
Meg. "He fought with General Putnam at the Battle of Brooklyn."

Momentarily stunned, Meg regained enough composure to ask
if she still had contact with him.

"No," Mercy shook her head vehemently. "I gave up my ties to
that side when I married my late husband."

Meg nodded. She had half-hoped Mercy would have been able
to write to her father and asked about Old Put and Aaron. "I see."
Meg wanted to ask her more about it, but Mercy gave another of
her laughs. "We all do what we have to for love, don't we?"

After the party, Meg had trouble falling asleep. She kept hearing
Mercy's voice saying so matter-of-factly that she had given up her
father to marry her husband. She wondered if Mercy ever regretted

that move now that her husband had died. Did Mercy, a Whig by upbringing, ever feel alone in a room full of Tory strangers? The opposite could have been Meg's fate, if only Aaron had agreed to marry her. Would it have been worth it to be Aaron Burr's wife, even if only for a short while?

Captain Moncrieffe was already seated at the table when Meg made her way down at midday the next afternoon.

"You're up late today, my daughter," he said by way of greeting.

Meg smiled sheepishly. "Sorry, Father. I think my feet are still exhausted by all the revelry."

He peered at her from above his bifocals. "I didn't see you do much dancing. It seemed you and Mercy spoke to Hercules Mulligan for a long period of time."

Meg pretended to be confused. "Oh yes," she said loftily. "The tailor."

Captain Moncrieffe steepled his fingers. "There is something about that man I do not trust. I am suspicious of anyone who can change their loyalties so easily."

His meaning was clear: stay away from Mr. Mulligan. "Yes, Father," Meg said.

"You missed our morning visitor," Captain Moncrieffe went on to state.

"Oh?" Meg perked up. Mayhap Aaron was able to get through the lines to deliver a message declaring his undying love.

"Mr. John Coghlan. He asked if he could call on you. I invited him to dine with us this evening."

Meg couldn't help wrinkling her nose.

Her father took notice. "That is enough now, Margaret—he is a fine gentleman."

Meg did not reply in lieu of saying what she was thinking, that he was a fine durgen but no gentleman.

Mr. Coghlan arrived promptly for dinner dressed in a similar velvet coat as the previous night, but this time in a garish purple.

After he was announced in the dining room, he immediately

went to Meg, who was standing next to Mercy, waiting for permission to be seated. He lifted her limp hand to his lips. "Good evening, Miss Moncrieffe."

"John," Captain Moncrieffe said. "We've set your plate next to Margaret." He nodded at his daughter, who took her usual place at the table, adjacent to her father at the head. Coghlan sat on her right.

"A drink!" Coghlan said, holding up his glass. The sudden movement caused powder from his wig to shower the air around him before landing on his shoulders. "To new acquaintances and the hopes they will become more."

Meg lifted her goblet half-heartedly before putting it back down on the table. No one noticed that she hadn't drunk from it.

Coghlan seemed pleased by the quality of the wine—he slurped from his glass and set it down before smacking his lips. As the Moncrieffe's serving girl, Athena, entered with the first course, Coghlan tapped his empty goblet and then turned to Meg. "Is that frock not in last year's style?"

"It is," Meg replied pointedly, laying her knife down with the blade on the plate, the way she'd been taught at boarding school. "I find that new dresses are hard to come by presently."

He tilted his head. "Perhaps you need someone who will gladly keep his girl in new clothes. A pretty girl deserves equally charming outfits."

"I am perfectly fine wearing last season's clothes," Meg said as Mercy raised her eyebrows from across the table. Meg turned her head as Coghlan dug into his meal with enthusiasm. Her former headmistress would be shocked at the number of etiquette rules Coghlan was breaking, including making small noises in his throat as he ate.

"Mr. Coghlan, why don't you tell us a little bit about yourself?" Captain Moncrieffe asked before setting his fork down.

"Well, let's see." Coghlan sat back and folded his hands over his wide belly as the servants cleared the table in preparation for the next course. "My father made his wealth as a merchant in Bristol."

You mean made his wealth selling slaves, Meg thought as the serving girl set down a plate of seafood in front of her.

Mr. Coghlan leaned over to sniff his food before he continued, "My mother is descended from Jones family. My great-great-grand-father was a member of Oliver Cromwell's Parliament."

The only person this served to impress was Captain Moncrieffe, who nodded enthusiastically before glaring at Meg as she picked up an oyster and then set it down again without eating it. The thought occurred to her that Coghlan was not that much different from the shellfish: slippery and likely to leave a fishy taste in one's mouth.

"I also sailed with Captain Cook on the *Resolution.*"

At this, Mercy gave Coghlan a polite smile as Captain Moncrieffe asked, "You sailed around the world?" before taking a drink of his Madeira.

Coghlan's eyes shifted to Meg, who once again pretended to be absorbed in her meal. "Well, nearly so. Life at sea can be challenging."

Captain Moncrieffe nodded. "I'm sure that it must have been quite an adjustment, given your background."

Coghlan slurped down an oyster before saying, "And then I joined the Loyalist militia to help suppress this rebellion."

"And your plans for the future?" Captain Moncrieffe asked.

"I'll be returning to Bristol when the war is over." He glanced again at Meg. "Hopefully with a wife and a babe in tow. Maybe two, depending on how long the rebels hold out. I need to find a fertile wife to beget me heirs."

Mercy covered her gasp at his brash words with a sip of water. Meg returned her friend's gaze with wide eyes.

Coghlan and Captain Moncrieffe spent the rest of the meal discussing the Howes' next possible move, whether it would be to follow the rebel forces into New Jersey and engage them or turn north to Philadelphia. Mercy appeared to be listening intently, but Meg tuned out, pushing her dessert of berries and cream around the bowl with her spoon.

After dinner the gentleman took leave to go into the parlor and drink their brandy. Mercy went off to bed while Meg sat staring at her embroidery in the living room. An hour or so later, Mr. Coghlan and the captain emerged from the parlor, along with a cloud of smoke. It seemed to Meg that Mr. Coghlan was ogling her as his customary smirk returned. She imagined the expression he wore was probably similar to that of his relatives as they sized up a slave to sell.

"Miss Moncrieffe, I must take my leave."

Her father frowned at her until she got up to bid Mr. Coghlan farewell. His lips seemed to linger on her hand as their servant, Noah, opened the door. "Until tomorrow, then," Mr. Coghlan said before donning his hat and exiting the house.

"Tomorrow?" Meg asked as Noah shut the door. "What does he want with me tomorrow?"

Captain Moncrieffe extended his hand toward the parlor. "Come, Margaret, I need to speak with you."

Meg walked into the parlor and sat down on the mauve loveseat. A pair of spent cigars were still smoldering in the ashtray on the table. She coughed daintily before asking, "Yes, Father?"

He settled in a wingback chair across from her. "It seems Mr. Coghlan, too, noticed you speaking with some…" he paused as he folded one leg over the other, "questionable characters last night. Both of us agreed that we wouldn't want your good name to be criticized."

"Father, you don't need to trouble yourself—"

"Now, Margaret, you know I worry about you while I'm on duty. I am quartered here for the winter, but what about next spring and the winter after?"

"Mercy is here now."

"Mrs. Litchfield can hardly vouch for your reputation, being the daughter of a rebel herself."

Meg wanted to question why he had Mercy move into the townhouse in the first place if that's the way he felt, but knew that would not be the way to win this argument. She was about to try her usual ploy, begging, but her father continued. "Mr. Coghlan had a reasonable solution: to ask for your hand in marriage."

Meg's tongue froze in her mouth. As if in a nightmare, her

father went on to state, "I agree that it is the best solution. He is well disposed to take care of you financially and will protect your standing socially."

Her tongue finally clicked into motion. "But Father, I hardly know this man."

"Most couples on the throes of marriage do not. That's what your newlywed year is about," he said with a wink.

He seemed particularly impenetrable this evening, as casual as though he were ordering a new suit, not planning a future she did not want. She bit back her panic to try a different tactic. "I'm not of marrying age."

He waved his hand. "Mr. Coghlan has connections with Governor Tryon and seemed to think that getting a special license would be no problem. He wants to have the ceremony in haste as he might be ordered to leave the city with the army in the spring."

Meg glanced at the chimney and imagined herself behind it, as though each statement from her father were another brick trapping her in. She felt as though she couldn't breathe and jumped to her feet to loosen the pressure of her stomacher. "But Father, I don't love him!"

Her father looked taken aback. "Love? What know you of love?"

Rather than confess her feelings for a rebel, Meg fled from the room.

She ran upstairs to her bedroom. Instead of flinging herself onto the bed and crying, she sat at her writing desk to compose a letter to Aaron, begging him to come rescue her. She wrote a whole page before she realized that she had no notion as to how he could receive it, and even then, he would have no way to get through the lines to save her. Despondent, she crumpled the letter and threw it across the room. After she dressed in her nightclothes, she lay in bed trying to find a way to avoid her new fate. She settled on the two best options—asking her Father to send her back to boarding school in England and politely but firmly refusing Coghlan's offer to his face—before falling into a dreamless sleep.

. . .

Coghlan arrived early the next day and awaited her in the parlor. Athena, the maid, acted as chaperone. She held a feather duster but made no shame of the fact that she openly listened to their conversation.

"Miss Moncrieffe," Mr. Coghlan said when she entered, dressed in a light blue gown over a cream-colored stomacher. This time he wore his red regimentals, complete with polished boots and sword.

Meg curtsied before settling herself in the loveseat. "Mr. Coghlan."

"I suppose you might as well call me John, now that we are betrothed."

Meg pasted on her best smile. "Mr. Coghlan," she said sweetly, "I mean, John, do you not want a wife who is of equal mind to yours?"

Coghlan unbuckled his sword and placed it on the table before settling into a chair. "There is no woman of equal mind to me."

"Of course not." Meg fought to keep the sarcasm out of her voice. "What I meant was, a woman who had as much affection for you as you have for her."

"I am not in need of affection. I am in need of a wife with a good family name."

Meg did not expect that answer. She paused for a moment before asking, "You do not wish to marry for love?"

Coghlan sat forward. "Margaret, I realize that you are very young, and new to matters of the heart, but a marriage does not necessarily spawn out of love." That was something Meg could agree with. "But, given time, love might spawn out of a marriage."

Not out of a marriage to you, Meg thought. She glanced at Athena, who stood near a corner bookshelf and pretended to polish the leather bindings of the books. Meg ventured to say, "John, I think you should know that my heart belongs to another."

He nodded before sitting back in his chair. Meg sighed inwardly, thinking at last she had won, but then Coghlan replied, "Again, it does not matter. Love is fleeting, but you will take my name forever."

"No!" Meg couldn't stop herself from crying out. "Can you not do the honorable thing and give up your pursuit of me?"

"Honor?" Coghlan asked with a sneer. "It is precisely to protect your honor that your father agreed to my proposal. And," he continued as he stood, "it is only your father's approval that I need. The wedding will take place in February."

Meg felt tears of defeat well in her eyes, but she would not let Coghlan see them. She blinked them back as he lifted her hand and kissed it before exiting the parlor. Athena gave her a sympathetic moue before turning back to the books. Meg wiped more tears with the sleeve of her dress. She sniffed and tried to gather herself. Obviously trying to reason with Coghlan did not work, but mayhap she could plead her case to Father. He was normally not so rigid in his views. Surely Meg could convince him to change his mind.

But just then her father burst into the parlor and marched toward her. "Margaret! What is this?" He thrust a crumpled piece of paper in her face. Meg recognized it as the letter she tried writing last night. "Who is Major Aaron Burr?"

"Father…" She reached for the paper but he crushed it in his fist.

"A rebel? You fall in love with a rebel and then refuse to accept the husband I wish to provide for you?"

Meg stood. "Father, you don't understand. Aaron's a good man."

"No rebel is a good man." Meg had never seen her father so angry. His face was as red as his uniform and spittle flew out of his mouth when he spoke. "I order you to your room to think very carefully about the choice I am about to give you: marry John Coghlan or I will disown you."

CHAPTER 23

SALLY

JANUARY 1777

 obert returned to Oyster Bay bearing supplies for the wedding reception of Major Green and Hannah. It had only been a few months' time, but it seemed to Sally that her brother was thinner, his cheeks more sunken, the circles under his blue eyes darker.

Papa led his son to the dining room so Robert could tell him the updates on New York City. Sally polished the pewter as Robert solemnly relayed the news of Washington's army. Since the evacuation of Manhattan, the Continental army had suffered great losses, including the forts of Lee and Washington. The disheartened rebels, pursued endlessly by Redcoats and Hessian mercenaries, had fled further into New Jersey and, according to Robert, were cornered on the east side of the Delaware River near Princeton. "The talk in Manhattan is that the war will not last much longer. Many of my Tory contacts predict Washington will yield early into this new year."

"He cannot concede yet," Papa said. "What of our cause?"

Robert let out an ironic guffaw. "Hordes of our soldiers are deserting every day. The recruitment attempts are disastrous: no one wants to be on the side of the failing army."

Papa sighed audibly. There was a few moments' pause as Sally continued in her work, rubbing the cloth endlessly across a fork. Finally Papa changed the subject by inquiring about the Townsend family business.

Robert stated that sales had been good. He had partnered with a woman who had recently become a widow. "Her husband fought for our cause," he continued in his quiet way. Sally saw a dimple on his cheek play in and out as it occurred to her that her normally stoic brother might actually have feelings for this woman, whomever she was.

"And your cover?" Papa asked.

"I enforce my neutrality whenever I can," Robert replied. "I have Caleb Brewster running supplies past the blockade."

"Caleb Brewster? That old smelly whaler?" Sally asked, setting down the fork. Caleb had been a childhood friend of her brothers', and therefore, to Sally anyway, a nuisance.

Robert turned to his sister. "You will probably never meet a man more loyal than old Cal."

Papa stood, gripping a candlestick in one hand and his gold-tipped cane in the other. "It is time for me to retire." He looked wearily at Sally and Robert. "Do not stay up too late, my children."

After she had put away the silver, polished to almost appear new, Sally joined her brother in the parlor. He was brooding, staring somberly into the fire.

"You care about this widow, don't you Robert?"

He did not turn away from the fire; the look on his face was as impassive as always, as though he hadn't heard her. She studied him, looking for any sign of emotion. Finally he stated, "I don't think she holds me in high regard. I maintain my Tory contacts. I know she does not approve of the British soldiers always coming and going in her husband's shop."

"Why Tories?"

He turned to her. "It's good for business."

"Hogwash," Sally said. Sally and Robert had always been unfailingly honest with each other. Theirs was the type of relationship in which they could tell the other anything and know they would not be judged for it. But whatever it was laying under the surface, Robert didn't let on.

After a few more moments, Sally got up to close the door. When she came back to her chair she stated simply, "If I could find out where General Green's battalion is to be placed this spring, do you think you could get it to the right person?"

Robert coughed as a log crackled and sparked. "Like who, General Washington?" The ridiculing big brother was back.

"I'm just asking." She was even not entirely sure she could provide Robert with that location, but something in her compelled her to ask, even if it was just to get a reaction out of him.

"Sally, you know that's treason talk. You'll be hanged as a spy." There was a hint of something serious behind the light teasing tone Robert's voice took on. "And besides, how would you even find out that intelligence?"

Sally stretched her cold fingers toward the fire. "When people live together, there's bound to be information to be shared."

"You'd be surprised at how much information one can hide when one wants."

Sally's head quickly spun to catch his meaning, but Robert was staring once again at the fire, his face inscrutable.

The next day was set for the sewing bee to finish Hannah's quilt top. As it was one of the most important rites of passage for an Oyster Bay bride-to-be, Audrey had been planning the bee ever since the engagement was announced. Eight girls fit comfortably around the quilt frame, so Audrey had to whittle her intended guest number down to only that. After the Townsend sisters, the bride and her sister, Almy, that left only three other girls: Mildred Underhill, Sally Coles, and Susannah Youngs. Although Sally had always been good friends with her, now that Susannah was married to a staunch Tory, she probably would have refused the invitation, but for the fact that the Townsend cousin was marrying an officer of the British army.

Audrey had commanded her younger sisters to set up the frames in the parlor, which had the best light in the house. The morning of the bee, Sally and Phoebe hung the frames across low-backed chairs of similar height. They stretched the backing of the quilt in the frames as tightly as possible and then laid the cotton fill above it.

"Queen Charlotte's Crown?" Sally asked when Hannah arrived with the top.

"Why, of course," Hannah said, casting a curious look at her cousin. "Beautiful Queen Charlotte is a woman to be revered."

Sally wanted to argue, but she supposed it wasn't the queen's fault she was married to a tyrant.

"What will your pattern be, Sally?" Susannah asked after the rest of the girls had arrived—dressed in similarly pastel colored dresses and all with their hair in casual updos—and were seated around the quilt. A maiden usually designed and pieced the tops of her future bedspread and then wrapped and put it away to await her engagement.

Sally shrugged. "I have not gotten many pieces together."

Mildred looked up. "How old are you now?"

"Nineteen."

The girls all exchanged looks. "I suppose it's difficult to find a husband when all of the best gentlemen are away at war," Mildred replied.

Audrey, temporarily forgetting about her betrothed, twittered, "Maybe there will be another handsome soldier when Major Green moves out." This inspired giggles from the rest of the quilting bee.

Sally stabbed her needle through the three layers. During the jubilant talk of Hannah and Susannah regarding the British triumphs in New York and New Jersey, the warmth of the fire could barely keep out the cold and Sally's fingers felt numb.

Sarah Underhill stated that she'd recently heard a story from Tunis Bogart, who had stayed at her cousin Amos's boarding house in New York City last September. "They were witnesses to the hanging of Nathan Hale, the pretend Loyalist who was executed as a spy."

Sally's heart sped up. She too had heard the tragic tale of Nathan Hale, and every time she thought about it, she couldn't help likening him to Robert. She recalled the clandestine conversation they had last night by the fire and suddenly realized what Robert's undertone had been trying to conceal. He was courting those Tory contacts in order to keep abreast of the movements of the enemy. She felt a fleeting burst of pride for her brother before the unwelcome image of Robert hanging from a rope beneath a maple tree followed. She stood, dropping the frame off her lap.

"Sally!" Audrey cried. "What on Earth?"

"I'm sorry, Aud." Sally put her hands above her stomacher. "Something is just not sitting right with me."

"The beef stock from supper?" Phoebe ventured.

Sally nodded. It was more the fear of Robert being called out as a spy, coupled with the seemingly light, but still Tory banter, coming from her quilting partners, but she could not tell her sisters that. She rushed out of the room.

Hannah would have preferred to hold her wedding ceremony in New York City at Thomas Buchanan's townhouse, but her father declared that to be an unnecessary peril. The wedding took place early in the new year, on January 7, 1777. Sally was slightly buoyed by Robert's news that Washington had finally crossed the Delaware and had successfully attacked twice: at the Hessian outpost at Trenton on Christmas Day and at Princeton four days before Hannah's wedding.

The Tory Reverend Leonard Cutting conducted the ceremony at the modest Christ Church on Main Street. Hannah had chosen an ochre brocade dress while her husband-to-be wore his British uniform. Sally had to admit that both of them looked exceedingly happy, but she secretly still seethed at the match. She felt that, in marrying the enemy, Hannah was betraying her new country. To distract herself, as Hannah took Major Green's hand in hers and began to recite her vows, Sally tried to picture herself at the altar. In only two years' time she would be of age. Audrey was nearing twenty-two and set on getting married just as soon as her betrothed got enough leave. Sally supposed her own marriage would follow soon after.

But who would be the bridegroom? Sally's eyes squinted, trying to imagine the man who would stand beside her at the wooden altar, but she couldn't picture him.

After the ceremony, the wedding party descended upon the Buchanan's fine home and feasted on oysters and duck. When the festivities had concluded, the Townsends returned home and Sally and Robert found themselves once again in front of the fire. As if reading her mind, Sally's brother nearly asked the same question she had inquired herself that morning: who might she marry.

"It won't be a British soldier, that's for sure. Or a Loyalist, for that matter," Sally added, thinking of Audrey and Captain Farley.

Robert nodded thoughtfully. After a while, he declared, "I cannot seem to imagine you marrying anyone."

"Maybe I'll end up a spinster."

"There are worse fates," Robert stated.

Sally, her thoughts turning again to Nathan Hale, silently agreed.

CHAPTER 24

MEG

*C*aptain Moncrieffe used his contacts to get the Governor of New York, William Tryon, to grant Meg a special license to wed John Coghlan. The wedding was to take place on the last day of February 1777, at Saint George's on Chapel Street in Lower Manhattan. Originally christened by Trinity Church to cater to their east side congregants, the church became the site for Dr. Samuel Auchmuty's sermons after the main chapel burned down. A Loyalist, Reverend Auchmuty had fled to New Jersey in late 1775, but returned with the British occupation. Meg had once thought the building, with its arched windows and towering steeple, regal. Now that she was being forced into marriage, Meg saw the church as a prison, and the Reverend her condemner.

Although Meg's robin's egg blue wedding dress was low-cut, she felt as though the lace at her bosom was choking her. Mercy, clad in navy velvet, helped her get dressed in Meg's room at the townhouse the morning of the ceremony.

She noticed Meg pull continuously at the bodice. "Are you nervous?" Mercy asked.

"Nervous?" Meg gave a hateful laugh. "No. Angry is more like it."

"Why go through with this, then?"

Meg sat in her vanity stool and looked in the mirror. Despite the fact that she'd barely slept for months, the young lady who stared back at her looked clear-eyed and calm, the hue of the dress agreeing well with her fair coloring. "Father says I have to."

Mercy sat down on Meg's bed. "It's probably for the best."

Meg turned to her friend. "Would you have done things differently if you could do it again?"

"You mean not marry John because my father disapproved?"

Meg nodded.

Mercy folded her hands in her lap. "I'm not sure. I did love him."

Meg lifted a pouf full of powder to her face. "Well, I don't feel the same for Coghlan, that's for sure. I love Father, but I don't know if I can go through with this."

Mercy hopped off the bed in a flurry of blue velvet. "Be right back."

Meg continued to powder her face. When Mercy returned, she stuck a silver flask under Meg's nose.

"What is that?" Meg cried, a delicate hand holding her nostrils shut. "It smells awful."

Mercy leaned forward to look at Meg's face in the mirror. "It's what will help get you through the day: whiskey."

Meg dropped her hand and wrinkled her nose as Mercy waved the flask at her. Meg took it from her and, tilting her head back, took a giant swallow. Immediately she began to cough. "It burns."

"Yes, but do you feel better about marrying Coghlan?"

"No."

"Just wait," Mercy said.

A few more sips from Mercy's flask and Meg was able to enter the carriage that was to take her to her doom.

The alcohol had begun to wear off when the organist played his opening notes and Captain Moncrieffe had to practically drag his daughter down the aisle. Each step Meg made felt more like a march to her condemnation. *John Coghlan must have been partaking in the whiskey himself that morning*, Meg mused as she met him at the altar. He stank of the alcohol and his eyes were rimmed with red. Throughout the ceremony, he swayed slightly in his place.

Meg tuned out the Reverend's sermon; her only thoughts were concentrated on how much she hated her soon-to-be husband. He wore a gray coat with wide lace undersleeves. The flounces that extended from his collar to his belt gave the illusion that he was even fatter. The entire look was not unlike that of a white breasted pigeon, save for the scowl that never left his face. Finally, Reverend Auchmuty's voice boomed over the congregation as he pronounced them husband and wife.

They were the last couple to be married by the man. Three days after the ceremony, Auchmuty died. Meg decided it was due to the part he played in the vile union of her and John Coghlan. Perhaps if she had been able to follow her heart and marry Aaron Burr, the great Reverend would have still been among the living.

CHAPTER 25

ELIZABETH

MARCH 1777

*E*lizabeth was restocking the shelves with coffee when Caleb Brewster, accompanied by a rather handsome man, dashed in. "Dame Grant is dead."

Robert, standing behind the counter, frowned at his friend. "There is a lady present."

"Sorry, ma'am," Brewster said, pulling off his hat as he bowed. "But the lady is precisely why we're here." He turned to the man beside him, who was dressed in a blue and buff uniform. "Mrs. Burgin, this is Benjamin Tallmadge, newly appointed Major of the Second Continental Light Dragoons by Washington himself. We grew up in Setauket together."

Elizabeth turned to get Robert's reaction to Brewster's introduction of the rebel officer, but Robert merely nodded.

Tallmadge bowed toward Elizabeth.

She curtsied back. "If you don't mind my saying so, you look quite familiar."

"Yes, ma'am. We met on the skiff to the *Jersey*. My brother, William, died aboard."

Elizabeth's hands tightened at her sides as she recalled that day.

"I was sorry to hear about your husband," Tallmadge continued. "In fact, I come in regard to the prison ships." He looked around the store. "Is there somewhere we can talk that is a bit more private?"

"We can go up to my apartment," Elizabeth replied, gesturing at the stairs.

Tallmadge nodded as Robert bent down and grabbed his keys. He went to the door of the shop and locked it.

"This is about Mrs. Burgin, Rob," Brewster said. "It doesn't necessarily concern you."

Robert flipped the sign to the 'closed' side. "That may be, but I don't want you to manipulate Mrs. Burgin into something without her being fully aware of the danger."

"What is this all about?" Elizabeth asked when they were comfortably settled around the dining room table. She'd sent Abby on a walk to drop off doughnuts at the Underhills'.

Tallmadge, seated at the head of the table, spread out his hands. "With the passing of Dame Grant, we are in need of a woman to help deliver supplies to the prison ships."

Elizabeth blew out her breath before replying, "And you are asking me."

From across the table, Robert told her that she could say no. "It's a dangerous endeavor."

Ignoring him, Elizabeth asked Tallmadge, "How would it work?"

Brewster leaned forward. "Once a week or so, we would climb into my whaleboat and I would row you and Higday across the East River to Wallabout Bay. Some of the more accommodating guards lower the gangway when they see us coming and we load it from the water. You would never even have to go aboard. And we'll pay you."

"It's a meager sum, straight from the funds of the Continental army," Tallmadge added quickly.

"But I hear the East River is filled with smugglers," Elizabeth replied. She did not necessarily need the money, not with Robert running the store, but was intrigued by the opportunity to help her country.

"Brewster knows those waters better than anyone," Tallmadge told her. "You will be safe."

From across the table, Caleb Brewster winked at her.

Elizabeth thought again of the sight of her formerly proud husband, reduced to skin and bones before dying a lonely death aboard the *Jersey.* "I'll do it," she said finally.

Caleb's face broke into a wide smile. "Your country thanks you for your service, ma'am."

"I just have one final question," Elizabeth continued. "How did Dame Grant die?"

Brewster and Tallmadge exchanged a quick glance. "It was the pox."

"You have been inoculated, haven't you?" Robert asked Elizabeth.

She shook her head.

Robert opened his mouth to say something, but Tallmadge held up his hand. "I can get access to the best surgeon in the army. She will be fine."

Elizabeth frowned. "I once brought up the idea of inoculating all of us, my children included, to Jonathan, but he refused, saying that it is God's will to take his subjects off the Earth when he wants."

This time all three men exchanged looks. "I suppose it is your decision to make now." Robert said.

Elizabeth considered that conversation so long ago, recalling Jonathan's argument. "Is there not a risk of actually contracting the disease through the inoculation?"

Tallmadge nodded. "Inoculation means that you are infecting yourself with the actual disease, although a weakened form of it. There is a chance that you could develop a full-blown case of the pox. But we've all been through it. Waiting to contract it the natural way is basically just waiting for a death sentence. Inoculation will protect you from that."

Elizabeth looked at Robert. "What do you think, Mr. Townsend?"

Robert seemed a bit taken aback at Elizabeth's asking for his advice. "Some people suspect that the British are infecting slaves with the pox and sending them out into cities like Philadelphia. Even if that's untrue, we do know that pox is affecting both armies. All you need is to come in contact with one infected soldier to be exposed." He paused for a moment before continuing, "I think, for the safety of your children and yourself, inoculation is the best solution."

Elizabeth turned toward Tallmadge. "Who is this surgeon you speak of?"

Dr. Charles McKnight was a well-kept man with a high fore-head and kind brown eyes. He reassured Elizabeth's fears that she was consciously endangering her family by telling her that he would use what he termed, "cowpox," a milder form of the disease, instead of the typical method of using pustules taken from an infected patient. Elizabeth decided to inoculate Abby, Johnny, and Catherine, but not Georgie, as he was still too young. Mary Under-hill took him into her boardinghouse while Elizabeth recovered.

From his bag, Dr. McKnight took out a small vial and dumped the contents onto a rag.

"Is that the cowpox?" Elizabeth asked. A few little black specks were scattered on the rag.

"Yes," Dr. McKnight replied. "These are the remains of blisters I scraped from a milkmaid's hand. She recovered quite quickly."

Elizabeth shuddered as the doctor took out what appeared to be a sewing needle.

"I grew up in a farming community in New Jersey," he said as he poked at the spots. "It's well known that maids who develop cowpox do not get infected with smallpox. I believe there is some-thing in these scabs that prevents that, much like a person who had smallpox once will not get it again. Hence the reason for inoculation." He peered at Elizabeth, a scalpel now in his hand. "You are nervous?"

"Yes, of course. I did not realize you were going to rub someone else's scabs on me."

"Not to worry," he said, his scalpel moving closer to Elizabeth.

Elizabeth recoiled and pulled her arm away from him.

Dr. McKnight set the scalpel down on a nearby table. "Mrs. Burgin, as an army doctor, I'm going to tell you the biggest threat to our military is not the British. It is smallpox. I've inoculated hundreds of soldiers with no problems, but thousands more will die because of the disease. This is the best protection I can offer you, as well as your children. Now, for all of your sakes, let me do my work."

When Elizabeth didn't move, Dr. McKnight stated that he could spare some laudanum. "It will put you more at ease. I try to only use it for emergencies, but, as you seem of a nervous constitution, I'd be willing to give you a dose."

"No," she replied, taking a deep breath. "I'd rather you save it for the soldiers who truly need it." With that, she held out her arm. Dr. McKnight used the scalpel to lightly scrape skin off of her forearm and then swabbed the needle with the cowpox into the scratches. He did the same to her other arm and then to the children and Abby.

"I will visit you each morning to make sure you are recovering well," he told Elizabeth as he packed up his medical bag. She felt queasy, but whether it was from the pox taking its hold or just nerves, Elizabeth was not sure.

After a simple meal of salted meat, Abby and the children went to bed early that evening, but Elizabeth wanted to keep busy. Feeling too weak to do any chores, she curled up in a chair to read Thomas Paine's newest pamphlet, *The American Crisis*. She agreed wholeheartedly with the opening words: "These are the times that try men's souls." *As well as women's souls*, she added to herself.

Someone knocked at the door. Fearing that it would be a British soldier, Elizabeth walked slowly to the hallway. "There's pox in this house," she called.

"I know. It's me, Robert Townsend."

Puzzled, Elizabeth opened the door.

"Good evening, Mrs. Burgin." He held up a plate covered with a kitchen rag. "I had my housekeeper make you some sweet cakes. I thought that you might not have eaten much supper."

As if on cue, Elizabeth could feel her stomach growl. "Thank you. And, seeing as we are business partners, you may call me Elizabeth."

"And I, Robert."

Elizabeth opened the door wider. "Come in, Robert. That is, if you think it safe."

He stepped over the threshold and headed into the kitchen. "My father had us all inoculated when we were younger."

Elizabeth settled into a chair as Robert poked at the fire. In a minute, he had it sparking fiercely, warming up the cool room. He put the plate with the cakes next to the fire and then sat down across from her. "Have you much of a fever?"

"No." Elizabeth touched her forehead. "I don't think so. But there are these." She held out her hand. A few light pink spots had formed between her thumb and forefinger.

Robert took her hand in his and examined them. "I don't think it's anything to worry about. At least we know that the inoculation has taken its hold," he said, releasing her. His hands had been warm and soft.

Elizabeth felt a bit light-headed. To compensate, she asked Robert to tell her more about his family. "I've met the handsome William," she said with a smirk. "And I've heard about your sister, Sally, but what are your parents like?"

"My father, Samuel, is a merchant as well."

Elizabeth nodded. That much she knew. "But what of his political leanings? Brewster mentioned that Sally was in favor of the rebel army. What of your father?"

Robert's face became even more guarded. "He was a Whig, but

was forced to swear allegiance to the Crown. I took the oath as well."

Elizabeth bit back a cutting remark about the King's tyranny as she studied Robert. He stared over her shoulder at the fire, avoiding her eyes. There had been a bitter tone in his voice when he spoke of the oath, and it occurred again to Elizabeth that there was something that Robert was not telling her. "And William?"

Robert chortled. "William's loyalties lie where the money is." He stood to retrieve the cakes, correctly guessing which cabinet the plates were stored in. He sat back down, handing Elizabeth a plated cake. "Now that you know more about my family, tell me a bit about you. Where did you grow up?"

Elizabeth took a hesitant bite of sweet cake. It was warm and filling. "In New York City. My father shopped at Jonathan's store. When Father's eyes started failing, he would bring me to help purchase his goods. That's when Jonathan made his marriage proposal. Father was only too pleased to have someone willing to take me in before he left this earth."

Robert swept a crumb off the table into his hand. "I worry about my own father. I think taking the oath was hard for him. He is very much a Patriot but unable to declare it."

"Why?" Elizabeth took her last bite of cake.

Robert stacked the two plates on top of each other and pushed them toward the edge of the table. "Politically, he doesn't want to alienate his customers but mostly, I suppose, because he is a Quaker. He's not supposed to fight." Robert finally met her eyes and Elizabeth realized he was not just talking about his father.

"There must be something he can do." Elizabeth, too, was not necessarily speaking of Samuel Townsend.

Robert stood. "I think what you are doing is very brave. It's not every woman who would willingly infect herself and her family with a dangerous disease in order to help American prisoners."

He had changed the subject again. This time Elizabeth fed him a genuinely warm smile. "Thank you, Robert. And thank you for the cake. The children will be excited to have some after breakfast."

After she let Robert out, Elizabeth went back to the fire to check the spots on her hand. They had spread further, and were now past her wrist and up her arm. She realized then, if she died, the sacrifice she had made in order to help her country would remain unknown. *Not unknown*, she reminded herself. There were three men with knowledge of what she had been willing to do: Caleb Brewster, Benjamin Tallmadge, and Robert Townsend.

CHAPTER 26

MEG

MARCH 1777

$\mathcal{T}$he few guests at the wedding—mostly men from Captain Moncrieffe's unit—and Mercy had retired to the Moncrieffe's townhouse after the ceremony. Coghlan did not own a house in the city. He had been quartered with a Loyalist family on the west side, but would be moving temporarily into Meg's room before most likely being commanded to relocate in the spring. That time could not come soon enough for Meg.

That night Coghlan took his liberties as Meg's husband. She lay still on the pink coverlet as he ripped off her wedding attire. When it came time for him to enter her, he did so forcefully, causing Meg to cry out. She fought back the urge to fight him and reminded herself that he was her husband now.

"You are still a virgin," he muttered more to himself than to Meg. By the way he slurred his words and the smell of alcohol on him, Meg knew he was still drunk. Consequently, he did not last long and when he spent himself, he climbed off of her, rolled over, and went to sleep.

Emotionally exhausted, Meg could still not enter the bliss of sleep, the area between her legs throbbed so painfully. Even with one candle she could already see bruises forming on her upper thighs where her new husband had grabbed her. She wiped away a lone tear and then lay back, staring at the chintz curtains, cursing her fate, the final words she had spoken to Aaron ringing through her head. Because she was a woman, she indeed would never be free. Both her father and John Coghlan were as tyrannical as the Whigs all thought King George was. For the first time since the war started, Meg sympathized with the rebel cause. If they could someday emancipate America and renounce the King, maybe perhaps she could share in a slice of that victory, as she would never be able to relinquish either her father or Coghlan's hold on her.

Coghlan seemed somewhat cheerful the next morning. Mercy took the opportunity to ask him about the possibility of visiting his troop's encampment as she and Meg ate breakfast with him in the kitchen.

"Whatever for?" Coghlan asked, a hint of amusement in his voice.

Meg dropped her eyes, trying to avoid her husband's sneer. That evil voice only brought back the pain of last night.

"I wanted to complain about the confiscation of some of my personal property," Mercy told him.

"It's all for the best cause," Coghlan replied.

"Yes, but I feel that since my late husband was a loyal soldier to His Majesty, they could have at least spared me my carriage."

Coghlan shrugged. "Why did you not bring this up last autumn at his social gathering?"

Meg, though only half-listening to the conversation, was thinking the same thing.

Meg saw Mercy wave her hand out of the corner of her eye. "I did not want to mix business with pleasure. And I thought that I could forgive His Majesty's soldiers, but now the Moncrieffe's carriage is in disrepair and we have no respectable way to get about town."

"I can see to it that you will have an audience with General Howe but I don't think that going to the encampment is the wisest way to go about it. It's a dangerous place for a woman."

"Meg will come with me." Mercy said.

Meg finally looked up. "Why?"

"To keep me safe," Mercy chirped.

Coghlan began to laugh. "Two women in an encampment is even worse than one!"

The next morning Coghlan declared that General Howe would be at the shipyard near the wharf. He walked the ladies outside and pointed toward the east side of the island. "I informed his aide-de-camp that some women wanted to speak to him." He narrowed his eyes at Meg. "I did not offer that one of them was my wife."

I wish I could deny that as well, Meg thought. She gave her husband a fake smile. "Thank you." The words were hard to get out.

Mercy pulled her hood up. It was a typical early March day: cold and gray. Coghlan retreated for the warmth of the townhouse.

"Here," Mercy said, handing Meg a red rosette. "Pin this on your cloak."

"What is it?"

"It acknowledges our loyalty to the King so that no one will bother us."

The wharf was only a few streets away. Near the shore was what Coghlan referred to as the "shipyard." Dozens of small skiffs no bigger than a whaling boat and in various stages of construction were nestled on the embankment. A few of them were not much more than wooden ribs and looking not unlike pigs after the feast had ended. Mercy headed for what must have been the sentry as he was standing at attention with a gun on his shoulder.

"Excuse me. Sir?" Mercy called.

Meg's breath caught as the sentry turned. It was Thomas Walcott, the soldier who had passed her message about the New York fortifications on to Admiral Howe.

"Miss Moncrieffe. Forgive me for not showing you the proper obsequies, but I am on duty," he stated.

"Actually, it's Mrs. Coghlan now," Meg replied dourly.

Thomas broke attention to look at Meg. "You're married?"

"Indeed." Meg curtsied. "We are here to see General Howe."

Thomas smiled. "You two don't exactly look like Mrs. Loring, but you might do for the general."

Mercy's jaw clenched, but Meg placated her by saying, "He's only jesting. Aren't you Thomas?"

He nodded and then turned to a soldier standing a bit farther down the shore. "Andrews!"

The young man glanced over. He had a baby face and did not look much older than Meg. "Take over my post while I escort these ladies to see the general," Thomas commanded him.

"Thomas," Meg hissed. "I don't want you to get into trouble."

"It's fine. He was supposed to take over for me soon, anyway. C'mon." He started walking east, creating a lane through the flat-bottomed boats.

"What are they building?" Mercy asked, her voice raised to be heard against the wind.

"They're called Durham boats. Good for navigating shallow rivers."

Mercy gazed at a nearly finished boat as they passed by. "Oh? I didn't think the Hudson was so shallow."

"No. It's for the Chesapeake Bay. Howe's planning on sailing up the Chesapeake to march on Philadelphia."

Meg watched Mercy's lips repeat the word "Philadelphia." When Mercy caught Meg watching her, she readjusted her hood and focused her eyes forward.

Thomas reached a large tent. "Visitors for General Howe," he told the Redcoat standing outside, who narrowed his eyes at the ladies.

"We have an appointment," Mercy added.

He shrugged and then ducked into the tent. When he returned, he announced that the general would indeed see them. He held the flaps back as Meg and Mercy entered. Thomas declared that he would stay outside. Meg figured that he would not want Howe to know that he had abandoned his post.

General Howe stood when they entered. He was slightly younger than his brother, the admiral, with softer features. He wore a regal red coat with heavy gold epaulets at the shoulders.

"How can I assist you ladies?" he asked in a booming voice.

Mercy curtsied and glanced at a group of men in the corner, who paid her no heed. "First of all, General Sir, I would like to thank you for seeing us. I know you are a busy and important man."

The general waved a large hand as he took in the rosette pins at their bosoms. "I am always willing to assist our Loyalists. Especially if they are beautiful ladies." He winked at Meg, who curtsied uneasily. She did not want to give her name for fear of being linked to either Coghlan or her previous activities with Thomas Walcott.

Mercy explained her carriage plight.

General Howe nodded. "So you say that your husband was a soldier? Did he die in battle?"

Meg looked at Mercy, realizing that Meg herself was also unaware as to the circumstances of Mercy's husband's death.

"Smallpox," Mercy ventured in a low voice. "In 1775."

"I'm sorry to hear that." General Howe put a casual hand on his sheathed sword. "I wish I could be of more help, but I will not be in New York for much longer."

Mercy tilted her head. "The army is moving on?"

General Howe gave her a tight smile. "I cannot divulge that, but we will do our best to see about your coach when the army returns for the winter. Isn't that correct, André?" One of the soldiers in the corner turned. Meg recognized the handsome gentleman with sand-colored hair from Howe's party in the fall. He walked toward them and bowed. "We will do our best."

Mercy nodded, her eyes on André. Meg noticed that she did not seem that upset about her carriage not being returned. She bowed and thanked both General Howe and André before grabbing Meg's arm to lead her out of the tent.

Thomas escorted them to the edge of the wharf. "I was sorry to hear about your marriage, Meg."

Meg bit her tongue back from telling him that she was too, but Thomas continued. "I was hoping to propose to you when you were of age, but I thought that you and that rebel Burr had something, the way he stood guard in the hallway when I first visited you."

Meg blinked hard. "No," she said finally. "We had nothing."

The trio reached Thomas's partner. "Are you ladies fit to return to your residence?" Thomas asked.

"We'll be fine," Mercy said. She led the way out of the shipyard. Instead of heading in the direction of the townhouse, Mercy turned the wrong way down Queen Street.

"Where are we going?" Meg asked.

Mercy stopped at a storefront and walked in without replying.

Meg peered at the sign above the door, which was imprinted with a threaded needle. The lettering read, "Hercules Mulligan, Tailor." She followed Mercy in.

Hercules was talking in a low voice to a tall, lean man. Mercy unfastened the rosette from her cloak and marched over to them. "Mr. Mulligan, I need this rosette mended. It's very important."

Meg gave a curious look to her friend. She hadn't noticed anything wrong with the brooch. Mercy's eyes were focused on Hercules, who took the rosette in his hands. "Is it urgent? I am with a customer." He gestured toward the tall man, who took a step backward.

"Terribly so," Mercy replied.

"My business can wait," the tall man said.

"Actually, I think I have some thread in the cellar that will do just fine for this rosette. Robert," Hercules turned to his customer. "I think this particular thread would be of interest to you as well."

Mercy eyed the man named Robert. "If you are sure he should be there," she said to Hercules.

"What about…" Hercules's gaze shifted to Meg.

"She can wait," Mercy said. "We won't be more than a minute."

Hercules led his two patrons to the back of the store. Meg went to a window and watched as they walked into the alleyway. Mercy and Robert paused as Hercules lifted up the door to his storage cellar and then they disappeared.

Convinced now that there was something much larger occurring than a rosette in need of mending, Meg glanced around the store. It

355: THE WOMEN OF WASHINGTON'S SPY RING

seemed like a typical tailor's shop: a few wooden dummies in various states of dress stood in the corner of the room and a shelf held bolts of fabric.

Mercy had been acting awfully odd, Meg mused. *But not all morning.* In fact, she was fine up until... just then Meg espied the cellar door opening. She stepped away from the window and pretended to be absorbed in a cut of wool on the counter.

They returned the way they left, through the back door of the shop. Their raucous chatter seemed a bit forced to Meg.

"Well, Meg, are you ready to leave now?" Mercy asked.

"Of course." Meg set down the wool. "Did you get your rosette repaired?"

"I did," Mercy said, not recalling that the original task was only to retrieve thread.

"Here it is," Hercules said, returning the intact brooch to its owner.

"I don't think we've met," the tall man said before bowing toward Meg. "I am Robert Townsend."

"Meg Moncrieffe, er, Coghlan."

"C'mon Meg," Mercy said, moving to the door. "Let us leave Mr. Mulligan and Mr. Townsend to their business."

Meg gave Robert a polite smile as she stepped out of the shop. She was pretending to go along with Mercy's ruse, but the best she could now figure out was that the fake rosette matter had something to do with the information about Howe's next move that Thomas had betrayed to them.

Mercy must be a spy was the conclusion Meg came to that night as she lay in bed. As usual, she had a hard time falling asleep, but when Coghlan came in after having drinks and cigars with her father, Meg pretended to be sleeping.

She hoped this would deter him from performing his marital rites, but he lifted up her dress anyway. She kept her eyes closed and bit her lip as he roughly entered her. When he finished, he slapped her. Startled, she sat up.

"What was that for?" she asked, putting a hand to her tender face.

"I knew you were awake the whole time. But that's no matter," he said, getting up. "I prefer my women not to talk."

"You're an awful man!" Meg spat out.

He shrugged. "At least I have money. You could be married to a poor brute instead of a rich one." He took his hat off a hook and put it on.

"Where are you going?"

"I'm going to find myself a whore who enjoys a rollick."

"But you were just intimate with me."

"Yes, I used my good seed on you. As soon as you get a babe in your womb, I'll give you a break and spend more time with my whores." With that, he left the room.

Bewildered, Meg pulled her legs to her chest before calling Athena for a cool rag and the chamber pot. She would be damned if she allowed his seed to take hold inside of her.

A few days later, Coghlan announced that he'd been given orders to leave for Philadelphia. Meg lifted her eyes to Mercy's face; the blank look Mercy held seemed contrived. Meg's smile was genuine as she gracefully offered to help her husband pack. Anything to get him away from her.

Coghlan left for places unknown that afternoon; Meg figured he frequented Canvas Town, the area once next to Trinity Church that was once known as The Holy Ground and was in all actuality anything but. Captain Moncrieffe was summoned to a meeting with Admiral Howe.

"Should we pay a visit to Hercules Mulligan, then?" Meg asked Mercy when she was sure they were alone in the living room.

"Why, Meg, whatever do you mean?" Mercy replied.

"I mean, I know what you are doing—" Mercy sat up straighter on the couch, but Meg continued, "And I want to help."

Mercy raised her chin and studied Meg's face. "It's dangerous work. If you're caught, you could suffer Nathan Hale's fate."

"I understand," Meg said firmly.

"Can I just ask one thing?"

Meg nodded.

"Why? This defies everything your father, and your husband for that matter, stands for."

"That's the first reason."

Mercy leaned forward. "And the second?"

"Aaron Burr."

Mercy sat back. "You are a married woman now, Meg. You will have to give up your hopes of ever being with Burr."

Meg rose. "I no longer have such designs. But I never met anyone as devoted to a cause as Aaron. It will be my one sacrifice, the one good deed I do in this world, to help him achieve his dream in any way I can."

Mercy stood as well. "Then let's go call on Hercules Mulligan."

CHAPTER 27

ELIZABETH

APRIL 1777

*A*fter a few days of a fever and mild achiness following her inoculation, Elizabeth felt much better. The spots on her arm had faded, and it seemed that the rest of her family would also survive unharmed. Elizabeth congratulated herself on making the right decision, difficult as it was.

When Mary Underhill came to return Georgie, she brought a well-dressed, dark-haired lady with her.

"Elizabeth, I'd like you to meet a friend of mine, Mrs. Mercy Litchfield."

"How do you do, Mrs. Litchfield?" Elizabeth asked.

Mercy curtsied prettily. She had the air of a debutante, and, as she looked around, Elizabeth saw her living room through Mercy's eyes: the shabby rug, the empty shelves where expensive knick-knacks once stood, the unpolished furniture. Although the store was doing well under Robert's guidance, Elizabeth had begun selling off many of Jonathan's prized possessions, including a mezzotint portrait of John Hancock and a sculpture of Julius Caesar, in order to buy more blankets and food for the prisoners. Elizabeth hoped both of the women realized that the unclean state of her apartment was due to her and Abby's recovery and not any slovenliness on her part. As Mercy focused her blue eyes on Elizabeth, Elizabeth noticed they were not unkind.

"George Washington," Elizabeth breathed, going toward her baby. "He's gotten so big!"

"He's walking now," Mary said proudly.

"Soon he too will be ready for inoculation," Elizabeth commented.

"How are you carrying on?" Mary asked, busying herself with tea in the kitchen.

Elizabeth gestured for Mercy to sit at the kitchen table. "Well, thank you." As Elizabeth was about to seat herself, she heard a knock at the door. "Who could that be?" Elizabeth asked aloud as she went to the door.

It was Dr. McKnight. "I've just come to check on you," he said. "General Washington has requested me to accompany the army on the next campaign, and I wanted to pay one last visit."

"Please do come in, Doctor," Elizabeth said, stepping aside of the door. "I have a few guests here, and Mrs. Underhill was just about to serve tea." Elizabeth led him into the kitchen and introduced him to Mercy Litchfield as he was already acquainted with Mary.

"I think," Mary said, setting a tray of tea and biscuits on the table. "I think we are all friends here." She looked at each person meaningfully after she sat. "I know Abby is a competent caretaker, but please let me know if you ever need me to look after the children. I must say, Elizabeth, what you are doing is extremely brave."

Dr. McKnight nodded. "I agree. The Redcoats burned my father's church and then imprisoned him. He died aboard the *Jersey.*"

Mercy put a mouth to her hand. "How horrible!"

As Dr. McKnight turned to her, Elizabeth could practically see a spark light between them. "'Tis what happens in war," Dr. McKnight replied.

Mercy dropped her eyes coquettishly. Elizabeth had always thought Dr. McKnight was good-looking and now it seemed the beautiful Mercy Litchfield agreed.

"Mrs. Burgin," Mercy reached out to put her hand on Elizabeth's. "Please do let me know if I could ever be of service. I believe we have more than Mrs. Underhill and now, Dr. McKnight," she paused to look over at him, "as friends in common."

Elizabeth gave her a puzzled look.

"Robert Townsend and Hercules Mulligan," she said, again with a glance in Dr. McKnight's direction. The doctor's expression did not change, but Elizabeth fought to keep her eyes from widening. She knew that Hercules Mulligan still frequented the store, but was unaware that Robert and Hercules had more than a casual acquaintance. Not for the first time, she wondered just what Robert Townsend was up to.

CHAPTER 28

SALLY

APRIL 1777

*W*ord spread of the injustices that Oliver De Lancey's Loyalist troops inflicted upon their fellow countrymen in Oyster Bay. The Townsends' neighbor, Joseph Lawrence, was arrested and put in jail after attempting to stop British soldiers from digging up his garden. Other families who were barely able to scrape by with what they had watched silently as De Lancey's troops stole their horses, harvested their wheat, and slaughtered their livestock. It was the same up and down Long Island: the Loyalists even robbed from Tories who professed loyalty to the King.

One day in early April, Sally was relaxing in the orchard after her chores. The day was unusually warm and she sought relief in the shade of the apple trees. She had just begun to doze off when she was startled by drumming. The commotion was coming from in front of the house and Sally rushed over to what looked like a crowd forming. Audrey was already there.

"What's going on?" Sally asked, breathless from her sprint.

Sarah Underhill was also among the crowd and came to stand

next to the sisters. "John Weeks from down the road was out after curfew. When the sentry stopped him, he refused to give the countersign and tried running away. He was caught by De Lancey's men and Judge Smith sentenced him to be whipped."

Sally's mouth flew open as two lobsterbacks shoved Old Man Weeks, his hands tied with rope, toward Papa's giant locust tree. "They aren't going to whip him right here, are they?"

No one replied as they watched the Redcoats manhandle their neighbor, a respected, kind man whom Sally had known her whole life. The soldiers roughly fastened another rope to the one between Weeks's hands and then tied it around the tree.

"No!" Sally shouted involuntarily. Weeks's adolescent daughter took up Sally's cry as well.

"Hush child!" Mrs. Weeks commanded her daughter. "That's not any help."

Sally caught sight of her father walking out of the house, leaning heavily on his gold-tipped cane as he came to stand next to Sally.

"Papa," she said, pulling on his lace sleeve. "Can't you do something?"

He merely shook his head as the rest of the crowd fell silent. The lead Redcoat, a man with squinty eyes and an invariable frown on his face now covered with sweat, brandished a cat o'nine tails and lifted it over his head. Sally covered her eyes with her hand as he swung. The sound of the whip cut through the air, followed shortly by a man's howl, and then a young girl's whimper. Sally peeked with one eye at John Weeks's daughter, who was sobbing. The girl's mother grabbed her arm and then led her away while the whip cracked again. Every fiber in Sally wanted to run, to find sanctuary under the orchard trees again, but she was unable to move. The awful whipping sound seemed to go on forever. Eventually Weeks grew silent and Sally could feel a cool breeze as the crowd dispersed. She finally opened her eyes again to see the soldiers mounting their horses.

"I hope you've learned your lesson," the lead Redcoat sneered from atop his mount. "But if you haven't, I'll hang on to this. And that goes for anyone else who dares disobey His Majesty's orders." He waved the cat o'nine tails before he pulled at the horse's reins and galloped away, his fellow officers behind him.

Weeks fell to his knees. Sally's mother appeared with a jar in her hand. She silently bent down and began rubbing the salve onto Weeks's wounds. He cringed but then managed to mutter, "Thank you, ma'am."

Mother paused to shoot a fearful look at her husband. He sighed and bent even more over his cane. To Sally, it seemed Papa had aged greatly in those few minutes. Instead of the stylish dandy she'd always seen him as, he now appeared every bit the old man, the cane more of a necessity than a fashion piece. Mother sent Audrey to go fetch Weeks's wife and daughter and let them know that it was over. It took Sally and both of her parents to help Weeks into the Townsend home and onto the living room couch. Mother instructed Sally to make Weeks some tea as she gathered all of the pillows she could find.

Weeks fell into a deep sleep as his family came in and sat silently beside him. Sally's heart sank as she watched the scene. They had all been wounded by the British soldiers' authoritarian presence in their town, but Weeks's scars would serve as indisputable evidence that the King's tyranny was still present in Oyster Bay.

The whipping episode of John Weeks forced Sally to become even more determined to do what she could to help the rebel cause. She paid a visit to the Youngs', hoping to pick up on some information about the Loyalist's plans, but all she learned about was that some of the British had raided a Patriot storehouse in Connecticut a fortnight ago.

Finally, near the end of spring, the Loyalist brigade began to move out of their winter quarters in Oyster Bay, presumably to Connecticut to fight General Benedict Arnold. The summer of 1777 dragged by for Sally. She learned of snippets of information, such as the British occupation of Philadelphia, from Robert, when he paid his family visits from New York City, or Daniel Youngs. In

August, Robert told her about the attack Caleb Brewster and company had made on neighboring Setauket, Caleb's hometown. Robert explained that the Loyalist Colonel Richard Hewlett had pillaged the church ministered by the father of Benjamin Tallmadge —another of Robert's acquaintances. Hewlett's men had looted the interior of the church as well as knocked over the gravestones outside. When the Patriots had descended on Hewlett, a gunfight ensued, halted only when someone forewarned Brewster that several British men-of-war were headed to Setauket's harbor. They managed to capture a few of the Loyalists' horses on the way out.

"That sounds a lot like Brewster Bragging," Sally replied when Robert had finished retelling the story. Caleb was sometimes known for embellishing his stories. He once told Sally about how a wounded sperm whale attacked his boat off Greenland.

Robert shrugged. "At any rate, it's a good story."

"Indeed," Sally confirmed, wondering who the person was that tipped off the Patriots regarding the descending warships. If the Loyalists occupying Setauket were anything like the oppressive ones here in Oyster Bay, she didn't blame Brewster's men in the slightest for attacking them.

The harsh news that the British took over Philadelphia was brightened a month later by the news that General Burgoyne surrendered to the Patriots in Saratoga, New York. Sally read about it in the *Gazette,* knowing that Rivington rarely printed anything positive pertaining to the rebel cause, so it had to be of consequence. Below that was an editorial by Rivington himself, predicting that, if the Patriot victory did indeed lead to an alliance with France —and Sally fervently hoped that it would—then King Louis XVI would then be crowned the American King and would force the women of his new country to wear cosmetics and heeled shoes like the ladies of his French court. Even Sally giggled at that.

CHAPTER 29

ELIZABETH

JUNE 1777

*E*lizabeth rose early one day in mid-June. Now that she had suitably recovered from her inoculation, it was time to take on the duty of visiting the prison ships. Robert met her in the street carrying boxes of supplies. He nodded at her but did not say anything more as they walked the few blocks to the wharf. The day was gray and rainy and Elizabeth, standing at the docks, questioned Brewster whether it was a good idea to venture out to the hulks in this weather.

"It's only a little cloudy," Brewster replied, glancing up at the dismal sky.

There was something about Brewster's unceasingly cocky manner that calmed Elizabeth. She took a deep breath before climbing into the whaleboat.

"You don't have to do this," Robert finally spoke as he set down one of the boxes in the middle of the boat.

"I know," Elizabeth said softly, "but it is my duty to my country."

From his spot on the dock, Brewster wound a few feet of rope around his arm. "Where's Higday? He's always late."

Robert put his hand over his brow to shield out what little sunlight there was. "I think I see him coming now."

Out of breath and empty-handed, Higday arrived and then sat on the other side of the whaleboat. Brewster unwound the rest of the rope from the pier and then settled in between the boat's rowing poles. "See you in a bit, Rob, ole' boy!" he called as he began to commandeer the skiff away from the dock.

After that, the passengers and rower fell silent. Brewster's oaring was rhythmic and swift. Soon Elizabeth could see the ship emerging as if it were a ghost appearing in the mist. It was low tide that morning and more of the hull was visible than she remembered. The bottom of the *Jersey* was covered with mud and seaweed from the surrounding tidal flats and appeared even filthier than the rest of the boat. The swampy stench of rotten eggs from the exposed muck reached them even before the smell of fear and dying men.

"I hate the hulks," Higday said, breaking the silence that had enveloped them along with the fog. "Evil lives there."

"There's nothing supernatural about them," Brewster replied. "And not much living to be had, either. It's a rare thing when one of those poor brutes finishes out his sentence alive."

"Still," Higday leaned over to the left side of the boat to address Elizabeth. "I dislike going there."

"So don't go," Brewster said. He had to drive the oars with more effort now that the water was shallower. "But we won't be paying you."

Higday shook his head and sat back, muttering about the price of fuel during this infernal war.

Elizabeth gazed anxiously at the ship. The gray fog was lifting, letting more sun in. From her vantage point, it seemed the Union Jack was stamped at every porthole, even if it was only the daylight reflecting off the barred windows. A few prisoners, emaciated and wearing rags, were on the deck, trying to get fresh air before the sun began to bake down on them. They shouted weakly at their comrades below that Brewster and Higday had arrived.

One young man, who couldn't have even been more than twenty, called to Elizabeth, "What's your name?"

"Mrs. Burgin." She wondered if any of them had known Jonathan. According to Brewster, the men who would have been imprisoned with her husband were most likely dead, victims of dysentery, smallpox, starvation, or just maltreatment and neglect.

"Thank you for your service, Mrs. Burgin," the young man replied. Other faces, more wretched and gaunt than the boy, leaned over and thanked her as well. Some of the voices came as scratchy whispers, so dehydrated were the speakers. Elizabeth's heart sank at the sight of the weakened men struggling to lower the accommodation platform. She was sure the skeletal forms before her had once been proud, robust soldiers and sailors, but the British army had purposefully neglected—or outright tortured—their prisoners of war. She fought back tears as Brewster and Higday loaded the boxes onto the plank. Elizabeth reached out to help them and found that her hands were shaking. She could not get the image of a desolate Jonathan leaning over the side, praising a different martyr for bringing him food and blankets. She hoped against hope that her husband did not die without knowing any form of kindness aboard that deplorable ship.

Their tasks completed, Brewster tipped his hat to the men on board as they called out more gratitude before he began to row away. Elizabeth felt a certain comfort as she watched Brewster maneuver the oars—his powerful arms were a welcome sight after the cadaverous forms of the prisoners. She tried to console herself with the fact that she had done a great thing, but at the same time, she could not wipe away the dread of knowing those men were likely to suffer Jonathan's fate.

When they arrived back at the dock, Robert was waiting in the same spot, as if he'd never left. He reached for Elizabeth's hand to help her out of the boat. She was so overcome with relief to be on dry land again that she threw herself into Robert's embrace. He folded his arms around her and she felt the soothing sensation of being in contact with an able-bodied man still in the realm of the living. She broke apart to ask, "How could anyone be so cruel to other human beings as to lock them up on that... thing?"

Robert stuck his hands in the pockets of his breeches, seemingly befuddled by the unexpected contact. "It's that bounder, Cunningham," he said finally. Recovering, he added, "Come, let's get you something to eat."

CHAPTER 30

SALLY

SEPTEMBER 1777

$\mathcal{A}$s fall approached, the Townsends grew even more apprehensive as to who they might be asked to quarter for the winter. Major Green had moved in with Hannah's family so Robert's former room had been empty all summer.

"German mercenaries!" Audrey announced one afternoon as she came into the kitchen. She had spent the morning visiting Hannah.

"What?" Sally stood up from the table, the dough she'd been rolling spread out in front of her.

"The Germans are to occupy Oyster Bay for the winter season."

Sally glanced at Mother, who had her hand held to her mouth. She pulled it away to ask, "Hessians?"

Everyone had heard of the stories of the hired German military men during the Battle of Long Island. After the Americans had realized they were trapped, they threw down their weapons and surrendered, but the Hessian troops charged them anyway, shooting down and then bayoneting the would-be prisoners of war. Now the barbarians were plundering through the countrysides of New York and New Jersey, burning any house or field in their path, after taking anything they considered valuable as part of their booty.

"Major Green said they were called…" Audrey wrinkled her forehead in thought. "Jägers?"

"The huntsmen," Sally said softly.

Oberstleutnant Ludwig Johann Adolf von Wurmb, the Lieutenant Colonel of the 1st Battalion Jäger Corps, was the commander who moved into Robert's room. Despite the residents' initial fears, over time they realized that the Jägers that came to Oyster Bay were not nearly as destructive or insolent as the Loyalist troops.

At tea a few weeks into September, Daniel Youngs told Sally of a story about their neighbor, Jonathan Haire, who fired upon the Hessians after they supposedly shot six of his sheep. "Lieutenant Colonel Wurmb ordered Haire brought before him."

Sally, recalling John Weeks's fate, stated that she could only imagine what had happened.

"No," his wife Susannah held up her hand. "Just wait to hear this, Sally."

"Wurmb then asked…" Youngs affected a German accent. "'Did you fire upon my men?' And then Haire replied," Youngs switched back to an American accent. "'I did indeed, as a result of them killing my sheep.' Wurmb said that he hoped Haire would not repeat his actions, but Haire told him that he would do so again."

"And what happened to Mr. Haire?" Sally asked.

"Wurmb gave him another reprimand, but allowed him to go about his business."

Sally put a hand to her mouth. "The Loyalists have killed men for much less."

"Indeed." Youngs took a sip of tea.

As the townspeople realized that the newcomers were in fact polite, friendly, and, most of all, fair, the prominent families of Oyster Bay began inviting the Jägers to dinners and gatherings.

During an outdoor concert, Lieutenant Wurmb presented all three Townsend sisters to the men of his Jäger Corps, the majority of whom were quartered nearby at Mudge's farm. Sally found one man, introduced as "Leutnant Ochse" to be particularly attractive. It was evident by Audrey and Phoebe's giggles that they felt the same. As Papa had recently announced Audrey's engagement to Captain Farley, Sally no longer felt threatened by her older sister. However, Phoebe, now seventeen, had turned into quite a lovely young lady. Sally knew the competition was over when Phoebe broke a ribbon on her shoe, and Ochse sang her a little ditty accompanied by fife and drum to cheer her up.

Although Sally had to admit to herself that the billeting situation could have been much, much worse, she found herself slightly dismayed by Ochse's preference for her sister. That and the fact that she was unable to garner much information from the reticent Wurmb to pass on to Robert contributed to the cloudy mood she exhibited for the next few weeks.

The regiments usually did not perform much action in the winter, so she was disconcerted to see Wurmb gathering a small group of soldiers near the churchyard in late November.

"Lieutenant Wurmb!" Sally called out without thinking. Already mounted, he gazed down at her, and Sally took advantage of the courteous smile he wore. "Lieutenant Wurmb, are your soldiers preparing to march?"

"Yes," he replied in his thick German accent. "The rebels are sailing through the Devil's Belt toward Setauket."

Sally glanced around. There were no telltale expresses or messengers that she could see, only a sea of Jägers in matching uniforms. "How do you know?"

A young boy walked up to Wurmb and gave him a piece of paper. As Wurmb scanned the words, Sally wished she knew what syllables were being formed by his lip movements. "We have signal beacons on Norwich Hill," he answered Sally before he stuck two fingers in his mouth to whistle loudly. He stabbed his spurs into his horse and ordered his men to move out.

Nothing much came of the raid: Sally heard later from Leutnant

Ochse that the rebels had already fled when his battalion arrived. In her mind's eye, Sally could almost see Caleb Brewster cursing and waving his fist at the Redcoats from the protection of his whaleboat.

The next afternoon Sally saddled Gem, determined to find more information about the "signal beacons" that Wurmb had mentioned. She told her mother that she was going to deliver some preserves to her Uncle James in Jericho. Norwich Hill was in the same direction as Jericho.

Now that she was looking for them, Sally could just get a glimpse of giant stacks of logs in pyramid shapes placed sporadically. She was unable to get a good look at them because they were up on the hill and each one had a sentinel near it. Once, when she halted for a better view, a soldier called out to her. His voice caused warm blood to cascade through her veins and she clicked at Gem to move faster, giving a backwards wave to the sentinel as her horse galloped off. As soon as she was out of sight of the sentinel, Sally laughed to herself.

After she arrived back home on a hurried round trip, she closed her eyes and tried to process the information. If the large stacks of wood were lit, the bonfire could be seen for miles. She surmised that the placements of the log pyramids could provide some sort of message to the British. *I've got to tell Robert!* was her thought when she opened her eyes.

CHAPTER 31

MEG

OCTOBER 1777

*W*ith Coghlan in Philadelphia, Meg felt liberated. Life in British-occupied New York was carefree and frolic-some. Hercules Mulligan introduced Mercy and Meg to hordes of high-ranking British soldiers and then stepped back to let the women use their considerable charms to ferret information. Hercules would then pass on a report to his handler, a man named Nathaniel Sackett, who somehow got the information directly to George Washington himself. Meg wondered what the Commander-in-Chief would say if he knew that some of the intelligence which guided his tactical decisions came from the feisty girl who once declined in front of him to drink to Congress.

Meg and Mercy would pay a visit to Mulligan's tailor shop a few times a week, ostensibly to shop for clothing. Mercy encouraged Meg to purchase something every time, just to keep up appearances. Because she refused to buy anything for her husband, Captain Moncrieffe's accessory collection grew by tenfold.

"Christopher Duychenik," Hercules said one day when they were safely ensconced in the storage cellar.

"Short, stout, friend of Governor Tryon?" Mercy seemed to have a stellar memory when it came to Loyalists.

Hercules nodded. "He claims to be one of us, under the cover of working for David Mathews, the mayor, who has ties to William Franklin." William was the illegitimate son of the founding father, Benjamin Franklin, but, unlike his Patriot sire, was a diehard Loyalist. He was the former governor of New Jersey and a suspected British spymaster, to boot. "We are not sure which way Duychenik's loyalties lie. If he is indeed a double agent, the information he feeds to the rebels could be deadly."

Hercules frequently spoke of the word "we." Meg was not entirely sure who he was working with, but she suspected it might have had to do with that tall man, Robert, who was in the shop the day when Mercy presented Hercules with her rosette.

"How exactly are we supposed to suss that out of him?" Meg asked. "It isn't as though he would say he actually worked for the British if we asked him."

Hercules shook his head. "It's more the impression he gives off."

"But if he is a spy should he not be very careful of his impressions?" For some reason Meg thought once more of Robert Townsend.

Hercules sighed and glanced at Mercy, who shrugged. He tried again. "It's—how do you say it—a woman's intuition. We just need to know if it's worth looking into. I want to know what you ladies think regarding Duychenik."

"Noted," Mercy replied. She poked Meg in the side with her elbow.

"Duly noted," Meg countered.

Hercules introduced Mercy and Meg to Duychenik at intermission during a play at The Theater Royale the following night. The suspect was dressed in the red and blue regimentals of the loyalist militia, and Mercy started off by commenting on his coat.

"The number of buttons in a row indicates the battalion number." He held out the navy lapel. "See, there are three, which means I'm of the 3rd Battalion."

Mercy reached out to finger the coat. "You must be so brave."

Duychenik laughed. "I haven't exactly been in battle. We're more tasked with keeping order in New Jersey."

Meg had heard about the havoc caused by the Loyalist militia on the island she used to inhabit. *Tasked with harassing the locals and stealing their food was more like it,* Meg thought.

Hercules took his leave of the ladies of the group, citing the need of another drink. Mercy squinted her eyes at Meg in a gesture that said, *You're not being very helpful.*

Meg turned a nearly bare shoulder to Duychenik. "I spent some time in Jersey last year. Are you on familiar terms with William Franklin?"

"I was," Duychenik said smoothly. "I met him through the mayor of New York City when they had some business to discuss."

"What sort of business?" Meg asked. She reached out and pretended to snag a loose thread from Duychenik's vest.

"Oh, just men's business, the type that would bore ladies of such grace." Meg caught the glimmer of sweat that had begun to form over his brow. "How do you know Mr. Franklin?" he asked, his eyes narrowed.

Meg giggled. "Oh, I don't know Mr. Franklin. I met his wife a few times. What was her name?" She pouted, pretending to have forgotten.

"Lizzie," Duychenik replied immediately.

"Ah, yes." Meg hid her genuine smile behind her fan. "That's it, Lizzie."

At that, Duychenik bowed and took his leave of the ladies. As soon as he was out of range, Meg whispered to Mercy, "He's lying."

"Indeed." Mercy hit Meg with the base of her fan. "See? Nothing to it."

"I guess there is such a thing as a woman's intuition," Meg murmured as a servant came to announce the end of intermission.

CHAPTER 32

ELIZABETH

NOVEMBER 1777

*E*lizabeth, Higday and Brewster continued to supply the prison ships every few weeks. The atrophied faces that lit up at the sight of them often changed, and Elizabeth knew that the absence of those familiar most likely meant their death and she soon stopped looking for them. She preferred not thinking of them as individual men with lives and families beyond the hulks. It was less painful that way, especially after the young man from her first trip failed to reappear. Instead, she studied the guards, noting that some were more cordial than others.

One day, Brewster surprised Elizabeth by calling out to one of the prisoners. "Selah Strong, you old bugger. What are you doing up there?"

The man who gave a half-hearted wave in return was tall and appeared somewhat robust from Elizabeth's vantage point. It was obvious he had not been held prisoner for long. "Ah, Brewster, it seems the Redcoats have finally caught up with me."

Brewster nodded. "They were never big fans of your politics, that's for sure."

Selah called out to someone on board and, as the accommodation platform began to descend, he leaned over the side of the *Jersey*. His face contained a great deal of emotion as he said, "Cal, will you please look out for my Anna while I'm confined?"

Brewster's tone was uncharacteristically grave. "Will do, Selah."

"You there!" Selah turned as one of the sentinels stationed on deck shouted at him. "Back away." Selah held up his hand mournfully before he disappeared from view.

As they began to row away, Brewster told Elizabeth that Selah was a fellow Setaukian, a Patriot judge.

"And Anna is his wife?" Elizabeth asked.

"Indeed," Brewster replied.

"Do they have children?" Elizabeth's heart went out to this Anna.

"Aye." Outwardly, Brewster did not seem overly concerned that his friend was aboard the hulks, but, as Elizabeth had learned from spending these boat rides with him the past few months, that was his nature. When he became agitated or aroused, the hint of Irish brogue grew thicker. "They must have four or five by now," he said, his words heavily accented and barely discernible.

Elizabeth glanced back at the ship as Brewster rowed away. From that distance, too far to see the tortured figures of the prisoners on deck or smell the surrounding water spoiled by human decay, the ship looked like any British man-of-war. Elizabeth wished fervently she could do more to help the men on board. A vision of the laudanum Dr. McKnight had given her appeared in her mind's eye. Suddenly, Elizabeth had an idea. It was a radical notion, and completely out of character, but plausible just the same.

As soon as they arrived back at the shop, Brewster pulled Robert into the storeroom. Elizabeth followed them, leaving Higday to the empty store. Neither man seemed to object to her presence.

Brewster shut the door before he declared, "Selah Strong is a long-time acquaintance of mine, and a friend to the cause. We have to find a way to secure his release."

Robert shook his head. "The only way for a man to get off that boat is in a prisoner exchange or else promising to defect and serve the British."

"Selah would rather die first." Brewster folded his arms across his chest. "Which brings up the other way: when they feed his dead body to the sharks."

Elizabeth listened as they went back and forth, hoping that Brewster's determination to free Selah Strong would be the impetus to convince them that her scheme could work.

Robert sighed. "I can use my Loyalist contacts to see if the Continental army has captured anyone of consequence lately. If so, perhaps we can negotiate an exchange for Strong."

Brewster shook his head. "He's not an officer and would not likely merit a prisoner swap."

"There is another way," Elizabeth finally spoke up. Both men looked at her blankly. The bell rang, indicating a customer had walked in. "But we shouldn't talk about it here."

"You don't mean—" Robert began.

"Tonight then," Brewster interrupted. "At your apartment?"

Elizabeth nodded.

Someone from outside the storeroom inquired, "Mr. Townsend?" Robert sighed before he headed out into the main room of the shop.

Later that night, after Elizabeth relayed her idea to them, Robert threw down his hands, slamming his palms loudly on the pinewood table. "It is too dangerous. I won't let you risk your life in that way."

Brewster got up from the table to pace around the room, rubbing his hand on his beard. "Rob is right: it is quite risky. That warden watches us from the deck like a hawk seeking its prey."

Elizabeth set the vial of laudanum in the middle of the table.

Brewster glanced at it before walking the length of the room. "We don't even know if Selah can get close enough to the guards to slip that in their drink."

Robert sat back and crossed his arms in front of him. "Let's say

Selah managed to get the drug into a few guards' drinks. He would need the help of many men to overthrow the rest of the sentinels. Men who would want to be rescued in return for the favor. We won't be able to bring them all back."

"The channel is too shallow for anything but small skiffs. And there would not be enough time to make multiple trips," Brewster added from the corner.

"There are a lot of complicated variables involved," Elizabeth agreed. "But if we put more thought into this, mayhap we can come up with as much of a fail-safe plan as possible. It is the only chance Selah has."

Brewster paused in front of the table and scratched at a spot on his temple. "I think we should bring Ben in on this. We could use his military expertise. And you, Rob." He turned to his old friend. "We'll need your sense of logistics. Will you help?"

"I don't—" Robert began, but as he glanced at Elizabeth's face, his own softened. After a moment, he sighed deeply and then nodded. "I will do what I can."

Brewster peered outside. "I'd best be getting going. Those Tories in the Devil's Belt aren't going to scare themselves." He bowed at Elizabeth and Robert before letting himself out of the apartment.

"I must be going as well," Robert said, but he made no move to get up.

"Do stay." The words slipped out of Elizabeth's mouth before she had put any thought to them. "I'll make some tea." Robert was silent while Elizabeth bustled around in the kitchen. As she sat down with a tray of teacups and biscuits, she could feel Robert's eyes on her.

"If you do not mind me saying, Elizabeth, you never fail to surprise me. There are not many women who insist on finding a way to rescue prisoners from their doom."

"And then make tea," she joked.

"Indeed," Robert said, reaching for a cup and saucer. "Again, if you don't mind my forwardness, you are handling the loss of your husband with the same competence as you grapple with everything else."

Elizabeth removed her own teacup from the tray. "As time passes, I find that Jonathan's absence becomes more tolerable."

"What about the rest of your family? I know your father is gone, but what about your mother? Any siblings?"

"I had two: a brother and a sister, but both have passed on. My mother died in childbirth when I was fourteen, and my baby sister did not live much longer. That's why, when the British invaded Manhattan, I had nowhere else to go."

"What about your husband's family?"

Elizabeth took a sip of tea. "Jonathan was an only child, and seeing that he was quite a bit older than me, both of his parents had died before we were married."

"It must have been a trying time." He looked out the window. "The harbor is not far away. You must have heard the cannon fire."

"Indeed, we did. It was just me, Abby, Johnny, and Catherine. George was still in here," Elizabeth said, gesturing to her stomacher.

Robert gave her an appreciative look. "Elizabeth, you are one of the bravest women I've ever met."

Elizabeth gave a nervous laugh. "I do what I can. I just don't want other families to suffer the way we have after Jonathan…"

Robert tilted his head toward her, changing the subject as smoothly as always. "You are very well educated as well. Did you attend school?"

Elizabeth reached for a biscuit and put it on her saucer without eating it. "For a bit. My brother had a tutor that came to the house. I would find excuses to not do my chores and listen in on their lessons. My mother knew about it, but never reprimanded me. And she never scheduled anything taxing while the tutor was there."

Robert's face finally relaxed as he pictured a young Elizabeth peeping at keyholes, trying to learn the classics. "What happened to your brother?"

"He died at Bunker Hill."

"I am sorry. Indeed you have sacrificed much for the cause."

Elizabeth set her empty cup down on the saucer. "And you. I've heard that you started writing for the *Gazette*. And there is the partnership with Rivington."

197

Robert avoided her eyes. "As a reporter, I have to travel the city with my pen and notebook at the ready, and interview the British officers to be informed of their intentions."

Elizabeth nodded slowly. Robert went on to explain how conflicted he had been when the war began; that he wanted to fight but his religion and family values had held him back.

There was a pause in conversation when he finished. Elizabeth stacked the tea cups back on the tray, deep in thought. He did not reveal which army he would have joined, but from the little information she's picked up, his family had strong Whig ties. Robert was too honorable to ever confess the real reason he courted all of those Tories, but yet was friends with dyed-in-the-wool Patriots like Caleb Brewster and Benjamin Tallmadge. Elizabeth surmised that somehow Robert had found another way to defy the British—an undisclosed method that he would never admit to. She cautiously reached out to put her hand over Robert's. He finally met her eyes over the candle flame, his pupils flashing with the understanding that Elizabeth knew his secret.

CHAPTER 33

SALLY

DECEMBER 1777

S ally did not know how to deliver the information she had gleaned to Robert. Luckily he invited her to stay with him at the Underhills' in New York City for a few days in December. Robert even told Sally to bring her best gowns as there would be balls and parties in honor of the season.

Caesar drove Sally, dressed in a fine blue camlet coat, in a cart to Dobb's Ferry. Upon reaching the checkpoint, two Redcoats in powdered wigs approached them, stopping near Sally's seat. The one whose face held the dourest expression asked, "What business do you have in New York?"

"I am to visit my brother, Robert Townsend," Sally stated smoothly.

The man broke into a knowing grin. "Ah, yes, Robert Townsend, of the *Gazette*. I have heard of him."

Sally wanted to ponder that comment, but the other soldier was ogling Sally. "Would you like a better chaperone than your darkie?"

Sally raised her chin. "No, thank you."

"Suit yourself," the second man replied. The first man had approached Caesar's side and was whispering in his ear.

"What did he say to you?" Sally asked Caesar as they pulled away from the checkpoint.

"He tole' me that if I would join their army, they could make me a free man."

Sally eyed the old man. He'd been a part of the family since before she was born. "And what did you reply?"

"I tole' him I'd think about it, even though I won't."

Sally nodded. As a Quaker, she was a bit uncertain of her feelings on slavery. On the one hand, she knew that the slaves provided necessary labor and her family had always been kind to their slaves. But on the other hand, she did not see how one person could claim to own another.

When they reached the harbor, Sally's heart sped up a bit. She'd always loved New York City, the hustle and bustle of it. It hadn't changed too much, but for the ensign on the flags waving in the wind. Massive ships lined the entryway into the port and the water sparkled in the December sunshine, promising the type of adventure she couldn't get in Oyster Bay.

Robert was waiting for her when they arrived at the wharf. He thanked Caesar and told him to give Papa and mother his regards. Caesar nodded before he handed him Sally's portmanteau and then climbed back into the ferry.

Robert pretended to almost drop the bag. "This is quite heavy, little sister. What do you have in here?"

"You told me to bring my best gowns!"

He smiled genuinely, causing Sally to search his face further. "You seem content," she told Robert. "Almost, dare I say, happy. And you have on a new suit." Instead of his usual plain Quaker garb, underneath his greatcoat he wore a royal purple vest that tapered at the waist.

"Do you like it?" Robert asked, affecting the manner of a Tory macaroni. "The tailor, Hercules Mulligan, advised me on the fit and color."

Sally nodded. "What has affected your change in mood?"

Robert subdued his grin. "I wouldn't say I was happy, exactly, not with the war still going on. But," he darted his eyes around to make sure no one else was in earshot. "When General Burgoyne was defeated at Saratoga, it was good to get some favorable news. Perhaps this will be the impetus that France needs to join us in the fight against England."

Sally folded her arms at her chest. Finally her brother was talking sensibly. The British had suffered a crushing defeat at Saratoga last month.

"General Arnold has shown himself to be an impressive field commander," Robert continued. As convincing as he might have been trying to be, Sally knew that his cheery demeanor was not just due to the Patriot victory. At any rate, she was glad that he was able to break his Tory façade, even if it was just temporary.

Robert led her to the Underhills' boarding house, a brick building in the Georgian style and bare of any fancy ornamentation. The front door opened into a cozy tavern, lit by an enormous fire. The tavern was nearly empty save for a slight young man sitting with one hand clasping the handle of a mug of ale.

Robert nodded when the young man looked up. He stood and Robert walked over to make introductions.

"Sally, I'm not sure if you remember Abraham Woodhull or not."

In contrast to her foppish brother, Abraham Woodhull's dress was very plain; he wore a waistcoat and breeches in neutral colors and his hair pulled back with no ribbon. Sally assumed that he was another one of her brother's peers, but his appearance first gave the impression that he was much older. His brow had a permanent furrow while beard stubble nearly obscured his thin mouth.

Sally curtsied. "I'm not sure I do."

Abraham bowed and said in a barely audible voice, "I visited your family in Oyster Bay a few times. I'm originally from Setauket."

"Mary Underhill is his sister," Robert continued.

"It is nice to see you again, Mr. Woodhull," Sally said.

His lips turned up at the corners as he attempted a smile. Sally noticed that his eyes darted nervously to the front door as the bell rang. A couple of Redcoats walked in and seated themselves at one of the empty tables on the other side of the room. Abraham raised a hand to greet them before sitting back down to his ale. He gave a faint wave to the Townsends as they took their leave.

Sally followed Robert as he headed upstairs, his long legs navigating the narrow steps two at a time. It was hard for Sally to keep up with him in her satin shoes. "He's a rather jumpy young man," she commented, a little breathlessly.

Robert reached the top of the stairs and extended a hand to Sally, who took it gratefully. "Who, Abe?" Robert snorted as he escorted her down the hall. "I suppose so. He's always been a bit fidgety, even when he was a boy." Robert paused in front of a door before leaning in closer to Sally. "You know he was General Woodhull's first cousin, right?"

"The one who was killed in the Battle of Long Island?"

Robert nodded before he unlocked the door. "This will be your room. I'm right next door if you need me." He walked in and set Sally's portmanteau on the bed.

She followed him into the simply furnished room. A single bed covered with a blue and white quilt was placed in the middle of the room while a desk was tucked into the corner, beneath a small window. Sally walked to the window to look out onto Queen Street. Robert came to stand beside her. He pointed below. "That's the shop I run."

Sally stood on tiptoes to get a better look. "Burgin's Wares? Who is Burgin?"

"That was the previous owner, Jonathan Burgin."

"The widow's husband, then?"

Robert's hand dropped to his side before he replied, "Yes."

"I'd like to meet Mrs. Burgin," Sally told him.

His face had taken on his usual inscrutable expression. "Of course. I believe she was invited to the ball tonight."

Sally pulled a pair of satin gloves out of her bag. "Who is giving this ball, anyway?"

"Mr. James Rivington."

"Rivington?" Sally asked indignantly. She thought back to the comment the soldier had made at the checkpoint. "Are you writing for his paper now?"

"Yes."

So much for the end of his Tory sympathizing, Sally thought, which reminded her: "Oh, Robert, I almost forgot to tell you the most important information!"

"What is it?"

She told him about the beacons she had spotted on her ride.

He swiveled his head from side to side, as if to check that the room was still empty. "Sally, you mustn't go gallivanting around, spying on the British. You could be arrested, or, worse yet, Papa could be blamed for your crimes!"

"Papa?" The thought had never occurred to her that she would place any of her family in danger.

"And did you actually make it to Jacob Townsend's with these preserves you promised?"

"No," Sally said sullenly.

Robert sat on the bed. "A cover is one of the most important pieces of what you were doing. If you'd told, say Major Green, that you were dropping off the preserves and he asked Jacob the next day about them, that would reveal your culpability straightaway."

Sally sat next to her brother and contemplated what he had said. It was just like him to reprimand her when she was only trying to help. After a moment of silence she asked, "Do you find the information about the beacons useful?"

Robert, his expression unchanged, nodded. "I do believe that is helpful." He stood up. "I'm going to get ready for tonight." He stopped halfway to the door and turned around. "Try not to put anyone off with your rebel banter, would you please?"

"Why, dearest brother," Sally pulled off a glove and waved her bare hand at him. "I would never."

Robert narrowed his eyes. "You would indeed." He folded his arms in front of him. "One thing you should remember, Sal. We are not betrayed by what we feel inside. It's what we express to others that may be viewed as deceitful." With that, he left the room, leaving his sister to ponder his meaning. Did he mean that his Tory views that seemed so deceitful to her were only a ruse? Or was it more of a caution, that she should curb her rebel views around his Loyalist friends? *Typical Robert,* she thought as she unpacked her things. *He doesn't speak much, but when it does, his words usually have a double meaning.*

"Why are we here?" Sally asked, peering out at the street. The coach Robert hired to escort them to the party had stopped in front of his store.

"This is where Mrs. Burgin lives," he replied, opening the door. "I offered to pick her up as she no longer owns a carriage. Would you like to meet her?"

"Surely," Sally said eagerly, taking his proffered hand.

As soon as they were introduced, Mrs. Burgin asked Sally to call her by her first name. Elizabeth's apartment, like her dress, was simple but dignified. She wore bronze damask with a linen petticoat and matching fichu. In contrast to Sally's blue brocaded gown that was strewn with yellow roses, the only flourish on Elizabeth's dress was a small burgundy bow that fastened the fichu to her bodice.

"Would you like a glass of sherry?" Elizabeth asked Sally, who accepted without hesitation.

Glass in hand, she wandered to the ornate tile fireplace in the living room. It seemed out of place in the otherwise sparsely decorated apartment.

"My late husband designed it," Elizabeth said, coming to stand beside Sally. "Long before the war, he liked to show off his wealth."

Sally smiled. "My papa was the same way."

Robert had seated himself at the kitchen table and Elizabeth and Sally joined him. Sally filled Robert in on the family's comings and goings. Elizabeth listened, periodically asking questions. Sally decided that Elizabeth was exactly the kind of woman she pictured Robert marrying: warm, stately, and generous.

As Sally brought up Audrey's upcoming wedding, Robert appeared agitated, taking a long sip of the claret he'd been drinking.

"To whom is your sister betrothed?" Elizabeth asked Sally.

"A man named James Farley," Sally replied. "He was a captain on the merchant boat with our brother Solomon in London. Captain Farley returned to America when Solomon fled to France. Solomon met Benjamin Franklin there," Sally could not help the pride from entering her voice.

"A man we would all like to meet," Elizabeth said, keeping her eyes on the table.

"Indeed." Robert rose from his chair. "Are you ladies ready to leave?"

CHAPTER 34

MEG

DECEMBER 1777

*J*ames Rivington was a good Loyalist contact for Meg and Mercy as his newspaper was extremely influential over the prominent Tory population of New York. Rivington himself was backed by his British officer supporters, who often wined and dined him in order to see their names printed in the *Gazette*.

Rivington was hosting a party in the tavern above his newest business venture: a coffee shop on Queen Street not far from the print shop. It was easy for Meg and Mercy to get invitations, given that Hercules was a regular at Rivington's coffee shop in order to meddle with the British officers who frequented there.

Upon arriving at the party, Meg spotted Robert Townsend amongst the sea of redcoated men and bejeweled women. He was deep in conversation with two women, one a stunning young maiden with copper-colored hair and the other appearing slightly older than her companion, with brown hair.

Mercy headed straight for their direction. "Robert!" she

exclaimed before curtsying. She turned to the brunette. "And Elizabeth! I trust you are suitably recovered from your ordeal?"

Elizabeth nodded. "We all made it through, thanks to Dr. McKnight." Her face lit up in a friendly smile that softened her features. "How is Dr. McKnight?"

Mercy cast a glance at Meg, who gave her a puzzled look. "Fine, thank you."

"Mrs. Coghlan and Mrs. Litchfield, I'd like to introduce you to my sister, Sally," Robert cut in, indicating the copper beauty.

Sally curtsied toward each of the women in turn. "Pleased to meet you both."

"And you as well." Mercy returned the curtsy. "Your dress is beautiful," she said, admiring Sally's blue brocade. She turned back to Robert. "Where is your handsome brother William tonight?"

Robert shrugged. "Who knows? William keeps his own counsel."

Sally nodded vigorously.

Rivington sidled up to the coterie. "Townsend!" He extended his hand toward Sally. "You never told me how beautiful your sister is."

Robert turned to face him. "Of course not," he replied as Mercy gave a tittering laugh.

Sally stuck her hand out, a bit reluctantly, Meg thought as Rivington kissed it.

"Have you heard the good news?" Rivington asked the group. As they shook their heads, Rivington continued, "Robert's decided to become a partner in the coffee shop!"

Meg cast her eyes around the little circle. It was Sally's turn to look puzzled. A frown darkened her exquisite face while Elizabeth tried to mask her expression by taking a sip from a crystal goblet. Only Mercy moved forward to congratulate Robert.

"Come, Robert. William Cunningham is here. I want to introduce you to him." Rivington put an arm over Robert's shoulders to lead him over to a heavy-set man in a frumpy coat.

"Cunningham," Sally spat out as soon as the gentlemen were out of earshot. "The provost of prisoners? I hear he sells their provisions to pay off his drinking debts."

"At any rate, he's the one who executed Nathan Hale," Elizabeth stated.

At the mention of the spy's name, four pairs of eyes glanced at Robert Townsend and then each woman quickly focused on different points in the room: Elizabeth on her hands, Sally on the refreshment table, and Meg on Mercy, whose eyes were, in turn, on the floor in front of her.

"How can Robert associate with either one of them?" Sally asked. "They are both such vile human beings. I have half a mind to go over there."

She gathered up her skirts, but Elizabeth put a gently restraining hand on Sally's arm. "As your brother might say, a silent mouth means an open ear," she told the younger woman.

Meg saw the wave of understanding come over Sally's face. *She didn't know,* Meg thought. *She might have suspected that her brother had another side to him, but she didn't fully grasp that he was a spy. Until now.*

Without speaking, each woman took one step closer, isolating the group even further from the rest of the party.

"When will your next run to the *Jersey* take place?" Mercy turned to Elizabeth.

Elizabeth cast a glance out toward the harbor, but the window had fogged from the heat the hundreds of candles had created. "As of late, the supply trips to the prison ships have been hampered by the ice over the harbor."

Mercy nodded consolingly. "I understand. And I'm sure the prisoners do too."

"The *Jersey*?" Sally broke in. "What business do you have with the prison ships?"

Mercy touched Elizabeth's hand briefly. "Elizabeth brings supplies to the fallen men who have been captured."

Sally turned a wondrous face to Elizabeth. "How very brave of you. I've heard of the tragic conditions aboard those ships, no thanks to that man." She nodded at Cunningham, still in conversation with her brother and Rivington. Robert's face was stern, but his eyes revealed no contempt for the two men next to him. "They say they are purposely starved and are shot on sight if they even think about speaking out against the King." She paused before continuing, her voice deepening with emotion, "I wish I could do more for the war effort than sew uniforms." She looked up, her lips pursed as if she longed to say more. Meg avoided her eyes by staring at the floor. She had the distinct feeling that each woman in the circle was contributing to the cause in their own, secret way. Including her.

"They introduced you as Mrs. Litchfield," Sally finally ended the silence that had enveloped them. "Where is Mr. Litchfield?"

"Major Litchfield is no longer with us," Mercy stated evenly.

"I am a widow as well," Elizabeth said, her smooth voice filling the awkward void that followed Mercy's reply. "My husband was captured at Long Island. He was stationed with General Woodhull at Jamaica Pass and then died aboard the prison ships."

"Oh, Elizabeth, I'm so sorry," Sally declared. To change the subject, she added, "I met General Woodhull's cousin the other day."

"Abraham," Mercy said. "I know of him."

"Quite a small world we live in," Sally continued, her voice echoing Mercy's cryptic tone.

Meg had stopped listening. Her heart, it seemed, had only just begun to beat again and she could feel the heat rise in her face. "If you will excuse me," she said as she rushed through the double doors that led to an outside terrace. Shivering, she enveloped her arms around herself.

"Meg!" Mercy burst through the doors, frightening Meg, whose heart was still racing, even further. "What are you doing out here?"

Meg turned to her friend with tears in her eyes. "Elizabeth's husband died at Jamaica Pass."

Mercy nodded before moving closer. "There are many that died there. Too many."

Meg turned toward the view of Manhattan that the balcony offered. She grasped the handrail, putting her heeled feet between the posts, and leaned over. *I could fall right now,* she thought. *Would anyone even mourn?*

Mercy put her hand on Meg's arm and pulled her down. "Meg, what are you doing?"

With her feet now back on solid footing, Meg's tears spilled over. "Oh, Mercy, I am so ashamed."

Mercy led her away from view of the windows into the darkness of the terrace. "Meg?"

Meg, desperate to tell anyone, even if she knew it might put her in danger, finally erupted. She told Mercy the whole story, how she'd overheard General Putnam discussing Jamaica Pass with Aaron and then told General Howe about it. She even divulged the part about the fortifications and Thomas Walcott.

"Meg, it's all right," Mercy said when Meg had finished. Mercy rubbed her friend's arm. "We all do bungle-headed things for love."

"Yes, but most do not get other people killed." Meg shrugged off Mercy's embrace to once again brace her body on the railing. "What if Aaron had died? I never would have forgiven myself. It's bad enough that a woman inside that tavern is a widow because of me."

Mercy moved to stand beside her. "You cannot accept the blame for this. The British might have already learned of Jamaica Pass through several sources and yours was only a confirmation, notwithstanding the mismanagement by the Americans to leave it so unguarded. This is not your fault."

Meg stared out at the landscape below. "I'm done," she said finally. "I'm finished spying."

Meg assumed her headstrong friend would try to convince her not to quit. She did not expect Mercy to reply, in a hardly audible voice, "I'm done, too."

Meg turned to peer at her in the dim light. "What do you mean?"

"That doctor Elizabeth mentioned earlier. Dr. McKnight. He has proposed to me."

"And you love him?" Meg asked, biting back a twinge of jealousy.

Mercy nodded. "He is a Patriot and cares for our sick and wounded."

Meg raised her chin, not needing her friend to say any more.

There was no way for Mercy to maintain her Loyalist contacts if she were to marry a rebel doctor.

"That's why I wanted to introduce you to Elizabeth," Mercy continued. "She is of our nature. But how could I have known..." Mercy, unsure of how to finish her sentence, knew her friend recognized her innocence in that matter. She put an arm around Meg. "Come inside, now. It's freezing out here."

CHAPTER 35

ELIZABETH

JANUARY 1778

*T*he winter of 1777-78 was one of the harshest Elizabeth could remember. Robert was unable to return to Oyster Bay in time for Christmas, and Elizabeth invited him to spend the holiday with her and the children. He bought them a wooden rocking horse, to the delight of all three. They exhausted themselves playing with it, and, as Abby put them down to bed, someone knocked at the front door.

It was Caleb Brewster, along with Benjamin Tallmadge who had returned to New York City. The ice that had crusted over the harbor still had not melted and they had been forced to delay the plan to rescue Selah Strong.

"The ice may actually help us in our task," Tallmadge said as he seated himself at the kitchen table.

"How so?" Robert asked.

"Well, one of your hindrances was getting a large boat to rescue as many prisoners as possible. What if instead of rowing them across the Bay, they could walk?"

Brewster nodded enthusiastically. "As of right now, the ice is thick enough, which means we have to put a plan in place as quickly as possible. But how can we communicate with Selah if we can't bring in a supply boat?"

The group fell silent. Part of the contingency was that they would use the boat as an excuse to contact Selah. Elizabeth was struck by inspiration. "What about a sleigh? Is the ice thick enough to accommodate a sleigh?"

Tallmadge raised his eyebrows at Brewster. "Caleb?"

He tilted his head. "In parts. If the sun is bright enough, I should be able to see which parts are too thin to carry the sled."

"So we choose a sunny day," Tallmadge said. Elizabeth got up to fetch him an inkwell and paper. He began to make notes. "What else?"

"We will need to conceal the laudanum and get that information to Selah somehow," Robert said.

"What if we prepare a package for Selah, saying it is from his wife?" Elizabeth asked. "We put the laudanum in a bottle of rum."

"The guards would confiscate the rum," Tallmadge added. "And drink it themselves." He turned to Elizabeth. "Brilliant, Mrs. Burgin."

Robert rubbed the back of his neck. "But Selah won't know any of this."

"Selah's not a stranger to espionage," Brewster said, lifting his eyes to Tallmadge.

"Indeed." Tallmadge leaned forward. "We write a letter."

Robert asked, "In sympathetic stain?" When he caught sight of Elizabeth's frown, Robert turned to her. "Dr. Jay in France supposedly had developed an ink that only becomes visible when you wash a reagent over it."

"Even if we had access to the ink, we couldn't get Selah the reagent without the guards becoming suspicious," Tallmadge replied. "The easiest way is to write a normal letter in a woman's handwriting, supposedly signed by his wife, Anna. We leave out key words and in their place reference certain lines in a book that contains the words you've omitted."

"We need a book that the guards would have no interest in," Robert added.

"*Common Sense?*" Elizabeth suggested.

Brewster shook his head. "They'd throw it overboard."

Tallmadge rose and walked to Elizabeth's bookcase, returning with a small leather book. Brewster picked it up and started thumbing through it. "Entick's Dictionary?"

"Why not?" Tallmadge asked. "It's innocuous enough. And it is guaranteed to contain the words we need. Hopefully Selah will decipher it in time to put the mutiny in place."

"He will," Brewster replied confidently.

"And after the prisoners are freed? Where will they go?" Elizabeth inquired.

Caleb thought for a moment before he said, "My crew will be out there every night, lying in wait by the shores. We'll get them across the Sound to Connecticut and then on to Valley Forge."

"I think Higday's got some connections up North," Robert added.

Brewster gave a dismissive wave of his hand. "Higday's a fool. We keep him around because he stands well with the guards. He will need to know of the sleigh run, but we shan't worry his pretty head about any of the rest."

Robert nodded in acquiescence. "Shall we begin, then?"

Tallmadge pulled a blank piece of paper toward him and began drafting the letter while Robert looked up the page numbers of words they wanted to disguise, such as "guard" and "bottle." Brewster left to let Higday know of the pending run and to procure some rum from one of his smugglers.

Robert noticed Elizabeth yawning. "Why don't you go get some sleep?" He nodded at Tallmadge. "We will probably be at this for a while."

"Yes," Tallmadge agreed. "We will need you to copy the end product in your handwriting, but you can do so tomorrow morning. If the day is clear, you might be able to make the trip to the hulks. You should get as much rest as you can tonight."

Elizabeth rose. "Then I will bid you all goodnight."

. . .

Elizabeth was awakened the next morning by Abby shaking her. "Miss Elizabeth, there are men in the apartment!"

Elizabeth was momentarily startled until she remembered the planning session from the night before. "It's only Mr. Tallmadge and Mr. Townsend."

"But why are they here?"

Elizabeth rose from the bed and went to dress. "I must accompany them again today."

Abby tilted her head and searched her mistress's face. "Are you in any danger?"

"No." Elizabeth paused, the ribbons at the bodice of her chemise in either hand. "But, Abby, if something were to happen to me, you must take the children to the Underhills. They will know what to do."

Abby nodded. "Do not worry about the children, missus. They are in good hands."

Elizabeth resumed getting dressed.

When she emerged from the bedroom, Robert and Tallmadge were already seated at the kitchen table. "Your maid," Tallmadge inquired. "Is she trustworthy?"

"Yes," Elizabeth said. She headed to the fire to warm up some bread. Brewster arrived and Abby showed him in as Robert declared, "Always in time for a meal, isn't that right, Cal?"

"Indeed!"

After Abby left to dress the children, Brewster pulled a bottle of rum from his satchel. He popped the cork and then took a swig. "What?" he asked the others as they peered at him. "Have to have room for the laudanum." Elizabeth retrieved the vial and handed it to him. He poured it in before replacing the cork and then used candle wax to reseal the bottle.

Tallmadge grabbed a blank piece of paper and ink from the kitchen desk before pulling the draft out of his breast pocket. He straightened it on the table. "The most important thing is to make sure the numbers are subtle enough that a cursory glance wouldn't

216

pick up on them." He grabbed the pen and, using the draft, showed Elizabeth. "Do you see how the numbers are part of the flourish on the last letter of this word? Page number first, then line number." Elizabeth practiced a few times before she started writing on the blank page. "That's good," Tallmadge stood over her and nodded his approval. "It's fine to make a mistake or misspell words. It's not like the guards would know Anna's an educated woman like yourself."

When Elizabeth finished the letter, Brewster picked it up and crumpled it in his hand explaining, "It's got to look like it's traveled all the way from Setauket." He tucked the letter into a bag along with the rum, the dictionary, and a blanket and then sauntered to the window to peer outside. The day had dawned bright and clear. "Shall we commence?" he asked.

Tallmadge nodded. "I'll send word to our sentinels in Connecticut to expect a horde of escaped Americans. We'll get them shelter and warmth."

Elizabeth knew that would be a lot to ask for, given the conditions in Valley Forge that had been reported. Still, she wagered the prisoners would rather freeze to death in Pennsylvania among their exalted general than be starved by enemy guards aboard the *Jersey*.

It took much longer to get out to the ship. Although Brewster was confident the ice would hold the weight of the sled itself, he hesitated to use horses and insisted that he and Higday pull it, with Elizabeth pushing from the back. The going was much slower than Brewster's rowing, but they finally made it to the hull of the ship. Sure enough, it was stuck fast in the ice. The deck seemed especially empty—presumably the prisoners were all huddled down below. Elizabeth thought she could hear them coughing from the stale, infected air.

"What is this?" one of the Redcoats shouted down at them. Elizabeth was grateful to note that he was one of the more amicable guards. "You are making runs in the dead of winter now?"

"Yessir," Brewster replied. "We figured the prisoners could use the extra blankets."

The Redcoat shrugged before gesturing toward another sentinel, who walked to the side of the accommodation platform. It made a wrenching squeal that cut through the winter silence and Elizabeth had the frightening thought that the platform was frozen in place, but she was relieved to see it finally descend upon them.

As Higday began to load it, Brewster stuck his fingers in his mouth and whistled.

"Yes?" The first guard leaned over the side.

Brewster held up the bag. "This one is for Selah Strong."

"Strong? Don't know him." Elizabeth's heart once again caught in the throat as he conferred with his comrade. *What if Selah had already died?* "All right. We can get it to him, but not before searching it, of course."

"Of course." Brewster nodded and then the guards raised the platform. There was another anxious moment as the trio below waited for the soldiers to examine Selah's package. Finally, the first one leaned over and shouted, "Thanks for the rebel rum! We guards will have a good night tonight."

Brewster tipped his hat sheepishly. "It was worth a try. In exchange for the rum, then, will you make sure Strong gets that letter? It's from his wife."

The friendlier guard—his comrade had disappeared from view —bent over to retrieve the letter from the bag. He tore open the seal and scanned it quickly before waving it at them. "Least I can do."

Brewster could barely contain his grin as he tipped his hat again. "G-day, gentlemen."

The guard saluted them before returning to his post at the bow.

Elizabeth and Brewster exchanged a quick, gleeful look before they resumed their positions to push the now empty sled back to Manhattan.

Elizabeth was awakened in the middle of the night by a frantic knocking at the door. After checking that Abby and the children were still sleeping, she pulled a robe around her and went into the vestibule.

Benjamin Tallmadge stood there, accompanied by a strange man. Elizabeth ushered them into the kitchen before asking in a shaking voice, "Did something go awry?"

"No ma'am," Tallmadge said, removing his hat. "In fact, everything went fairly according to plan. Selah led an attack on the few guards who hadn't passed out from the rum. Most of the prisoners came down on the accommodation platform while some tied the blankets you gave them in knots and used that as a makeshift ladder."

"How many in all?"

Tallmadge glanced at the man next to him before replying, "I would venture to say some two hundred. Any man that was in good enough health was made aware of the plan."

Elizabeth sat down, blinking back tears. That was two hundred men—and their families—who were spared Jonathan's fate. "And the consequences for the rest?"

The unfamiliar man spoke up. "The guards don't venture down below: they are too afraid of catching a disease. They also don't keep good records as to who is aboard—or who has perished, for that matter."

Tallmadge added, "We are hoping they are too embarrassed that a bunch of sick men got the better of them to report it to their superiors. The rest of the prisoners might suffer a bit, but they are already at death's door."

"A small sacrifice to make for the liberation of good, strong Americans," the man said. He bowed deeply. "I was one of the prisoners, only recently aboard, but very grateful to end my stay, thanks to you."

Townsend gestured toward the man. "Mrs. Burgin, I would like you to meet Mr. Leonard Van Buren."

Elizabeth curtsied. "How do you do, Mr. Van Buren."

He bowed in response. "Much better now than I was a few hours ago."

Tallmadge turned to Elizabeth. "Mr. Van Buren is a former

219

deputy commissary from Albany. It is my intention to arrange safe passage for him to return, but I need a few days. I was hoping he could remain here."

"Of course," she replied.

Van Buren reached out to grasp her hand. "You are too kind to me, Mrs. Burgin."

Van Buren was a gentleman and amiable to Abby and the children. He stayed in the apartment the whole time he was a guest at Elizabeth's. He did not dare venture outdoors because due to his activity before he enlisted, he wasn't "to be had in this Tory island." He told her of the framed copy of the *Gazette* in his possession back home. Rivington had written in glee of his capture, stating that Van Buren "was well known for persecuting the Loyalists in this city."

One day after Abby had taken the children to play in the park, Elizabeth implored Van Buren to tell her more of life on the *Jersey*.

"Major Tallmadge told me of your husband's fate. I'm not sure you want to know the details," he replied.

"I would," Elizabeth said firmly. "And please do not feel the need to skim over some of it because I'm a lady."

Van Buren chuckled. "Tallmadge also told me you were a headstrong woman. I am quite inclined to agree with him."

Elizabeth brought him a cup of tea and then seated herself opposite of him at the kitchen table.

Van Buren took a sip of tea and stated, "The day would begin with an officer shouting down the hatch, 'Bring out your dead!'"

Elizabeth's stomach immediately curled like spoiled milk, but she forced herself to listen as Van Buren described the circumstances.

"Every morning I was there, we lost anywhere from one to six men during the night. I only had to endure the winter, but I'm told the summer was insufferable. Men would strip down naked to stay cool and would then get so scorched by the sun they would get blisters." Van Buren looked over to see her reaction.

Elizabeth had propped one elbow on the table and put the other hand on her mouth. She took it away to implore Van Buren to continue.

"I was told there was a period this past summer when the air was so toxic below that candles would not light and men lay dead for multiple days before anyone discovered them."

Elizabeth clasped both hands together underneath the table, remembering what Brewster had told her once. "Did they get thrown overboard?"

"Supposedly the exceedingly rancid bodies did, but I never witnessed that myself. Their custom was to sew the bodies into blankets and take them ashore to bury them. The able-bodied men would clamor to be chosen for grave-digging duty. I never was chosen."

Elizabeth nodded slowly, wondering if that shore was Jonathan's final resting place.

"The food was rotten, along with the water. They dumped all of the waste in the bay, and this is the water that was hauled up for drinking."

Elizabeth had enough description. "Tell me one last thing, Mr. Van Buren. The supplies that were delivered the day of your escape. Were they conveyed to the prisoners?"

Van Buren's eyes, which had dropped to his lap, brightened as he looked up. "Oh, yes, Mrs. Burgin, they were indeed. I was quite happy just to receive an extra blanket before Selah approached me later that night."

"Thank God in heaven," Elizabeth said aloud, thinking of the poor souls who were left behind.

"I cannot thank you enough for all you have done, and hope to repay you someday. If there is anything you might need, please let me know."

"I will," Elizabeth said as she rose from the table.

CHAPTER 36

MEG

MAY 1778

*L*ife took a turn for the worst when Mercy married Dr. McKnight. She moved out of the Queen Street townhouse about the same time that Meg's husband returned from Philadelphia. The time that had passed only served to make Coghlan more of a brute. He seemed to take it as a personal affront that Meg did not become pregnant and continued his nightly assaults of her. Occasionally Meg would fight back, but that only made him angrier. Most of the time he was careful to only hit her where it would not show under her clothing, but one night he grabbed her roughly by the wrist and left purple marks where his fingers had clutched her skin.

In the daytime, he reported to his unit, and in the nighttime, after he had his fill of Meg, he would go carousing about the city. Captain Moncrieffe had been called away, so the only people who knew what was happening behind the closed door of the bedroom were the servants, who would never say anything.

Meg entreated her father to help her, in much the same way

she'd written to him when she left Elizabethtown to house with Mrs. De Hart. Back then he had come to her rescue by arranging for her to stay with General Putnam. But this time he wrote back that it was her wifely duty to lie with Coghlan. Captain Moncrieffe concluded by saying Meg now belonged to Coghlan and, as her father, he could offer no more assistance.

After a fortnight of this treatment, Meg decided she could not carry on this way. Deep in thought in the parlor one morning, she was startled to hear the doorbell ring.

"Mrs. Coghlan," Noah appeared in the sitting room. "There is a British soldier who came to call on Mrs. Litchfield. I explained that she no longer resides here and he then asked to see you."

Meg rose from her spot on the loveseat. "I will come to the door."

She recognized the Redcoat as the sandy haired soldier from General Howe's command. She joined him on the portico, shutting the door behind her.

"Mrs. Coghlan," he bowed with a flourish and then stamped his boots to attention. "I am not sure if you remember me, but I am Major John André."

"I do remember," Meg replied after her curtsy. His manner now reminded her even more of Aaron Burr. For a moment she thought maybe her father had changed her mind and sent another hand-some soldier to rescue her. *But,* Meg chided herself, *originally André asked to see Mercy.* "What is it that brings you here?"

He gestured toward the street and then turned back to flash her a dashing smile. Meg noted that, despite his light hair, he had a swarthy complexion that was not quite English nor American. "I've come to return Mrs. Litchfield's carriage."

Meg opened her eyes wide. "Oh," she said, emphasizing the pucker of her lips on the syllable. She gave André her most coquet-tish expression. "Mrs. Litchfield is no longer living at this residence. She was married this past month, to a rebel doctor. Can you imagine?"

André shifted so that his legs were shoulder width apart and put his arms behind his back. Meg thought briefly that such polished mannerisms gave him an older air that contrasted with those boyish good-looks. "Indeed, I cannot imagine Mrs. Litchfield cavorting with a rebel. At any rate, shall you give me her address so I can drop off her carriage?"

Meg folded her hands in front of her stomacher. "She has left the city with the army. I am not sure where she has gone."

André seemed in no hurry to leave. "Well, then, I guess we should lodge it in your coach house until such time when you have more information on her whereabouts."

"Indeed." Meg, too, was anxious to find an excuse for André to stay. "Would you like to come into the living room for tea?"

André looked uncertainly at the sentry standing next to the carriage and then shrugged. "I would never pass up the chance to have tea with such a lovely lady."

Meg led him into the living room and then rang the bell for Noah. After she'd directed him to prepare the tea, Meg sat in the loveseat while André settled into a nearby chair.

"What brings you back to New York City?" Meg asked him. "I hear you were recently stationed in Philadelphia."

"Indeed. But General Clinton has taken over command. One of General Howe's last acts was to order the evacuation of Philadelphia, as it did not help our position as much as he would have liked."

Meg tilted her head as she recalled something Mercy had told her about André. "And you threw General Howe the most marvelous going-away party. What was it called? The Meson-something?"

"Meschianza."

"Yes, that's it." Mercy had been derogatory, saying how awful it was for the British to be throwing such elaborate parties while the Americans were starving at Valley Forge. The extravaganza required the ladies to dress as Turkish mistresses (as though in a harem, Mercy had related) and even included a mock joust, portrayed by the soldiers themselves, who wore knight costumes. While the Redcoats and Tory ladies of the city danced the night away, the Marquis de Lafayette led his men to Barren Hill, just a few miles outside of Philadelphia. *What was it Mercy had said?* It was like Nero fiddling while Rome burned.

"Mrs. Coghlan," André lifted his teacup to his mouth with impeccable English elegance. "There actually is something I wanted to ask you."

"Yes, Major André?" Meg asked, batting her eyelashes.

André set his cup down and leaned forward "It is about your husband."

Meg could not keep a scowl from forming.

André nodded, as if the expression on her face had answered an unasked question. "I spent some time with him in Philadelphia." He took her arm to examine the purple bruises. His hands were soft and Meg felt a tingle from his touch. It was a pleasant experience to be handled so gently by a handsome soldier once again. "Normally I would not dare ask such an intimate question of a lady and her affairs." He frowned as he released her arm. "But, I feel that it is my duty as a gentleman and a soldier, considering your husband seemed a bit—how shall I say this? Unhinged." He glanced over at Meg and saw her grimace deepen. "I am well to assume the marriage is not a happy one?"

Meg nodded. Most men would shun asking a woman about the state of her marriage, but she had quickly ascertained that John André was not like most men, American or British. The idea flashed in her mind that he could be her savior. Since they had already gone beyond the breeches of etiquette, she was going to be as frank with him as she could. "I consider it more along the lines of—dare I say —honorable prostitution?"

If Major André were shocked to hear the vulgar words come out of Meg's mouth, he hid it well. He drew up a booted leg and set it atop his other knee. "And your father? Does he know he hurts you?"

"My father was the one who forced me into this arrangement. It is more important for him to not admit he is wrong than to annul the marriage." It was her turn to lean forward. "My only hope is that Coghlan will die in battle."

This time André did not camouflage his surprise. He crossed

himself before saying, "Mrs. Coghlan, one does not wish a soldier to perish in combat." He lifted her chin so that their eyes met. "No matter how hated the man," he finished as Meg began to cry softly.

She reached again for his hands. "Major André, is there no way for you to help me? He will be returning tonight, and every night thereafter to mistreat me."

He squeezed her hand and then pulled away to sit for a moment, deep in thought.

"Major André?" Meg asked after a minute of silence.

He stood, looking a bit perplexed. "I've never left a damsel in distress and I do not intend on doing it now. However, this might require some maneuvering on my part." He reached into his bag and pulled out a small flask. "Slip some of this into your husband's drink tonight. I will return at dusk with a solution."

It was not easy for Meg to follow André's directive. She had to invent an excuse to the servants as to why she was in the kitchen in the first place. She told them she wanted to check the supply of silver for a party she was planning. Noah did not question her. She'd concealed the vial in the ruffles of her gown, and then, after the wine was poured, convinced Noah that she'd heard the doorbell. Meg waited until Athena was not looking and then emptied the contents of the flask into Coghlan's glass.

He fell asleep at the table, face down into a plate of ham. Meg told Athena that he'd had too much wine, which seemed to soothe the servant's startled demeanor.

André, true to his word as Meg knew he would be, arrived soon after. After Noah had led him to the dining room, André glanced from Coghlan's immobile form to Meg. He bowed. "Mrs. Coghlan, I've made arrangements for you to stay at General Clinton's residence."

Meg nodded.

"If you don't mind, we must make haste." His gaze settled again on Coghlan. "Gather what you need for immediate use and I will send for the remainder."

It did not take long. She took a few fine dresses and jewelry and then left instructions for Noah to arrange the packing of the rest.

"Are you leaving us, Madame?" Noah asked as Meg headed back downstairs.

"For a little while." She did not tell him where she was going, not that she knew exactly where Clinton was quartered. The less information Noah knew, the less Coghlan could demand of him.

In the hallway, Noah handed Meg's things to André. He managed all of it while still being able to hold out the crook of his arm, which Meg took as he escorted her to the carriage.

"It's Mrs. Litchfield's," André said, pausing at the curb before he loaded her bags in the back with the help of the Redcoated driver. "I didn't think she would mind."

André came around to offer Meg his aid in climbing into the coach. As they began to move forward, he cleared his throat. "There is one thing you must know."

"Yes?" Meg asked, moving the curtain aside so she could see out the window.

"In order to convince the general of your need to stay, I had to tell him a small fib." André attempted a smile that did not reach his eyes.

"And that is?"

"I told him you were my mistress."

Meg let out an uncomfortable giggle. "Why, Major André—"

He put a hand on her knee before withdrawing it quickly. "I'm sorry if that embarrasses you."

She gave a lilting laugh. "It is of no consequence." Meg was well aware that many British officers took on mistresses while overseas. At this point she had not given thought to whether she wanted the fib to turn fact or not. She was just glad to once again be away from Coghlan's grasp. *Still*, Meg thought, glancing at the soldier across from her, *André was a mighty handsome fellow.*

The carriage came to a halt. All Meg could see out the window was an iron balustrade that looked vaguely familiar. "Is this…" she began to ask as André, already on the ground, held out his hand.

"One Broadway," he said proudly as Meg emerged from the carriage. "The erstwhile Kennedy mansion."

"Oh," Meg replied as she once again looked up at her former— now present again—residence. The Union Jack still flew as haughtily in front as it had during General Howe's stay; not much else had changed. Her heart began to beat in trepidation as she recalled all that had happened there: sewing with Mrs. Putnam and the girls in the parlor, flirting with Aaron on the rooftop, learning military secrets in Old Put's office.

André showed her to her old room. "This is where Mrs. Loring stayed while General Howe was here," he told her. Meg nodded, too overwhelmed with emotion to be disdainful of Mrs. Loring's relationship with the general. After André had taken his leave, Meg walked over to the desk where she'd once drawn images of the Yankee's fortifications of the city. Ironically, now that she was being housed at British headquarters, she was in the best position possible to spy for the Patriots. *But I'm done,* she reminded herself. *I will be the cause of no one else's pain or death.* Not even her husband's.

CHAPTER 37

ELIZABETH

AUGUST 1778

*R*obert seemed somewhat fearful after the prison ship escape and begged Elizabeth to end her runs to the *Jersey*, to which she finally consented. Robert informed Higday that he too must lie low but declined to tell him the reason why. Higday was understandably upset as the price increases of food that summer were unbearable. The inflation was mostly due to the presence of the blockade by the French fleet at Sandy Hook, as well as the population swell in Manhattan resulting from the mass exodus of Loyalists from Philadelphia. Bread was scarce in the city; the British were feeding their men rice and oatmeal instead of flour products. Somehow Elizabeth's family, the Underhills, and Robert Townsend were never in want of these products, thanks presumably to Caleb Brewster and his whaleboats in the Devil's Belt.

But Higday was not so lucky and insisted that he needed some way of earning income for the family. He entreated Elizabeth with his request, who promised to pass it on to Robert when he returned. Robert managed to get him a job at the coffee shop. He told Elizabeth that Higday complained endlessly when he was out of earshot, but was polite enough to the faces of the British officers that frequented there.

Elizabeth no longer frowned when Robert mentioned his Tory contacts. She was not exactly sure what Robert did, but his disappearances from the store increased in both frequency and duration until he ceased to come in every day. As she was convinced that his loyalties matched hers, she did not question his absence. Plus, Elizabeth now felt more than capable of managing the store by herself.

Robert took on the task of educating little Johnny, now seven. He would come over in the evenings, brandishing books in Latin and Greek. It was not long before Robert noticed that Abby often crept into the kitchen as well. Abby could read enough to get by, but she had always considered herself "unlettered." When Robert learned this, he brought Abby paper and ink and gave her daily assignments to practice her handwriting.

Elizabeth set about teaching Catherine to embroider. They would sit in the living room as Robert, Johnny, and Abby occupied the kitchen table. True to form, Elizabeth never called out her daughter when she seemed distracted by the instruction in the next room. Both would be silent, intently listening as Robert's voice, rich with enthusiasm, expounded on the classics.

Elizabeth taught Catherine her letters and numbers, which the little girl then stitched onto her sampler. Catherine was particularly adept at sewing and Elizabeth, who was not, soon ran out of stitching patterns to instruct.

She paid a visit to the Underhills' to inquire if Mary had any of interest.

"Indeed," Mary replied. She had been manning the tavern, but her husband, Amos, had arrived shortly after Elizabeth. "It's upstairs in the attic bedroom. My brother Abraham has been staying there."

"I do believe Abraham has been out and about on business," Amos interjected.

Mary gestured for Elizabeth to follow her up the staircase. "Abraham is a farmer and comes into the city to sell his goods."

"He must find a good market with them now, considering the French blockade," Elizabeth commented.

Mary was out of breath by the time they reached the attic. "It's just in here," she said, opening the door.

Elizabeth started as she heard a shout followed by a loud crash. Peering into the room, she caught sight of a man standing next to an overturned desk. He grabbed a handkerchief from his pocket and wiped at something. Although an inkwell was lying on its side, Elizabeth did not see the telltale spreading stain of spilled ink.

Mary rushed to the desk to help. "I'm sorry, Abraham, I did not realize you were in here."

"Yes, well, considering the hazards of my occupation, you would do well to knock first." The man's voice seemed shaky; it was obvious he'd been quite spooked at his sister's sudden entrance. He stacked up a few scattered papers and then held them close to his chest.

Elizabeth, standing in the doorway, thought that an odd reply for a farmer. And why was he so protective of that pile of blank papers?

As Mary moved past him to her trunk, Abraham grabbed a utensil off of an empty plate and squatted to spoon clear liquid from a puddle into the inkwell.

"Can I help?" Elizabeth asked from her post.

Abraham obviously hadn't spotted her previously. He jumped to his feet and glared at Mary. "Who is this woman and why is she here?"

Mary looked up from her forage in the trunk. "Abraham, I'm sorry, this is Mrs. Burgin. She is a friend of Robert Townsend's."

Upon hearing the name, Abraham seemed to relax. "Forgive me, Mrs. Burgin, but you both gave me quite a fright." He resumed his prior task of rescuing the liquid.

Mary located the sampler and straightened up. "We will leave you, then, Abraham."

"It was nice to meet you," Elizabeth said with a curtsy.

Abraham gave them a listless wave before Mary shut the door.

"I'm sorry for that, Elizabeth," Mary said, beginning to descend the stairs. "Abraham tends to be a bit... jumpy sometimes."

"Is he also a friend of Robert's?"

"Indeed. As you know, Long Island is a tight-knit community. Abraham and Robert had quite a few mutual friends so it was only natural they would make acquaintances of each other."

Elizabeth, reflecting on Abraham's absurd behavior, had a feeling that those mutual friends might be named Benjamin Tall-madge and Caleb Brewster.

As Abby was putting the children to bed after their nightly tutoring session, Elizabeth made tea as usual, but that night's topic of conversation between her and Robert would be unexpected, at least on Elizabeth's part. "Who is Abraham Woodhull and why was he using the sympathetic stain you had mentioned to Benjamin Tallmadge?"

Robert, taken aback, glanced quickly around the room. "How do you know—"

"I saw it with my own eyes. Do not try to placate me, Robert. You know I am a trustworthy individual and loyal to the cause. Is Abraham a spy? Are you?"

Robert pinched the bridge of his nose and sighed. It was the most visible sign of emotion she had ever seen come from him. "Yes."

It was Elizabeth's turn to be momentarily stunned. She had long suspected that he was indeed, but never thought he would admit to it.

"Both Abraham and I operate under code names, which I will not divulge for your safety."

"And Brewster and Tallmadge?"

"Caleb is our courier. He delivers the message to Ben, who then, I'm told, gives them to Washington himself."

"You correspond with the Commander-in-Chief?"

"Yes, but again, he only knows me by my code name. I've received direct instructions from him, though, to mix among the officers and Loyalist refugees. As I've told you, my work at the paper allows me to travel about the city without question."

Elizabeth exhaled a long breath. "Are you in danger?"

Robert gave a wry smile. "Of the noose? Yes. But we take great precaution so as not to strike suspicion in anyone."

"Such as using codes?" Elizabeth asked, remembering the ease of which both he and Tallmadge had written the cipher to Selah Strong.

"Yes, often, for the stain is expensive and hard to come by."

That explains why Woodhull was so concerned about saving the spilled ink, Elizabeth thought.

"Ben, Abraham, General Washington, and I are the only ones who have the cipher," Robert continued. "We also employ covert ways in which we pass on the information. I do not want to go into too much detail, for if you were ever questioned, you could honestly say that you do not know."

"I will worry about you," she said quietly.

Robert reached out and put his hand on hers. This time he did not remove it. They sat that way for a few minutes, both in awe of the other's sacrifice for their country. Finally, Robert got up to leave.

"Will you stay?" Elizabeth asked. "In the guest room?" She had a sudden fear that he would be harmed in the street.

Robert hesitated. "Yes," he said after a moment's pause. "I will."

CHAPTER 38

MEG

*M*eg's new life at her former residence was even more gay and pleasant than it had been the first time. Dinners given for the high-ranking British officers and their mistresses began at four and lasted well into the night. She attended concerts, balls, and card games on the arm of André, who proved to be a most deferential companion, even if Meg was not his true mistress.

Ironically, many of the attendees were the same people Meg met during her spying days. But now she forced herself to stay away from Robert Townsend and Hercules Mulligan, try as they might to pull her into a corner. She clung to the illusion that she was the same ardent Loyalist she was at the beginning of the war.

As André was aide-de-camp to the new commander, Sir Henry Clinton, he always seemed to be buried in paperwork. To keep up appearances, André would visit Meg's room, where they would sit by the fire and simply talk, as he was ever the true gentleman he gave the impression of being. One night he told her about the woman he had once planned to marry back home in England. He pulled a small trinket from his breast pocket and handed it to Meg. It was of a young girl, painted in meticulous hand, on ivory.

"Her name was Honora Sneyd. You look not just a little like her, actually," André said.

Meg took a closer investigation of the painting. The girl had blond hair and blue eyes, true, but there was an innocence about her that Meg never quite associated with.

"She was one of the most intellectual women I've ever met. We were engaged to be married," André added.

"What happened?" Meg asked, handing him back the ivory piece.

He took another affectionate glance at it before tucking it back into his waistcoat. "Although we were betrothed, her father did not think I had enough finances to support her. He pressured her to end the engagement, which she did. I recently heard she wed a man who I'd met a few times while he was still married. The ceremony took place only a fortnight after his first wife died in childbirth."

"Scandalous," Meg replied, noting the slump in André's shoulders. "Is that why you joined the army?"

He nodded. "What about you? Did you love anyone before you married that brute?"

It was Meg's turn to become melancholy. "A rebel in every sense of the word." She briefly described their relationship.

"What was his name?"

"Aaron Burr."

André repeated the name. "If you want, I can use my contacts to find his whereabouts."

Meg reached out to grab his sleeve. "If you could, please." She knew it was too late for them as a couple, but it would give her a great peace of mind to know that he was still alive, out there existing in the world with his dapper charm and ambitious heart.

André rose and grabbed his sword off a nearby chair. "I will take my leave of you now. There are many promotions and leave of absence requests awaiting my signature in the morning."

"Sounds titillating." She sat up, gathering her skirts. She felt that she was on good enough terms with André to ask him something that had been bothering her for quite a while "What know you of the pillaging done by your regiments?"

André set his sword back down. "Pillaging? I'm not aware of such behavior by our troops—it would go against the notion of a gentleman's war."

Meg snorted. "Gentleman's war? Clearly you are unaware, then, of the plundering committed by the Loyalist and Hessian troops. Mayhap you should find the occasion to step out of the office and into the field." She was careful to say that last part gently, for she respected André as a man, even if she held the rest of the British army in contempt.

André frowned and Meg immediately regretted the harshness of her words. He moved toward his sword as he replied, "I will look into it, as well as inquire of Aaron Burr. It will lend a bit more interest to my day."

"Thank you, Major André."

He turned to her and bowed. "Goodnight, Mrs. Coghlan."

It was less than a fortnight later when André returned to Meg's room brandishing a folded paper. He placed it on her desk and told her she probably wanted to get into a comfortable position before she read it.

It was a report on Aaron Burr. Meg scanned it, her heart pounding. She was not surprised to hear of his military exploits, a few he had been victorious in. There was also mention of Aaron's bad health—which seemed to originate from heat stroke during a battle in August—of which Meg was sorry to read. At the bottom was a report on his personal affairs. It seemed André's source had gathered mostly local gossip, but it focused on Aaron's frequent visits to the house of a married woman in New Jersey. The missive included a quote that called this woman, Theodosia Prevost, "the object of Burr's affections."

"She's the wife of a British officer!" Meg exclaimed as the letter fluttered to the floor.

"And a good ten years older than him, with two offspring by that officer, to boot."

"Is she pretty?"

In lieu of replying, André picked up the report and walked over to the fireplace. "Do you object?" he asked as he held it near the fire. When Meg shook her head, he tossed it in. Both of them watched in silence as the paper was consumed by flames.

"So that is what has become of the honorable Aaron Burr." Meg smoothed the lace on her skirt. Then again, had Aaron commissioned a report on her, he might read of her disastrous marriage and then of her being taken up as André's supposed mistress. "Life certainly does take its turns, doesn't it?"

"Indeed it does." André sat down next to the fire and patted the spot beside him. "I looked into the alleged pillaging, as you called it, by our army," he said as Meg joined him. "I was quite shocked at what I found. Goods have been taken from houses of the infirm, destitute, widowed, even from our own Loyalists. Such acts can only bring on acrimony, which in turn can lead to revolts. I prepared a full report and handed it to Sir Henry today. I also urged the formation of a board of inquiry with the intent of distributing reparation to the victims."

She folded her hands in her lap. "That was very noble of you."

"Perhaps a bit foolhardy as well, as I think there are many among the general's personages that will be most displeased by my revelations."

"I would assume these would be the officers who allowed such behavior to occur."

André stretched out a booted leg and rotated his foot.

"Do you have much pain?"

He flashed her a quick smile. "Sometimes. It is the burden of a soldier." He seemed to be studying her. "There was something else I wanted to ask you."

"Yes?" Meg's heart started to flutter. Did he somehow uncover information about her previous wartime activities, or was it something of a more passionate nature? And if it was indeed a romantic proposal, would she accept?

"Have you ever acted?"

She let out a peal of laughter that disguised the relief washing over her. "Every day of my life."

His smile broadened. "I mean, on stage."

"I did a bit while at boarding school. Mostly skits: I was one of the witches in *Macbeth*."

"Perfect. We are in need of females at the Theatre Royal. A few like-minded officers and I have formed a company."

"And they don't play female parts?"

"Well, we do have some junior officers with high voices." He batted his eyelashes at her. "I think I myself might make a beautiful lady."

Meg took in his thick, curling hair and wide brown eyes. "You would indeed."

"We placed an ad in the *Gazette*, but I thought you might be inclined to the stage."

"For all that you have done for me, Major André, I would be glad to assist."

CHAPTER 39

SALLY

NOVEMBER 1778

*W*ith the campaign season steering to a close, Sally's family prepared to billet yet another officer for the winter. William was frequently absent and spent most of his time in New York City. Robert, busy with his store, coffee shop, and writing for *The Gazette,* was seldom ever home. With Audrey now married to Captain Farley and Solomon still in France, the large house was even more subdued than it had been previously.

It was a clear autumn morning when Sally awoke to the sound of horses trotting. She peered out the window. The blue sky was unmarred by clouds, and some of the trees still held the vestiges of burnt orange leaves. Below them a troop of mounted men in green coats paused. Sally watched as Papa approached them. The man in charge—all Sally could discern was a bulky figure and a powdered wig—dismounted and pointed at the house. Sally's hand tightened on the curtain as she could clearly see her father's face fall. She rushed downstairs, still in her chemise.

"Papa?" she asked as he walked in.

"Sally." He was too weary to notice that she was not dressed. He gestured toward the front gate where a muscular man was tethering a horse. "That's Colonel Simcoe. He will be quartering with us this winter."

"Samuel?" Sally's mother appeared from the back of the house. Upon spying her daughter, she shouted, "Sally! Get some clothes on!" She then commanded Phoebe to put the kettle on. The Townsends were about to receive yet another British houseguest.

Sally dressed quickly, throwing on the same pale blue dress she wore the day before, and then watched her parents greet Colonel Simcoe from her post at the top of the stairs.

He stood at attention, his black boots gleaming in the sunlight filtering in through the windows. "I assume I will have a room to myself?" he asked impatiently.

Sally's chest swelled with indignation. *How dare he be so rude!* she thought. As if he could hear her thoughts, Simcoe shifted his eyes toward the steps, but Sally ducked out of view just in time.

She heard Papa murmuring something, just catching her name before he called up to her. "Sally? Will you please show Colonel Simcoe to his room?"

Sally counted a few beats before she started down the stairs. She knew it was important to maintain a peaceful atmosphere, for both her father's safety and for the chance, however small, to glean information that would be of use to Robert. Consequently, she kept her eyes downcast, afraid that Simcoe would be able to see how much she hated being forced to house the enemy.

After introductions were made, Sally led Simcoe to Robert's old room downstairs. It was a modest room, done in Quaker style, but furnished with touches such as a Turkish carpet and homemade quilt. Both Major Green and Lieutenant Wurmb had roomed here without any complaints, but now Simcoe, after gazing around the room, asked since there was no fireplace, may he have another quilt?

Sally frowned. Inwardly she was thinking that it was just like an

Englishman to not be satisfied with what he had, but outwardly she told him that she would fetch him one shortly.

Simcoe went to the bookcase and pulled out Robert's copy of *Common Sense*. Holding it between his two fingers and making a face, he asked Sally, "Might this be removed straight away?"

She came forward and grabbed it from him, clutching it tightly to her chest.

Simcoe went to his bag and extracted a few of his own belongings to put on the shelf. Sally stepped closer in order to read the titles of the books Simcoe thought appropriate. A few Shakespearean works were mixed in among the treatises on military strategy. Sally set *Common Sense* down to retrieve *Romeo and Juliet* and flipped through it.

Simcoe had stopped his unpacking to peer at her. "One of his finest," he said, nodding at the book in her hands.

Sally, refusing to get pulled into a conversation with him, slid the book back into its spot and picked up *Common Sense*. "I will go see about that quilt," she said, giving him the slightest curtsy before leaving the room.

Papa told Sally and Phoebe to set the dining room table for dinner, thereby ending the cozy kitchen meal times. After he joined them, Simcoe informed the Townsends that he commanded the Queen's Rangers, another troop composed of mostly American Loyalists. Sally had heard of them. They were formerly under the direction of Robert Rogers, a man who supposedly assisted in the capture of Nathan Hale.

Sally watched her parents' eyes meet over the meal and knew what they were thinking: another tyrannical Tory unit, like that of De Lancey's, had come to Oyster Bay.

Phoebe politely inquired why Simcoe wore a green uniform.

He turned to Phoebe. "I'm glad you asked. General Clinton recently asked the same thing." He addressed his next statement to the table as a whole. "The Queen's Rangers under my command are not just like any infantry. It is my belief that they should be able to remain concealed until such times when the situation causes them to charge or evade the enemy."

You mean the chicken-hearted "hit and run," strategy, Sally thought. "Green coats are fine to hide in the spring, but what about autumn?" Sally gestured toward the window, where those leaves that remained on the trees had turned bright colors.

"Much like the brilliant spring fades, or the amber leaves of autumn, a coat—when worn constantly through downpours and the blazing sun—will fade as well." Simcoe bestowed a disarming smile onto Sally.

"Or how a lady's beauty fades with time," she added.

"I could not imagine your beauty ever fading." Simcoe gestured toward Phoebe. "Or that of your sister's."

A wave of jealousy unexpectedly passed over Sally. She shook it off. Simcoe was an arrogant louse, although… Sally studied him as he speared a piece of meat with his fork. His sturdy shoulders and bronze coloring gave off a strong, competent aura. He looked up suddenly and caught Sally staring at him. She focused her eyes on her own meal and did not glance up again.

At breakfast the next day, Simcoe was already ruddy and sweaty. He'd obviously been up early.

Sally sat awkwardly across from him. They were the only ones at the table as Mother was busy in the kitchen and Papa rarely rose in time for the morning meal nowadays. Sally gave an inward sigh of relief when Phoebe joined them.

"Tell me, Miss Townsend," Simcoe was, once again, directing his attention to Sally. "What sort of delights are to be found in Oyster Bay?"

"Oysters, of course!" Phoebe replied.

"Do you shuck them yourselves?"

"No," Sally said. "We do a lot of things in the kitchen, but Caesar's always been the one to shuck them. It's dangerous: you could cut yourself badly if you are unskilled."

Simcoe nodded sincerely, as if this piece of information was of great importance. He wiped his mouth with his napkin before he said, "I must apologize if you thought me rude yesterday. I was feeling a bit tired from the journey."

Sally looked up at this unexpected apology.

"Oh, no, Colonel, we did not think you rude at all," her sister replied.

He nodded at Phoebe's comment, but his eyes were on Sally.

She stood up and grabbed her plate, stacking it on the counter before starting for the hallway.

"Miss Townsend?" Simcoe called.

She stopped, an apology on her lips, albeit a much more insincere one than his. She'd hoped to avoid having to acknowledge Simcoe's atonement, but apparently he would command her as he did his Rangers. She would have no choice but to obey. But when she turned, he asked, "I was hoping you could point me in the direction of the fortification Lieutenant Wurmb had begun. Part of my orders this winter is to complete it."

Sally's stomach, full from breakfast, turned over. Was he actually asking her to accompany him to observe his troops construct battlements? A wide smile formed as she realized how fortuitous that could be for her mission to provide Robert with information. Simcoe seemed pleased by her reaction as he echoed her beam.

"Can I come as well?" Phoebe asked.

Sally narrowed her eyes, but her sister did not seem to notice as Simcoe stated, "Why, of course. The more lovely Townsend ladies that accompany me, the better. Wasn't there a third sister?"

"Audrey," Phoebe told him. "But she married as close to her twenty-first birthday as she could."

He turned to Sally standing in the doorway. "And how old are you?"

Phoebe answered for her. "Twenty, and I'm nearly eighteen now."

"Quite nearing marrying age, then." Simcoe said before he stood. "I will meet you two presently, if you don't mind. I like to accomplish much of my work in the morning."

Phoebe pushed her plate back. "I shall go tell Caesar to get the horses ready."

Sally had two riding habits. She chose the red one, not necessarily for the color but because it was more close-fitting than the other. Both she and Phoebe spent extra time arranging their hair, Sally twirling ringlets to dangle under her felt hat. It was not often they had admiring male eyes to impress.

When they emerged from the room, Simcoe was waiting for them at the bottom of the staircase. "Such enchanting sisters," he commented before leading them outside.

Wurmb's men had begun reinforcing a small hill across from Main Street near the Townsend home. After they arrived at the prospective stronghold, Simcoe dismounted to get a closer look. As he walked around the bottom, he nodded and muttered to himself. Sally and Phoebe exchanged bewildered looks. The hill was only about 60 feet high and had been there as long as Sally could remember. Wurmb's troops did not do much besides add a small number of vertical wood planks to the base of the slope. When Simcoe finished his survey, he told the ladies that it indeed offered a good view of the waterfront. "We shall erect a fortification that would help protect the town from attacks by rebel whaleboat men."

Sally grinned to herself as she pictured Caleb Brewster harassing Tory sympathizers. She was not afraid of the whale-boaters that terrorized the Devil's Belt. Indeed, the greatest threat to Sally's family was Simcoe himself. If Sally's befriending the British officer kept her father out of danger, then so be it.

When Simcoe's Rangers were not working on the breastworks of the Main Street hill, they drilled endlessly in the fields nearby. Sally often rode Gem out in the mornings to watch, thinking that any knowledge of the Rangers would be useful to Robert. Simcoe, for his part, seemed pleased that Sally was taking an interest in his work. He always greeted her graciously and would then explain the purpose of the formations he directed his men into or how the redoubt would look upon completion. Simcoe reiterated that his goal for the Rangers was for them to be agile and quick. During these encounters, Simcoe was all business, but at family meals, he would often seat himself next to Sally and engage her in conversation.

One night, a week after Simcoe's arrival, Sally had trouble sleeping.

"Sally?" Phoebe's voice, coming from the opposite bed, sounded slightly muffled. "Are you still awake?"

"Yes."

"What is going on between you and Colonel Simcoe?"

Sally propped herself up on her elbow to peer across the room, but Phoebe's form was ensconced in shadow. "What do you mean?"

She could hear a rustle, and, as Phoebe's voice increased slightly in volume, Sally surmised that her sister had turned toward her. "It's obvious that he is quite taken with you."

"Obvious how?"

"Sally, don't you notice how his eyes light up when you walk into the room? That he only talks to you at dinner?"

"That means nothing. We are friends."

"You might think that is all it is, but I'm not certain Simcoe would agree." Sally heard Phoebe turn back over and realized that was the extent of the conversation.

The next day Simcoe informed Sally and Phoebe that he'd secured a carriage so that the sisters might accompany him on a scouting tour around the island. Simcoe was still convinced that Oyster Bay was in danger of being attacked from rebel-held Connecticut, which was only seven miles north of Long Island. On these trips, the Townsend ladies learned much about Simcoe's early life, including his stints at Eton College.

"Do you have many siblings?" Phoebe asked him.

"No," Simcoe replied, his eyes, as they often were, on Sally. "I had three siblings that died in childhood. I have no idea what it must be like to have such a big, boisterous family as yours must have been growing up."

Sally smiled wistfully, remembering fishing and riding with her brothers and the crowded but affectionate family meals. She had to admit that Simcoe's presence had livened up the empty house a bit.

When he was not sharing stories from his childhood, Simcoe would enlighten them on his designs for barricading the island. Occasionally he would ask the driver to pause the horses and he would get out, lifting a spyglass in each direction. Upon climbing back into the carriage, he would make a mark in his notebook, telling the ladies that it would make a logical landing spot for the rebels. As they continued their trips, Sally noticed that British sentinels would be placed in these areas Simcoe had pointed out.

Since Sally was usually seated beside Simcoe, she would watch what he recorded and, when they returned home, would go to the desk in her room and write down—and sometimes even sketch—what she had seen. She kept these papers hidden in the bottom of a broken clock, knowing that her hope chest—where she stored old birthday cards and her quilt tops—would be too obvious a spot should anyone become suspicious.

Even as they formed a tenuous friendship, Sally was ever the more wary of Simcoe, especially when he revealed during one of their rides that another of his purposes was to expose any instances of suspected spying activities.

"Do you believe there are spies in Oyster Bay?" Sally asked, trying to emulate Robert's neutral tone.

Simcoe shrugged. "According to John André, the head of British intelligence, there is information being passed from New York City to the front, and it is believed to be routed through Long Island."

"Do you know Major André?" Phoebe inquired. Every girl in the state of New York knew of André's reputation of being a rogue with the ladies.

"He is a good friend of mine," Simcoe answered. But Sally was no longer listening, realizing that Simcoe's presence at the house was now more of a threat to Robert—and her for that matter—than her father.

Still, she was determined to do what she could to help the cause, stopping short of searching Simcoe's documents. She could think of no reasonable excuse for her to go through his personal belongings, and, besides, she also knew how methodical he was. If she left any paper or inkwell in the wrong place, he would know immediately that something was amiss in the Townsend house.

CHAPTER 40

SALLY

DECEMBER 1778

*I*n mid-December, as was custom, the Townsends decided to host a celebration both in honor of the upcoming holiday and for Simcoe and his Rangers. The day of the party, Sally was dawdling over her breakfast when Phoebe rushed in, breathless. "The apple orchard!" she managed to gasp.

Sally started at the sight of her normally composed sister. Her cheeks were flushed and she had a frantic air about her. When she finally caught her breath, Phoebe told Sally that the Rangers were chopping down Papa's prized apple orchard.

"What?" Sally stood. Now it was her turn to run, rushing toward the orchard located on the west side of the property.

Just as Phoebe had said, most of Papa's trees had already been felled. A pair of green-coated soldiers were carrying a trunk in the direction of the redoubt while other Rangers were bent over at the waist, sawing at the bases of the few trees that remained. Sally approached the closest soldier. "What do you think you are doing?"

He stood up. "Miss Townsend?" Despite the cool winter air, a line of sweat dripped from below his felt hat.

Sally looked up to see her parents peering down at the scene from their bedroom window. "I demand you cease this destruction at once," she told the soldier.

"I'm sorry, miss, but I cannot. I have orders from Colonel Simcoe himself."

"Colonel Simcoe?" Sally gathered up her skirts and headed toward the redoubt. As she approached, she could see the soldiers sharpening the newly razed trunks into sharp points. It was clear that Simcoe was to use the trees as a rampart around his hill.

When he spotted Sally, Simcoe gave her a casual wave, which only served to heighten her anger. "How dare you do this?" Sally cried. "Just when I was beginning to think you were a decent human being, even if you are British." She was too upset to realize that her last line could be construed as Whiggish.

Simcoe held up his hand as he walked toward her. "I am a decent human being."

Sally kicked at a bevel lying near her boot. "You are not. You are deliberately destroying my family's property, after all we have done for you." She noticed that the soldiers around her had paused in their work to observe the scene.

Simcoe waved at his men, but none of them moved. "Miss Townsend, you must understand—"

"Understand what? That you think you are entitled to take whatever you need? You are just the same as all of them: Tories, Loyalists, Redcoats, thinking that the townspeople owe you. You pretend to have honor, but you, sir, are just a heartless brute."

Simcoe reddened. Sally took a deep breath and prepared for another tirade, but Simcoe said, "Enough!" in a voice that was just a shade lower than a shout. "I am sorry for the destruction of your father's trees, but, as military commander, I have the authority to confiscate them at will. Now, if you will excuse me, Miss Townsend, I have work to see to."

Sally, her mouth hanging open, was speechless as she watched him saunter away. She tried to rein in her fury for Papa's sake but found it was not easy to do. At any rate, she would have no more qualms about feeding Robert the information about Simcoe's fortifications. In fact, she walked around the barricade to observe the work in progress, under the guise that she was making sure the trees were being put to good use. The entire orchard had been destroyed and there was nothing she could do about it, other than make sure the rebels knew of Simcoe's plans for Oyster Bay.

The party was to take place that evening. Sally wanted to follow her father's lead and retire to her room, but she forced herself to get ready. Papa depended on her to keep the peace, even if he himself was unable to bring himself to act as the gracious host for Simcoe and his regiment.

She plastered a smile onto her face as she walked downstairs with Phoebe. Mother had borrowed a few slaves from the Buchanans to help prepare food and run it back and forth from the kitchen. All the chairs of the house had been gathered in the parlor. The small table the Townsends brought out on such occasions was placed in front of the built-in cupboard and already stacked with sweet meats and bread. Colonel Simcoe was standing in the living room, conversing with another fellow whom Sally recognized as an officer with the Rangers. Upon catching sight of the ladies, he requested them to come be presented to his companion, Captain McGill.

"You are so lucky, sir, to be billeted in the house with the most beautiful sisters in all of Long Island," McGill said after the introductions were made.

"I completely agree with you," Simcoe replied.

Sally had to concentrate to keep from frowning as she felt her heart ice over.

"Do you still hold me in low regard?" Simcoe asked as Phoebe and McGill fell into conversation.

Sally said nothing as she walked to the refreshment table. She pretended to be busy wiping down a spotless pewter plate with a rag she had grabbed from the corner cupboard.

"Miss Townsend." The contrite tone in Simcoe's voice caused Sally to finally look at him. His eyes, normally so commanding, looked sorrowful. "I'd like to explain my earlier actions, if you don't mind." He seated himself in a nearby chair.

Sally remained standing. "I believe you've made yourself quite clear. You think you have the right to confiscate other people's property, and we can do nothing but watch."

"Yes. There is that. And also, Lieutenant-General Erskine, who commands our forces on Long Island, told me only the day before that the Rangers would be moved to Jericho. I thought that an unwise move—Jericho is too far away from the shore to provide adequate protection from raiding parties. The only way for me to fully assure him of Oyster Bay's potential was to fortify the redoubt. Your father's trees were too convenient for that purpose to pass up."

She wanted to reply that she would have preferred them all to be relocated to Jericho and out of her town, but she held her tongue. The trees were gone and nothing she could say would change that.

"I do want to say," Simcoe continued, "that I have much cherished your presence on my daily excursions and would have missed them greatly had I been commanded to depart Oyster Bay."

The words did little to melt the ice around Sally's heart but she forced a conciliatory smile anyway. "I accept your explanation, Colonel Simcoe." She adapted the same supercilious tone he had used that morning at the redoubt to add, "If you will now excuse me, I have more things to see to before our guests arrive."

In the absence of Papa, who claimed to be sick and stayed in bed, Sally, Phoebe, and Mother greeted their non-military guests and introduced them to the newest British officers to occupy their town. Sally was apprehensive that the Loyalists might still be uncertain of Papa's allegiances, especially given his nonattendance. Consequently, she went out of her way to appease them, turning on the charm by batting her eyelashes and over-serving their Madeira.

As the evening wore on, the guests—Tories, Whigs, and officers alike—dropped their guard and chatted over innocuous topics like the weather and if it would be a good harvest this year.

"Sarah," McGill whispered to Sally as she rearranged some of the baked goods on the table.

She looked at him in surprise. "Are we addressing each other by first names now? If so, then you should probably know that most people call me Sally."

McGill's eyes, slightly bloodshot now that he was deep in his cups, widened. "I'm sorry. Your mother mentioned something about her daughter, Sarah." He bowed. "And I am John."

"Mother usually only calls me by my real name when she is upset with me. She is the original Sarah Townsend." Sally glanced about the room for Mother, but only caught sight of Simcoe, who was watching them from across the room.

"Sally, then." McGill leaned in closer to her. "Are you close with your brother Robert?"

Sally nodded, fear washing over her.

"Do you think you could get him to print an article on my behalf?"

Sally let out a quiet breath. "You mean in the *Gazette*?"

"Yes," McGill replied as another officer, obviously overhearing their conversation, sauntered over.

"Of course, Robert Townsend of New York City. I did not make the connection until now." The man bowed toward Sally. "I am Captain Wilson. I've met Robert several times at Rivington's coffee shop. In fact," he took a small diamond ring off of his finger. "I won this from Rivington himself in a poker game."

Sally took the proffered ring and held it up to the light. "It's quite pretty." She handed it over to McGill, who also admired it.

"Do you know what is unique about diamonds?" McGill asked. Both Wilson and Sally shook their heads. "They can cut through anything."

"Anything?" Sally demanded. "Even glass?"

"Of course. I can prove it, if you'd like." McGill headed over to the bay windows in the middle of the parlor. He held the diamond up to the window and began to etch. Phoebe and Sally Coles also came over to watch. McGill made a show of his movements, stepping back once he'd finished.

"The Adorable Miss Sally Townsend." Phoebe read aloud. "But of course, you must sign your handiwork."

McGill assumed his position, this time signing "J. McGill," at the bottom with a flourish before turning to grin at Sally. He put an X through the word "Sally," and wrote "Sarah" right above it.

"Write something about me," Phoebe commanded. She'd obviously had a glass or two of Madeira herself and did not seem to mind that McGill was writing on her family's windows. Sally, for her part, was stunned by the phrasing McGill had used. Did an almost stranger really find her adorable? McGill now scratched the words, "Miss P.T., the most accomplished young lady in Oyster Bay."

Phoebe beamed as McGill glanced over at the remaining girl and wrote, "Sally Coles," before pausing in thought.

"Captain McGill," a gruff voice spoke out. Simcoe had joined them. "What exactly do you think you are doing?"

"Just having some fun with the ladies, here." Remembering his place, McGill clicked his boot heels together, adding, "Sir," before handing the ring back to Wilson.

Simcoe reached out to rub at the beginning words on Sally Cole's window, to no avail. "These will never come out," he said, dropping his hand. "You dare to deface our kind hosts' property?"

Sally furrowed her brow at Simcoe. How could he carry on so? A few scratches on the window were nothing compared to the destruction of an entire orchard.

"I'm sorry, sir." McGill addressed Sally. "Please accept my sincerest apologies, Sarah." He couldn't keep the grin from spreading as Sally relaxed her face. "I mean, Miss Townsend."

Sally had not truly believed that the diamond etchings would be permanent, and, as she had imbibed in the wine as well, returned the smile. She would worry over Papa's reaction to the windows in the morning. For now it was nice to have a handsome officer describe her as "adorable."

Simcoe turned to Sally. "While I agree with Captain McGill's sentiments, I must declare that it is time for my men to return to their post. Thank you for the party." He bowed at Phoebe and then

Sally Coles before glaring at McGill as the young captain followed suit.

"Maybe next time you could finish recording your thought," Sally Coles giggled as McGill took his leave of her, kissing her on the hand. As the officers walked away to say their goodbyes, she said to the sisters, "That McGill is something else."

"Indeed," Phoebe agreed. "But all the while, his lieutenant was practically shooting daggers out of his eyes at him. I have a feeling that, with Simcoe in charge, McGill's life in the regiment will not be easy going from now on."

CHAPTER 41

MEG

DECEMBER 1778

*T*hat holiday season, the Theatre Royale performed Shakespeare's tragedy *Julius Caesar*. Meg took on the role of Calpurnia, the wife of Caesar—played by André—who tried to warn him before he is assassinated that she dreamt of his death, to no avail.

Shortly before the dress rehearsal, Meg was astonished to see the set designs, which included the Parthenon and beautiful Roman countryside. "Who painted these?" she asked, slowly rotating on the stage to take it all in.

"I did," André said, entering in his toga.

"You speak German, French, and English, draw, paint, act, and have the finest military mind this side of the Atlantic." Meg took an appreciative glance of his form before asking, "Is there anything you can't do?"

"I cannot juggle."

Meg smiled. "But mayhap you will learn someday."

"Mayhap."

. . .

The rehearsal went well, and André, heady from both his spotless performance and the Madeira the cast had to celebrate afterward, was especially talkative at the fireplace in Meg's room that night.

He confided in Meg his other reason to celebrate: "Clinton has just made me his chief intelligence officer!"

"Congratulations!" Meg lifted her glass to his.

"Yes. I do not believe that the Yankees take much stock in their newly formed alliance with France and now, with their currency practically worthless, they shan't hold out much longer. One more decisive victory in our favor and I think the war will be over."

Meg plastered a fake smile on her face and clinked his glass again. She hadn't realized that the tides had turned that much. If her husband ended up on the winning side, she supposed they would return to England. Whereas she once fervently hoped for that outcome—albeit with a different beau—now she was not so sure she wanted to leave America.

"Of course," André lifted his glass to his lips and took a sip. "There is the problem of intelligence slipping out of Manhattan."

Meg practically choked on her wine. "Pardon?"

He didn't seem to notice her disconcertion. "We've intercepted a letter intended for Washington mentioning a man named Samuel Culper Junior who has access to information on our troop sizes and the comings and goings of our warships. Apparently there exists a Samuel Culper Senior who also provides such intelligence. My men are on the lookout for a father/son spy team."

"The Culpers?" Meg's astonishment was not false. "I've never heard of them."

André let out a giggle, followed by a hiccough. "It didn't occur to me that you would have."

She covered her confusion the best way she knew how. She tucked a stray ringlet behind her ear and slid closer to André. "Do you have any suspicions as to who these spies might be?"

"No." He stood up. "But as chief intelligence officer, it is my job to find them."

262

Meg's lips formed a pout. "Are you leaving so soon?"

He shot her one of his easy grins. "I have to. I need to get up early tomorrow and continue my search."

Meg barely noticed him leave, she was so concerned about the danger to her friends. Mercy was out of the city, but could Hercules Mulligan be one of their suspects? As far as she knew, his father had passed on and his sons were too young. *But the Culpers could merely just be a code name.* And with that, one of André's lines from the play popped into her head:

Yond Cassius has a lean and hungry look.

He thinks too much. Such men are dangerous.

Closing her eyes, she could see an image of Robert Townsend's lean, dark-haired figure. Whomever these Culpers were, Meg had an intuition that Townsend was somehow involved. But instead of being afraid for him and his contacts, Meg felt a rush of fear for André. Shaking it off as Caesar did, she turned down her bed in preparation for sleep.

CHAPTER 42

SALLY

S ally had been avoiding Simcoe as best she could and no longer joined him on scouting missions. Simcoe had been absent for most of the family meals, choosing to bestow his presence at the tables of prominent Oyster Bay Loyalists. He celebrated the Christmas holiday with his regiment, leaving Papa, Mother, Sally, Phoebe, and William to dine in the kitchen.

The ice that formed over the harbor meant that Robert was unable to come home until after the New Year. The night he arrived, Sally was setting the table for five—as William had left for the city again—when Simcoe entered. He approached Robert, who was sitting near the fire, to introduce himself. "You must be the famed Robert I've heard so much about."

Sally looked up from her chore, hoping that her brother would not think she was gossiping about him to Simcoe. But Robert remained as outwardly at ease as ever as he shook Simcoe's hand. "And I've also heard much about you and your Rangers."

"Colonel Simcoe, will you be joining us for dinner?" Sally asked.

She wanted to show her brother that she could still be gracious to their houseguest.

Simcoe glanced at her, obviously surprised at Sally's change of heart. "Yes I will, if you don't mind." He walked off in the direction of his room before pausing in the doorway. "Mr. Townsend, I do believe I am occupying your room."

Robert held up his hand. "I am fine on the couch in the parlor. And, please call me Robert."

At dinner, Robert sat beside Sally, with Simcoe seated next to Phoebe.

"Tell me, Colonel Simcoe. What do you do for leisure?" Robert inquired as their servant brought out the first course.

"Not that I have too much time for leisure, but I do enjoy reading. Shakespeare, to be more specific."

Robert nodded. "I particularly enjoyed *Julius Caesar*."

"I would be inclined to agree with you. My friend, John André, played him last month at the Theatre Royale," Simcoe replied.

"Actually, I attended one of the performances," Robert said, digging his fork into his venison. "He did quite well."

"Yes, André is a real artiste." Simcoe took a bite of food, and after a sip of wine, addressed Papa, "I must ask something I have been curious about. Are you of the Raynham Hall Townsends from Norwich?"

Papa chewed thoughtfully. "Yes, I believe my ancestors came from that area. But the Townsends have been in the colonies since before 1640," he added proudly.

Simcoe nodded. "Charles Townshend, the Chancellor of the Exchequer, was of Raynham Hall."

Sally's fork clattered to the plate. Charles Townshend was also the designer of the detestable Townshend Acts, the Parliament bill which proposed to tax the colonies for such necessities as paper and tea. The bill had induced riots among the outraged colonists and resulted in the Boston Massacre of 1770.

Papa held a tight smile. "I believe that Charles Townshend was a cousin."

A proud American all of her life, Sally usually gave little thought to her family's origins. She now thought it ironic that one of her relatives was responsible for the act that had so stirred the emotions of her countrymen. She glanced at Simcoe, wondering what his purpose had been for mentioning the fact. Was he indeed that curious or did he want to remind Papa that he had Loyalist blood? But Simcoe's eyes were steadily focused on his plate.

After dinner, the female Townsends commenced sewing near the fire in the parlor. Sally waited until both Papa and Simcoe retired before asking Robert to accompany her to her bedroom upstairs.

Once there, Sally went to the broken clock and pulled out the documents she had collected.

Robert sat in her desk chair to flip through the papers, peering at Sally's drawings of the redoubt and estimated troop numbers. "How did you come across this information?"

"I accompanied Simcoe on some of his excursions," Sally said, keeping her eyes down as she felt Robert studying her. "But I forfeited going with him after the apple orchard incident." She related what had happened to Papa's trees.

Robert sat back. "I figured as much when I saw the cuttings. The British believe they can have access to whatever they need, whenever they need it," he continued bitterly. "But," he folded up Sally's papers and put them in the pocket of his waistcoat. "We must keep those thoughts to ourselves. This information will be of great value to my contacts."

"Who—" Sally began, but Robert held up his hand. "It is best if you don't know. I recommend pursuing your friendship with Simcoe."

"But I despise that man!"

He gave her a meaningful look. "I said *friendship*, and nothing more. You can try, can't you, Sal? In order to help the cause?"

She sat on the bed. "I suppose so."

He gestured toward the broken clock in the corner. "That's a good spot for hiding. In fact," he picked up a quill and dipped it into the inkwell on her desk. "I'm going to leave this piece of paper with you. It will allow you to disguise anything you might say that would be of interest to our enemies. If you feel it necessary to contact me, you can deliver the message to Daniel Youngs."

"Youngs? He is a staunch Loyalist."

"It would appear so, wouldn't it? But Sal, make sure to conceal the papers in the horse's saddle bag, not on your person. Do not make the mistake of putting important documents in your shoe. That would be the first place they search, not that they would have cause to search a woman. And this code will prevent an immediate recognition of intelligence."

Sally nodded bravely.

Robert rose to leave. "And Sal? Be careful. Simcoe is a crafty man. You must make sure he never knows your true purpose, or you will be putting us all in danger."

Sally drew herself to her full height. "Of course."

CHAPTER 43

ELIZABETH

JANUARY 1779

One night in January, Robert did not show for the nightly tutoring session. Elizabeth's puzzlement increased to genuine worry as the hour grew late. What if he had been discovered? Finally there was a knock on the door. After Abby answered it and led Robert into the kitchen, she gathered all three children and started to lead them into their bedroom.

"Mr. Townsend," Johnny cried in anguish. "Are we not to learn tonight?"

Robert went over and ruffled the child's hair. "Not tonight, Johnny, m'boy. Tomorrow."

Catherine escaped Abby's clutch to hug Robert's legs. Abby managed to free her and bid him and Elizabeth goodnight. Robert kept his eyes on the door for seconds after Abby shut it.

"Robert?" Elizabeth asked. "What is it?"

"Abraham Woodhull's father was accosted at his farmhouse a few nights ago. I have only just now heard."

Elizabeth's hand flew to her mouth. "How do they——"

His next words made her blood run cold. "It was a raid led by Colonel Simcoe, the man who is billeted in my family's home."

"Oh, Robert." She went to hug him, but his form remained stiff in her arms.

"Only a fortnight ago I told Sally to befriend him in order to get information."

"Is Sally in danger?" Elizabeth broke her embrace to look him in the face. "Are you?"

He sank into a nearby chair. "As far as Brewster knows, it was a smuggler who had the misfortune to be captured by the British. He gave up Woodhull's name to save his own hide. Luckily Woodhull was in the city, staying with the Underhills, and had no papers in Setauket to be found, but that did not spare his father."

"How goes Abraham's father?"

"He is badly beaten but he will survive."

Elizabeth sat down across the table from Robert. "And this smuggler... how did he get Abraham's name?"

Robert shook his head and looked down at his hands. "I don't know."

She reached out to clasp his hand. "You must stay here tonight, just to be safe."

"No." His voice was adamant. "I have caused my loved ones much danger." He dropped her hand. "For your own safety, we must no longer associate."

Elizabeth cleared her throat to keep her next words from getting caught. "That will be very difficult for me to do, considering that I've fallen in love with you."

Robert's face crumpled briefly before the stoic mask reappeared. "I would never forgive myself if something happened to you because of me."

"Robert——"

"Think of the children. They need their mother. They don't need a spy in their midst, threatening their very foundation." He stood up, his long legs striding toward the door.

Elizabeth struggled to keep up with him. "Robert," she tried again in the hallway, but he held up his hand. He unlocked the door and opened it before turning back to her. "I do feel it is necessary to state that I love you too." And with that, he walked down the stairs and out of Elizabeth's life.

CHAPTER 44

SALLY

*a*t Robert's urging, Sally resumed her friendship with Simcoe. As they drilled, she estimated the number of the soldiers in the way Robert taught her: to count only the greencoats in one section of grass and then multiply that by the number of sections. It was not easy, but it was less confusing than counting each individual soldier as they marched by in their varying formations.

Simcoe took his eyes off his troop in order to watch Sally. She realized she'd been unconsciously pointing with her finger as she counted.

"About 450," Simcoe told her. "One hundred on horseback."

"So many!" Sally cried out, trying to distract him if he was at all suspicious of her true purpose. She next tried flattery. "And all under your command."

"Indeed." Simcoe's chest puffed out like a pigeon. "They would die for me with no qualms."

"How… nice," Sally said, for lack of anything else.

Simcoe captured her hand in his. "I would die for you, as well."

Sally refrained herself from snatching her hand back. "I do not require that of you." She turned her head back to the troops, feeling Simcoe's eyes on her.

That night at dinner, Simcoe informed the Townsends that he would be expecting a houseguest in the next few days. "My friend, John André. He recently was appointed Adjutant General of the army, and it seems his new duties have gotten to his psyche. General Clinton suggested he take some time away, and what better place to recuperate than the fine town of Oyster Bay?"

Papa merely nodded his acquiescence. Ever since the apple orchard incident, he had grown ever the more reticent around Simcoe.

Phoebe had the opposite reaction. "Major André is coming here?" She looked at Sally excitedly, who shrugged in return. Phoebe turned to Simcoe. "How are you acquainted with him?"

"We met when we were stationed in Philadelphia," Simcoe replied smoothly.

"Where will he stay?" Mother asked. "We have a small attic room where William and Robert sleep occasionally, but it is cold up there."

Simcoe held up his hand. "He will stay in the extra bed in my room. I would not want to put your family out more than I have already."

"I will make sure he has the best blankets and coverings that we have," Phoebe stated, almost to herself.

Simcoe laughed. "I'm certain he will appreciate that."

Phoebe held her hand to her lips. "Oh, Colonel Simcoe, I did not mean…"

"It's fine." He wiped his mouth and stood from the table. "I, too, must prepare for André."

Phoebe sat back with satisfaction. Sally knew she had watched with envy as first Hannah and then Audrey got married and started new lives with their husbands. With most of the boys they had grown up with now off fighting on either side of the war,

Sally knew Phoebe worried that she was approaching prime marrying age. None of them wanted to end up like Lydia Jones, their distant cousin and neighbor who, at 30, was considered too old to marry. A spinster, she had been dependent on her father to house her and take care of her expenses, but when he died, she was forced to take a position as a maid to earn her own keep. Sally knew that Phoebe had hoped the Jäger Lieutenant Ochse would have proposed to her, but he left without much of a goodbye when his troop was called away. Sally, too, feared the fate of becoming a spinster, but not as much as being forced into a marriage with the enemy.

The next morning the elegant Major André appeared at the Townsends' door. Phoebe had risen early and put on her best chintz morning gown and curled her hair. Sally had rolled out of bed in her usual manner and thrown on whatever dress was handy. Both girls positioned themselves in the hallway, eager to lay their eyes on the celebrated André for different reasons. Simcoe led André into the living room. As the companions stood opposite to shake hands, Sally could not help but compare the two. Where Simcoe was broad, André was slim; Simcoe had frizzy hair that often escaped his unadorned queue, André's hair was styled with two curls at each temple and the rest tied back neatly with a ribbon; Simcoe had a wide face whereas André's was narrow, with evenly sculpted features. Indeed, André was as handsome as the rumors implied.

Simcoe, on catching sight of the sisters, gestured for them to enter.

"Major André, may I present two of the famed Townsend women, Phoebe and Sally." After they curtsied, André kissed their hands in turn. Was it Sally's imagination or did André's lips linger for just a few seconds longer on her? She dropped her eyes to the floor and then raised them back up the way she'd often seen Audrey do. André returned her glance, his brown eyes reminding Sally of a doe facing down the barrel of a rifle: wide and almost sorrowful. The image disappeared as André's perfectly shaped lips expanded into a grin. Sally's face heated as she realized she was still holding her hand up. She dropped it to her side as André chuckled.

"Shall I make you gentlemen some tea?" Phoebe asked.

Simcoe, who had been watching Sally as always, frowned. "No, I think we will head to the back bedroom to discuss a few military matters."

"But I do look forward to seeing you both at dinner," André said with a bow. His gait, quickened to catch up with the striding Simcoe, had a jauntiness that belied the major's confidence.

"I do not believe I have ever met a man like Major André," Phoebe said when the two men had retreated down the hall.

"This time I quite agree with you, sister." Sally said, watching as Simcoe led André into the room. André tipped his hat at her before walking in and closing the door.

At dinner that night, André and Simcoe chatted amicably. Occasionally André would ask Papa questions on neutral topics—naturally avoiding the subject of war—but Papa would only return one-word answers. When André inquired as to what he thought of the newest fashions coming from the French court, Papa replied that he paid no such mind to fashion. Sally exchanged a worried glance with Phoebe. A year ago he would have been eager to discuss the wardrobe of the French king.

Mother sought to put André at ease. "Shall we plan an afternoon tea for your men this Wednesday?" she asked Simcoe.

Simcoe nodded before wiping his mouth. "I would be much obliged, thank you, Mrs. Townsend."

"I'll make my famous tea cakes," Phoebe said.

"I cannot wait to taste them," André replied. Phoebe simpered and Sally recalled her sister's victory, although short lived, with Leutnant Ochse's affections. But then André turned to Sally and asked, "And what is your specialty?"

Sally, whose knowledge of baking was quite limited, murmured something about olykoeks, a round treat of fried dough.

"Ah, yes," André's smile seemed to brighten the dim room. "My mother, being from France, used to call them 'crispies.' I will very much look forward to tasting them." He winked at Phoebe. "And of course, your sweet cakes."

Phoebe raised her shoulders and looked smug while Sally refrained from rolling her eyes.

Phoebe spent the next day baking and preparing the table for the following afternoon's tea. She retrieved her mother's best china from the cupboard in the parlor and then set about polishing the silver teaspoons until they gleamed as if brand new. She looked up at Sally, who stood empty-handed near the door to the hallway. "I'm finished in the kitchen."

"Thank you, but I'm just going to make the olykoeks tomorrow."

"Won't they need time to cool?" Phoebe held up a spoon to the light, frowned, and then rubbed at it again with her cloth.

"They'll be fine as long as I start on them in the morning. I was going to see if André and Simcoe wanted to go for a ride this afternoon."

Phoebe's face turned downward. "That's just like you to be out gallivanting instead of cooking or sewing. You will make a poor wife someday." Her voice rose on the last part as Major André walked into the room.

"Any man would be beyond pleased to have Sally as his wife," André stated. "I'd much rather have a riding companion."

Sally's heart expanded in her chest as Phoebe frowned. "Are you up for a ride now?" Sally asked.

"Of course," he said, winking at Phoebe before he linked his arm through Sally's.

"Who will cook and clean for you if your wife is always on her horse?" Phoebe called as the pair began to saunter off.

"Isn't that what maids are for?" Sally tossed the words over her shoulder as André chuckled.

"I am going to change into my riding habit," Sally told André when they reached the hallway. She found that she was reluctant to have her arm back.

"And I will extend the invitation to Colonel Simcoe."

"Surely," Sally said, trying to keep the disappointment out of her voice. Although it would be considered improper to go riding alone with a near stranger, she would have liked for their chaperone to not be Simcoe. *Still,* she thought, climbing the steps, *at least he did not ask Phoebe.*

Simcoe, desiring to show off his work at the redoubt to André, led the way for the ride. André rode beside Sally.

"You know something, Miss Townsend?" Sally glanced over to see Major André staring intently at her. "Your profile is quite breathtaking."

Sally felt her face heat up underneath her bonnet as she focused on the path in front of her.

"I dabble a bit in silhouettes. Would you mind if I did a cut-out of you sometime?"

She looked over at him again. André rode confidently, holding the reins with only one hand. "I'd be delighted."

That evening, when Sally came to dinner, she was surprised to spot a folded paper at her plate. Upon opening it, she gasped to see it was a drawing of her in her riding habit and signed by John André.

André entered the room and caught her studying it. "I'm afraid it does not do you justice."

"Oh, it is beautiful. Thank you, Major André."

"A beautiful picture for a beautiful girl."

He does flatter so. "Tell me, Major André, a man of your demeanor must have all the New York City girls fawning over you. Have you one in particular?"

André paused for a brief moment. "I have become quite taken with Mrs. Coghlan, actually." He said the words so matter-of-factly that Sally could not imagine there was much passion between them.

"How wonderful for Mrs. Coghlan," Sally replied, giving no recognition that she recognized the name. Inwardly she was curious as to what Meg was up to.

"But my heart still has room for more affections," he said with a wink.

"Phoebe will be glad to hear of it."

"And are you?"

Sally peered at him. The question seemed to come out of sincerity and she wondered if he knew that Simcoe might have designs on her as well. "Mayhap," Sally said in a neutral tone as she set off to place the drawing in a prominent position in her room.

The next morning Sally rose early to prepare the olykoeks. She rolled the dough—a mixture of eggs, yeast, and raisins—into little balls before putting them into a lard-filled iron cask. After a few minutes over the fire, the dough balls turned a delectable brown. She then sprinkled them with sugar before setting them on the kitchen table to cool.

Sally—thinking again of Major André's brown eyes, as she had been all morning—spent extra time on her hair and dress, choosing a lavender lutestring with a cream underskirt. When she went back downstairs, Phoebe had arranged the sweet cakes she made in the middle of the dining room table. She pointed to an empty charger off to one side. "I would have put the olykoeks there, but I could not locate them."

"They are on the table," Sally said as she passed by her sister. But when she got into the kitchen, she did not see them. "Did you move them, Phoebe?" she called.

"No."

That is odd, Sally thought as she began opening cabinets. When she did not find them, she asked her mother, but she had not seen them either. After one more search, Sally walked back into the dining room where Phoebe was fussing over the placement of the cake plate, moving it an inch to the side before moving it back.

Sally put her hands on her hips. "I know you took them," she said accusingly.

"I did not." Phoebe did not look up.

"Yes you did," Sally's voice rose.

"Sally," Phoebe turned to her sister, the picture of innocence. "I did not."

"What is all of this?" André asked as he and Simcoe entered the dining room, each dressed in their respective uniforms: André's coat in red and Simcoe's a moss green. Both of the men glanced appreciatively at the table.

Sally did not want to burden the gentlemen with their domestic dispute, but Phoebe pointed at her and said, "Sally somehow misplaced the olykoeks and now she is blaming me."

André tipped his head back and roared. "Oh Sally, how could you? Have you checked everywhere?"

"I did."

He walked over to the built-in cabinet. "Even in," he opened the two bottom doors with a flourish, "here?" And there, placed directly in the center of the shelf, were the olykoeks.

"You hid them!" Sally said with a laugh as she came over to stand beside André. After retrieving them, she set them next on the charger. "There appears to be some missing."

André patted his vest. "And they were delicious."

Simcoe watched the exchange, his face growing darker and his frown deepening. He walked over to the plate and grabbed an olykoek. He popped it into his mouth and declared it "excellent" before casting his eyes at his friend.

André, obviously unaware of the showdown developing between him and Simcoe, asked Phoebe if he could be of any service.

"No, of course not. I have it all handled," she said, with an emphasis on the "I".

A heavy knock sounded on the door. "I will get it," Sally said. She led Captain McGill and another soldier into the dining room and Simcoe introduced them to Major André.

· · ·

After a few more Rangers arrived, Phoebe invited the men to sit at the table. André, presumably unknowingly, took Simcoe's usual place next to Sally. Phoebe, seating herself at the head, seemed dismayed by this until McGill, at her right hand, complimented her on her pink dress.

"Thank you, Captain McGill. I am also responsible for the table settings," Phoebe said as she leaned over him to pour tea into his cup.

"Clearly you have exquisite taste," McGill replied.

"Did I mention that I have met your brother on several occasions?" André asked Sally.

The blood in her veins momentarily chilled. "Oh?" she asked.

"Yes, at Rivington's coffee shop. I've also had a few poems published in the *Gazette.*"

"Ah," Sally said, reaching for an olykoek. Phoebe gave her a dirty look, probably for lunging across the table.

"He's quite a reticent man," André continued. Sally gave him a tiny smile, wondering if the chief of British intelligence had more than a passing interest in her brother or if he was just making casual conversation. "Ah, Bohea." André took a sip of tea before setting his cup down. "My favorite," he said, bestowing a grin on Sally and then Phoebe.

When the pleasant exchanges at the tea table turned to military matters, Sally and Phoebe fell silent and pretended not to listen. The way the soldiers spoke about a visit they paid to a gentleman in Setauket, Sally gathered that it was not an amiable social call.

"Woodhull was not there, but I think we made our message clear by our treatment of the old rebel," Simcoe stated.

To Sally, it seemed as though Simcoe had ordered, or even participated in, the harming of a helpless elder and yet showed no remorse. But there was something else he said that perked Sally's ears. The words, "Abraham Woodhull?" came involuntarily out of her mouth as the men at the table exchanged glances. *Why did I say that?* Sally asked herself. "I've met him," she added, careful not to mention that Robert introduced them. She realized that Woodhull must have come under their suspicion, so Sally sought a way to affirm his innocence. "He's as loyal to the Crown as they come," she continued, an affected hint of dissent in her voice.

"You speak of that like it is distasteful," McGill commented from the end of the table.

"Why, Captain McGill," Sally replied. "That would imply I knew anything about politics."

"You don't?" André asked.

She batted her eyes at him. "I don't bother to fill my pretty little head with such trifles," she said, pleased when, after the men's laughter died down, the talk turned back to more nonpartisan topics, including the impending Valentine's Day.

"I shall pin bay leaves to my pillow this year now that I am nearing a marrying age," Phoebe said.

"Bay leaves?" McGill inquired.

"If you have bay leaves on your pillow and you dream of your sweetheart, you shall be married," Sally told him.

"And what happens if you don't dream of him?" André asked.

Sally shrugged.

"Such a strange tradition," André stated. "Last night I dreamt of my horse. Does that mean I shall marry him?"

"Only if you had bay leaves on your pillow and only if it is the night before Valentine's Day," Phoebe replied.

"Have you performed this ritual before?" Simcoe inquired of Sally.

"I never had a beau to dream of," she said softly.

"And this year?" McGill asked.

Sally, feeling the eyes of everyone in the room on her, looked down at her hands before nodding.

After she finished helping Phoebe clear the table, Sally put on her wool-lined cloak and went outside. Her favorite place to think had always been the apple orchard, so she sat down on a stump to contemplate all that she heard at tea. Simcoe was clearly a dangerous man and she hoped her comments on Woodhull would afford him some protection. She recalled the kindness of Mary

Underhill, Woodhull's sister, and could not imagine how awful it must have been to hear of the ill treatment toward her father. Her resolution to keep Simcoe in good company was ever the more important now, both for Papa and Robert's safety.

That night when Sally headed up to her room to retire, she noticed a small card had been slipped under the door. It was her silhouette, cut by Major André and accompanied by a note: "If you put this under the pillow strewn with leaves, mayhap you should dream of me." The dreams she had that night did include the major, but instead of Sally and him riding off into the sunset, Sally saw him and Robert dueling with swords. She woke up in a cold sweat, unsure of the outcome she would have wished for.

Simcoe sought her out after breakfast. "I wrote this for you, Miss Townsend," he said, handing her a neatly folded piece of paper.

"What is it?" she asked as he led her into the living room. He motioned for her to sit on the couch and then boldly sat beside her. "Open it."

As Sally unfolded it, she saw that it was a sketch in Simcoe's own hand of two hearts, one with the initials S.T. and the other J.G.S., spliced by an arrow. Underneath was a poem.

"Read it aloud," Simcoe commanded.

Sally began, her words stumbling over the beginning:

Fairest Maid where all are fair,
Beauty's pride and Nature's care;
To you my heart I must resign'
O choose me for your Valentine!

The poem went on to declare Simcoe's "pure, unchanging" love for Sally, comparing her eyes to lightning fire and invoking images of fields strewn with roses and lilies.

"Sally," Simcoe took the valentine and put it on the table before he placed his hand over hers. Sally balked at both the use of her proper name and the physical contact. "I am to be called away for the summer, but hope to return in the fall." Her heart swelled at the ability to drop the facade of her possessing affection for Simcoe, even if it were to only be a temporary reprieve. "If our relationship continues, and if you would permit me, I would then ask your father for your hand in marriage."

Sally gasped aloud as she put her other hand to her chest. At that moment, Major André passed by in the hall. Sally looked up to see him stop his stride and then switch his course to the living room. "What is all of this?" he asked as he walked in, glancing at Simcoe's improper proximity to Sally and then dropping his gaze to the valentine on the table.

Simcoe seemed to have taken Sally's reaction for acquiescence. He patted her hand before rising. "I have just declared my love for Miss Townsend and asked to marry her."

"And she accepted?" André gave Sally a puzzled look.

She decided to cover her confusion with a giggle. "I have not yet consented, but will promise to give it much thought these months that you will be gone."

"Deployment?" André asked Simcoe.

He nodded.

"Actually, I came to tell you that I too must leave Oyster Bay and return to the city." André said loftily, as if he had not been heading outside before he spotted the two of them.

Sally felt like a chicken caught between two foxes. Agreeing to marry Simcoe meant protection for her family, but she was not sure she could stomach the thought of being his wife. On the other hand, there was the dashing Major André, who had gone out of his way with all of those affectionate gifts. If she could manage to cast her loyalty aside and begin a relationship with André, it would only serve to anger Simcoe more. And there was the major's reputation as a hopeless flirt and that mention of Meg Coghlan, to boot. She decided to take the path of neutrality.

"I shall mourn both of your absences," she said, rising from the couch and venturing toward the hallway.

"Miss Townsend?" Simcoe had reverted back from calling her by her Christian name.

"Yes?" she asked, turning around.

"Do not forget your valentine," he said, holding it aloft.

She curtsied before walking to retrieve it. "Thank you."

André left the next day, but not before gifting Sally yet another representation of his artistic accomplishments. He had boldly placed a poem, entitled "The Frantick Lover," under her pillow. Upon discovering it, Sally quickly scanned through it, a few lines leaping off the page and into her heart.

The star of the evening now bids thee retire;
  Accurs'd be its Orb and extinguish'd its fire!
  For it shows me my rival, prepared to invade
  Those charms which at once I admired and obey'd.

My insolent rival, more proud of his right,
  Contemns the sweet office, that soul of delight.
  Less tender, he seizes thy lips as his prey,
  And all thy dear limbs the rough summons obey.

Sally clutched the missive to her chest, realizing that she was not just another of André's paramours and that his feelings, much like hers, ran very deep. The rival he referred to was undoubtedly Simcoe. If only she could convey that she did not want to obey his "rough summons," but doing so might put her family in danger of Simcoe's wrath.

CHAPTER 45

ELIZABETH

MARCH 1779

*R*obert had not returned to the store for more than a month. Elizabeth had to come up with an excuse for Robert's neglect to her saddened children, saying that he had gone away on business.

One afternoon in late March, she was surprised to see James Rivington enter the shop. "Mrs. Burgin," he called, an unmistakable urgency in his voice. "You must come now!"

"Come?" Elizabeth asked as she came out from behind the counter. "What do you mean?"

Rivington's head swiveled at a customer in the corner before he grabbed Elizabeth's arm and pulled her into the stockroom. "You are in grave danger. Higday has given your name to the British, and they are searching for you as we speak. We must fetch your children and I am to take your family to the Underhills.'"

Elizabeth's hand flew to her mouth. "How do you know this?"

"Robert contacted me. He is arranging someplace for you to

stay on Long Island. More can be explained later—we do not have much time now."

"Right." Elizabeth hurried upstairs, shouting for Abby. The two women grabbed what little clothes they could fit into a small valise before rushing back downstairs, Abby holding the hands of the bewildered older children and Elizabeth with the baby in her arms. Rivington had gotten rid of the customer and stood waiting next to the door. He shouldered the valise and explained that everyone needed to be calm and act as though nothing was amiss.

"What about our dog?" Johnny asked as Rivington opened the door and began to usher the children outside.

Rivington cast his eyes to Elizabeth.

"My husband's since before the war." She found her voice was shaky.

"I will take care of it," he said. The gruff words seemed to satisfy Johnny and he went out into the sunshine.

Elizabeth found that remaining calm was difficult once she saw all of the Redcoats in the Underhills' tavern. Rivington set the valise down next to the counter before he went to greet the British officers. Elizabeth walked to the desk, her bonnet pulled over her face. "I'd like a room, please," she told Mary, pretending as though she didn't know her.

"Certainly," Mary glanced at Rivington before glancing down at the ledger. "For you, the maid, and the children?"

"Yes." Elizabeth looked down at Catherine, who seemed stuck to her side. Johnny stood next to her, uncharacteristically holding his sister's hand. "One night only. We will be leaving very early in the morning."

Mary nodded as she handed her a key. "We only have the top room available. Shall I show you up?" She came around to fetch the valise.

"That is most kind of you," Elizabeth said.

Abby went to pick up Georgie, who had toddled toward a table of Redcoats, their mugs of ale nearly empty. "Come along, children."

Once they were safely behind the closed door of Abraham Wood-hull's former room, Mary sat the valise on the bed. "What is going on?"

"I'm not sure," Elizabeth replied. "I was of the mind that you would know more."

Mary shook her head, eying the children, who, under Abby's supervision, were wandering the small room in investigation. "Robert rushed over here to let me know that you would be arriving and that it would be best to act as though you were a regular guest."

"It was something about Higday."

"Do they know about the prisoners?"

"I don't know." Elizabeth was unaware that Mary herself knew about the mutiny on the *Jersey*. "Mary, I am afraid," she stated in a low voice.

Mary gave her a brief embrace. "Robert will take care of it." They both looked down as little Georgie pulled on his mother's skirt and announced that he was hungry.

"It's best not to let on that you are afraid," Mary said, bending down to tell the boy that she would bring them a snack. "I'd better get back downstairs. If anyone was watching, it should not take me too much time to show you up here."

Elizabeth nodded.

As soon as she left, Abby asked to know what Mary meant about the prisoners. "Are they upset with you for bringing them blankets?"

"I am not sure." Elizabeth affected a lofty air. "We will have to wait and see." She pulled a book out of her valise and then sat on the floor to read to the children.

An hour later, Elizabeth and Abby were trying in vain to get the children to nap when there was a knock on the door. Elizabeth answered it, expecting to see Mary back with refreshments. But it was Robert who strode into the room.

The children shouted, "Mr. Townsend!" and ran to embrace his legs.

"Shh," he said, bending down to greet them each by name. "I

have a present for you," he said, brandishing a small spinning top. Johnny took it from him and rotated it on the floor. Robert nodded a greeting at Abby. "Children, make sure you take turns and be sure to keep the noise down. I've got to speak with your mother."

They retreated to the farthest corner of the little room as Abby bent down to oversee the children's playing.

"What is going on?" Elizabeth was anxious and not a little upset that she had not seen Robert for weeks and now they were to meet under these circumstances.

"Near as I can tell, some time ago the British intercepted a letter from Washington intended for Ben. The general must not have had the code book available when he wrote it because he mentioned Higday by name as a person that could be of use to the ring."

"And how do the British know of me?"

"They arrested Higday. His wife, in an attempt to lessen his punishment, gave up your name as helping Higday assist the prison ships. That is all they know currently. I don't believe Higday has knowledge of the escape, but we cannot be sure. I've arranged for William to accompany you to Oyster Bay. You will stay there for a fortnight or so while I locate a more permanent residence for you, some place far away from here."

"No," Elizabeth stated resolutely. "I did not leave during the siege and I will not remove my children from their home."

"Elizabeth." Robert met her gaze. His face looked anguished, even more pale and gaunt than the last time she'd seen him. He reached up as though to touch her hair and then reconsidered, his hand falling back to his side. "I'm sorry, but to do that is to put you and the children in grave danger. You must leave the city as soon as possible. William will meet you at the wharf tomorrow to bring you to my friend Daniel Youngs' house."

"I will not depend on the pity of others," Elizabeth replied, this time a bit more weakly as she took a sidelong glance at her children.

"Youngs will be well compensated for the additional mouths to feed, and William has volunteered. The sentries at the ferry are familiar with his comings and goings, and, as he will claim you as a cousin, it should not arouse suspicion." Robert, too, cast his eyes to the group playing on the floor. "I wish I could accompany you to Oyster Bay myself, but there are stirrings amongst my contacts that lead me to believe the British might be making a large move in the future."

Elizabeth nodded. "The cause must come first." She sighed. "I will go to Oyster Bay with the understanding that this might be a storm that blows over as quickly as it came in."

Robert set his lips in a firm line. "Thank you." He let out a breath. "With that, I must be going."

Elizabeth could not help throwing herself into his arms. This time his hand entangled itself in her hair.

"Why are you crying, Mama?" Catherine asked. She had grown bored with the top and now stood next to them.

"It is all fine, little Kitty," Robert said, ruffling her curls. "You are going to take a vacation in my hometown." The smile he bestowed on her did not extend past his mouth.

Elizabeth ran her fingers under her eyes and then wiped them on her apron. "Children, come say goodbye to Mr. Townsend."

CHAPTER 46

MEG

APRIL 1779

*I*n early April, Meg and André met for an afternoon tea
and found themselves alone in the room. General Clinton
and many of his officers and hangers-on had taken advantage of
the weather and had gone quail hunting in the countryside. André
had declined, wanting to get some rest. As the maid poured their
tea, Meg asked how his new position as head of intelligence was
going.

"Well," he replied, "We managed to intercept some papers
addressed to Benjamin Tallmadge, and written by Washington
himself. We found one of the spies he mentioned. A man by the
name of George Higday."

Meg spooned sugar into her tea. Her heartbeat had sped up
when he said the word, "spies," but she was unfamiliar with anyone
named Higday.

"We had him in Bridewell prison for over a week, but he refused
to give us any more information. His wife, however, on hearing of
his arrest, gave up another name. A woman who supposedly was the

mastermind of a prison ship coup. Can you imagine? They keep such poor records aboard the ship that no one knew that so many men had disappeared."

"What was the woman's name?" Meg managed to ask, even though her throat seemed suddenly obstructed and her chest tight.

André rolled his eyes to the ceiling, trying to remember. "Bergen. Eliza Bergen." Meg refrained from correcting André as he continued, "We visited her place of residence, but it looks as though she might have fled, probably for the countryside. Clinton is offering a reward of 200 pounds if she can be apprehended. He has it in his head that she can lead us to the Culpers, though I personally don't think a woman could be involved with Washington's main ring."

Meg set her spoon down. Pushing her tea setting aside, she searched desperately for a reason to leave. She would have given anything to shed decorum and run from the room, but doing so would only invite André's inquiry, and possibly end his ability to talk so freely with her about the Culpers.

André, unaware of his companion's anxiousness, mentioned that a Loyalist acquaintance he had in Philadelphia had recently married General Arnold, the American hero of Saratoga.

"Oh?" Meg asked, pretending to be absorbed in the conversation. "What sort of acquaintance?"

André smiled his golden grin. "Not that kind. Peggy Shippen was well educated, like you and Honora. However, I wish she would have put some of that knowledge to learning rather than social climbing." He raised one eyebrow as he glanced at Meg.

"Another woman falling in love with a man of the enemy's army," Meg murmured, momentarily forgetting her plight. "Do you know if her family approved?"

"Well, they were quite strict." André took a sip of tea before delicately setting the cup in the saucer. "Peggy could not even go to the Meschianza ball because a few Quakers pleaded with her father that it was too indecent." His voice reflected the bitterness he must have felt of that declaration. "But even if they are strict Loyalists, becoming the wife of the military commander of Philadelphia has its own perks."

"Are his fortunes still secure even after that court martial?" Many British officers had derided the fact that the Continental army was accusing one of their own generals of stealing from them and the matter had been fodder for gossip at One Broadway for weeks.

"Fortunes?" André roared. "Arnold claims the army owes him that in back pay. He barely has a penny to his name." André set his teacup down. "I wonder…" He rose from the table so abruptly that his chair fell over.

"Major André?" Meg called at his retreating back, thankful for the end of their conversation, though a bit perplexed by André's sudden exit. As soon as she heard a door slam down the hallway, she left the tea table and hastened to her room. Despite Mercy's assurances, Elizabeth's husband died in part due to Meg's treason. She was determined to help her any way she could, even if it meant sacrificing her own safety.

The maid was still clearing the tea cups when Meg came back downstairs. "If anyone asks, please tell them that I've just stepped out to run an errand," Meg commanded her. The maid nodded demurely.

Once on the street, Meg realized that she had no way of getting to the other side of the city besides walking. She recalled the heady days before the occupation when she and Aaron would ride out together. *Now he's traipsing about with a married woman!* Meg thought. Her heart caught in her throat as she thought of Aaron's dark eyes. *I hope they're happy,* she thought before she turned toward Queen Street.

She was used to riding about town on horseback or in a carriage; the view from the ground was very different. Most of the beautiful trees that once shaded the avenues had been cut down for firewood last winter, and the April sun heated her bonnet and the back of her neck. Meg wrinkled her nose as the wind blew, bringing with it an overwhelming smell of decay, likely from the Sugar House and Bridewell prisons only a few blocks north. Mercy had once told her that the prisons were so crowded with Americans that there was not enough space for all of them to sleep and they had to take turns lying down. *Still,* Meg thought as she crossed Smith Street, *it must be better to be detained in a land jail than on those hulks in Wallabout Bay.* She recalled what André had said about Elizabeth. She knew Elizabeth's husband had died aboard the *Jersey* and Mercy had once mentioned that Elizabeth brought blankets and food to the prisoners. Meg did not have much more information than that, but she knew where to go to find more.

"Robert Townsend," Meg gasped as she finally made it to Hercules Mulligan's shop. She put a hand to her side. "I must speak to Townsend."

"Meg?" Hercules came from around the counter. "Look at you. You're covered in sweat," he added distastefully.

"I had to walk."

"From where? Your sanctuary with André?"

Meg straightened her posture. "Do not start with me, Hercules. You know what my husband is like."

He cast a quick look around and then said in a low voice, "Yes, but m'dear, you are now in the perfect position to resume your old work."

"No," Meg said vehemently. "I need to find Townsend."

Hercules shook his head. "He has become quite the scarce man these days. You might try over at the Underhills.' It's only a few blocks that way," he said, extending his thumb north. "Why are you so interested in finding Townsend?"

"I need to tell him something. It's extremely important." She quickly filled him in on what André had told her at tea.

Hercules nodded. "C'mon. I'll take you there."

They soon arrived at a simple brownstone and Hercules led her inside. There was only one man sitting in the tavern area. A middle-aged woman with a round face was behind the counter. "Hercules!" she exclaimed upon spying him. "What brings you here?"

"We're looking for Townsend," he said in a low voice.

Mary Underhill frowned. "I have not seen him lately." She nodded to the man in the tavern. "Perhaps my brother Abraham can help. He's known Robert since they spent some time in Culpepper County, Virginia."

Meg gasped when she realized that by Culpepper, she must have meant Culper.

Hercules raised his chin in recognition. "Not here, though."

"That's right, I do have a room available for a few hours," she said loudly. "Abraham, I cannot leave my desk right now. Can you show this kind couple up to the attic room?"

Abraham got up slowly. With his sallow complexion and untidy hair, Meg would not expect him to be in the line of work he followed. At any rate, she supposed, he was of the type that could be easily overlooked. "Abraham Woodhull," he said when they reached the attic. He bowed briefly and shut the door behind them. "I take it you have some business?"

"I was originally looking for Robert Townsend," Meg said, "but your sister said you could help. It concerns Elizabeth Burgin."

Woodhull gave an almost imperceptible nod. "Go on."

"She is in grave danger. Clinton has a price on her head!" Meg's voice rose in panic as she thought of the peril Elizabeth might be facing.

Woodhull's eyebrows knit together. "Are you aware of anything else that might be of importance?"

Meg drew in a deep breath. "André mentioned that she might be of assistance in uncovering who the Culpers are."

This finally caused a real reaction in Woodhull. His face fell as he staggered into a nearby desk chair.

"Do you know where she is?" Meg cried.

"For now, she is in a safe place, but now we must convey her out of the city as soon as possible."

"She should go to West Point," Hercules interjected.

Abraham put his chin in his hand. "The military garrison?"

"That way there will be no Loyalists to give her away," Hercules said as Meg searched her head for where she had heard those words before. She scrunched her face before her eyes widened. *Of course!* In her last letter, Mercy had mentioned that Dr. McKnight had been recently stationed at West Point to manage an inoculation clinic. "I have a friend there," she said.

Woodhull reached into the desk and pulled out a piece of paper and a vial. "I will get this to Robert as soon as I can." With that, he turned his back and began scribbling. Meg noticed that his pen must have run dry because no ink was showing up on the paper. Before she could point this out to him, Hercules pushed her out of the room.

CHAPTER 47

ELIZABETH

APRIL 1779

*T*here had been no time to pack. Someone had knocked roughly on the Youngs' door in the middle of the night. Elizabeth, awakened by the noise, went out to the hallway and listened as a gruff voice asked for her by name. She did not want to cause the Youngs any more danger and hurriedly threw on some clothes, prepared to accept her fate if the unexpected visitor was a Redcoat. But it was Caleb Brewster who stood in the doorframe. Both he and Daniel turned as she hastened downstairs.

"We must go now, tonight," Brewster said. He was, as usual, dressed all in black, but now his look was complete with a floppy black hat and mud darkening the features of his face not covered by his heavy beard.

"Just let me wake the children and Abby," Elizabeth replied.

"No," Brewster said firmly. "My instructions are to bring you only."

"I've already arranged with Caleb that they can stay here as long as necessary," Daniel told her kindly.

Elizabeth's eyes filled with tears. "I cannot leave them!"

"You can send for them as soon as the scandal dies down."

"Scandal?" Elizabeth's throat closed and she struggled to get the next words out. "Has my name appeared in the *Gazette*?"

"Not the *Gazette*," Brewster said, placing an arm on her shoulder to urge her out the door. "But pretty much every other paper in the city. One of our contacts told us Clinton offered two hundred pounds for your seizure." He nodded at Youngs, who wished Elizabeth good luck before he shut the door. The sound of the lock echoed through the outside darkness. "If I didn't like ye so much, I'd as like to turn ye in as well. It's good money, thar." The Irish brogue was back, which meant Brewster was more nervous than he was letting on.

"Where are we going?" Elizabeth asked in a loud whisper as Brewster held up the lamp to find the path.

"Eventually, West Point."

Elizabeth stumbled on a rock. "Across the Sound? In the middle of the night?"

"Aye. Luckily it's cloudy." He again took hold of her arm to lead her to the water where his whaleboat was docked. "I was in Setauket earlier today. Anna got the message straightaway and Woodhull came as soon as he heard." He steadied the boat and Elizabeth climbed in.

"Anna?"

He followed her in and grabbed the oars. "Anna Strong, Selah's wife. She hangs a black petticoat on the line along with a certain number of handkerchiefs. That's how Abraham knows which cove I'm in. There are six of them, and I dock in a different one each time. Hence why the British haven't caught me yet. Shh!" Brewster said suddenly, as if she were the one talking and not him. "Get down!" he commanded, and Elizabeth ducked as low as she could after catching sight of another boat entering the waterway a few yards down. "Damned Oyster Bay and its exposed waters. That's why I don't come this way much." He paused and Elizabeth lifted her head to see him peering down at her. "Don't ye worry, I can outrun 'em."

After several nerve-wracking minutes, Brewster told Elizabeth she could raise her head.

"Why West Point?" she whispered after she had sat up again.

"Dr. McKnight is there, not to mention that it's probably the safest place to be in America right now, besides in General Washington's own tent."

Elizabeth nodded. She was trying to keep her mind off the three sweet, innocent heads sleeping the night away in the Youngs' guest bedroom. *If anything happened to them because of me, I'd never forgive myself.* But the British could not be that cruel, could they? Elizabeth tried to banish all of the horrible rumors she'd heard of the Hessian troops murdering women and children in their beds.

A splash erupted in the quiet darkness. Brewster's oars halted above the water before he motioned for her to duck down again. This time she could hear men shouting from the other boat, followed by a noise so loud it felt like Elizabeth's teeth shook in their gums. *A gunshot!*

Brewster paused to haul his rifle up onto his lap before he somehow found the strength to increase the rhythm of his rowing and the voices soon faded. Elizabeth squeezed her eyes shut, imagining herself in the middle of a gunfight. *Home,* she thought, keeping her eyes closed. She pictured her apartment that, while spare of furnishings, was filled with love. Behind her eyelids, she saw an image of Robert instructing Johnny and Abby while Catherine curled up to read a book on Elizabeth's lap, and the baby slept in the corner. Suddenly, she felt the boat slow down. She raised her head, expecting to see a boat full of Redcoats beside them, but, instead, Elizabeth saw only mud and grass. They were ashore.

Brewster let out a wolf whistle. In a moment, a responding whistle sounded from a nearby tree.

"Bolton?" Brewster called.

"Here!" the voice was closer now. Elizabeth could discern a tall figure making his way through the undergrowth. As he approached their vicinity, Elizabeth recognized him. "Major Tallmadge?" she asked, the confusion obvious in her voice.

"Bolton's his code name," Brewster said. "In case anyone is listening."

"Are we in danger?" she asked.

"Not presently," Tallmadge said. He held out his arm and Elizabeth clutched it and climbed out. She turned to Brewster and noticed he was still sitting in the boat. He tipped his hat at her. "This is where I leave you, Mrs. Burgin." Brewster, having safely delivered his cargo, was back to his American accent.

"Thank you, Mr. Brewster."

Tallmadge stepped toward the boat. "Any reports?"

"No," Brewster replied. "But Culper Junior says something big must be going on in the city. The rank and file seem restless."

Tallmadge nodded. "Keep us informed."

Brewster touched his hat once more before he set his oars back in the water.

Elizabeth wondered who Culper was but didn't say anything as Tallmadge led her to where two horses were tied.

"I'm sorry, Mrs. Burgin," he told her wryly. "The army doesn't own a sidesaddle or pillion, so you will have to ride in a gentleman's way."

"It's fine, Major Tallmadge," she told him before she mounted. She may have grown up a city-girl, but her father had taught her to ride when she was little.

They traveled for an hour or so before stopping at an inn. Elizabeth was doubly thankful for the soft beds they provided, although the feeling of still riding a horse and the threat of nightmares made it somewhat difficult to sleep.

They set off early the next morning, traveling north along the Hudson River. Because of its proximity to New York City, with routes to almost all of the New England states, Elizabeth knew that West Point was important strategically to the Continental army. Tallmadge seemed well familiar with the area and knew where to stop to water their horses or rest. The countryside was quite pretty, with columbine and wild geraniums blooming, but Elizabeth was too worried over the fate of her children to notice much. They finally arrived at a fine mansion situated between two large hills.

"The Robinson House," Tallmadge stated before dismounting.

Elizabeth followed suit and felt the familiar ache in her legs from a long day of riding.

Dr. McKnight greeted her warmly and, after Elizabeth had some food, took her on a tour, filling her in on the history of the mansion. He'd been stationed there for a few months; Mercy had recently had a baby and was currently with her family in New Jersey until the time the baby was old enough to travel. The Robinson House, or "Beverly," as Dr. McKnight called it, was a few miles south of the military stronghold and was once a summer house belonging to Beverly Robinson, now a colonel with the British army. Like many other fine Loyalist houses, the mansion had been confiscated when the Robinson family fled for the city. "Oddly enough," McKnight told her, "Robinson is at this minute on the British-man-of-war the *Vulture*, stationed down the Hudson a little ways," He inclined his head toward the north. "An early commander of West Point, General Putnam, resided in this house, and General Washington occasionally stayed here, but now it, along with the multiple outbuildings scattered around it, houses sick and wounded officers."

"Smallpox?" Elizabeth asked as Dr. McKnight showed her to the room in which she would be staying.

"No," he replied. "I have the ones suffering with the disease isolated in the lazaretto barracks at the base. I've turned one of the huts into an inoculation room." He nodded at her. "I might reassign you there soon, since you are no longer in danger of catching it."

"I'd be happy to help." *Anything to keep her mind off of missing the children.* The room was simple, with whitewashed walls, and only a desk and chair and the bed for furniture. She went to the window, espying some of the outbuildings Dr. McKnight had mentioned. "How does it that I get my own room?"

"There aren't that many women at West Point other than the camp followers and the 'girls of the night' out of Fishkill. Since you'll be working with me, it was decided that you would get the Robinson's maid's room instead of housing in the barracks. Besides," he continued with a wink, "General Robert Howe, West Point's commander, had a soldier in his troop that was rescued from the *Jersey*."

Elizabeth had trouble getting to sleep that night. She was not used to the noises of the country—it seemed a cicada was garrisoned right outside the tiny window—and her mind kept straying to her family. Every time she closed her eyes, she saw Georgie's smile, Catherine's dimples, the way Johnny's eyes would light up when Robert... *No. Mustn't think these thoughts.* She knew that there must be laudanum stored in the medicine closet Dr. McKnight showed her earlier but she did not want to deprive a soldier in pain. She settled with counting in her head, getting to over five hundred before she finally fell into a restless sleep.

Nursing was difficult work, but the seemingly ceaseless tasks of purging chamber pots, administering laudanum, cleaning the airless rooms, and making sure the patients were adhering to Dr. McKnight's prescribed diets soothed Elizabeth. She would often fall into her bed at night so exhausted she would go right to sleep. She often dreamt of the children and Robert, waking with an aching need to be with all of them. She would then throw herself into more monotonous duties, and the pattern would repeat again.

She received only a fraction of what Dr. McKnight made as the resident surgeon, but that and the rations she received for her duties allowed her to gain a bit of dignity. Because of her situation, she was unable to send the money to Oyster Bay, but she stockpiled it in an old shoe to one day pay back Youngs for his kindness.

CHAPTER 48

MEG

*A*lthough Meg had washed her hands of military matters—the rescuing of her Elizabeth notwithstanding—it seemed like information drops were happening daily right in front of her. With General Clinton back in New York, the opulent dinners resumed at One Broadway. Clinton's mistress, Mary Baddeley, often joined them. The other officers' wives had gossiped to Meg that Mrs. Baddeley had been John Hancock's maid in Philadelphia. When Clinton confiscated the Hancock house, he confiscated the maid as well. Her complacent husband had been promoted up the ranks in the British army and was now a captain in Colonel Beverly Robinson's regiment.

The dinner included ham, duck, and pigeon as well as potatoes, other vegetables, and fresh bread. After the requisite toasts to His Majesty and General Clinton, and an ambiguous toast from the other end of the table to "the Hudson River," small talk commenced while their dinner companions—more than fifty by Meg's count—indulged in the food and drink.

"Are you all set for your trip, André?" one of the officers across from her asked.

"Indeed," André said after a sip of wine.

"Trip?" Meg asked, turning to the major.

"Ah, the lady did not know!" the man—De Lancey was his name, Meg remembered—exclaimed.

"I'll be vacationing in Oyster Bay with Colonel Simcoe for a few days and then I'll be heading north after that."

Meg nodded. She knew that he stayed before with Simcoe at the Townsend House and found it not a tad ironic that the chief intelligence officer was billeted with an enemy spy's family. The first time André returned from Oyster Bay, he seemed pensive for a few days, as if something bothered him. When Meg inquired as to his mood, he insisted that it was nothing and recovered soon after.

De Lancey shot André a winning grin. "André's got something cooking up there that could end the war in a matter of weeks."

"That new contact that you mentioned?" Another man in epaulets from down the table asked. The wine, it seemed, was functioning to loosen the officers' tongues. General Clinton, from the head of the table to André's left, listened silently, his lips in a tight line.

"Soon enough we will be referring to you as 'Sir André,'" De Lancey said.

"Is it risky, this business of yours up north?" Meg asked.

"Risky, maybe, but well worth it," André replied. Meg was of the mind that nothing in this pointless war was worth risking a life for, especially not the possibility of being knighted by a redundant King, but she affected a sympathetic shake of her head.

André's manner in the days before he left belied his nervousness. He showed up late for tea, forgetting his usual impeccable mannerisms and lifting his tea cup with shaking fingers. He and General Clinton often met behind closed doors until long into the night, candlelight showing under the door frame after everyone else had gone to sleep. Had Meg been of her former passion, she would have immediately reported such goings-on to Hercules Mulligan, but doing so, she was painfully aware, might put André in danger. Whatever his task was, she hoped that it would not result in André's capture—or worse. Although she did not relish a British victory, she realized a swift end to the war could bring a stop to this madness.

CHAPTER 49

SALLY

AUGUST 1779

"Colonel Simcoe has returned!" Phoebe exclaimed one day in August upon coming into the room.

Sally clamped shut the book she had been reading and sat up. "He is here?"

"Yes, and his first question to me was regarding your whereabouts."

She had been restless all summer. She had not heard from Major André—or Colonel Simcoe, for that matter—since they left Oyster Bay last spring. Even Susannah Youngs was unavailable for visits as she was taking care of a convalescent relative. *At least Simcoe's presence would liven up this dull summer.* Sally sighed and went downstairs without checking her appearance in the looking glass.

Simcoe had lost a great deal of weight, and his green uniform hung loosely on his now gaunt frame.

"Colonel Simcoe?" Sally inquired, pausing on the middle stair.

"Ah, Sally," he said in a weak voice. "How I have missed seeing your beautiful face. Did you worry much over my captivity?"

"Captivity?"

Simcoe frowned. "I was taken hostage by the rebels after my horse was shot out from underneath me. I've only recently been released."

Sally proceeded the rest of the way down the stairs and stood in front of him. His shoulders slumped forward and he did not meet her eyes. Some of his overconfidence had given way to defeat, giving him the ego of a normal man.

"Come," she told him. "Let's get you something to eat."

After André had left last spring, Sally pestered Simcoe with questions as to where he might be deployed for the summer. He took it as concern for his safety and would simply reply that wherever he went, he would return for her. He asked one more time for permission to speak to Papa about marriage, but Sally insisted that they should wait until the war was over.

As he now broke apart a piece of bread, hardened from the time that had passed since breakfast, he told her that the end of the war might be in the near future.

"How do you know that?" Sally inquired, but of course, Simcoe was enigmatic, only saying there had been recent developments that would result in Britain's favor. His lips turned upward. "And then we could marry."

Sally contrived a smile as inscrutable as Simcoe's own.

There was no way Sally could ever marry Simcoe. She never once believed that Britain would actually win, meaning that Simcoe would be forced to return to his native country in disgrace, and, if she were his wife, her fate would be the same. She would have to leave her beloved home for an alien country she had grown to despise. But telling Simcoe she had no interest in becoming his wife would be the final blow to his ego and most likely culminate in him lashing out in hurt and anger. So she kept up the charade, keeping him at arm's distance without ever discouraging him. She began accompanying him again to the redoubt, which had been untouched in his troop's absence. A few days after he himself returned, Simcoe informed Sally that André was expected in Oyster Bay the next day.

"Major André?" her heart sped up in the pleasure of speaking his name. While she looked forward to flirting with the handsome soldier, she also knew that his presence greatly complicated the tactics she employed to keep Simcoe clueless of her true feelings. "Why is he coming here?"

"He is traveling from Gardiner's Bay on his way north, and asked to speak with me about something."

"Does this something have to do with the end of the war you mentioned?"

Again that ambiguous smirk appeared on Simcoe's face, the one that Sally was quickly beginning to hate.

André's demeanor had also changed. Instead of being the mischievous rogue who had once hid Sally's olykoeks, he too had taken on a more serious mind. As soon as André had arrived, he greeted her loftily and then he disappeared with Simcoe into Robert's room, where they spent the entire afternoon.

Dinner that evening was a quiet, dreary affair. Mother was warm enough to Major André, and of course, Phoebe tried her best to engage him in conversation, but after the small talk ended, silence ensued. As soon as her parents left, Sally rose from the table. "Enough!" she shouted. "Why do you two insist on ignoring me?"

Phoebe shot her an incredulous look that quickly turned smug. She was evidently pleased that her sister's once adoring suitors had cast her aside to continuously discuss whatever it was that brought André to Oyster Bay in the first place.

Sally threw her hands up in dismay and began to stomp, most unladylike, out of the room.

Simcoe grabbed her arm. "I'm sorry, Miss Townsend. It's just that Major André is only here for a short time and needs my opinion on some military strategies he is thinking of employing."

She cast a dark look at Major André, who gave her a subtle wink before turning back to Simcoe. "What military strategies?"

He dropped her arm. "Oh, just some troop formations. It's all very boring and tedious."

She knew that whatever it was that was prompting their cryptic behavior, it was much more than discussing humdrum troop formations, but she was also aware that neither man would reveal their actual topic of discussion.

Simcoe continued, "Major André will be leaving the day after tomorrow and then I will have more time to spend with you."

Phoebe, obviously cognizant of the undercurrents flowing in the room, looked at Major André to get his reaction, as did Sally. André took a long sip of wine and gave Simcoe a tight smile. "But not too much time," he reminded his friend. "I will be requiring the presence of the Rangers on my mission as well."

"Will you be gone long?" Phoebe asked André.

"Hopefully not," he replied. "This should be a quick one," he said, glancing at Simcoe, who nodded.

"Well, then, we must give you a proper sendoff," Phoebe stated. "Sally, we don't have much time to prepare."

"Are you going to bestow your olykoeks upon us, then?" André looked at Sally, his eyebrows raised and a miscreant glint in his eyes.

She returned his smile. "Only if you promise not to hide them."

Phoebe rushed out with the intent to plan another fete, leaving Simcoe to shift his eyes back and forth between his intended and the major, his frown deepening.

It was not long before the men excused themselves and, once again, disappeared behind the closed door of Robert's old room. This time Sally could not help herself and paused outside to listen. She carried an extra blanket—in case anyone should catch sight of her, she could claim that she wanted to make sure Major André was comfortable. She was able to pick up a few snatches of phrases here and there, such as "'tis settled then," and "fall to the Empire." *What would fall?* Her heart fell into her satin slippers as she realized the importance of their discussion. She crept even closer, putting her ear on the door.

Simcoe's voice had grown louder with excitement. This time she distinctly heard the words "West Point," and "Hudson River." André's voice, murmuring something in agreement, sounded as though he was near the door. Sally pulled the blanket to her chest and hastened as quickly away as she could without resorting to running. She slowed to a walk as she crept up the stairs, casting a worried look down upon the empty hallway before heading to her room.

Sally knew that West Point, with its key position on the Hudson River, was the most important American military base and stored vast amounts of equipment for the army. She quickly surmised that André's mission had something to do with the fort. Sally got up to light a candle and then fetched a paper and a quill. Her intention was to dash off a quick missive to Robert about the possibility of a British attack on West Point, but then she remembered his warning to code any future information. She retrieved the slip of paper he'd left her in the bottom of her clock and then sat down, putting Robert's sheet as close to the candle as possible. On one side was a list of numbers and opposite, their meaning. The word "careful" was represented by the number 87 and "advise" by 234, and so on. On the other side was a cipher to disguise other important words that were not given a number.

She began by addressing the letter to "723," the way Robert had told her. She wrote the body of the letter haltingly, occasionally pausing to consult the sheet and add a number instead of a word. She frowned when she got to the most important part. New York was coded by 727, and Long Island was 728, but there was no number for West Point. She flipped to the cipher and then scrawled the letters that corresponded: Yiuv Rqcpv, before underlining them twice with her quill. It was all a bit disconcerting to Sally, but Robert had told her this was the customary way of conveying intelligence within his circle. When she had finished, she wrote the number "355" as instructed at the bottom of the message instead of signing her name. She had just returned everything to her clock when Phoebe entered.

"I've been looking everywhere for you," Phoebe told her pointedly. "I've decided, with Mother's permission, that we will throw Major André a going-away party."

There goes Phoebe again, planning parties when the fate of the Continental army is at stake. Sally bestowed a fake smile upon her sister. "I will go with whatever you desire."

"Just make your olykoeks again," Phoebe told her in a voice that implied that she had no other party-planning skills, which suited Sally just fine. She had to find a way to get this message to Robert, and quickly.

The house was quiet the next morning. Papa left to meet with a customer and Mother and Phoebe had gone to extend invitations to their neighbors for the party. Simcoe and André had already departed by the time Sally started baking her cakes in the kitchen.

The surety of her missive last night had begun to give way to doubt. If she indeed found a way to deliver the message to Robert, she now feared that it might have dangerous repercussions for André. While she knew her dedication was ultimately to the American objective, she had affectionate feelings for the major and the last thing she wished was to cause him harm. She wavered back and forth, reminding herself that André might not come to personal injury, but if West Point fell, that could result in the swift end of the war that Simcoe had hinted at.

By the time the olykoeks were cooling on the table, Sally had once again convinced herself to ride out to the Youngs' place to secure the message to Robert. She went upstairs to retrieve her letter and was about to start down again when she thought she heard the front door open. She maneuvered out of sight of the doorway and tucked the note into her bodice. She peered downstairs, expecting to hear the chatter of her mother and Phoebe, or even the masculine voices of Simcoe and André, but there was only silence. The man she spied from her view at the top of the stairs was dressed in dirty homespun and wore a hat that covered most of his face. Sally angled her head and edged down the stairs, watching as the man skulked into the parlor. She moved yet another step down when she realized she could see the man's reflection in the parlor mirror. He walked toward the built-in cabinet where André had once hidden her olykoeks. The thought occurred to Sally that he too was going to hide her baking endeavor, as if André had hired a stranger to commit this newest prank. Instead, the man took a slim piece of paper out from the pocket of his waistcoat and, opening the bottom doors of the cabinet, stashed it inside. He made to close the cabinet, but then thought better of it and shoved the paper deeper inside the cupboard before shutting the doors and replacing the latch. Sally hoisted herself back onto the landing as the man looked around the room again, obviously preparing to leave. She stayed out of sight until she heard the front door click shut.

She sat at the top of the stairs for a minute, breathing heavily to catch up for the moments she'd held her breath. *What was that stranger doing in her house?* He was not a soldier, or if he was, he'd dressed as a commoner for this occasion. Sally made up her mind to retrieve the letter under the guise that she needed a charger plate for this afternoon's tea. She crept downstairs and into the parlor in the same manner as the man who had just left. She kept her eyes on the front door as she moved the latch and opened the cupboard before groping around its insides. Half-expecting nothing to be there, indicating that she had been imagining the whole thing, her fingers finally closed upon the paper. She pulled it out, still breathing hard. The envelope was addressed to "John Anderson," and sealed with wax. With a sigh, Sally replaced it, knowing that she could not undo the seal without arousing the suspicion of the intended recipient. She hazarded a guess that it was meant for the major—John Anderson must be a code name for John André.

Her suspicions were confirmed when, soon after André returned, her olykoeks disappeared once again. André entered the kitchen directly after her, waiting for her reaction. She stood before the empty plate and put her hands on her hips as André laughed. Sally pretended to storm out and marched straight to the parlor cupboard. She pulled open the doors with shaking hands. While the olykoeks were in there, the envelope was not. André followed her, and she masked her surprise at the quick disappearance of the letter. As Simcoe was still occupied at the redoubt, André was obviously the one who had retrieved the missive.

She excused herself, saying that she needed to change out of her apron. She was about to start upstairs when André called out, "Sally?"

She turned to face him. His brown eyes looked sorrowful. "Are you truly planning on marrying Simcoe once the war is over?"

She dropped her gaze to her hands, which were folded over the soiled apron in front of her. She was not sure how to answer. Was he asking for Simcoe's benefit or did he have a different motive? If she answered truthfully: that she did not want to marry Simcoe, it might open the door for André to ask himself. But then again, the same dilemma of her moving to England would confront her, notwithstanding that spending her life with André was a much more inviting prospect. She would never willingly leave her family or her country but to tell him the truth would reveal the patriotism that ran through her veins. "My heart does not know what it wants," she called out before rushing upstairs.

She was absolutely certain now that, in trying to save West Point, she was endangering André and his mission. But Sally shut out whatever feelings she might have for the handsome soldier as she added a postscript with the name "John Anderson,"—"Dqbp Ephiluqp" written with the cipher—and the mysterious circumstances of the letter to the bottom of her message. She quickly scrawled a separate note to her brother, asking him to procure some Bohea, Major André's favorite tea, as soon as possible as he would be leaving Oyster Bay shortly. She also wrote that she was enclosing the packet of paper he had requested. It made no sense for Sally to be sending her brother stationary since his store sold the exact same brand, but this was how Robert instructed her to convey her intelligence should she ever find the need. She dug the packet out of her hope chest and carefully opened it. Robert told her to put the paper after the 21st sheet, in honor of her own birthday in May. She counted the pages and then tucked in the coded message before resealing the packet as best she could. She placed the innocuous note regarding the tea on top and then wrapped the entire package in brown parcel paper, also supplied by Robert.

Simcoe had still not reappeared when Sally headed back downstairs. She went out to the stable and saddled Gem by herself, mercifully not encountering André again. She rode Gem to the Youngs as Robert had instructed. Sally did not fully understand how Daniel Youngs, the Loyalist militia captain, factored into Robert's affairs, but she trusted her brother implicitly.

There were a few militiamen roaming about the Youngs' farm, as well as three small children playing with chickens in the side yard. Although Sally had never seen them before, the little girl reminded her of someone, but she could not place who it was. A woman in a loosely laced stomacher watched them with a forlorn look on her face.

"Sally!" She turned to see Daniel walking out from the house.

Sally dismounted and took the package from Gem's saddlebag. "I have a rather urgent message for Robert," she stammered, proffering the bundle to Daniel.

"What is it?"

"Oh, a request for tea for Major André. He is quitting Oyster Bay very soon."

"Ah," Daniel replied, turning the parcel over in his hands. "That sounds quite important." He motioned for one of the Loyalist soldiers and Sally's face heated up. She was sure she was caught, but then Daniel handed him her package and told him to rush it to Robert straightaway. "We would not want Major André without his tea, would we?" he asked, winking at Sally.

As the man moved out, Daniel tied Gem to a tree and offered Sally some lemonade. "Are you sure?" Sally asked. "Susannah mentioned that you had a sick relative."

"Oh," Daniel said, glancing at the young woman near the chicken coop. "She is not contagious, so I would not worry too much."

After a brief interlude with Susannah, in which Sally invited her to the party, and Susannah asked a few questions about the impending departures of André and Simcoe, Sally headed back home.

The major was sitting on the steps of the back porch, and Sally's heart caught yet again in her throat. André seemed out of sorts as he fanned himself with a piece of paper. He stood as she approached. "I've been looking for you. Where have you been?"

She readjusted her bonnet, pulling it over her heated face. "We are out of Bohea," she told him as smoothly as she could. "I wanted to make sure we had a supply for your party, and requested Robert to send us some."

His smile didn't reach his eyes and Sally felt the familiar hammering in her chest. *Did he know what she had actually been up to?*

"I'm sorry to tell you this, Sally, but I have to leave for my appointment as soon as possible."

"Now? But what about your party?"

He hesitated before saying, "We will have another when I get back." He handed her the paper he'd been fanning himself with. "One last gift for my beautiful host."

As Sally took the paper, Simcoe rode up. "Ready, Major André?" he asked. André nodded and then headed for the stables. Sally did not meet Simcoe's eyes as she strode into the house.

When she got to her room, she unfolded the paper, wondering if it had anything to do with the letter in the cabinet. But there was no seal and no address on the front. It was another poem, written in André's handwriting.

If at the close of war and strife
My destiny once more
Should in the varied paths of life
Conduct me to this shore;

Should British banners guard the land,
And factions be restrained,

And Clivedon's mansion peaceful stand,
No more with blood be stained,

Say! Wilt thou then receive again,
And welcome to thy sight,
The youth who bids with stifled pain
His sad farewell tonight?

Sally refolded it and tucked it into her hope chest, praying that she would indeed be able to welcome Major André into her sight, but only after an American victory.

CHAPTER 50

ELIZABETH

AUGUST 1779

In mid-August, Elizabeth was informed that General Benedict Arnold would be taking over command at West Point. As he would soon be joined by his wife—the former debutante of Philadelphia, Peggy Shippen—and his young son, the hospital was relocated to the fort. Elizabeth's temporary quarters were moved to one of the outbuildings on the grounds of Beverly, which suited her fine, as she had heard that Mrs. Arnold could sometimes be difficult to get along with. Dr. McKnight told her that he would send for her when the nurses' huts were completed.

Now without a job, Elizabeth spent her days wandering the countryside around Beverly. A beautiful cliff was located nearby, and, after scaling the rocks, she could observe the military garrisons and barracks of West Point. The first time Elizabeth had seen the fort, there were men—appearing to her vantage point as dots in colorful uniforms—constantly marching, as if they were ants swarming a hill. Now that General Arnold had taken command, the bevy of soldiers had scattered amongst the woods near the strong-hold, presumably cutting firewood or foraging for horse fodder.

One afternoon soon after Elizabeth had relocated to the cabin, she was summoned by a sentinel at her door. "Major Tallmadge is here to see you. He is awaiting your presence in the apple orchard."

Elizabeth nodded and rushed outside.

Tallmadge was in full uniform, his horse tied to a nearby tree and munching on forage from the forest floor. Upon seeing Elizabeth approach, he removed his feather-topped helmet and affected a polite smile. "Mrs. Burgin, I bring a message for your eyes only."

Elizabeth took the sealed letter. "Who is it from?"

"Your maid, Abigail."

Elizabeth's heart jumped into her throat. "Is something wrong with my children?"

"I do not believe it is your children that are of concern."

Puzzled, Elizabeth frowned, but just then both of them spotted a heavyset man walking out of the great house, supported by an ivory topped cane.

"General Arnold." Tallmadge saluted.

Elizabeth curtsied obligingly before tilting her head to study the military hero. He was a large man and she thought that his cane would have been necessary even before he was shot in the leg, as that barrel chest seemed too broad for his tiny legs to sustain.

"Major Tallmadge," he returned in a gruff voice. "I need to speak with you briefly." He stopped short a few paces of Elizabeth, who took the hint and found a shaded spot in the trees, ostensibly to read her letter. Tallmadge walked forward to converse with the general. Whatever it was they were discussing displeased Tallmadge, Elizabeth noted, as she saw the major repeatedly shake his head. Finally he said in a loud voice, "I will not inform any person on earth of their names," before stalking toward Elizabeth. Arnold watched him, but did not say anything else. After a moment of contemplation, he clumped back to the house.

"I never trusted that man," Tallmadge stated. "And you should not either, Mrs. Burgin. Do not ever tell him of the *Jersey*. He claimed that as commander of West Point, he should be informed of my contacts' names."

Elizabeth knitted her brow. "Why would he need to know their names?"

"He doesn't," Tallmadge said, moving to untie his horse. As he led his horse away, Elizabeth unsealed the envelope, pleased that Abby could write a letter on her own. Her pleasure quickly turned to shock as she read the first sentence: "Missus, I regret to inform you that I am of a womanly way." The note went on to say that the child was William Townsend's, although he claimed that it wasn't. *I always knew there was something foul hidden behind that beautiful face,* Elizabeth thought to herself. However, Abby went on to write, Robert had somehow found out about his brother's indiscretion and promised that he would help her and the unborn child in any way that he could. At the bottom, Abby went on to assure her that the children would be fine, and that Robert wanted her to know he was working out a way to reunite Elizabeth with her family.

Elizabeth sat the letter in her lap, reflecting over its contents. She was disappointed in Abby for sure, but knew that the sins of pleasure were often hard to ignore, especially for someone like Abby, who had a harlot's blood in her. Perhaps Robert could persuade his brother to do the honorable thing and marry his mistress. At any rate, her hope of seeing her children, Abby now notwithstanding, had been renewed as she had complete trust in Robert.

CHAPTER 51

ELIZABETH

SEPTEMBER 1779

*T*he inhabitants of Beverly were in an uproar at the end of September. Servants rushed by Elizabeth in a hurry, and supplies arrived by the wagonful. The kitchen chimney seemed to smoke all day and night. It couldn't be in preparation for the arrival of General Arnold's family, as they had been living there for a month already, though Elizabeth only occasionally caught a glimpse of the beautiful Mrs. Arnold and her infant son.

"What is the cause for your haste?" Elizabeth asked a serving wench as she scurried by her with a bucket of water.

"The general arrives this morning!" she shouted as she tossed the contents of the bucket at the base of an apple tree.

"General Arnold?" This was puzzling as Elizabeth knew Arnold left Beverly every morning, traveling in his barge upriver to the fort, and then returned the same way every evening.

"No," the girl gave Elizabeth a curious look. "General Washington himself. He is to break his fast with General Arnold and his family."

"Oh!" Elizabeth put a hand to her mouth.

The girl tossed her a wry smile over her shoulder as she headed back inside. "And now you know the reason for my rush."

Elizabeth withdrew back to her little cottage, pulling up a chair to the window. She desired a glimpse of the great man, but the heat of the morning made sitting outside uncomfortable. After half an hour of waiting, Elizabeth stood and moved the curtain back when she saw horses approach. Puzzled, she watched two men dismount in front of the house, neither of them the famous general. She reasoned that the arrival of the Commander-in-Chief would require guards by the tenfold, not two men. She recognized one of them from the papers as the general's aide, Alexander Hamilton, but was unsure of the identity of the other. They tied their horses to posts and then went into the great house. Not long after, another man with the urgent speed of an express arrived. He clumsily tied his horse next to the others and then, after presumably delivering his message, the express galloped away as quickly as he came.

Another half an hour ticked by. Elizabeth grabbed her copy of *Common Sense* and began to read. Not too much more time passed before she heard a commotion, but this time it was coming from the back of Beverly. She hastened to the bedroom window where she caught sight of General Arnold exiting the house through the parlor. He shouted something to Hamilton—who had come outside to the little portico—before mounting his horse and riding away. Not a minute later, Elizabeth heard the thunderous sound of many horses. She ran outside to see Washington's concierge riding up from the opposite direction in which Arnold had disappeared. Elizabeth watched as Colonel Hamilton approached Washington.

This was all rather unexpected, Elizabeth thought to herself. *Why did General Arnold gallop off like that if he was awaiting his commander?* It must have had to do with the express—maybe West Point was in danger? But if so, then General Washington must not have thought much about it because he and his entourage of a dozen men—including one in a French uniform that could only be the Marquis de Lafayette—disappeared into Beverly. Again the servants began going in and out of the house, and Elizabeth figured the breakfast was taking place—without General Arnold.

Yet another express arrived. *Goodness,* Elizabeth thought, *Beverly is quite the busy place!* This express did not soon reappear, and Elizabeth settled back down with her book, hoping to get another glimpse of the heroes of the Continental army before they left.

A knock sounded on Elizabeth's door in mid-afternoon. Hastening to open it, she was puzzled to see Dr. McKnight there. "Hurry, Mrs. Burgin," he told her. "Mrs. Arnold is in a state of advanced fright and I need a woman's help."

Elizabeth joined him outside, shutting the door behind her. Dr. McKnight led the way to the main house and then up the stairs to the master bedroom. Startled, Elizabeth took in the scene. Mrs. Arnold lay on the fine bed in a flimsy shift. Although she had been rumored to be one of the most beautiful women in America, her hair was currently in disarray and her eyes were held wide, giving her an unblinking, wild look. The fireplace was lit, and the over furnished room felt hot and stuffy. Colonel Hamilton, standing next to the bed, cast a bewildered look at Dr. McKnight. "She keeps repeating that I've been ordered to kill her child."

Dr. McKnight rushed to the bed. "No one is going to hurt Neddy, Mrs. Arnold. General Arnold will soon be returning from West Point and everything will be back to normal."

This seemed to soothe Mrs. Arnold. She closed her eyes and began to breathe heavily, as though she had fallen asleep.

"Actually, Doctor…" Hamilton tilted his head at Mrs. Arnold and then gestured for him to come near the fireplace. Elizabeth followed, feeling sweat pinprick her face.

Hamilton threw out his hands. "General Arnold has gone over to the British."

"What?" Dr. McKnight's mouth dropped open in surprise as Elizabeth put her hand over her own gaping jaw.

"He has betrayed General Washington and our country," Hamilton said mournfully before taking a deep breath. "Apparently a British spy named John Anderson was caught in the neutral territory of the lower Hudson carrying sketches and notes of West Point's fortifications—in Arnold's handwriting!"

"Dear God," Dr. McKnight said. He pinched his lips between his fingers, as if to forcibly keep them closed, and furrowed his eyebrows.

Elizabeth was too stunned to speak. General Arnold had been a well-respected leader of the Continental army and he had nearly given up West Point. His betrayal could have ended the war and guaranteed a British victory. Elizabeth said a silent prayer of thanks that West Point was still in American hands.

The doctor removed his hand to ask, "Where is Arnold now?"

Hamilton shook his head. "We were eating breakfast this morning, waiting for Washington's arrival, when an express came with a message. Arnold read it and then ran upstairs before he quitted the house, saying that something at the fort required his immediate attention. He left both his wife and child here to deal with his treachery. No wonder she has been behaving so peculiar," he added, glancing at the form on the bed.

At this, Mrs. Arnold opened her eyes and commenced shouting "Benedict, Benedict!" over and over.

The three of them rushed back to her bedside. Elizabeth's hands were shaking—she'd never seen anyone in such a state of shock. She supposed Mrs. Arnold's behavior was well founded, considering her husband had betrayed his family as well as his country, but all the same, the ear-piercing screams were beginning to strain Elizabeth's ears. She found a washcloth and wet it in a basin of water before applying it to Mrs. Arnold's forehead. Again Mrs. Arnold fell into a calm which only lasted a few seconds before she sat up in bed, causing the washcloth to fall into her lap, and pointed to the ceiling. "General Arnold is up there with hot irons on his head!"

"He will someday be in hell for his crimes, but we are not that fortunate yet," Colonel Hamilton whispered under his breath.

As Mrs. Arnold's head fell back into the pillow, Elizabeth replaced the cloth. Mrs. Arnold touched it. "And I too have hot irons on my head!" she shrieked. "Only General Washington could rid me of this torture." She reached out to grasp Elizabeth's arm, her nails cutting into Elizabeth's skin. "I must see General Washington at once!"

Dr. McKnight and Colonel Hamilton exchanged a glance.

"General Washington!" Mrs. Arnold shouted.

Hamilton nodded. "I will fetch him. Maybe he can bring an end to this madness."

But when the good general arrived in the room, Mrs. Arnold insisted that it was the Commander-in-Chief himself who had the intent to kill her child.

"Mrs. Arnold," The general began as Elizabeth balked at the sight of the tall, graceful man bent over the frantic woman with the tear-stained face. "General Arnold has escaped. Have you any knowledge as to his destination?"

She pointed to the ceiling.

General Washington turned to Hamilton. "He fled to his barge, and then presumably to the *Vulture*, and where he will go from there, we are not sure."

"What shall we do about her?" Hamilton asked, nodding at Mrs. Arnold.

"We will send her back to her family." General Washington rose to his full height. Turning to Elizabeth, he continued, "Mrs. Burgin, will you accompany her to Philadelphia?"

Elizabeth could only nod her assent. She was amazed that the general knew her name, but, then, she quickly surmised, he was the head of the entire Continental army.

"I thank you for your duties to our prisoners," the general continued. "I know Mr. Culper Junior was working on a more permanent spot for you in order for your children to join you. He has found a home by the way of a Mr. Thomas Franklin, our commissary of prisons in Philadelphia. We will secure a safe route for you and Mrs. Arnold."

Elizabeth curtsied, keeping the multitude of questions that sprang into her head, including the identity of this Culper Junior to herself. "Thank you, your Excellency."

Mrs. Arnold commenced screaming again, and Dr. McKnight

rushed to her side. "Mrs. Arnold, take a sip of this." He slipped the contents from a small vial into her water before handing it to her. She drank deeply, water dribbling down her chin, before dropping the glass on the floor. It shattered and Mrs. Arnold began shrieking that her child was dead.

"I gave her some laudanum," Dr. McKnight said, his calm voice a welcome contrast to Mrs. Arnold's hysterics. "It should take effect soon."

"I will leave you to it, then," General Washington said, moving to the door in a few long strides. "Again, Mrs. Burgin, thank you. Please let me know if you ever need assistance." He nodded at Hamilton. "Now if you will excuse us, Colonel Hamilton and I must locate General Arnold and deal with this John Anderson character."

Beverly was once again a flurry of activity the day following Arnold's defection. Elizabeth was aware that Colonel Hamilton thoroughly investigated all of the servants, including Major Franks, General Arnold's former aide-de-camp. Hamilton must have satisfied himself that Franks was innocent of helping General Arnold commit his crimes because he asked him to escort Mrs. Arnold, Elizabeth, and a few other servants to Philadelphia.

Franks cautioned Elizabeth before they left that it would be difficult to find lodging along the way. Most of America had become aware of Arnold's flight, and despised him for it—the Whigs for nearly betraying the greatest American fort and the Loyalists for the plight of John Anderson, revealed to be John André himself, the brilliant adjutant to General Clinton. He was now being held prisoner by the Continental army.

The carriage ride was deathly quiet, save for the whimpering of the baby in Mrs. Arnold's arms. No one had anything to say for fear Mrs. Arnold would become hysterical again. Elizabeth stared out the window at the countryside, knowing that each step of the horse brought her further away from New York and her children. Despite the crowded carriage, Elizabeth felt lonely, her heart as heavy as lead.

They stopped at dusk in Paramus, New Jersey to stay at Hermitage House, a large brick farmhouse owned by friends of the Shippen family. Elizabeth, her legs stiff from the journey, assisted the servants in getting Mrs. Arnold out of the carriage. As a maid carried the baby inside, Franks whispered to Elizabeth that the woman of the house, a Mrs. Theodosia Prevost, was married to a colonel in the British army currently stationed in Georgia, but frequently entertained American officers.

A handsome man in civilian clothes came out of the house and then wrapped his arm around Mrs. Arnold's shoulder. He guided her toward the door as she, nearly collapsing in his arms, said, "Aaron, it's horrible, so horrible."

"I know, Peggy," he replied.

Franks caught Elizabeth watching them walk inside. "That's Mr. Aaron Burr," he said. "Formerly Major Burr, but he quit army life to become a lawyer. He is often a houseguest of Mrs. Prevost."

"I see," Elizabeth said, quickly grasping his meaning.

From the interior of The Hermitage, Mrs. Arnold's shrieking began again, so loud that it seemed as if she were outside.

"Here we go again," Franks said with a sigh.

Elizabeth pulled out the vial of laudanum that Dr. McKnight had slipped into her bag before she left.

Franks nodded approvingly. "Anything that will allow the household to get some sleep. We are all exhausted."

When Elizabeth and Major Franks entered the house, they could see that the table had been set for dinner. Mrs. Arnold was standing next to her place setting, her hands on her face, claiming that her food had been poisoned.

A woman who looked to be a few years older than Elizabeth, approached her. "I don't know what she's talking about. Aaron and I have both known Peggy since she was a girl. I've never seen her like this."

"But it is somewhat understandable," Aaron Burr appeared next to the woman Elizabeth inferred must be her hostess, Mrs. Prevost. "Given the circumstances."

Mrs. Prevost extended her hand toward the table, and Burr went to the head. Franks lifted his eyebrows at Elizabeth before grabbing Mrs. Arnold's goblet and bringing it to the side table. Elizabeth followed. Franks filled the glass halfway with wine, and then Elizabeth retrieved the vial from her bag and added a few drops. Franks put the goblet back at Peggy's plate and poured the rest of the wine into the glasses.

"Please sit," Mrs. Prevost said to her guests. "We are pleased that you are here."

Burr lifted his glass for a toast, but then seemed at a loss for words. Normally Whigs drank to George Washington's health while Loyalists exhorted the protection of His Royal Majesty. Due to the mixed company, Aaron Burr decided to go a safer route. "To Mrs. Prevost."

"Here, here," the other people, including Mrs. Arnold, agreed. One by one, each of them toasted another person at the table. Mrs. Arnold drank liberally while Elizabeth took tiny sips. She would have given anything to be back in New York amongst her friends and family, but here she was, in a different state, with this incongruous and awkward crowd.

A plate of duck was brought out. Elizabeth barely touched her food while Major Franks and Mrs. Arnold ate heartily. Burr and Mrs. Prevost exchanged frequent glances across the table. British husband notwithstanding, their love was clear to Elizabeth, and she had to stop herself from thinking about Robert.

In the middle of the next course, Mrs. Arnold held up her glass. "To John André," she said. The other people at the table gazed at each other with wide eyes. Burr was the first to return the gesture. "Here," he said.

"Here," the rest of the company followed suit. No one quite knew what would become of the man who had been caught as a spy behind enemy lines.

"I knew," Mrs. Arnold said quietly. All heads swiveled toward her. She set down her wine before she continued, "I was the one who encouraged Benedict to defect." She gave a little laugh. "After all, John André and I were acquainted with each other. And you," here she pointed to Franks, "treated my poor Benedict so badly."

She turned to her friend, Mrs. Prevost. "He was owed so much by the Continental army, and then they had the audacity to court-martial him and accuse him of stealing money." Although she singled out Franks again, Elizabeth caught on that Mrs. Arnold meant the entire army. "Of course he sold off supplies. He needed to compensate for the money Congress owed him. You know he paid his soldiers that fought with him in Quebec with his own inheritance." She took another sip. "He's a good man, my Benedict."

Franks obviously thought she had gone too far. "Mrs. Arnold," he said.

"Major Franks. He's a good man too," Mrs. Arnold turned to Burr. "He didn't have anything to do with Benedict changing sides. I'm the one who told him to."

"Peggy—" Mrs. Prevost started, but Mrs. Arnold waved her hand. "I'm tired of it, Theodosia. I'm tired of the deception. My throat hurts from screaming, but I had to do it, to give time for Benny to get away."

"Enough, Peggy," Burr said, rising from his chair. "We are all exhausted and I think you need to retire for the night."

"I am not finished, Aaron," Mrs. Arnold said. She had begun to sway from side to side.

Burr exchanged a brief glance with Mrs. Prevost before marching over to Mrs. Arnold. "Let's get you to your room."

"No." Mrs. Arnold picked up her fork and knife, but Burr pulled them from her hands and set them down. He grabbed her shoulders and tried to lift her to her feet, but when that did not work, he commanded Franks to get on the other side of her. Together the two men managed to get Mrs. Arnold upstairs before she revealed any more secrets.

"I am sorry for that, Mrs. Burgin," Mrs. Prevost said casually. "Peggy has always had a flair for theatrics." She took a drink of wine before continuing, "Did you know that Peggy's uncle, Dr. Shippen, raised Aaron and his sister after their parents died?"

"I did not." Elizabeth took a bite of meat, going along with Mrs. Prevost's charade that everything was perfectly normal, and that

Mrs. Arnold did not just admit to a table of people that she played a part in General Arnold's betrayal.

When Burr and Franks returned, they also resumed eating. Finally Burr spoke up. "As I said, we are all exhausted from the events of the last few days. Evidently Mrs. Arnold does not know what she speaks. If anyone was aware of what she has told us, it would make her life even more difficult than what she is about to face."

The rest of the table nodded in unison. Burr's meaning was clear: tell no one what they heard that night. Elizabeth knew he spoke the truth about her life becoming more burdensome and she did not envy the woman. Mrs. Arnold was practically a widow now, with a small baby on her hands. But instead of dying a hero's death, Mrs. Arnold's husband had become a traitor, hated on both sides. Whether or not Mrs. Arnold was a willing accomplice, she would have enough to deal with as it was. Elizabeth had her own worries and did not feel the need to make another person's life harder.

CHAPTER 52

SALLY

SEPTEMBER 1779

The party in André's honor was rescheduled and changed by Phoebe into a going-away feast for Simcoe. It was clear that something was afoot as Simcoe spent every waking hour drilling his troops, preparing them for the mysterious mission.

Sally fully suspected that he would be relocating to West Point. She had no idea whether Robert had received her message. She encountered quite a few sleepless nights, alternating worry over her letter arriving in time with her concern for Major André on his journey. Perhaps her information would indeed lead to an American victory. André would be a disgraced British soldier, but surely Robert, or even Papa, could find him work. In time, people would forget André's former occupation and he and Sally could marry… she knew it was all just wishful thinking, but those happy thoughts allowed her to finally drift into a blissful sleep.

Simcoe had been acting edgy all week, constantly sending his men off with messages to and from New York City. Each time they returned carrying a small paper which Simcoe would unfold, his frown deepening as he read it.

The family was interrupted at dinner by one of these expresses a few days after André's departure. The messenger walked in through the back door without bothering to knock and handed Simcoe a sealed letter. Simcoe opened it and scanned it quickly before rising. "I must leave immediately," he told Papa. Sally thought she detected panic in his usually measured voice.

"But the party…" Phoebe protested. It was supposed to take place the next day.

Simcoe had already left the kitchen and did not return to say goodbye. After they heard the front door slam, Sally and Phoebe hastened to Robert's old room. Simcoe's books still stood on the bookshelf, but the wardrobe door had been flung open, exposing an empty interior. The sisters exchanged a bewildered look, wondering what could have been in the note that caused Simcoe to behave so oddly.

Phoebe decided to proceed with the celebration as planned, changing the theme to "An Autumn Harvest." The day of the party dawned bright and clear and Phoebe had Caesar relocate the tables of food to the garden outside, on the other side of the house from the barren field that had once been Papa's apple orchard. Simcoe had informed the family at breakfast a few days ago that he had paid for new saplings and he would have his men plant them when they returned. Both Mother and Papa seemed pleased, but Sally could only nod her thanks, thinking that he would not have had to go through the trouble to plant new trees had he not cut them down in the first place.

At midday, the guests began arriving: the Coles, the Greens, the Buchanans, and the Youngs. Daniel approached Sally and told her that her package had been delivered to Robert as requested. She nodded and thanked him again.

They had just sat down to eat when one of Youngs' Loyalist militiamen rode up. Daniel rose and walked over to him. Sally watched as Daniel's face fell after the soldier spoke. As an afterthought, the soldier pulled something out of his saddlebag and handed it to him.

Daniel approached the table. "Attention everyone, attention." The guests paused midway through conversation to turn their eyes on Daniel. "I have just been informed that General Arnold has defected to the British." A few cheers from the Loyalist guests went up and Sally had to stop herself from glaring at them.

"However, John André has been captured by the Americans and is undergoing a trial as we speak."

"Captured?" This time Sally had no control over her emotions. "Is he going to be released soon?"

Papa looked forlornly at Daniel. "He was behind American lines?"

Daniel nodded.

Papa said, practically to himself, "He will suffer Nathan Hale's fate, then."

"No!" Sally stood up from the table. "He can't. They cannot hang a man as fine as André."

"That is up for General Washington to decide," Papa told Sally before she ran into the house.

Sally trudged upstairs to her room, feeling as though her heart might break. The capture of André had been her fault and she was not sure she would ever be able to forgive herself for it. Sally had never been in love before, but she was quite sure she had loved John André, and now she would be the one to send him to the gallows.

As Sally's storm of tears subsided into sobs, she heard the door creep open. She sat up in bed and looked over to see Papa standing in the threshold. "I'm sorry, Sally," he said, setting something on her dresser before he walked over to the side of the bed with the help of his cane. "I know you cared a great deal for Major André. I think we all did."

Sally's tears began fresh again. Papa had no idea the depth of her feelings, let alone what she had done.

He held her until her tears ebbed once more, patting her before saying he needed to return to the few guests that remained. "As you can imagine, the party has taken quite a turn after the announcement was made." He paused at her dresser. "I almost forgot. This was a package that Daniel's messenger brought for you." He set it on the bed before he left.

Sally peered at the package. Her name and address were printed neatly on top, in Robert's handwriting. A sense of dread built in her chest as she undid the brown paper. It was exactly what she thought it was: a container of Bohea tea. Another tear slipped down Sally's cheek as she realized that André would never drink the tea she procured for him.

CHAPTER 53

MEG

OCTOBER 1779

*A*t One Broadway, Meg anxiously awaited the fate of her supposed paramour. The myriad of officers that always came and went was at an even greater number now, but a few of them took pity on her and filled her in on the news as it came. André had been taken prisoner and was now in Tappan, New York, under the guard of Benjamin Tallmadge, a fair man by all reports. One morning Colonel De Lancey marched into the mansion, a deep frown on his face.

"Guilty," was all he said when he passed by Meg.

Clinton had appealed for a prisoner exchange, but the only man Washington wanted in his place was Arnold. "Of course I cannot hand over that duplicitous traitor," Clinton shouted so loud that all of Broadway could have heard him. "What would it say to the other duplicitous traitors thinking about betraying their supposed country in our favor?"

In the end, nothing could avail André and he was hanged as a spy in the beginning of October. One of his last acts was to pen a letter to his commander, which General Clinton graciously let Meg read. She took comfort in the words he wrote before he mentioned his mother and sisters:

I am perfectly and tranquil in mind and prepared for any Fate to which an honest Zeal for my King's Service may have devoted me.

He was as noble and faithful to his King at the throes of death as he was in the crux of life.

The man who brought the letter to Clinton witnessed his death and filled the sorrowful guests in on André's last moments at dinner that night. "He was brave to the last moment," the officer said. "The only time I saw him falter was when he saw the gallows. He had begged Washington to be shot as an officer, but the villainous general insisted that he hang as a spy."

The rest of the table murmured their agreement as to the man's opinion on Washington.

"André's last words were, 'I pray you to bear me witness that I meet my fate like a brave man.'"

"Enough!" General Clinton roared from the head of the table, setting his wineglass down with such force that much of it spilled onto the white tablecloth. Meg was astonished to see the great general put his face in his hands. "Excuse me," he said, getting up from the table and heading out of the room.

Meg decided then and there that she'd also had enough. The only tie she had to the British army had been Major André. And now he was gone. She spent the rest of the night packing her bags, refusing the aid of a servant. The next day she arranged for transport back to the Queen Street townhouse. Nothing remained for her at One Broadway, and the constant reminders of André, the closest friend she'd ever had, wreaked havoc on her fragile heart. Even being under the jurisdiction of her barbarian husband would be more welcome than the endless mourning over André.

CHAPTER 54

SALLY

OCTOBER 1779

Simcoe returned to Oyster Bay only long enough to arrange for the transport of his things. With his puffy eyes and somber demeanor, it was obvious that he too was heartbroken over the loss of André. To Sally's relief, he made no more inquiries for her hand in marriage. After the Rangers quit Long Island, Sally never saw John Graves Simcoe again.

Robert came home to Oyster Bay after the news of Arnold's defection had reached New York City. Sally waited until after dinner, when it was just her and him by the fireplace, to query why he came back.

Robert said simply, "We do not know what Arnold knew."

"Are you in danger?"

"I'm not sure. Ben assured me that Arnold knew nothing about the ring, but at the same time, Hercules Mulligan was arrested."

Sally's grip on the chair tightened.

"Don't worry," Robert told her with a wry smile. "Mulligan's been arrested before and somehow always manages to get released."

His smile faded as he continued, "I just could not face seeing that traitor Benedict Arnold walking around Manhattan in a British uniform."

She wanted to inquire more about André, but wasn't sure how to approach it. Instead she asked about Elizabeth.

Robert's face fell. "She's headed to Philadelphia now."

"You must go to her, Robert."

"I can't. The war is not over yet, and my presence might put her in further danger."

"I'm sorry." Sally knew what it was like to not be able to be with the one you loved most in the world.

Robert turned to her. "You mustn't blame yourself for André's death, Sal."

Just hearing his name caused her heart to feel as though it could explode. "Did you——"

"As soon as I got your message, I sent it through the proper channels. Ben had already heard of "John Anderson"—Arnold informed him that a man by that name would be coming through the lines with a pass from him. André was caught by a bunch of criminals in the neutral ground. One of them was wearing a Hessian coat he'd stolen, and André, assuming they were Loyalists, revealed himself as a British officer. The men searched him and found Arnold's treasonous information in André's shoe." His lips curled into a sardonic grin and Sally remembered Robert's warning not to hide papers on her person. "Ben told me he would have known the man they captured was an officer anyway, even if he did not get our message about André/Anderson. It was his walk that gave him away. Ben said that he watched him pace up and down the little room and soon knew that the man was no ordinary soldier."

Sally, remembering that confident stride, felt her heart sink even lower when she realized that André would walk no more.

Robert paused for a moment and stared mournfully into the fire. "André was of a most amiable character," he said finally. "But he made a lot of mistakes that became his own undoing. The only thing we can do is learn from them and move on."

Sally nodded, tears once again filling her eyes. They had all been playing the same treacherous game, but André had lost.

"Sally," Robert rose from his chair and walked over, bending down in front of her. "Just think of what could have happened if the British gained West Point."

"They would have won the war." Her words came out with a sob.

"Exactly," Robert said, patting her leg before returning to his chair. "Years from now, when the pain has subsided and you reflect back on this time, don't think about sacrificing the life of your friend John André. Think about how you saved America."

EPILOGUE

THE TRUE FATES OF THE CHARACTERS IN 355

THE WOMEN

*E*lizabeth Burgin was granted permission to return under a flag of truce to collect her children, and upon returning to New York, discovered that her clothes and apartment had been confiscated and given to Loyalists. After she arrived in Philadelphia, she found herself in an unfamiliar town with three children, no clothes or money, and no friends. As Elizabeth herself wrote, "Helping our poor prisoners brought me to want, which I don't repent." Leonard Van Buren, one of the men Elizabeth helped rescue, heard of Elizabeth's plight and gifted her $500 as a thank-you. General Washington himself appealed on her behalf in early 1780, stating in a letter to the Continental Congress "From the testimony of different persons, and particularly many of our own Officers who have returned from captivity, it would appear that she has been indefatigable for the relief of the prisoners and in measures for facilitating their escape. For this conduct she incurred the suspicion of the British, and was forced to make her escape under disturbing circumstances." Finding it still hard to get by a year later, Elizabeth petitioned Congress, altruistically asking to be paid for "cutting out the linen into shirts... for the army." Instead of a seamstress job, Congress then awarded her a pension, making her one of the few women of the Revolutionary War to receive the annuity. Nothing more is known about her after 1786.

Margaret Moncrieffe Coghlan sailed to England where she later claimed she was subjected to "barbarous treatment" by her husband. After they docked, Coghlan abandoned her for two weeks. In typical fashion, she wrote to a former New York acquaintance, Thomas Clinton, to appeal for help. The two purportedly had an affair and Margaret was advised to flee to France. Two years afterward, she returned to England and was rumored to have begun yet another affair with a man named Charles James Fox. More affairs and liaisons with other men of means followed. Years later, while writing her memoirs in 1793, she had this to say about Aaron Burr: "With this Conqueror of my soul, how happy should I now have been! What storms and tempests should I have avoided (at least I am pleased to think so) if I had been allowed to follow the bent of my inclinations and happier; oh ten thousand times happier should I have been with him!" She died in 1795* (most likely date), at the age of 33.

Sarah Sally Townsend never married and lived out the rest of her life in her family's house in Oyster Bay—later named Raynham Hall by her descendants—with her bachelor brother Robert. She kept Simcoe's poem—which was purported to be the first Valentine written in the United States of America—as well as André's silhouette of her until her death in 1842, at the age of 82. Both were heavily creased, as if she frequently opened them. The window addressed to "The adorable Miss ~~Sally~~ Sarah Townsend" can still be seen at the Raynham Hall museum in Oyster Bay.

Margaret Shippen Arnold was banned from Philadelphia soon after she arrived after fleeing West Point. She joined her husband in New York and, in 1781, they moved to England with their two sons. Five more children were born afterward, with three surviving past infancy. In 1789, she made a brief visit to her family in Philadelphia, where she was not given the warmest welcome: it was reported that old friends and acquaintances snubbed her while others jeered her on the streets. She died in 1804, at the age of 44, three years after her deeply in-debt husband left this world.

After her death, Aaron Burr came forward to state that he was at the Hermitage the night she stayed with Theodosia Prevost and heard her confess her own participation in her husband's treason. Defenders of Peggy Arnold's innocence have long claimed that Burr's accusations came out of spite. They claim that Burr once made advances on Peggy only to be spurned by the beautiful debutante. In the 20th century, several letters in the Sir Henry Clinton collection came to light that make it clear Peggy knew of Arnold's plotting and most likely encouraged and played a hand in it.

THE MEN

Aaron Burr married Theodosia Prevost and moved to New York City after the British evacuation to open a law practice. After losing the 1800 presidential election to Thomas Jefferson, Burr became the vice president of the United States. He blamed Alexander Hamilton for his lack of success in politics, and challenged him to a duel in 1804. After Burr famously shot and killed his rival, the resulting scandal ended Burr's political career. Although he was later indicted for treason, he never went to trial for the murder of Hamilton. He died in 1836, penniless and partially paralyzed from an earlier stroke.

. . .

Caleb Brewster married Anne Lewis, the daughter of the wharf owner where he had made most of his landings, and moved to Fairfield, Connecticut, where he became a blacksmith and farmer. In 1793, he joined the predecessor to the U.S. Coast Guard and commanded the USRC *Active* during the War of 1812 before retiring to his farm in 1816. Unlike his fellow, more tight-lipped, members of the Culper Ring, he was known to boast about his involvement as a courier and sometimes intelligencer. He died in 1827 at the age of 79 and was survived by eight children.

Hercules Mulligan was able to talk his way out of jail as Benedict Arnold could present no evidence against him. He had breakfast with George Washington when the general returned upon the British evacuation of New York, thereby putting a halt to any plans the Whigs might have had to tar and feather the supposed Loyalist. Washington declared Mulligan a "true friend of liberty," before he ordered a suit from him. A sign proclaiming that Mulligan was "Clothier to Genl. Washington," hung outside his Queen Street shop until Mulligan's death in 1825. He is buried at Trinity Church near his good friend Alexander Hamilton.

James Rivington was referred to as "726" in the Culper code book. Whether the notorious Tory printer participated in the Ring out of patriotic sympathy or to deepen his own pocket remains a mystery lost to time. Like Mulligan's shop, Rivington's printing press was spared of any looting when the Americans returned to New York City. His newspaper, however, could not find a following in the new nation and he was forced to serve time in a debtor's prison. He died at the age of 78 in 1802—perhaps a tad ironically—on July 4th.

John Graves Simcoe returned to England shortly after André's death. He married the heiress Elizabeth Posthuma Gwillim in 1782 and won a seat in Parliament, where he advocated for organizing more militia akin to the Queen's Rangers. In 1792 he became the lieutenant governor of the mostly Loyalist Upper Canada, where he passed the Act Against Slavery, leading to a full abolition of slavery in that region by 1810. In 1806 he was named Commander-in-Chief of India, but fell ill on his journey there. He returned to Devonshire, England, where he died at the age of 54.

Benjamin Tallmadge was promoted to the rank of lieutenant colonel in 1783. Shortly after, he married Mary Floyd, the daughter of the Declaration of Independence signer William Floyd, and fathered seven children. He became a member of the U.S. House of Representatives, representing Connecticut in the Federalist Party for eight terms. Although he wrote a book about his experiences during the Revolutionary War, he was notoriously vague regarding his intelligence sources. He died in 1835 at age 81.

Robert Townsend, like his sister Sally, also never married. Due to the reticence of most of the ring after the war, Robert Townsend's role was lost to history until historian Morton Pennypacker uncovered it in the 1930s. Ironically, it was Townsend's handwriting that gave him away as Culper Junior—in life, one of his biggest fears was that his secret identity would have been discovered due to his unique penmanship. At his death, Townsend left a considerable amount of money to a man named "Robert Townsend Junior." It is unclear exactly who fathered him: Robert's older brother Solomon, in a journal in the possession of the Raynham Hall Museum, speculated the boy actually belonged to William Townsend.

A note to the reader: Thanks so much for reading this book! If you have time to spare, please consider leaving a short review on Amazon. Reviews are very important to indie authors such as myself and I would greatly appreciate it!

·   ·   ·

Read on for a sample of *Women Spies Book 2- Underground: Traitors and Spies in Lincoln's War*

AFTERWORD

A NOTE ON 355 BY THE AUTHOR

Abraham Woodhull's cryptic mention of a 355, translated from the Culper Code into "lady," has puzzled historians for centuries. I first heard of her when I researched "forgotten women of history," and was immediately hooked. There are a myriad of theories for the identity and personality of 355. In his book *A Peculiar Service*, published in 1956, Corey Ford wrote that he "liked to picture 355 as the opposite of the reserved and sober young Quaker (Robert Townsend): small, pert, vivacious, clever enough to outwit the enemy, but feminine enough to give Townsend a brief interlude of happiness that he would never know again." According to Brian Kilmeade and Don Yaeger, authors of *George Washington's Secret Six*, 355 was the sixth member of the Culper Ring. All of this misinformation seems to stem from amateur historian Morton Pennypacker and his 1948 volume of the Culper Spy Ring legend. In it he cites 355 as being Robert Townsend's paramour, who was imprisoned aboard the *Jersey* and later died. However, Pennypacker provided no proof for this wild tale—there is no record that women were ever even held aboard the prison ships let alone anyone who would fit 355's description.

I chose Sally for my 355, as it was not unlikely that Abraham Woodhull was acquainted with Culper Junior's sister and both Simcoe and André were guests of the Townsends shortly before Arnold's treason. While we may never know to whom Woodhull referred, it is clear that the women of this book, and countless others, played a crucial role in the fight for America's freedom, and I have dedicated this book to them for that reason.

UNDERGROUND: TRAITORS AND SPIES IN LINCOLN'S WAR

WOMEN SPIES BOOK 2

Kit Sergeant

UNDERGROUND CHAPTER 1

HATTIE

FEBRUARY 1861

$\mathcal{B}$altimore's men were up in arms. Even at the unseemly early hour of three in the morning, shouts from angry secessionists echoed through the slats of the depot, drowned only by the train whistles announcing each new arrival.

"It will be coming soon, boys," a man in a straw hat and full beard announced. "Remember," he told the men who gathered around him, "no damned abolitionist shall pass through this town alive."

Hattie Lewis's eyes shifted to her friend and supervisor, Kate Warne, who stood just to the right of the mob. Kate's face held her usual inscrutable expression, but Hattie could tell from the way she gripped her handbag that she was as uncomfortable as Hattie. Most of the employees of the Pinkerton Detective Agency had arrived in Baltimore only a few days prior, but the depth of the anti-Union sentiment had greeted them almost as immediately as the concierge at the Barnum Hotel. Maryland was a swing state, and its rebel proclivities had boiled over with the election of the anti-slavery Lincoln to the Presidency.

Hattie turned at the sound of horses approaching. A plain coach stopped near the tracks, the horses whinnying as the driver pulled them to a halt. She hurried toward them. As she entered the coach, snatches of Dixie followed behind her, ceasing mercifully when she shut the door.

"No doubt there *will* be a good time in Dixie, by and by," a deep voice offered.

Hattie gave the man a tentative smile. The President Elect was dressed in a simple traveling suit, the shawl draped over his head taking the place of his stovepipe hat, which was placed beside him. She'd read multiple descriptions of Abraham Lincoln in the papers —most focused on the newly grown beard in response to the young lady Grace Bedell's request for him to cover his sunken jaw—but none of them had properly described his dignified manner, nor the fact that the beard still grew sparse over his gaunt cheeks. His eyes held an amiable crinkle as they focused on Hattie. She regretted that the tight quarters of the coach offered no room to show Mr. Lincoln the proper obsequies. She introduced herself to Mr. Lincoln and then told him, "Miss Warne has arranged an empty sleeping car for our purpose."

He nodded. "I am to be your brother, then," he stated, addressing Hattie.

She cast a sidelong glance at the man sitting beside her, her employer, Mr. Allan Pinkerton. He leaned forward. "It is for your safety." Even though he'd been in America for nearly two decades, his accent still resonated Scottish when he was anxious.

"I still think it is all nonsense." Ward Hill Lamon, Lincoln's personal bodyguard, sat back into the ripped velvet of the coach. "And ridiculous for our new President to be skulking about a city, unknown, in the middle of the night."

"It would be even more ridiculous to have our new President not arrive at his inauguration alive," Pinkerton replied evenly. He opened the door to the coach. With a swish of her satin skirts, Hattie scooted past him to retrieve the wheelchair the driver had unloaded. Lincoln looked down and sighed before climbing out of the coach and arranging himself into the chair. He made to replace his hat, but Hattie pulled the shawl up to obscure his face instead, knowing his customary hat would only serve to give him away.

"Brother, I believe our train has arrived." Hattie's hands tightened on the chair as she pushed forward toward the station. Lincoln was so tall he nearly reached Hattie's height sitting down. She did not look up, even as she passed by Kate, who stood in line waiting to board a car near the front of the train.

"May I be of assistance?" Hattie was about to refuse the train operative who loomed in front of her until she recognized him as another Pinkerton employee, Timothy Webster.

Hattie affected a Southern accent. "We have reserved the back car. My brother here needs to be isolated."

Timothy, with his usual capableness, bent down to hoist the front of the wheelchair up the steps to the car. Hattie, pushing forward, peeked at the man in the straw hat. He and his companions stood with their arms crossed, searching the crowd. According to the posted schedule, Lincoln's train was not due to arrive for another several hours. After uncovering a potential assassination plot, Pinkerton had insisted on rescheduling and sending the President-elect in on an earlier train from Philadelphia. Hopefully the man in the straw hat would not realize he'd been outwitted until long after Mr. Lincoln arrived at the Capitol Building for his inauguration speech.

At last Mr. Lincoln was safely ensconced in the sleeping compartment. Webster locked the door behind him as he left, and Hattie allowed herself one sigh of relief before retrieving the small pistol hidden underneath the seat of the wheelchair. Lincoln had boarded the train, but that did not mean his life was no longer in danger.

Mr. Lincoln had to double up his legs to fit in the sleeping berth, a position that, when Hattie dared to cast her eyes at him, seemed too lowly for a man of his status.

She stretched her cold hands to the warmth of the stove as she heard the cargo door bang shut. She immediately cursed herself for leaving her gun out of reach. *Amateur.* But the intruder was only Allan Pinkerton, coming to check on the precious cargo. As usual, the heavy smell of Cuban cigars clung to his clothing and beard. Hattie assumed he'd been chain smoking them on the bridge.

"How does he sleep like that?" Pinkerton wondered aloud as the train whistle blew.

"How does he sleep at all, knowing what he knows?" Hattie asked in reply. It was not just that his life was in danger, but he was about to take on a nearly impossible role. Seven states had already seceded from the Union in protest after his election. It was up to him to try to repair the conflict that was building between the North and the South and to solve the moral question of slavery as a whole. Hattie knew she and Pinkerton were of the same mind as Lincoln, but that the rest of the country would not come to an agreement so easily. "I am fairly sure I will not be able to get a wink in myself."

Her boss smiled wryly. "The nature of the job. We Pinkertons never sleep." He went to the window. A flash of light broke through the darkness. He tapped the window. "All's well," he said, turning back to Hattie. She knew Pinkerton had placed several operatives at train stations along the way. They were instructed to flash lanterns stating that no known evil forces were at work.

Hattie glanced again at Mr. Lincoln, visions of all the ways the plotters could still attack temporarily blinding her. They might be out of Baltimore, but henchmen could still burn bridges or derail the train. "Let's hope it stays that way."

The train arrived in Washington, mercifully without incident. The Pinkerton detectives unloaded from different cars, avoiding each other's eyes, but silently congratulating each other nonetheless. Hattie marveled that no one would ever know of the danger their new President had been in, and that the threat of murder could have been resolved not by apprehending the alleged criminals, but by a mere switching of the train time table.

And yet the guilty parties walk free, Hattie reminded herself as she scanned the people surrounding her. Mr. Lincoln was still wrapped in his shawl and the crowd seemed blissfully unaware that the potential savior of the Union was the man in the wheelchair.

A man dressed in a fitted frock coat walked rapidly toward Mr. Lincoln. Hattie fingered the pistol in her handbag. The man extended his hand and was about to give a salutation when Hattie stepped forward.

"Sir?" she asked quietly.

He looked Hattie up and down before turning back to Mr. Lincoln. "Mr. Presi—"

"My brother here is very tired," Hattie declared, conscious of the lanky figure in the wheelchair attracting multiple pairs of eyes.

"This is Miss Lewis. She is a friend of the railroad company," Mr. Lincoln told the man.

The man, obviously catching on to Mr. Lincoln's double meaning, nodded. "Your carriage is waiting, sir."

Pinkerton appeared next to the man. "Miss Lewis. You can ride in my car."

Hattie relinquished her grip on the wheelchair as her boss and the man exchanged pleasantries.

Mr. Lincoln reached out to grasp Hattie's hands. "I am aware that you put your life at risk for me last night. I truly thank you for your service," he said in his quiet tone.

"Thank you for yours," Hattie replied. She wanted to say more, that she knew he had a lot riding on his shoulders, although if anyone could save the Union, he could. But, knowing her place, she kept quiet.

Pinkerton had one final question for Lincoln. "Mr. President, shall we move forward with arresting the would-be assassinators?"

Mr. Lincoln focused his solemn eyes on Pinkerton. "No. I do not wish to make martyrs out of cowards and madmen."

Pinkerton bowed his head. "As you wish."

They followed Lincoln's carriage to the Willard Hotel off 14th Street and watched Lincoln exit, glancing up and down the street as he did. He was still in disguise and seemed curious as to why none of the passersby paid him any note. Lamon, his chief of security, came out of the hotel and hustled him inside. Pinkerton gave Hattie a wry smile before nodding his head at Pennsylvania Avenue just behind them. "Lincoln's only steps away from the White House now," he said with a wink.

Hattie sat back. "Thanks to you."

"And you, Miss Lewis. You have proven yourself."

She nodded, pleased. She'd been with the agency for nearly a year now, but the Lincoln plot had been her first major assignment, and one of national importance at that. Hopefully she had indeed finally shown her fellow agents what she was capable of.

The Pinkertons were off-duty for the inauguration, but Hattie could see many policemen spread far and wide over the city, watching for any sign of trouble. The day had dawned gray and rainy, but it was now bright and sunny. *Just like our country: what began today in darkness as a fractured nation will now come together in light and jubilance under our new President.* There were thousands of people spread on the grounds of the unfinished Capitol building: the vivid parasols of women sprinkled throughout the neutral suits of the men. When Mr. Lincoln appeared on the platform erected on the eastern portico of the building, the crowd greeted him with thunderous cheers. After the marine band played "The Star-Spangled Banner," Senator Baker introduced the new President. Mr. Lincoln walked to the front of the podium and bowed to the enthusiastic approbation. He put on his spectacles and rearranged the papers in front of him before beginning his speech. Lincoln's booming voice had a musical lilt to it, and, despite her distance from his podium and the hordes of people in between them, Hattie could hear him clear as day. As she had predicted, Lincoln urged reconciliation and discouraged secession. He closed by saying:

We are not enemies but friends. We must not be enemies. Though passion may have strained, it must not break our bonds of affection. The mystic chords of memory, stretching from every battlefield and patriot grave, to every living heart and hearthstone, all over this broad land, will yet swell the chorus of the Union, when again touched, as surely they will be, by the better angels of our nature.

As he spoke, Hattie could not keep her eyes from shifting over to that fire-eating Texan, Senator Wigfall. If anyone was Lincoln's enemy and not friend, it was he, who leaned against the Capitol building with his arms crossed over his chest. Hattie felt heat rise in her face. Texas was the most recent state to secede from the Union and, along with the rest of those deserters, had formed the Confederate States of America. Consequently, he should not have even been there. *You have your own slave-holding, supposed president,* Hattie thought. *What do you want with ours?* Wigfall made a sudden movement and Hattie pulled her bag, with the gun concealed within, closer. But Wigfall merely nodded to himself, as if he had made a silent decision.

UNDERGROUND CHAPTER 2

BELLE

APRIL 1861

"*B*elle! Belle Boyd!"

Belle looked up from the book in her hands. She'd been trying to read it for half an hour, but the delightful Baltimore spring day had proved much more interesting than perusing the treatise on femininity she'd been assigned. Her best friend at school, Virginia, was running toward her. Belle smiled, thinking what the author of the tome would say about a young woman running through the mud, skirts hiked up and showing more than a little ankle.

Virginia reached the tree Belle had been using for shade. She bent at the waist in an effort to catch her breath.

"What is it, Ginny?" Belle demanded.

"Shots have been fired." Virginia gasped, still breathing heavily. "Fort Sumter. War has started."

Belle waved her fist in a most unladylike manner. "Finally! Maybe now we can get that rail-splitter Lincoln out of office."

Virginia straightened. "But what will become of us? We are in

Northern territory here." She crumpled a handkerchief in the palm of her hand. "And God hates the Yankees."

"Yes, why don't they just leave the South alone? They can let those darned abolitionists have their way and let us keep the traditions laid down by our forefathers." Belle cast her eyes around the campus of Mount Washington Female College, as if the lush landscaping could belie the official political leanings of the school. Maryland was still a slave state, but its proximity to Washington made its status as Union or Confederate unclear. "I must get home to Mother as soon as possible."

Virginia shook her head. "You know Headmistress Staley is a staunch Unionist. She will not allow you to go home as long as your tuition is paid up."

"We shall see about that," Belle said, hiking up her own skirts and heading toward the headmistress's office.

"Absolutely not." As predicted, Headmistress Staley refused to let Belle leave the school grounds. "There is a war brewing in our fair Union. It would not be safe to let you leave."

"But Headmistress—"

"Your parents have entrusted me as your guardian. You are under my care, hence you will obey my command." Never once in Belle's tenure at the school did Headmistress Staley ever waver in her principles. Miss Staley ruled the girls under her like a temperate overseer, molding them into submission with threatening words instead of fists while teaching them both the classics as well as how to be a proper lady. As the attendees were from both the North and South, Belle often felt that the mannerisms she was taught contradicted greatly with the feminine ideal of a Southern woman, but that was no matter, since Belle herself was in contradiction to those same ideals.

Realizing she was as likely to change Staley's mind as she was to take up arms and join the war effort, Belle gave a half-hearted curtsy before exiting the headmistress's chambers.

Virginia was waiting for her outside. She need not ask for the outcome of Belle's plea since the disappointment was written on her face. Virginia joined Belle's quick pace and walked beside her. "What shall we do now?"

Belle stopped and stared helplessly at the sky. She could see the entrance to the grounds, the starred-and-striped flag that graced the hill, flapping in the breeze just beyond the driveway. Belle felt a sudden rush of hatred for that once beloved symbol of a country that no longer felt like hers. A plan began to form in her mind. "Ginny, do you still have that pearl-handled pistol your father gave you?"

Virginia nodded. Her father manufactured such items back home in North Carolina.

"Go and fetch it for me."

Virginia, used to Belle's odd demands, did as requested.

"You aren't going to shoot anyone, are you?" Virginia asked when she returned with the gun.

"No." Belle walked quickly across the sprawling green lawns of the college. "I won't be shooting a person." She paused near the flagpole and peered up at the flag. Squinting against the bright sunlight, she grasped the pistol with both hands and took aim. Belle shot the gun with the expertise of someone well accustomed to a firearm, not even startling at the kickback. Virginia glanced up, noting the bullet hole that was located where one of the Union's stars should be. Belle repeated the gesture and managed to take out another star. The lawn soon filled with young women chattering at a safe distance from the line of fire. Belle used up the entire round, managing to take out four stars in total.

"Miss Boyd." The headmistress, who had waited until there were no more bullets left to shoot, appeared next to Belle.

Belle opened the chamber and held the gun handle toward Staley. "I suppose now you will choose to expel me?"

Even after three years of Belle's antics, Staley was clearly surprised by this newest one. She merely nodded. "I will make the arrangements immediately."

Belle nodded and headed to the dormitory to begin packing.

Enjoyed the sample? Purchase Underground today! Thank you for your support!

Books in the Women Spies Series:
    355: The Women of Washington's Spy Ring
    Underground: Traitors and Spies in Lincoln's War
    L'Agent Double: Spies and Martyrs in the Great War
    The Spark of Resistance: Women Spies in WWII

Sign up for my mailing list at www.kitsergeant.com to find out more information on my newest releases!

SELECTED BIBLIOGRAPHY

Berkin, Carol. Revolutionary Mothers: Women in the Struggle for America's Independence. Vintage Books, 2006.

Ford, Corey. A Peculiar Service. Little, Brown and Company, 1965.

Kilmeade, Brian, and Don Yaeger. George Washington's Secret Six: the Spy Ring That Saved the American Revolution. Sentinal, 2016.

McCullough, David. 1776. Simon and Schuster, 2005.

Misencik, Paul R. Sally Townsend, George Washington's Teenage Spy. McFarland & Company, Inc., Publishers, 2016.

McGee, Dorothy Horton. Sally Townsend, Patriot. Dodd, Mead, and Company, 1952.

Moncrieffe, Margaret. Memoirs of Mrs. Coghlan. New York Times, 1971.

Pennypacker, Morton. General Washington's Spies on Long Island and in New York. Scholar's Bookshelf, 2005.

Rose, Alexander. Washington's Spies: the Story of America's First Spy Ring. Random House Inc, 2014.

Schouler James. Americans of 1776. Corner House Historical Publications, 1999.

Read on for a sample of the next book in the Women Spy Series, *Underground: Traitors and Spies in Lincoln's War*!

ACKNOWLEDGMENTS

First and foremost, I'd like to thank folks at kboards.com and to all of the people who nominated this book during its Kindle Scout run.

A special thanks to my critique partners: Ute Carbone, Theresa Munroe, and Karen Cino, for their comments and suggestions. Once again, I am eternally grateful to Rhonda Sergeant for being the best proofreader in the world.

And as always, a special thank-you goes to my loving family, especially Tommy, Belle, and Thompson, for their love and support.

Made in the USA
Las Vegas, NV
01 February 2025

17365193R00225